Cursed on the Taiga

The Earthen Calamities: Nizhny
Book 2
E. Anders

E. Anders

Cursed on the Taiga / E. Anders — 2nd ed. New Cover

ISBN: 979-8-9891807-5-2 (Paperback)

ISBN: 979-8-9891807-4-5 (eBook)

*To anyone out there who had a pregnancy that wasn't
what they expected/hoped/dreamed
it might/could/should be.*

This one's for you.

The Earthen Calamities

In the spring of 2016, the **Aperien Event** forever altered Earth.

In an inexplicable moment, everything humanity anywhere in the world had ever imagined became real. No one understood why or how, but the who, what, and when were cataclysmic.

Every myth, every monster. Every story and every dream. All the things that went bump in the night and the virtues descended from various heavens. Gods, demons, vampires, dragons. Magic powers, dangerous alchemy, and a dozen recipes for the elixir of life. Wishes, witches and wendigos. Undead, rebirth, immortality. Apocalypses. Lots and lots of apocalypses.

If there'd been a story about it at some point in human history, it suddenly existed. All of it. All in the same instant.

And as one might imagine, it was a mess.

Cursed on the Taiga

In **2244**, the world has largely settled after two centuries of apocalyptic events and heroic interventions.

The **Aperiens**—manifested beings from the **Aperien Event**—exist everywhere. **Dusters**, the result of unions between humans and Aperiens, outnumber pureblood human beings ten thousand to one. The **Icelandic Citadel of Knowledge** oversees the **Accorded Territories**, the nations which rose from the ashes of the Aperien Event. The Citadel enforces a set of magically binding laws called **the Accords**. Examples include the **Human Protection Accord**, the **Anti-Apocalypse Accord**, and the **Vilestars Accord**.

Nizhny is a rare **Independent Territory**, operating outside Accorded Law. Founded seven years earlier, the settlement continues to grow via trade with the Accorded Territory **Moscow Dominion**.

Content Warning

This story contains violence, PTSD, explicit sex scenes, a brief conversation about abortion, a pregnancy with complications, mother and unborn baby in dangerous situations, and childbirth.

Chapter 1

All Audrey managed was to shuffle backward through the slush and mud until her back hit a pine tree. There was nowhere left to crawl.

The angel Kushiel was beautiful and horrible, white-winged, fueled by righteous desire and a longing for revenge so deep, the well knew no bottom. He opened his Heaven, golden beams of light filtering through the canopy of the Siberian taiga, the bluebird sky a pale comparison to his piercing gaze. Haloed and bright, infinite and brutal, Audrey realized then she'd never known an Aperien at their full, unsuppressed power until this moment.

That same Aperien, who hated her, who hated everything she'd done in her very short life and everything she loved, drew a holy blade and laced it with hellfire.

Was this how she died?

Despite the friends and powerful beings that had come to her aid. Despite Jonathan, the man she loved, who just needed more time to understand he loved her too. She knew it in her bones, felt it in every way he took care of her and kept her safe. In how he stood before an Aperien angel, undaunted and ready to die for her, a simple, unimportant human girl.

Then all hells broke loose.

Kushiel stabbed at her, but the blade went deep into Jonathan's chest instead of hers. At the same time, Rina called out and threw her treasured sword to Jonathan, who caught it and cut off the angel's head in a single upward stroke.

She didn't have heightened senses like Jonathan, but she'd learned details she never wanted to know and would now never forget.

How pine needles tasted when they evaporated. What holy steel looked like when it boiled. The smell of hellfire devouring living flesh. The way blood felt when it ran in rivers, when it pulsed out of a body in time with their heartbeat.

The sound of Jonathan screaming as he died.

"I have the flames!" Virtue called. The Aperien was a nightmare in her full Aperien form, more so when she wrenched her clawed hands through the air and sucked the hellfire from Jonathan's body, all the flaming trees, and the burning leshy.

The leshy Aspen, who'd trusted Audrey's intentions when she came to him on behalf of Nizhny, whose territory she'd ran to for help, now burned.

Virtue let out a hiss and took flight, the infernal flames following her as she rose on demon wings. The air dropped from sweltering to frozen.

Jonathan slumped against Audrey, the molten metal sizzling through his body as he howled. The steam rising from his chest was black.

E knelt in front of them, the dverger shoving the angel's headless corpse aside like it was nothing as he dropped Mjölnir, Thor's hammer, into the slush and blood, like the weapon of legend didn't matter.

Audrey's head swam, her vision blotting out as she clutched Jonathan's coat.

"Please," she whispered. "Please don't let him die. I'll give you—"

"Don't tempt, lass," E murmured, his eyes glowing with residual electricity and ancient power. "Not all can resist."

She didn't care; she'd give him anything. She would have gone with Kushiel and given her life for the man who'd saved hers, over and over.

"Steady on," E said, more to himself than Audrey, flexing his open hands over Jonathan's chest—who passed out from the pain, or oh gods, or was he already dead?

Audrey blinked a few times, trying to clear the hot tears pouring down her cheeks now that the hellfire wasn't evaporating them before they fell. Her breathing stuttered.

E was smithing the metal inside Jonathan's body.

It cooled to silvery-white, silken smooth as it bent and wrapped and sunk deeper into Jonathan's chest, a fresh river of black blood rushing over his charred skin. E's hands glowed now, the same color as what remained of the holy sword, his fingers twitching, sweat beading on the smith's furrowed brow.

His braided gray beard had been almost entirely singed away.

Why that made her sob harder, she didn't know.

Her heart was breaking to pieces.

She clutched at Jonathan. His head lolled as she pressed her cheek to his forehead.

"Please . . ."

Audrey didn't know how much time passed. E muttered words she didn't understand. Jonathan was a dense, unmoving weight against her, his skin colder and colder under her cheek.

"Audrey."

She felt hands on her shoulders, shaking her gently, pulling at her. Rina? She heard other voices, too, telling her to let go. Aster was there, saying they needed to bandage and move him.

"No." She refused to open her eyes, holding tighter. She wouldn't let him go. She couldn't.

"Audrey, sweetheart."

A deep, resonate voice. A hand brushed the sweaty hair away from her forehead.

"I'm right here. Wake up."

She did with a jolt, the darkness cut by moonlight through the open window, her back pressed into softness, not tree bark. Large hands held her face. A body against the length of hers, warm and alive.

"Breathe, baby, I got you."

She felt the rumble of Jonathan's words where their bare chests pressed together, felt the way he breathed deep and slow, the steady rhythm of his heartbeat. Alive.

Alive, alive, alive . . .

It didn't stop her from pushing against his shoulders enough that he leaned back, bracing himself on one elbow on their bed as she frantically ran her fingertips over his scars. As she traced the lines marking when she almost lost him.

No boiling metal, no hellfire, no burning flesh. Just Jonathan, alive and whole and healed.

Audrey shuddered. Sweat cooled on her skin, the sheet tangled around their legs. She blinked up from his chest to his face, and there he was. Jonathan.

Her Jonathan.

His brow knit, those stern, handsome features concerned but calm. The pitch black of his eyes, the telltale marker of his vileblood, which had never frightened her because she'd always seen the man beyond the monster society had labeled him. She traced his cheeks, his slightly crooked nose, dark eyebrows, and full lips, reassuring herself this was real.

Jonathan kissed her fingertips when they touched his mouth. "Right here." His deep voice soothed. "You're never getting rid of me, sweetheart."

"I know," she whispered, closing her eyes as the dream—the memory—faded with wakefulness.

"There you are," he murmured, kissing her forehead before surrounding her with his strong, massive body. She couldn't help a hiccupping sigh as she buried her face against his neck. He didn't crush her, but it was a near thing with how tight they held each other. "What do you need?"

Audrey shivered against him, her voice a pained rasp when she answered, "You."

It had been six weeks since she told him she loved him only a day before he nearly died at Kushiel's hand. Since he lived, told her she was everything to him, and made love to her the first time. They'd rarely gone to bed without sex since. Audrey was still slick between her legs from both of their releases a few hours ago.

When Audrey had this same nightmare for the first time, leaving her mind unable to claw back from that dark memory, they'd figured out sex helped. The physicality of it, the undeniable reminder than he was alive. They were alive, and together, exactly where they belonged.

Her body was soft and warm with sleep, welcoming Jonathan as he shifted her thighs wider and slid inside her with an uninterrupted push until they were hips to hips.

Audrey's breath left her lungs in a rush; it always did. The size of him, the way he filled her to her limit. The way he never failed to growl against her throat when he did, as lost as she felt. Every single time. They stayed there, hearts beating against one another, hers shifting from a panic to desperate arousal—not so different, apparently.

"I'm here," Jonathan crooned, sipping at her skin. One hand tangled her hair and opened her throat to him, so he could sink his teeth in enough to bruise. Audrey whimpered, her body clenching around him, an involuntary response to how he marked her skin so everyone knew she was his. He let out a grunt in reply, the rolling pump of his hips pushing himself deeper into her body.

Alive, alive, alive.

"Beautiful girl," he whispered, breathing against her lips. He built a gentle rhythm as he praised her, loved her. "I could never leave you. Never."

He nipped at her chin as her head fell back and she lost herself in the feeling of him. So, so close. Part of her. Together. She fluttered around him already, still in disbelief at how well he knew her body, how easily he pulled pleasure from her. Tingles raced through her veins, an aching warmth spreading low in her tummy. Audrey tightened her arms around his neck, and Jonathan shifted his body in answer, pinning her to him. His hips stuttered once before resuming the perfect pace, the perfect friction along parts of her she never knew existed until he showed her.

"Jonathan . . ."

"You're mine, sweetheart. Mine."

" . . . yours."

"That's right." A harder thrust followed that growl of his, her affirmation awakening the more feral side of him—the side Jonathan did his best to keep her safe from, even now. His voice, his words, they drove her mad with desire. "Come around my cock, sweet thing. Let me feel you."

She did; she was helpless to resist him. Audrey gasped his name as she climaxed, burning back the dark dreams, because the closeness of this moment, the way he entirely controlled her? It was nothing compared to how her stoic protector shuddered and groaned as she shattered around him.

"Yes, Audrey. Gorgeous, baby."

She felt hazy and a little lost, her bloodstream still racing with adrenaline and now sweet relief, but Audrey noticed when Jonathan slowed his strokes and stilled. He kissed her cheeks, her nose, soft brushes of his lips over her closed eyes.

"Don't stop."

"You're tired," Jonathan mumbled, his body still hard as steel inside hers, her center fluttering around him in tiny aftershocks. He was wound tight, his shoulders tense as she ran her fingers along his sweaty skin.

"I don't care. Keep going."

Jonathan groaned, his forehead falling to her shoulder. She smiled where he couldn't see, looping her calves around the back of his before he got any more ideas about trying to sneak away. He did this, for all the beast he liked to call himself. He always tried to deny what he needed during sex, convincing himself his own desires and satisfaction with their lovemaking was less important than her own.

She might have been inexperienced when she first came to his bed, but she'd learned him as much as he'd learned her.

Audrey dug her nails into his skin; he arched into the touch like a cat, rolling his hips in response and biting at her shoulder.

"Audrey."

She almost giggled when he cut off in a grunt as she clenched herself around his cock, tight as she could. Her cheeks blazed, her mouth dry, but she somehow whispered, "Please, come inside me."

"Fuck. *Fuck*, woman," Jonathan bit out, right before he looped an elbow under her knee and proceeded to—for lack of a better way to put it—fuck her into the mattress while she clung to him, coming again when he poured himself into her body with a desperate, hungry noise that always made Audrey's heart stutter.

Afterward, he slumped against her, nipping hard enough at her jaw to make her squeak. "You're a menace," he grumbled, but he didn't sound very upset about it. After they'd both caught their breath, he cupped her cheek. "Alright?"

"Yes." Looking up at his tender expression, the flush on his pale skin, and the line between his furrowed brows, how could she not be? He was alive and hers. "I am now."

When Audrey smoothed a finger across his forehead, Jonathan smirked down at her. "Sleep?"

She shook her head. No, she wouldn't go back to dreams, not tonight.

Jonathan understood without a word. "I'll make tea."

"Thank you." Audrey grinned, knowing he wouldn't drink a sip, instead making his own bitter, black, horrible coffee after he finished preparing her drink.

Chapter 2

After a shower, freshly dressed and bundled in a fur blanket, Audrey wandered into the kitchen. The house was warm, always so thanks to E's handy rune work and their wood-burning stove. For a cabin in the middle of Siberia, Audrey lived like a queen.

Especially given the view and the company, she mused, watching Jonathan as he finished making his coffee, clad only in a pair of sweatpants hanging dangerously low on his hips. She grinned to herself, appreciating all those pretty muscles under his pale skin while purposely avoiding lingering on his scars.

"Get a good look?" Jonathan asked, not bothering to turn, and she rolled her eyes as she took her seat. Her tea was ready, sweetened with honey just how she liked it. She held the mug, letting it warm her fingers.

They'd just finished the renovations on their home the previous week. They'd kept the two bedrooms and bath the same, extending the main living area to nearly three times the space. It allowed for a larger table, a rectangle with eight chairs instead of two. Her single bookshelf was now a library along the north-facing wall, though she'd barely filled a single set of shelves despite her ever-growing collection. The trap door down to their basement storage occupied a corner of the kitchen, which was relatively small aside from the stove, ice chest, and sink. Near the bookshelves was her modest desk, on it a beautiful vase of blue cornflowers. They were a gift from Aster, Nizhny's resident cornflower wraith and tavern keeper.

The other side of the room was all Jonathan. A weapon rack in tidy order, free weights and a bench, a bar built into the ceiling for his calisthenics routine. Audrey sipped her tea—the perfect temperature, a light chamomile this very early morning, which she knew he'd picked in case she tried to sleep again. She wouldn't, and she hoped Jonathan would let her do stretches instead of pushups later this afternoon.

Her life before Nizhny seemed like a faraway place, and she was glad for it, she thought as Jonathan sat down across from her, his coffee steaming. Not that she'd ever forget being a no-name girl sold into an indenture factory, later a runaway living in the Eastern Seaboard Conjunct slums.

Her hands tightened on her mug as she stared down at the curling steam and inhaled the flowery fragrance. She felt Jonathan's gaze on her from across the table, recognized his deep inhale as he tasted her scent—his many traits as a vileblood duster included extremely heightened senses, so much so that he could read emotions and intentions through a person's scent. Audrey smiled up at him, knowing her expression was a bit sad because she'd never insult him by lying. It would also be pointless, as he'd know, anyway.

"Just thinking," Audrey offered. He'd lit the oil lamp in the table's center for her, as he could see as well in the darkness as in the light. She glanced at the antique clock above their front door, the numbers illuminated with enchanted paint. It was just after three in the morning.

When she didn't elaborate, Jonathan leaned back in his chair. "About?"

"My life before I ended up here."

"Hmm."

She smiled at him. Jonathan was so serious so much of the time, and a man of few words. Unless they were in bed, of course, where he'd turned out to be deliciously vocal. Her cheeks warmed; his brow perked. She stuck her tongue out at him. He gave her a minute to elaborate, and when she didn't, he shifted the conversation.

One more reason she loved him. He knew her as well as she knew herself, and while she would have waded into those memories if he'd asked, he understood she didn't really want to.

"Theo should be here in another day or two. Fucker can't be bothered with the train."

"Jonathan," Audrey huffed his name around a laugh. He just shrugged those broad shoulders of his, but he was smirking at her as he drank his coffee. He really was unfairly handsome. "Would you take a train if you could fly?"

He seemed to give it genuine consideration, then just shrugged again.

"You're impossible."

When he flashed her a grin, toothy and mischievous, her heart fluttered. Too handsome, indeed.

Once they finished their drinks, Audrey shooed him off so he wouldn't hover, and he disappeared into their basement storage area to work. He didn't need as much sleep as she did, yet lingered in bed when she did, just another reason she loved the man. With terrible memories in the past where they belonged, Audrey set about preparing breakfast for their inevitable company.

Audrey made biscuits, blood sausage, a dozen of the chocolate chip cookies she'd become famous for in Nizhny, and prepped a fresh coffee pot. Dawn came, the nights still lengthening as they shifted toward springtime, and she was sitting at the table reading when a knock sounded and the front door swung inward.

Audrey didn't need heightened senses to detect the wet dog smell that assaulted her, but she didn't mind it a bit as the chuchuna family blundered inside. Zhadan, the large male, strode in first, shouting his greeting. "Little!"

She couldn't help but smile up at him, the giant he was, more caveman than the snow-white yeti of some mythos. He had a huge head and mouth, all snorts and chuffs around his words, and he crushed her against his hairy chest, his open coat damp with snow.

Audrey laughed, patting his arm. "Good morning, Zhadan." She craned her head around his wide body, greeting the rest of the family. "Hello!"

Lyubava looked exhausted, very much a mother of three young cubs, and gave Audrey a bleary nod as she shooed the trio inside. The cubs chirped and squealed when they smelled the cookies. Like Zhadan, Lyubava was covered in dark body hair from head to her enormous feet, bare despite the cold of the taiga.

She fluffed snow off her winter clothing, snorting in Russian. "<<*You spoil them with your cookies, Little.*>>" Lyubava scolded, but her expression was warm as she took a seat at the table.

True to form, the triplets already scrambled over each other and onto the tabletop with grabby hands. Unlike their parents, they were still mostly hairless, a bit wrinkly, and reminded Audrey of newborn puppies. If one ignored the fact they'd been running and wide-eyed at two days old. Aperiens were interesting, top to bottom, Audrey thought as she watched the children.

Two boys and a girl, they were two months old now and growing at an alarming rate. Biserka, the daughter, was the loudest and largest, snarling at her brothers as she mounted the table, claimed a cookie between her teeth and one in each fist, then jumped to the floor with a triumphant, muffled roar.

Audrey had trouble telling Pyotr and Ignat apart, but they were always in cahoots and made off with the rest of the plate together, fleeing down the hallway when Zhadan gave chase, thundering like a moose over the wooden floorboards.

Lyubava sighed.

"<<*Nap?*>>" Audrey asked. She made a point of speaking Russian as much as she could around the chuchuna, at least when she wasn't giving Zhadan his English lessons with Tomas.

The chuchuna snorted. "<<*My brood would eat you alive, make you come crying to my den in moments.*>>"

The door swung open again, their other nearby neighbor letting himself in. Tomas kicked the snow off his boots as he peered at the table. "They took them all?"

"Early bird and the worm and all that, lovely," Innocence tutted from behind him, the incubus sliding into the cabin with his uncanny grace. He inclined his head toward Audrey, then Lyubava, his perfect golden curls shimmering in the early light. "Ladies."

Audrey blushed despite herself; Aperien biology was what it was. Innocence was a duster, which meant he was part human, but his incubus blood ran heavy. She wasn't sure she could *not* find him attractive, even when he wasn't overtly trying to be seductive. He was beautiful in an ethereal way, flawless and lean, with sea-green eyes that glowed in any light.

To Audrey, he was nothing compared to Jonathan, which worked out well for everyone because the incubus was helplessly in love with Tomas—who grabbed a biscuit and shoved it in his mouth like he'd never eaten before. Tomas held up the other half toward Audrey in cheers. It sounded like he said "thanks" through his full mouth, getting crumbs all over the table. Only two years younger than Audrey at eighteen, his mop of black curls was a riotous mess, and his black eyes twinkled good-naturedly.

He was a vileblood and, like Jonathan, hardly the monster the world would believe them to be.

Innocence sniffed. "Honestly, Tomas."

Tomas just hummed at him in question, right as the chuchuna boys came howling through the main room and out the front door, with Zhadan thundering after them.

"Fucking hells," Jonathan said, dropping the hatch to the basement closed behind him. "Sounds like a gods-damned battlefield up here." His expression was all disdain, but Audrey knew better; it had taken him time—long, long months—to understand he belonged here in Nizhny with all those who'd become their friends. Their family.

Innocence tried to make excuses, but Tomas dragged him into a chair and shoved a coffee into his hands. They argued for a few minutes about who kept whom up the night before. Lyubava sat with Biserka cuddled and cooing in her lap while she ate her cookies, content now that her brothers were out of the way. Her mother hummed to her, rocking the cub. Audrey brought Jonathan a fresh mug of coffee after he finished washing his hands at the sink. She leaned into him, his arm a natural fit over her shoulders as she smiled at the chaos and warmth filling their home, a mere subsect of the life they'd built together in Nizhny.

When she'd thought of a future all those years ago as an orphan and runaway, she'd never imagined her life ever feeling so full. Audrey rested her head against Jonathan's chest, feeling his little grunt at the full room—the reminder that he did all this *begrudgingly*.

A few minutes later, Zhadan burst back in with the two boys, one on each bicep, both of them biting at him. The chuchuna begged and pleaded until Jonathan 'saved' him from his sons, using them as weights for his morning exercises while Zhadan sat beside his mate and nuzzled his daughter.

Audrey gathered the books for their morning lessons. She'd been teaching Tomas to read and write, and working on Zhadan's English by proxy. Most days, after breakfast was over, Lyubava took the cubs so Tomas and Zhadan could actually study, and Innocence would depart out of boredom shortly after. Other times, everyone lingered longer, and this morning felt like one of those times. The train wouldn't come until tomorrow, with most hunting quotas and other responsibilities met for the week, creating a sort of lull that came and went.

Audrey stole a glance at Jonathan again, who was doing pull-ups now, a squawking cub clutching each ankle as he ignored them. She laughed, wondering, not for the first time, if he would have made an amazing father.

Of course, they could never have children together. His vileblood made it impossible. His kind was part of a power curse designed to wipe out humanity. Any human woman who became pregnant by a vileblood was doomed to a terrible death after giving birth to a twisted monster or a new generation of vileblood to carry on the curse.

Jonathan never would have touched Audrey, let alone slept with her, if she didn't have magical protective runes on her skin, one of which protected her from undesired pregnancy.

And while Audrey wouldn't trade what they had for anything, every once in a while, she couldn't help but dream of what it would be like if she could have children with the man she loved. Children that would never have to fear being abandoned like she was or forsaken like he'd been.

It was a pleasant dream.

Chapter 3

As much as Audrey missed Theodore, one of her dearest friends, the reason for the Archivist's visit wasn't a pleasant one. Dread curdled in the pit of her stomach as she pulled on her coat, her gaze fixed on the floorboards as she tugged her gloves into place.

The Aperien Kushiel, an angel and Accorded Warden of the Manhattan Penitentiary of the Eastern Seaboard Conjunct, was dead and buried in the taiga, not five miles north of Nizhny's border.

Jonathan delivered the killing blow, but the entire town had played a part in the angel's death, herself included. It was only a matter of time before a missing angel, especially one so important, drew attention and powerful beings came searching for answers.

Nizhny was an Independent Territory, outside the jurisdiction of the Accorded Laws. The other side of the same coin left Nizhny without Accorded protection. The frontier town, founded deep in the Siberian wilds, was a self-proclaimed town of outcasts and miscreants and monsters. A home for those whom no one else wanted.

Who would be believed: a holy Aperien war hero? Or the paroled vileblood who cut off an angel's head to save the woman he loved?

Audrey didn't want to know the answer.

Well, she already knew the answer. She didn't want to watch justice fail once again. She hadn't spent her whole life fighting injustice only to watch it play out against those she cared about again and again.

But she wasn't a fool. They couldn't ignore the situation. Theodore would have ideas about what they could do, as well as what consequences might be unavoidable.

"You should at least try to look happy to see him," Jonathan drawled as he opened the cabin door for her. "You know I won't."

She pressed her lips together even though she knew he scented her amusement. "You're still impossible," she said as they walked out into the day.

"Ain't that one of those things you like about me?" he teased.

"Love," Audrey corrected, because she would always, always remind him.

For being a hybrid Aperien, the child of a living god and a dragon, Theodore Avialian was rather unassuming. A slightly taller-than-average Black man with a shorn scalp, he always dressed in elegant silk robes. Aside from the faint sheen of iridescent scales on the back of his neck, he appeared entirely human.

Jonathan once told Audrey that Theodore was exceptionally skilled at masking his strength, magical or otherwise, because without his sense of smell, he might have mistaken him for a duster. Unlike dusters, Aperiens and hybrid Aperiens didn't have a drop of human blood.

All of these things made Theodore no less than one of her truest friends. She grinned behind her scarf, waving like an excited child as they approached the station proper. Rina, Nizhny's leader, and Theodore both waved back from within a mess of puppies, the wolves and wolf-hybrids barking and jumping, being trouble as normal.

"Letting the new ones scent him," Jonathan noted as they walked. "Must be driving the whole pack nuts, smelling a dragon out of nowhere."

True, since Theodore would have flown into Nizhny in his dragon form to avoid being tracked by the train logs coming from the Moscow Dominion.

"Come on, you're too slow," Audrey said, tugging his arm. When Jonathan only grunted, she laughed and jogged ahead without him.

The station building, Nizhny's beating heart, towered over the taiga, a holdover from the pre-Aperien era that survived when most of Siberian Russia fell to the early chaos and calamities that followed the Aperien event. Katerina Yaga, Rina for short, fought back a dirge of monsters and myths to reclaim Nizhny as an Independent leader. Just over seven years later, the frontier town was thriving, thanks in part to trade moving back and forth along the Trans-Siberian Railroad's connection to the Moscow Dominion.

Rina herself was a sight, as if she'd stepped right out of Norse mythos with her stark blond braids, icy blue gaze, and the enchanted greatsword always strapped across her back. Theodore looked positively tame beside her as he knelt and petted the puppies.

A reminder that, in their world, appearances rarely determined the truth of a matter.

While a fierce warrior and the daughter of Baba Yaga and the Aperien legend Ilyes Muromets, Rina had no magic to speak of beyond her inherited blade. Theodore could easily slay her and the entirety of Nizhny without blinking.

Theodore stood as he shushed the six eager pups. They all sat obediently at his heels, and Rina tsked.

"There's the real magic. Takes years to get these beasts to be anything but terrors." Rina scowled down at the puppies, waving them away. In Russian, she said, "<<*Off with you, you've had your snacks. Tell Yuri and Liral all is well.*>>" After a few more whines, they darted off deeper into the field of dens to find the pack leaders.

Theodore gave Rina an appreciative nod as Audrey and Jonathan approached. "Impressive pack, and they heed you well. A boon for Nizhny." Then he turned his attention to Audrey, giving her a brilliant smile. "There you are." He opened his arms as she stepped up to hug him. He was very warm given that he stood outside in little more than silks. "You look well."

"I am well." She stepped back and pulled down her scarf so he could see her smile.

Theodore's attention shifted over her shoulder, his expression changing from warm to cordial. "Gunnar."

"Theo," Jonathan drawled.

Theodore's lip twitched. "Well-mannered as ever, I see."

Audrey rolled her eyes. As much as the pair pretended not to get along, she knew they respected each other. Without Theodore's help to change the Vilestars Accord, Jonathan would still be locked in the Manhattan Penitentiary, rotting away in the dark with nothing more than sustain potions to keep him in a half-life. Without Jonathan, Audrey would have died long before she and Theodore ever met.

Without either of them, well, Audrey wouldn't be here. Or happy.

Rina saved them from standing out in the cold. "No pissing in the snow, boys. We've got more important business, yes? Aster prepped a meal, come." Then she left them, her boots heavy on the snowpack.

Audrey watched her go, unable to help a shiver, as this wasn't a casual gathering. Jonathan slung an arm over her shoulder, tucking her close. Theodore observed with a curious expression, which made Audrey blush. She had a feeling Theodore would have questions later. When he'd last seen them after they fled the ESC, she and Jonathan certainly hadn't been as close as they were now.

Audrey cleared her throat, her cheeks burning. "Shall we?"

Theodore inclined his head, his expression far too knowing, not that she had any reason to be embarrassed. She'd all but begged him to add the fourth rune to her skin, the one that protected her from undesired pregnancy, and by proxy had allowed her and Jonathan's relationship to progress.

That didn't mean she wanted to answer questions about her sex life. She wrinkled her nose at the absurdity of *that* being a concern when Theodore had come for much more important matters.

The station was warm and smelled amazing as they stepped inside, the first room beyond the entryway repurposed into a tavern which acted as the town hub for residents and visitors. As it wasn't a train day, there were no guests, only Nizhny residents, and not all of them.

Rina was a dictator, and despite her general willingness to listen to counsel from those of her inner circle, she determined Nizhny's fate. Audrey often wished some sort of democracy might find a place here, but such uncompromising forms of leadership made up most territories in the post-Aperien world.

As Audrey took her seat at the gathering of magical beings, the only human in Nizhny who'd somehow found a place at this table, she still couldn't help the apprehension deep in her belly.

They'd killed an angel to save her. Whatever befell Nizhny, her home, and her friends? She was the cause.

Chapter 4

After a few cursory items regarding hospitality, although Audrey doubted Theodore needed such reassurances, they all sat around Aster's beautifully crafted feast. Rina took the head of the long pine table and motioned for everyone to eat as she spoke.

"This is Archivist Theodore Avialan of the Icelandic Citadel, for those who aren't acquainted. He's come at my request for advice on a certain," Rina paused, her grin a bit menacing as she continued, "guest who has overstayed their welcome."

Audrey focused on filling her plate, the murmurs from around the table a mix of emotions. She didn't care for Rina being flippant, but she knew it was in part performative. As much as Theodore came as a friend, he represented the Accorded Territories. He was beholden to powers bigger than Rina.

Rina went on, unmoved, gesturing first at the blazing fireplace. "As you know, those rugs over by the fireplace are Yuri and Liral, the alphas of the pack." Neither of the dire wolves reacted beyond flicking their ears; it wasn't the first time Audrey thought they acted more like cats than dogs. "Aster here is our tavern keep and all-around welcome wagon. You can thank her for the good food."

Aster inclined her head, and like Theodore, she appeared remarkably human despite her nature. The cornflower wraith helped ensure their crops grew well and no one hungered under her care. Audrey couldn't help smiling at the Aperien who'd become one of her good friends. Aster included the cookies Audrey made as part of the feast, near the table's center in a place of honor. Snickerdoodles, because Audrey recently discovered how much Aster loved cinnamon.

Rina jerked her chin at the ceiling. "Celaeno is my scoutmaster," was all she said to introduce the harpy, who preferred to be neither seen nor discussed. Theodore gave the fellow Aperien a nod that wasn't returned, red eyes glowing from the rafter's shadows.

"Frode and Hertha represent all Clan Bödvar matters here," Rina went on, "and supply the mead, lucky for us."

The Úlfheðnar nodded, the older berserker pair husband and wife. Audrey's bite of bread stuck in her throat. Úlfheðnar magic didn't grant immortality, both Frode and Hertha showing their age compared to the immortals.

Hertha was a thick woman with stern features, and Audrey didn't think she'd ever seen her without the bear-head armor across her shoulder. She kept her head shaved on one side, an intricate tattoo across her scalp of four bear cubs. A red ink line cut one in half, as her eldest son was executed for his crimes against his Clan. Two were simple black ink, but the third had recently changed, overwritten with luminescent blue.

Njal. Her youngest son, who died defending Audrey and Nizhny from Kushiel.

Hertha met Audrey's gaze from across the table, likely feeling her staring at the woman with her smothering guilt. Audrey blinked a few times, trying to seem anything but desperately, painfully sorry. It surprised her when the old warrior's stony expression softened.

Eyes burning, Audrey stared back down at her food. She was grateful when Jonathan's hand found her knee and gave a gentle squeeze. She wove her fingers in his and squeezed back, lifting her chin. They needed to make sure none of Hertha and Frode's other children or grandchildren suffered the same.

Frode offered a toast then, to resolutions, the giant man warm despite the recent loss, always the balance to his wife.

"You've met Virtue." Rina motioned to the Aperien seated at her right hand. Virtue smiled, all seductive grace and beauty, even when all she did was sit in a wooden chair.

Today, Virtue wore an exquisitely embroidered mink-lined cloak, which Audrey knew the details about because Rina had asked for her help in arranging the gift. While Virtue was a succubus-incubus hybrid Aperien who serviced the town residents in return for feeding on their life force, she and Rina were more than just lovers. The near miss during the battle with Kushiel had only strengthened that relationship, whatever they called it, because the pair were inseparable, and the cloak wasn't the only gift Audrey had helped Rina secure from the Dominion. On the next train day, Virtue would receive a crate of persimmons and thirteen handcrafted teas.

Audrey wondered if Rina was working up to a larger question.

"We've met," Theodore said, lifting a glass toward Virtue. "I was one of many voices opposed to the Accorded action against the Velvet Emporium during your oversight."

Virtue hummed, swirling her glass. Her sea-green eyes—the same color as her half-brother, Innocence—gleamed in the tavern's low light. Unlike Innocence, who was golden-blond and white as snow, Virtue's coloring was several shades darker than Theodore's. In moments like these, when Virtue let a bit of her innate power leak out so those gathered remembered exactly who and what she was, she reminded Audrey of a living, breathing shadow.

"A shame wiser minds didn't prevail," Virtue said, her voice barely a whisper, the words cold and clipped.

"A conversation for another time," Rina said.

Audrey didn't know for whose benefit she cut off the exchange.

She introduced E next, the dvergar smith at the table's opposite end, appearing as nothing more than a bored, dirty dwarf. The knowing look Theodore and E exchanged made Audrey wonder if the pair knew each other from before Nizhny. If Theodore knew E was Eitri, one of Odin's legendary smiths. Being that Odin was alive and well, and part of the Icelandic Citadel of Knowledge's pantheon, which Theodore served, it wouldn't be a surprise.

At the invading memory of Jonathan dying, metal boiling in his chest as E worked his magic, Audrey swallowed a few times. A cold sweat broke out across her forehead and the back of her neck.

Jonathan squeezed her hand again under the table, outwardly focused on the continuing conversation between creatures of legend and myth, all casually seated around the table, covered in every inch by a lavish feast that should have been impossible in the middle of nowhere.

For all Audrey spent her life around Aperiens and dusters, sometimes she felt out of her depth as a mere human, masquerading as if she belonged at their table.

Theodore dabbed the corner of his mouth after a drink, then cleared his throat. "It may be best for an accounting, top to bottom, of what occurred."

Audrey wondered if they would play word games the entire time he was here, but then Rina waved a hand, dismissive as she took another bite.

"Tomas and Mateo were the start of it," Jonathan started off. "Two vileblood stowaways on the train heard this town was a safe harbor for our kind. No lies on either of them, so Rina gave them a fair shake, let them stay to see how they'd fit."

Audrey almost laughed at the streamlined version of events.

"They settled in without causing trouble," Virtue confirmed, an idle hand playing with Rina's braided hair. "They partook of services from my brother and myself, met their quotas, and kept to themselves otherwise. Then Innocence tasted blood madness on Tomas."

"We wanted to help him," Audrey said.

"Then Mateo was a fucker," Jonathan drawled. "Tried to kill me, used his brother as a smokescreen, figuring shit would end up better? Who fucking knows. The kid wasn't so far gone, and Rina arranged for a blood mage to come in from the Dominion to cure him. And I killed Mateo."

Images flashed in Audrey's mind, along with the gleeful croons that the man she loved was dead. Visceral sounds of a body being taken apart. So much blood, dark black blood. Her head swam as she drew a shaking breath, reminding herself Jonathan was alive and Mateo was dead and gone. She squeezed his hand tighter, her palm damp with sweat.

Jonathan pressed his lips to her temple. "Hey, I'm right here." She closed her eyes and nodded. The room stayed quiet beyond the scraping silverware against plates and the hearth fire popping. Yuri whined once. Audrey recognized his tail thumping against the floorboards.

"Sorry," she whispered.

"Don't be," Jonathan murmured against her hair before he looked over her head toward Theodore. "He trapped her in the house, told her I was dead. Wasn't time for anything but taking him out, so she saw the whole fucking thing." There was a growl to his words, a tension thrumming in the air, in his body, his barely contained rage.

Audrey patted his chest. "I'm okay. It's just difficult to think about, that's all." She turned on Theodore, offering him a wan smile. "We think he saw Tomas's blood madness as an opportunity."

Theodore wasn't eating, instead leaning forward on the table, fingers steepled at his lips, and for all his outward calm, Audrey recognized his fury. Unlike Jonathan, Theodore kept his anger carefully concealed. She knew the posture from countless meetings fighting for the Accorded reforms when his patience ran thin with arrogant Aperiens who refused to listen to the most basic, reasonable requests.

"An odd chance for two vilebloods to show up here, of all places, looking for sanctuary," Theodore said in that quiet way of his.

"He sent them; he admitted it later," Rina said, still avoiding mentioning Kushiel by name. "He must have learned Gunnar ended up here and needed a reason to come all the way out to Nizhny without drawing attention to himself. He went on and on about his duty to check in on the vileblood under the new Accord, about Gunnar breaking his parole by burning down Audrey's apartment and supposedly killing her in the blaze."

"He admitted to setting the hellfire loose," Audrey whispered. Theodore's grim expression suggested this didn't surprise him.

"Mateo was already dead at that point, and we figured if he came across Tomas," Rina went on, "he'd put the boy to the sword for being blood mad. He threatened me openly, ready to take me in for breaking the Accords by not turning in Gunnar." Rina rolled her eyes. "Gunnar intervened, was all set to go back to the ESC, which seemed exactly what the bastard was after."

Audrey's brow furrowed at Jonathan, who met her gaze head-on without a hint of remorse.

"He didn't know you were alive. I went quietly, Nizhny was safe, and you its best-kept secret." When she opened her mouth to protest, he smirked. "Like you wouldn't have done the same damn thing. I know you wouldn't have let Rina take the fall to save your own ass, let alone the entire town and everyone in it."

Audrey pursed her lips. When she turned to glare at Rina—a silent *you knew about this*—she only quirked a brow. Theodore chuckled.

Rina pointed her fork at Audrey. "Gunnar's right. He didn't know you were here. He seemed to lose his mind when he found out."

Another memory Audrey wouldn't soon forget.

She'd never expected to see Kushiel again, yet there he was, striding down the station stairs from Rina's office as if he belonged in Nizhny, as if he'd existed here the entire time and she'd somehow missed him. Like always, the angel dressed impeccably, everything about him perfect. The deepest, dearest dreams of humanity made flesh.

Then he saw her, and everything angelic and beautiful about the Aperien faded to ashes. Fury replaced shock, twisted and dark and age-less. Hatred, raw and eternal.

For all she'd disliked Kushiel during her arguments to free Jonathan, she'd never feared him. She feared his attempts to sabotage their efforts might bear fruit and feared the influence he had over the penitentiary holding Jonathan. When he spared her from the strip search in a dark back room after she mistakenly brought contraband into the prison, she feared what might happen to her if she messed up again. But she'd never feared him, not directly.

She knew in that moment he meant to kill her. For all Kushiel's hatred for the vileblood, the Vilestars War, and Jonathan by proxy, the angel hated her more. Audrey tasted the lengths he would go to, his willingness to kill every single person she'd ever cared for, on the warming tavern air.

She did the only thing she could think of, the only chance to save a few lives. Audrey knew Jonathan would follow them, but maybe she could spare the rest.

She ran.

Audrey blinked a few times, the surrounding conversation continuing on. They talked through the battle now, but not too much in the way of specifics. Rina herded the conversation away from giving more information than necessary about any specific person's involvement. She mentioned Aspen, the leshy, and the dire wolf pack's losses. Frode spoke of Njar, followed by an old Norse prayer, and then recounted how Jonathan beheaded Kushiel with Rina's sword.

They breezed by Jonathan almost dying.

Audrey wasn't sure if she felt relief or frustration at having those circumstances diminished.

Theodore was respectful in his attention, no matter the speaker. Aster began cleaning up, and Audrey leaped at the chance to do something, anything really, besides stare at her hands and shake like a leaf.

Virtue laughed, the sound fanged. "Please, his sense of justice died somewhere on the bloody fields where his sword found Lamashtu's heart. It's been a century, more than, and he's had plenty of new fascinations. He's a warmonger, like the rest of their kind, provided the sword cuts."

"Come now," Theodore said as he reclined now. Non-threatening, Audrey recognized, as she piled up a few plates. "We can't lump all angels together any sooner than we can all vileblood."

Audrey grinned at Jonathan's snort, but Virtue wasn't amused.

"He had no qualms about labeling his self-proclaimed righteousness above the truth of what happened here. Said it, plain as daylight. He would call a tribunal, lie in earnest, and see us all burn because his 'merits' surpass our own." Virtue waved a hand, which Rina caught and held. "There was no doubt in his mind your pantheon would align with him unquestioned. Not unlike the Velvet Emporium purge."

"I'm not arguing with you, Virtue," Theodore appealed, his expression grim now. "Merely stating that you can't expect all who sprung from the same faith to fall in line with one angel's thinking."

"You make it sound simple," E chided, gruff as he drained his mead horn. "He is—was—well-supported across the Accorded Territories. There's never been a change in the Penitentiary Wardens. All of 'em have kept their post since the Citadel appointed them. That's a hell of a resume against a fresh Independent."

"All of which is secondary." Rina rubbed her face. "It's been six weeks now. How long do we have? Is our time already up?"

"Not as such," Theodore replied. "He left the Manhattan Penitentiary in the hands of his second, the angel Pyriel, taking time away for personal matters."

"Yeah, that doesn't stink," Jonathan said. Audrey patted his shoulder as she moved by him, gathering up more used dishes.

"That said, it's been long enough now that there are questions, especially since unobtrusive scrying can't seem to locate him. His holy blade is also unaccounted for." Theodore rubbed his jaw. "No official requests for investigation yet, but there's an ongoing dialogue between Pyriel and the Citadel. This behavior is an outlier on Kushiel's part; being untraceable is practically an announcement."

"Then it is working," Rina asked, brows lifted, unable to stop herself from glancing in E's direction. The old smith shrugged.

"I'd like to verify myself," Theodore said, "Some things are less reliable under a closer inspection."

E grunted. "How's the room read to you now?"

Audrey bit her lip as she stepped behind the bar while Theodore glanced around the tavern.

"I was under the impression the body isn't in Nizhny proper."

"The body, no," Jonathan said, his black eyes gleaming at the irony of a holy sword melted down and reformed inside of a vileblood's chest.

Audrey braced herself against the bar, her nose suddenly burning. Metal, liquid and boiling, mixed with flesh and evaporating blood . . .

A cool hand touched her cheek, and Aster offered Audrey a clean, wet cloth. She took it with weak smile, wiping at the fresh sweat.

"Give yourself time," Aster said, quiet enough for her ears only. "That night was difficult."

"Thank you," Audrey murmured.

Theodore's laugh cut through the haze. "May I ask how?" Jonathan's shirt was open, Theodore perusing the scars. Audrey looked away, following Aster to gather the last of the dishes.

E's only answer was: "You don't melt metal down, remake it anew, and call it the same damn thing."

Theodore hummed. "A novel approach."

"A necessary one," Rina corrected. "Hellfire and holy steel don't mix so well when they aren't controlled."

"He set fire to the forest as if it cost nothing," Aster added, retaking her seat as Audrey brought the leftover bones and gristle from the roast to Yuri and his mate. Both licked her hands, happy with the offering. "He flung his power around like a child." Aster rarely showed intense emotions, but she fumed now. She'd spent the weeks since that battle nursing Aspen's forest back to health. Helping the leshy recover was an ongoing process. "To be so cruel and claim to be just? And to know we were nothing in the face of his weight." Aster spit, garnering more than a few surprised reactions, her voice a low hiss when she added, "And you on high wonder why we seek freedom on the fringes."

"She's got a point," Rina said, all pride and self-satisfied, but the conversation didn't sit quite right with Audrey.

"He was also grieving," Audrey said, quietly, but not so much so that the entire gathering didn't turn on her. She shivered head to toe, because they might be her friends, but it reminded Audrey exactly how small and human she truly was. She cleared her throat though, and found her voice. "For all he was wrong, for all he sought to use the system favoring him to his advantage, I don't think it was out of spite, or power for power's sake.

"I don't know who he lost in the Vilestars War, but his pain was real. Even after all this time, he grieved." She blinked a few times, her eyes stinging. "I thought Jonathan was dying." She didn't look at him now, she couldn't, instead walking her gaze between the Aperiens and other dusters at Rina's table. "I can't imagine living with that kind of loss for a hundred years.

"Maybe the human colloquialism is 'time heals all wounds,' but we're mortal. And what we dreamed, we dreamed within the constraints of that mortality. There's no forgiveness or Heaven for angels because we never imagined they would need it. Or maybe we never imagined beyond what *we* needed from the mythos we created? I don't know, but there wasn't an end to his suffering and grief. He had eternity stretched out in front of him, without whoever was supposed to be part of that future.

"It's not an excuse," Audrey went on, "but worth remembering about those who come looking for answers. If his death might be justice to us, injustice elsewhere, or maybe heartbreak to one who might force that pain on others in retaliation."

"Eloquently spoken, as always," Theodore said, and she blushed under his pride. He'd always believed in her, hadn't he? From the first time they met, an archivist sent to assess a report filed by a no-name human girl seeking to overhaul Accorded law. He pushed back from the table. "Perhaps a walk in the woods is amenable then? Before it gets dark, of course."

Chapter 5

It wasn't required that Audrey accompany the small group to the deep woods, to the space that had been haunting her dreams and waking hours, but she needed to go. She needed to see that the forest was healing, to see Aspen and apologize for the mess she'd dragged to his feet. She pulled her fur jacket tighter, snuggling down into her scarf. The sky remained clear, but it smelled like more snow was on the horizon.

Jonathan led them, Rina and E close on his flank, while Audrey walked with Theodore a few paces behind. She couldn't help but grin when Jonathan glanced back—again—as he'd been doing every few steps since they passed by their cabin and reached the trees.

Theodore chuckled.

"I know you're just waiting to pry," Audrey said as he took her hand and helped her climb over a fallen tree.

"We can speak plainly," he replied. "No one will hear us."

She pulled back her mitten-covered hand. "Why would that matter? I'm not hiding anything." Her cheeks warmed. "We're together now, if that's what you're asking."

"That much is clear," Theodore said with another chuckle, along with a nod at Jonathan, who glared at them both now. "Seems he's noticed he cannot hear us anymore."

"Is this an excuse to bicker with him then?" Audrey rolled her eyes.

"Honestly, you two fight like children."

"No. I simply wish to know if you are happy, Audrey."

"I am," she said as she stuck her chin out. "Why do you think that question needs to be answered under some kind of secrecy?"

"Because happiness can be complicated, and I assumed you wouldn't want to discuss private matters with an audience."

"And I thought we'd moved past this distrust when you brought us to Nizhny, together." Audrey tried and failed to keep the annoyance from her tone.

Theodore was silent for a beat, and when he spoke again, there was a dangerous edge to his voice that could only belong to a powerful Aperien. "Did he know about the rune I gave before or after he took you to his bed?"

Her cheeks flamed now, partly with embarrassment, because Theodore was right, she did not feel comfortable discussing sex casually, as it was only her and Jonathan's business. But she was also furious at his blatant questioning of Jonathan's character. After everything, after they'd fought together to change the Vilestars Accord, after Jonathan saved her life a second time and brought her to Theodore for help, he still saw Jonathan as a threat.

"You still don't trust him," she said, unable to mask the hurt as Theodore rested a gentle hand on her elbow. "Why not?"

"Perhaps I've lived too long," he answered, "and seen too many good things collapse when pushed. Or I've become jaded. Maybe I care about your welfare enough to risk insulting you, so long as it ensures your safety."

"You left me with him in a frontier town of self-proclaimed monsters and trusted him enough to keep me safe then. What changed?"

"Yes, I left a human woman in the hands of a vileblood when that vileblood would sooner cut off his own arm than lay a finger on you.

A man who shied away from offering you the barest physical comfort because he understood the boundaries of the curse in his blood. Clearly, *that* has changed."

Jonathan walked toward them now. His expression was neutral, but Audrey knew him well enough to read the tension in his entire body.

Part of her wanted to tell Theodore it was none of his business; she was a grown woman, not a child, no matter her age when he met her, no matter how long he'd lived compared to her. He was her friend, not her father, for all their relationship might feel like it at times, and the magic Theodore put on her skin should have rendered this entire conversation moot.

But it didn't, she knew, because it wasn't a question of whether she'd been safe from Jonathan's blood when they had sex. It was a question of Jonathan's character, both because of and despite his bloodline.

Because in a world where gods walked, taking things on faith had become a bit more complicated.

Theodore had only known Jonathan in the prison visitation room, chained to a chair, unbelieving his life could change until it did. He'd been there for the argument in the hall, when Jonathan was ready to bolt, not understanding why Audrey wanted to help him beyond some sort of debt solution. And yes, Jonathan saved her life a second time from the hellfire attack on her apartment, brought them both to Theodore to escape the ESC, but that saved his own life as much as hers.

How much of Theodore's faith in Jonathan had really been faith in her?

"He knew before," Audrey said, her expression firm as she stared up at her mentor. Putting her faith in him. "He asked what they meant, and I told him, and he still didn't make any advances. Unless holding me through my nightmares counts. And I told him how *I* asked *you* for the rune protecting me from getting pregnant. And I kissed him first, and when things went too fast for me, he stopped when I asked. He didn't understand at first when I told him I loved him."

She shook her head, smiling despite herself at the memory of his utterly befuddled expression when she confessed her feelings. "I explained I couldn't have sex with him if he felt nothing for me. He didn't touch me again, not until after he almost died to save my life and told me he loved me back."

Jonathan reached them, growling as he asked, "There a problem?"

Theodore replied, "No, not in the least."

Jonathan stayed at her side for the rest of the walk, into the bowers where the shadows stretched and the snow mixed with fallen pine needles. No one spoke much, each of them diving into memories of that night. Or, in Theodore's case, quiet respect for what came to pass within these woods. Aspen's trail was a clear path if one knew where to look.

That said, it was a bit overgrown now, tangled with weeds and gnarled roots, a warning almost, and the forest air carried a distinct foreboding she didn't recall feeling the other times she'd visited Aspen's territory. She shivered despite her furs and the days' ever-so-slow creep toward spring. Jonathan's hand found the small of her back as they maneuvered around the overgrowth, and she was thankful for his steady presence and ability to sense her mental state.

She wondered if coming back to this place where he almost died troubled him. As per his normal, he remained outwardly stoic and unmoved by anything around him, his black gaze fixed ahead. A survival mechanism he'd built up over the years? He'd never stayed in one place unless forced. When in solitary confinement for ten years, Jonathan had existed in torpor. Once released, he'd been ready to run again, never looking back and always waiting for the next shoe to drop.

Until he decided Audrey was worth the risk a second time, and then they'd come here to Nizhny, now their home. A place where he'd found friends and the love between them.

All it cost him was a blade through his chest and a near-death experience. Who knew what it might cost next, when the Accorded came calling over a dead angel?

Audrey imagined he'd remain much the same as he'd always been in her eyes: unshakable.

"Almost there," Rina said to Theodore, who walked shoulder to shoulder with her now. Audrey caught bits and pieces of their conversation, mostly about the status of Nizhny, their successful trade endeavors, and how their reputation grew.

Theodore hadn't attempted to persuade Rina to join the Accorded Territories yet, even though Audrey knew he considered it.

It wasn't just about the accolades Theodore would garner for bringing a new player into their fold. Not like he needed any, given his birthright and his prestigious work since the Citadel's inception. He genuinely believed the Accorded Territories would benefit from fresh views, and Rina would certainly bring that in spades. Audrey understood Rina's desire for independence, along with her distaste for Accorded Laws and past actions of the Accorded Territories, but her stance put Nizhny at odds with most of the world. At the very least, with the most powerful Aperiens.

Audrey shook her head—thoughts for another time.

The clearing was nothing like where she'd fled from Kushiel now.

The forest had been at its most dense here, lush with the leshy's magic. Old-growth trees thick with moss despite the heavy snows. Ice on the branches shimmered like glass, the air warmer than the taiga should be, a frosted wonderland to Audrey's human senses, and yet somehow welcoming as a warm and well-tended hearth. Granted, her first visit to Aspen's forest had been laden with good intentions and hope, peace her primary focus, and she'd put herself on the line for a better solution than violence for Nizhny.

When Aspen had stepped from the woods and took a seat on a stump shaped like a chair instead of a throne, he was what she'd imagined a grandfather might be like. A long and lean man made of bark and old magic, he sat with her, a human girl, and talked about her hopes, ate her cookies, and never once begrudged her very terrible Russian grammar.

Now, the same clearing was more of a meadow than a cultivated gap in the trees for visitors. The old growth was gone, the once-proud trees knocked down or burned away with hellfire. To the north, the trees parted in a deep line, charcoaled trunks and missing branches, deep trenches in the soil covered by snow where the canopy no longer touched. But young evergreen saplings sprouted in the churned soil, a woman kneeling among the greenery.

Aster had beaten them here, her cornflower blue dress pristine as she rose from the mud. She glowed under the overcast skies, particularly her vivid blue eyes, but Aster seemed less vibrant than normal. Tired, no doubt helping Aspen recover taking a toll on her magic.

That was when Audrey noticed Aspen's chair stump remained on the clearing's edge, and the leshy sat atop it. What was left of him.

Audrey dashed through the fresh growth, avoiding the tiny trees and sinking to her knees in front of the stump. "Oh, Aspen. I'm so sorry."

The leshy, a spindly thing no bigger than a rabbit, ran his twiggy fingers through his tiny beard. Aspen's gaze still brimmed with magic, an eerie verdant light shimmering like faceted emeralds.

"For what, child?" It was strange how deeply his voice resonated, given his diminutive size.

Audrey wiped her cheeks, sniffling as she rocked back on her muddy heels. "I led him right here to this beautiful place, and he destroyed it. He burned your forest. He hurt you."

"Did I not seal myself to the bonds of agreement between my forest and your Nizhny?"

"Rina's Nizhny," Audrey corrected. "And yes, to defend the territory if anything crossed into your forest." She pressed a hand against her chest. "Kushiel came from the railway. He would have never come here if I hadn't."

"And you believe my interpretation of being part of the Nizhny Independent Territory would allow for me to stand by during an attack on Nizhny proper so long as the clash remained beyond this soil?"

Audrey hesitated, because the last thing she wanted was to offend Aspen on top of everything else. "This soil was yours long before Nizhny. When I drafted the agreement, I worded it in a way that granted you as much leeway as acceptable for Nizhny's expansion plans to be satisfied without risking any further border conflicts. I left those obligations vague intentionally, despite your agreement to consider Rina your sovereign as long as she holds Nizhny. Neither you nor Rina challenged it."

The leshy hummed, the sound shaking the trees, pine needles sprinkling the air. "What is it you fear, child? That you have angered me?"

"My entire purpose in negotiating a peace was to avoid violence against you." She waved a hand. "And then I brought it here myself. I'm so sorry, Aspen."

"Wounds heal. Trees grow. And the dead are not always a burden alone."

"But—"

"Look closer, child. Tell me what you see."

She turned against the stump. Aster smiled as she sat beside Audrey and patted her knee. Rina, E, and Theodore remained at the clearing's edge, talking. Jonathan stood beside them but watched only her.

It didn't take long for Audrey to notice how the trees around the edge of the clearing shimmered, silver and gold, almost like filigree buried in the bark cracks. The saplings were the same: delicate glowing veins within the new wood, and the flowers. They were all beautiful white lilies.

"He feeds the recovery of the wounds he wrought," Aspen said. "Yes, this forest will always bear the mark of his hatred, but as it grows, as it meets with the purity of nature, the uncomplicated simplicity of life anew, it changes."

"How much of him is left?" Rina called across the clearing. Ever the sledgehammer, Audrey thought, shaking her head at the bluntness of her question.

"By the solstice, he will be entirely renewed," Aspen answered.

Audrey did the mental math—middle of May now, the summer solstice would be in late June. A few weeks and the angel's body would be gone.

"The overlaid warding is impressive," Theodore said for everyone's benefit. "I can barely see the threads at all, not without knowing where to look, and standing here, inches from the grave, I sense nothing." He rubbed his chin, circling a small space, and Audrey realized then if she squinted just right, she could make out silver strands no thicker than a spider's thread, coming together to form an oblong lattice. "I've never seen such fine craftsmanship."

"By solstice, it won't matter," E said with a grunt, his arms crossed. For being one of Odin's legendary smiths, he was the most subdued Aperien Audrey had ever met.

"Would you consider—" Theodore started, his tone curious, but E cut him off.

"No." He held up a thick hand when Theodore seemed ready to push. "I'm not giving it a name. I'm not giving it to you or anyone else. And I'm sure as hells not telling you a damn thing about how I did it. And when it's done, no one will ever find the metal I used."

The air shifted, heavy in a way that made Audrey's insides twist. Power, magic, danger, was all her human instincts gave her, while Jonathan grinned like a cat with the cream because anything that involved Theodore being put in his place was bound to make his entire week.

"I respect your decision." Theodore went as far as bowing, and that uncomfortable feeling in the air dissipated. To Aspen, Theodore asked, "And this won't have lingering effects on your forest?"

Tiny Aspen considered long enough that Audrey wondered if he was going to answer at all, but then he shrugged, the gesture so human-like she couldn't help but smile. "Many things have come and gone in these woods, fallen to become a part of the whole. It exists, echoes of old power, but when a tree falls, it cannot stand up and become a tree again, no matter what comes from its rot. This clearing will bear the mark of his passage, same as the trees bear the scars of his hellfire. Perhaps a being well attuned enough could pace through my trees and tell you what fueled their growth, what death became their life, but trees do not remember names."

"And the lilies?" Audrey asked. "They aren't from this climate."

"No, they are from his blood," Aspen agreed. "When I am able, the road through my forest will change to keep such secrets."

"Thanks," Rina said then, giving the leshy a nod with a certain formality about it. "Audrey was right to bring the fight here. It saved a lot of lives and gives us a chance to make sure what really happened gets out there. You have Aster as long as you need her and she's willing."

"Not much longer now," Aster offered. The tavern had been quiet without her, everyone looking forward to having her back behind the bar.

"It is best you return now," Aspen said, his voice carrying less than when they arrived. He was tired, Audrey realized.

"I'll make sure Aster has cookies for you next time she comes up," Audrey said as she rose. She bit her lip. "And thank you for helping me."

"You are most welcome, Audrey Doe of Nizhny." The leshy smiled, still the gentle grandfather despite how small he was at the moment. She looked forward to visiting him again after he'd fully recovered, because she really wanted to give him a hug. "And your Russian is much improved, child."

She blinked, realizing that she had, in fact, been speaking Russian the entire time. Everyone had. Hearing it spoken so much must finally be sinking in.

Audrey bid Aspen and Aster a last farewell, walking wide around the thin metal warding E contrived to keep prying eyes away from Kushiel as he decomposed and fed the forest he destroyed.

She spared a single glance to where Jonathan almost died, the tall pine tree stained pitch where roots met soil, the dirt darker and bare of snow.

A single black lily rose from the loam.

Chapter 6

Audrey didn't realize she was staring out the oval window over their sink at nothing until Jonathan came up behind her. He reached around her to shut off the running water overflowing her teapot, his broad chest warm as he pressed against her back. That done, he rested his hands on either side of the counter around her.

"Okay?" The word was a feeling as much as a sound this close. Audrey shrugged as she leaned back into his sturdy presence.

"What about you?" she asked instead of answering.

"What about me?" he mumbled, running his nose along her throat. She squeezed her eyes shut and shivered.

Jonathan Gunnar kept composed at almost all times. Audrey had rarely seen any public displays of emotion from him that didn't involve carefully controlled aggression, annoyance, or anger. Otherwise, he was aloof or intimidating. Outwardly removed and cold. Feral and almost feline in his apparent disinterest in everything around him.

But she'd known him long enough now to recognize his behavior wasn't for lack of interest or emotion. If there wasn't immediate danger that called for action and snap instincts, Jonathan turned inward and processed. What surprised Audrey was when Jonathan stopped hiding from *her* when he did this internal prowling.

He let things seep from around his edges with her, as if he dropped his guard just enough for her to know where his head was at, all without releasing the full landscape of his thoughts. Like right now.

Not even an hour ago, they'd returned to the battlefield where he almost died. Where she'd held him while he bled out in her arms and an Aperien forged a new wonder around his heart. *What about me* was his default kind of deflection. And maybe he wasn't bothered the same way she was bothered, but he felt *something*.

Audrey sensed it all over his motions, which she only now recognized because she'd experienced the man completely and utterly relaxed. *With her.* Jonathan told her things now without words.

In the way he crowded her, pressed against her bodily, a hand drifting down to squeeze her hip and hold her against him. When he inhaled under her jaw, deeper when she opened her throat to him and sank further into his arms. How he ran his teeth over her skin. How he bit down, just there, where her shoulder and neck met, the place he loved most to mark her skin.

Mine, the movements said, each and every one of them possessive. Obsessive and reverent in the way he held her. Audrey wondered if others might find this behavior concerning, her lover almost aggressive in his need to reiterate, over and over, in a hundred different ways that he'd never, ever let her go.

Should it have bothered her? She was a woman, not a thing, after all. Feminism and all that, alive and well despite all the Aperien founding mythos striving for the contrary. But the truth was, she loved every second of his attentions. If she'd thought loving him from a distance drove her crazy, having his focused affection only reinforced her own intense feelings.

And for them, the intensity made sense. They were both castoffs, unwanted and shunned in different ways, forgotten in others. Isolated without love for much of their lives, believing themselves either unworthy of such a thing or doomed to never encounter it, either in a human lifetime or immortality's gifts. Against all odds, they'd found each other and filled the missing piece in the other. Maybe they didn't know any other way to love but with *everything*.

It was perfect.

Audrey laced their fingers. "Did going back there bother you?"

Jonathan left off her neck and pressed his cheek against her hair. "Not bothered by going back there, but that asshole's a problem even dead in the ground. He'll still be a problem when he's gone from the dirt completely. Don't like it, having a threat just hanging out there like that." When she hummed in agreement, he moved his hand from her hip, pressing it against her stomach and pulling her closer to him, like he wanted her to be a part of him. "Kinda like before you got the Accord changed, but instead of running, gotta dig in. Protect what matters."

Audrey felt his heartbeat thrumming at her back, steady but faster than normal. "We'll figure it out," she said, and meant it. She believed Theodore would help them find a solution. She believed the truth mattered, and she also wanted to believe in the end, the truth would be enough.

"You?"

"I'm glad I went. I needed to see Aspen."

"He didn't like you calling him chicken."

She huffed, smiling despite herself. "That's not what I said, and you know it. But I needed to apologize, even if it seems silly to everyone else."

"It's not silly. It's complicated, and human and good of you. Why a lot of those fuckers don't entirely get you all the time but like having you around." Another kiss on her temple. "Or love having you around."

Of course, he smirked down at her. She grinned back, but the mirth faded after a few seconds. "I didn't like going back to where you almost died."

Jonathan grunted. "I wondered if it might help with the nightmares, seeing it again. Maybe wouldn't seem so big in your mind."

That made some sense. It was just a forest—well, a leshy forest, fed and nurtured by a decaying angel's corpse, but still. "Maybe," Audrey offered, but she didn't sound very convincing even to herself. "It's not about the forest, not really. I just . . ."

"I'm right here."

"You almost weren't. The thought of being without you . . ." Audrey made a frustrated noise. "Things were getting better; *I* was getting better after that mess with Mateo. He might not have hurt me, but the idea that you were dead . . . And then you really did almost die, right in front of me. I just can't seem to get out from under it."

"Hasn't been so long."

"How long is long enough? How long will I be stuck with these horrible dreams?"

"You aren't used to all this shit, sweetheart. Sure, you lived on the streets for a bit, but not everyone is built for violence. Saw it in the pens plenty of times when I was in the general population." He rocked her as he spoke, chin on the top of her head. "They'd throw in new inmates, and didn't matter if they were dusters or low-level Aperiens, some just shut down. Fight or flight, yeah, but there's also freezing, or giving up everything to make the threat stop. You kept your shit together when it mattered, Audrey. Ran when you needed to run, and you didn't check out when I needed you."

"All I did was cry," she whispered.

"Far as I heard it, you held me while I was covered in hellfire."

"I'm immune, remember? Theodore's runes."

"Yeah, and? You helped keep me still while E worked his magic."

"I'm pretty sure you passed out from the pain."

"You stayed," he said against her hair. "But all that was about helping everyone else, not you. I know damn well you didn't run from Kushiel to save your own ass. You lured him away."

Audrey couldn't deny as much. "He would have burned the entire town to ash."

"Then you took care of me for a week."

"Of course I did."

"Probably running on adrenaline the entire time, barely eating or sleeping. I know you never showered." She pinched his forearm, and he chuckled. "You're working through it, that's all. Delayed a bit, maybe. However long it takes, I'm here."

"I know, I just . . . We've only just found this," she said, lifting their joined hands.

Jonathan nodded; he didn't dismiss or attempt to diminish her feelings, irrational as they seemed here and now in his arms. He just nuzzled her hair again and sighed. "Yeah, I get that part."

They both stared out the window, the snow painted in warm sunset colors, as if it might mask the bitter cold.

"Doesn't bother me the same way," Jonathan offered. "But I think about being a second late. His sword through your chest instead of mine."

He'd said nothing about this to her before, but she'd wondered a few times when she'd woken in the middle of the night to find him pacing the room. He'd sense her awake, crawl back under the blankets, and soothe her as if she'd had a nightmare, even if she hadn't.

"Didn't happen. He's dead, so he won't get a second chance. Going back there today, though, my instincts are up." He chuckled, the sound dark and rumbly. "Gets me a little feral thinking about something happening to you too. Being without you." His teeth found that spot on her throat again, which already thrummed with a fresh bruise. "Makes me need, I think. Need you."

"You have me," she whispered.

Jonathan's breath was warm along her skin, his hands tighter now on her body. "Meaning, more specifically, inside you. And soon."

She blushed; the heat ran all the way to the tips of her ears.

Audrey hadn't told him his deep voice was one of the many things she loved about him, but he'd figured it out all on his own. Especially when he combined the rumbling growl with his bedroom talk. He could be filthy. This right now was mild for him, and there was no denying it aroused her to an obscene level.

"That alright, sweetheart?" The breathy, gentle question was a whisper against her ear, all pretense gone when he checked in with her. He always, always did, which directly coincided with what she loved most about Jonathan: he kept her safe.

Audrey nodded—a bit desperately, but she didn't care.

"Need your words."

"Yes, that's more than alright."

His hum of approval was another dangerous weapon, one he wielded with as much precision as any he ever utilized. It didn't help matters when he nipped at the now-tender spot on her throat, then moved her hands so they both rested on the countertop. One large palm settled low on her stomach, his calloused fingertips playing with the lacings of her doeskin leggings.

Audrey had mentioned in passing she found the leathers made from local beasts rough on her skin. She wasn't complaining, just making plans to order materials on the next train out. He told her not to bother. Jonathan brought back the doe the next morning, then took a trip down to Clan Bödvar's campground for tips on keeping the hide extra supple and soft. Once the hide was treated, he'd brought Virtue by the cabin, had her help with Audrey's measurements and make sure the stitching looked nice.

The pants were one of the most thoughtful gifts she'd ever received and her absolute favorite piece of clothing.

Right now, she wanted them *off*.

Audrey squirmed, Jonathan moving painstakingly slow as he undid the ties of her pants. "You don't have to wait."

"Wait for what?" Jonathan drawled the question, reminding her of a cat, and not for the first time. How he acted entirely disinterested despite being focused on whatever held his attention, which was currently her. She knew he liked to tease her; he knew what she meant, what she wanted, but as much as she loved when he used his voice for seduction, she also knew it drove him entirely wild when she mustered the courage to speak to him in that manner.

It never mattered how mild her words were compared to his, or if she stumbled over them. Audrey wasn't putting on an act. She'd never be a seductress, by human standards or otherwise. And as comfortable as she was with Jonathan in their bed, she wasn't sure she'd ever overcome the innate shyness she felt around sex. She didn't want to take control in their bed. She wanted to be his, entirely.

But Audrey loved to please him as much as he pleased her, so she bit her bottom lip, then whispered, "To have me. To be inside me."

His reply was a muffled growl against her shoulder, his hips pressing her into the counter, grinding his erection against her backside. The hand on her stomach tightened, digging into her skin, and she reveled in stirring such an intense reaction from him.

"I'm never in that much of a hurry," he crooned, his tone at odds with the way he jerked the ties undone, his hand muscling down the front of her pants and underwear at the same time.

Audrey let out another whimper as his fingertips found her center and stroked, ever so softly, his free arm snaking up her body and taking her jaw in a firm hold.

"Besides, gotta be careful with you, being so tiny compared to me."

Audrey huffed out a breathy laugh, but she learned a long time ago that Jonathan didn't bother with unfounded boasts. Then she was having trouble thinking at all as he petted her. She was embarrassingly wet for him already, which only made her blush more and try to hide her face. He held firm, her head tilted back just so, forcing her to meet his heated gaze.

"You can't hide from me." He licked at her mouth, then nibbled on her bottom lip as he slipped a finger inside her body.

Gods, he knew how to touch her so, so well. The heel of his palm put pressure just right as he found a firm rhythm, in and out, and she gasped, pinching her eyes shut. Her head swam as he rubbed her cheek with his, his skin rough with his evening shadow.

Jonathan tsked against her lips, and she knew his smirk without seeing it. His words were scolding, but they held nothing but affection. "You thought I was just going to bend you over this counter and fuck you?"

Audrey shivered, panting now, keeping her hands flat on the countertop without being told—he'd said where he wanted them without words earlier—even though her arms and legs already quaked.

"Did you?"

"I don't . . . know," she managed, "I just wanted . . . you."

"You have me. Everything I am, everything I have, it's yours." He slipped a second finger inside her, curling them both. Tingles already raced through her blood, warming her head to toe. Lost, floating. All while he kept her anchored right here, safe in their home, secure in his arms. "But you can't have my cock until you come for me at least once, sweet girl."

Despite his words, he slowed his motions, gentling the touch to a sparking, delicious tease. Audrey tried to chase the friction, take more of what he offered, but he kept her still. With his arms around her like this, pressed firmly against his powerful body, she couldn't move at all.

It drew a strangled little sound from her throat, no longer embarrassing to her because she'd learned her noises turned him more ravenous. More possessive in the way he'd claim her. He grunted in reply, which shifted into a snarl before he took her mouth as if he needed her kiss to breathe.

Audrey moaned, a pleading sound, but he remained infuriatingly steady. When their lips parted, she nearly whined at him.

"Jonathan . . ."

"Yeah?"

"W-why are you . . . *oh, gods* . . . teasing me like this? If you need?"

"Want to savor it," he said, gentle, loving. At odds with the lewd way his fingers pumped inside her, how slick she was against his palm. Vulnerable in the way he watched her as she fluttered her eyes open, gazing up at the predator who owned her body and soul yet treasured her as if she was the most precious part of his life. "Someone like me getting to touch you at all."

"Don't do that." Her words came out breathless instead of stern. "You know you're the only one." She ended in a choked gasp, his efforts between her legs shifting from gentle petting to a pointed assault. "Jonathan . . ."

He still held her, his arms a vise, his body a wall, his mouth at her ear when he bit out, "I'm never letting you go; you know that." He sounded as wrecked as she felt, her entire body stiffening as she came hard, his words sending her over the precipice. Heat filled her limbs, that delicious tingle racing through every nerve in her body, her head falling back on his shoulder as she slumped into him, his name her mantra.

Jonathan didn't waste time, already stripping her pants and underwear off, using his foot to wrestle them down to her ankles. Her shirt went next, tugged roughly over her head, and she heard his hit the floor after hers did, her naked back pressed against his muscled chest, his lungs heaving like bellows. He nipped at her throat, her ear, her jaw, the sensation of his teeth dragging over and pinching her skin making her clench between her legs.

"Fuck, I love how the more I have you, the more you smell like me. Still want to be fucked over the counter?" he growled as she felt his hands at her bottom, wrestling himself from his pants, his fist and erection bumping her as he stroked himself and rubbed her bare skin with each jerk.

Audrey swallowed a few times, but her voice had abandoned her, so she nodded, frantic movements as her body quivered with the aftershocks of her release. A thick thigh wedged between her legs, forcing them apart.

Then he kissed her nape, mumbling against her hair, "I'd never hurt you sweetheart," before he adjusted their bodies just so, slickening his cock against her wetness. When he bumped her clit, again and again in a steady, teasing slide, a strangled cry slipped out. She bit her lip, spreading her legs wider for him, restrained by her pants at her ankles, restrained by his free hand taking her hip and squeezing tight. She'd bruise, but that wasn't hurt. It was one way he loved her: hard enough to leave marks on her skin, so she'd remember the next morning, the next day, forever.

"Please," Audrey sobbed. It was almost too much, the remnants of her orgasm making her ache in time with him spooling her up all over again. He never felt satisfied unless he pulled two or three from her. More, sometimes, when his moods were less feral and more patient, as if the entire world could wait when he tasted and pleased her. "Jonathan, love me, please."

"I do," he crooned, "I am," he added with a deep grunt, nudging himself inside, and she moaned as he speared her open wide. Every time took her breath away; he was larger than life in so many ways, he'd always been, and sex with him was no exception. His cock was no exception. Even on the tail end of her orgasm, he stretched her, more and more as he sank deeper, an amazingly torturous slide to fill her up entirely.

Jonathan took his time, his other hand smoothing up and down her spine as she collapsed onto the counter, her arms shaking so much she couldn't hold herself up all the way. She buried her face in her elbow, keening as he bumped up against her cervix, a gentle tap, before he growled and ground his hips against her rear, the sounds all satisfied male.

"Look at you, taking me so well. Fucking gorgeous."

She whimpered into her arm, face burning as he praised her. Gods, his praise, the unadulterated pleasure in his voice. She fluttered around him, wetter now, so impossibly pushed to her limit, but if he had more for her, she'd take it. She'd take everything he'd ever give her.

"Come on, sweet girl," he whispered as he tangled a fist in her hair, urging her up, but not yanking her to where he wanted. He asked instead, guiding her, and she let out a distressed cry as she pushed herself up from the counter. "That's it, baby." Her reward was his body caging hers, that huge hand commanding her jaw again, and a searing kiss that left stars behind her eyelids. Gods, he hadn't moved yet, and when she squirmed, he hummed at her, almost a purr. "Open those eyes, beautiful. Look at yourself."

Jonathan tilted her head forward, away from him, which confused her at first, until she remembered where they stood.

In front of the kitchen window.

Audrey's breathing hitched, and she kept her eyes pinched shut. Oh gods, could she do this?

Jonathan's other hand shifted from her hip, palming one breast entirely before giving her nipple a firm pinch. "I want you to see what I see."

"Jonathan," she whined his name.

She had no illusions of what she was: a human woman in a world of wonders. And she'd never really wanted to be anything spectacular or magical. She'd just wanted to be enough. But if she opened her eyes now, what would she see?

A plain, skinny girl with unremarkable brown hair, a few too many freckles, and normal hazel eyes. Ridiculous, wasn't it? Her being the fixation of this beautiful man behind her, inside her, loving her back.

"Open your eyes, sweetheart. For me."

Anything for him, she'd decided that a long time ago. Her cheeks burned, but she forced her eyes open, her brow furrowed when she met her own reflection. Her hair was tousled and wild, her cheeks pink, her eyes glassy. Her entire breast swallowed by his huge hand as he toyed with her, as if they had all the time in the world to stand in this kitchen with his cock buried inside her and not go absolutely insane.

Jonathan loomed behind her, and his expression was what stalled her embarrassment. The hunger in the depths of those black eyes as he drank her in. His pale skin against her slightly darker complexion, his fingers stroking her jaw, his arm muscles on sharp display in the hard shadows of sunset. How his mouth hung slightly open, his breath coming in harsh pants.

"Perfect," he said, and Audrey's breath caught because as she looked at them together, how they fit, how she tucked against him and he surrounded her? How he stared at her like a man obsessed and she watched him back with the same endless longing?

Yes, perfect.

Jonathan leaned closer when a tear raced down her cheek, whispering, "Okay?"

"Yes."

"Good," came another purr as he licked the tear away and gave her a slow, dragging thrust out and back into her heat. She mewled, grabbing at his arms, needing to hold on to him or she'd fly apart. "Keep watching, Audrey. Watch how perfect you are when I fuck you."

And she did.

Chapter 7

On the day before train day, Jonathan woke Audrey just before dawn, like she'd asked. He needed to hunt a bit more for his quota, delayed by their trip to the leshy's forest and visiting with Theodore. He'd walked her down to the station despite her telling him she'd be fine, but he didn't like her outside alone during the night or the between hours. Audrey didn't really argue over it because it made good sense. Most of the nasty things around Nizhny might stay away from the town proper, but nearly every one of them stemmed from a mythos that really enjoyed eating or drowning or otherwise murdering humans.

Now, tucked behind the tavern bar, Audrey hummed to herself as she ran through the list of train day preparations Aster left for her. She'd offered to help while Aster assisted Aspen with his recovery, and prepping didn't require a magical touch. And Audrey liked it. Not just helping, but cooking and the fact that it gave her purpose.

Becoming an esquire, a magical lawyer of sorts in the Eastern Seaboard Conduct, had occupied nearly half of her life. Her education had been extensive, and while Audrey thrived on learning and study-ing, being an esquire had a single goal behind it: changing the Vilestars Accord so that she could secure Jonathan's parole.

She'd succeeded with flying colors, but there'd been no time to consider what she might or might not do next with her education.

When her apartment building was burned to the ground by hellfire the night after Jonathan was freed, they'd had no choice but to flee the ESC. They'd landed on their feet in Nizhny, but barely six months went by before everything upended again, first with unexpected vile-bloods arriving in town and the complications they brought with them. Shortly after, Kushiel arrived, hells-bent on revenge.

And while Jonathan and Rina reassured her, adamantly, she had more than carried her weight since they'd arrived, Audrey couldn't help feeling a bit rudderless. Sure, she helped around town. Her education helped her assist with trade issues and negotiate a treaty with Aspen. Everyone loved her baking, especially chocolate chip cookies, and she truly was happy with her life in Nizhny, her relationship with Jonathan the obvious highlight.

She still longed to find a better niche for herself. Helping Aster out was nice. It was good having a backup, so to speak, and while she wasn't a fighter and didn't have any magical talents, she could step in for nearly any job the town required that wasn't hunting or guard duty. Rina was pleased with Audrey's offer to tutor anyone who wanted to learn English, but so far, she only had Zhadan and Tomas as students.

Audrey would just have to keep looking. She'd figure it out.

She pulled out a teapot and set the water to boil, then fetched the bread dough Aster left rising overnight.

Not everything could be as dramatic as overhauling an Accorded Law.

And that definitely wasn't how she wanted to spend all her time. As much as she loved being able to overturn injustice, the political maneuverings and endless games? Audrey might have learned to navigate them in her short time as an esquire, but she didn't like the grimy feeling that came with compromising herself in small ways to succeed at the bigger goal. She'd let Theodore handle as much of that part as possible, but she hadn't been able to avoid it completely.

Audrey's skin prickled. Even muted human instinct recognized being watched by something dangerous.

Virtue yawned as she slid onto a barstool, dressed in a stunning emerald-hued robe with gilded thread. Otherwise unadorned, the color complemented her dark skin and ethereal green eyes.

"Good morning," Audrey said, smiling, trying to ignore how she blushed.

Virtue wasn't doing anything but sitting on the stool, but her mere presence was enough to make Audrey feel . . . tingly. She tried her best to hide it, even though the Aperien no doubt sensed the arousal she inspired simply by existing. Audrey also knew Virtue and her brother, Innocence, held their natures in tight control at all times. Reminding her of what she couldn't help just seemed rude.

"Aster mentioned your tea. The kettle is ready. Did you want to steep it yourself?"

Virtue waved a hand, the motion all flawless grace. "Go ahead, if you aren't too busy." She offered a kind smile, then shrugged. "Perhaps a holdover of mine, once being so important." Virtue chuckled. "It's nice to be waited on now and again."

"I'm happy to," Audrey replied, and she meant it. She'd learned a long time ago lying, even little white lies, tended to be pointless with Aperiens. Like Jonathan, Virtue had extremely attuned senses. "Sugar? Cream?"

"No sweetener, but yes to the cream." Virtue yawned again. "Enough to make it obscene."

Audrey laughed. "Coming right up."

They kept a companionable silence as Audrey prepped her drink, smiling to herself as she poured her own cup. This black tea was mixed with orange, clove, and cinnamon, and Audrey enjoyed it in the mornings with extra honey in place of sugar or cream. She finished Virtue's drink first, pouring until the mixture was almost a latte, and brought it over.

"*Merci*," Virtue said with a sigh, holding the cup in both hands, inhaling with closed eyes.

"*De rein*," she answered without thinking. She must have picked up more than she'd realized from one of her newer books, an overwrought tome about old French mythos she'd traded the Dominion's head bookkeeper for ink.

"Audrey?"

She turned back to Virtue with a frown, because the Aperien sounded upset. "I'm sorry, too much cream?"

Virtue set the cup down as she stared, danger in her gleaming eyes. She went as far as to push the tea off to the side, canting her head. "No, the tea is fine. Would you . . ." She gestured her closer.

Dangerous as Virtue might be, Audrey didn't fear her. She did look very tired, though. Audrey wondered if she needed to feed, but she'd never ask that from Audrey. Nizhny might be Independent, but feeding on humans in any form was outlawed by the Accords. Risking it didn't make sense, even outside the Accorded territories. Not to mention Jonathan would have an aneurism.

She stepped up to the bar. "Are you alright?"

Virtue ignored her question, her stare entirely too intense for Audrey's liking. She shifted her feet under such close scrutiny, for a second wondering if it had to do with the bruise on her neck. Jonathan had worked that spot more than usual the night before, but it was just a hickey. Her cheeks heated again because she really, really didn't want to talk about her sex life with Virtue, especially when the Aperien had shared Jonathan's bed out of necessity when they first came to Nizhny.

Then Virtue leaned back, huffing out a sharp breath before she tapped her nails on the bar top. She seemed to come to some sort of decision then.

Audrey wasn't expecting her to ask, "When was your last cycle?"

"My . . . what?"

"Your monthly blood."

"I know what you mean," Audrey mumbled. "I just . . . why are you asking?" Her tummy did a little roll, because given her rune from Theodore, it wasn't something she'd been paying particular attention to, but now that she stopped and thought about it . . .

Her cycles had always been light and not particularly regular, and she'd have no reason to give them much attention until very recently. But now, as she ran through the days, then the weeks, Audrey frowned. "You know I'm protected."

Virtue nodded. Rina had insisted that they make the knowledge public. She didn't want anyone in the town to get ideas that she'd let a vileblood bed down with a human without good reason.

"I am aware of the spell work, yes."

Audrey's frown deepened, the knot in her stomach tightening. "Then why are you asking?"

"Audrey," Virtue started, then paused as if reconsidering her direction.

Why was she suddenly sweating? Audrey rubbed her forehead.

"My kind can read pheromones, as it helps us keep in tune with our lovers. It also helps us determine who is safe to feed on. Feeding on a pregnant woman would be catastrophic, as their life energy or soul, however you deem to classify it, is delicate. As is the life within them."

Audrey's lips felt numb. She counted the days again. More than a month.

"I can't be, the runes are . . . Theodore's magic . . ."

Her vision swam, and when Audrey regained herself, she sat on the floor behind the bar, Virtue crouching in front of her and pressing a cold, damp cloth to her forehead. Her expression calm but stained with blatant concern.

"You're sure?" Audrey whispered.

"I am." Virtue wiped her forehead, the sides of her neck. "Don't wait to tell him."

Jonathan. Audrey hiccupped. She was pregnant, and Jonathan was the father.

A vileblood.

The curse in Jonathan's blood was going to turn her into a twisted monster while their baby grew inside her, and then one or both of them would die when the child was born.

Chapter 8

Ten Months Earlier

Theodore's townhouse had become a second home to Audrey during their time working together on revising and challenging the Vilestars Accord. It held a minimalistic charm, mostly because he rarely spent more than a few days on the property during his visits to the ESC York hub. Over the year and a half they'd worked to revise the Accord and arrange for Jonathan's parole, the Archivist spent more and more time here. She'd watched the odds and ends stack up, like extra towels and toiletries in the bathroom, the cactus she'd bought him on the windowsill of his otherwise empty kitchen. He'd even kept a few items specifically for her in the guest room for when they'd worked late and he didn't want her on the streets alone.

Audrey stood in the guest room now, drying her hair, shivering despite the warm sweatpants and shirt she'd taken from her stash in the dresser. Her arm ached from the hellfire burn despite the fast-acting healing ointment and potions. Her feet were also sore from being in the slums for nearly three days without shoes before Jonathan and she safely made it here, to the upper streets of the York hub.

The thought of Jonathan made her smile despite her exhaustion, despite just losing everything she had to her name. He'd saved her life a second time, and when he could have left her behind, he laid out a future for them instead.

A knock sounded on the door. She shook her head, trying to focus on now even though she felt like she might fall asleep on her feet. They needed to plan how to get out of the ESC. All the flashing news screens talked about was the esquire's murder and the vileblood responsible.

Audrey opened the door to find Theodore changed from his dressing robes to his normal archivist attire, both of the handwoven, authentic silk outfits worth more than her pittance of a yearly salary. Before her career burned to ashes.

But more importantly, Jonathan wasn't here anymore. Audrey instinctively knew. The man just took up that much space in her attention.

"He left?" Audrey didn't bother hiding her alarm.

Where had he gone? Had he changed his mind after being forced to take care of her in the slums? Did that future she'd seen go up in smoke as well?

"Breathe, Audrey. A few notice-me-nots and illusions in place, and a quick memory repellent, and Mr. Gunnar was safe to send for supplies. You'll need them where you're headed." He paused, not missing how she nearly collapsed in relief. "And you're certain about this? Siberia? Under an Independent keeping a town full of self-proclaimed monsters and outcasts?"

Audrey mustered herself a bit, smoothing her sweatshirt even though she was pretty sure Theodore had used some sort of magic to keep away wrinkles. "Sounds like the perfect place to me. After all, how much more outcast can I be than dead?"

"Fair enough. And I'm sure Mr. Gunnar will fit in just fine." Theodore stepped inside, shutting the door behind him. She didn't like how he studied her now; she felt like an ant. "I do have a request, however. An insistence, actually, before you head off to the ends of the known world."

"Honestly, Theodore. I'm not worried about living without twenty-first-century technology just because I'm human."

At that, he laughed. "By far my least concern. I wish to offer you protection, as I cannot watch over you. It would be best for both of you if I played the outraged mentor, furious at the death of my protégé."

"While reminding the ESC media vilebloods can't use hellfire?" She crossed her arms, her chin up. It was absurd how quickly the news blamed Jonathan for the hellfire. When Theodore didn't comment, she said, "Right?"

"I would be best that I faded from attention with little comment and returned to the Citadel as I intended. I will not grant interviews."

"So you won't defend him?"

"I won't do anything to draw any more attention to your fate, being that you aren't actually dead and by concealing that fact I, as an archivist of the Icelandic Citadel of Knowledge, am ignoring my obligations to truth."

Audrey winced. Well, that made sense. But other truths mattered, too, like how vilebloods couldn't use hellfire.

"We digress. I'll be out of reach, and I want you protected."

"Jonathan will protect me."

"I want you protected from things he cannot defend you from." Theodore held up a hand before she argued. "Permanent runic innovations on the skin. Firstly, immunity to hellfire. If whoever came after you learned you were alive, they may strike again."

Audrey's mouth snapped shut, her head spinning a bit. Theodore would be binding part of his essence—his life, his soul, his magic—to her. While she bore his runes on her skin, he would no longer have access to that part of himself. He'd be diminishing himself for her benefit.

"Theodore, I can't ask you to do that."

His smile told her he'd foreseen her reaction. "You're not. I am insisting. I would also like to insulate you against possessions and persuasions, both common tactics of less savory magical beings on humankind." Theodore rolled up the sleeves of his outer robes, then removed a silver dagger from one pocket and a fired clay bowl from the other. He set them on the dresser. "Siberia is wild with Slavic mythos, much of it dangerous. There are no Accords so far out in the wilds that protect human life, and even beasts who might understand law have no regard for it, anyway."

"Katerina Yaga must? I can't imagine you sending me to a town with an Aperien who doesn't care for humans."

"She is honorable, but she is also bent on staying outside the Accords for the very purpose of bucking their demands. Do I believe she would harm you for being human, or allow others to hurt you? No, she takes care of those who join her Nizhny and holds her residents to reasonable standards for all the barking about monsters out in the dark. It's the actual monsters that concern me, Audrey."

It made sense. She'd be a fool to pass up such protection, from a demigod no less, who was asking for nothing in return. Audrey bit her bottom lip—better to be sure.

"No cost?"

Theodore nodded in approval at her question. "No, I offer this freely. You owe me nothing."

"And what if I said no?"

That, he didn't like. It was easy to forget just how powerful her friend was and how Aperiens, even second generations like Theodore, disliked being disobeyed. "Then I would refuse to take you to Nizhny. I would take Mr. Gunnar alone for his safety, and you would return to the Citadel with me and take up archivist training."

Audrey chafed at the finality of it all. How he believed he could just decide her life like this, not unlike when she'd been an indentured child, her contract owned by an unconcerned factory owner with dozens of other abandoned human children. Welfare, indeed, the ESC's way of adhering to the Accords by the bare minimum.

She had it better than pretty much any other human she knew.

Whistelae, the healer who saved her life and helped falsify her paperwork to free her from her childhood indenture, later sponsored her schooling so she wasn't sent back to the slums for an adult contract she'd never escape. Few humans rose above menial labor without the sponsorship of an Aperien or a duster with clout, at least in the Eastern Seaboard Conduct. And she'd earned the patronship of an archivist who believed in her and cared about her enough to help her even after she'd fulfilled her purpose as his esquire assistant.

She still didn't like it, but when gods walked and magic saturated everything, those who wielded power controlled the outcome. Audrey knew when it was pointless to fight, and despite her initial apprehensions, Theodore had always held her best interests at heart.

But she'd realized she could take some power for herself through her education. How becoming an esquire had given her a foothold and shown her that being brave wasn't just about swords and fighting. Sometimes one had to push when it would be easier to fold.

"Alright, but I have a condition."

Theodore's lip twitched; he was doing his best not to smile as he motioned for her to continue.

"I want a fourth rune," she said, then quickly amended with, "Please."

"For?"

"I want you to make it so I can't get pregnant."

He blinked several times, stunned by her request. She watched as his mind walked through her reasoning, and how his expression darkened. "You're asking me to sterilize you? For what? The hopes that this man might one day return your affection?"

Audrey's cheeks burned. "I'm in love with him." There was no dancing around it anymore. She'd suspected after she'd accidentally brought contraband into the prison and Jonathan had put his freedom on hold, more concerned about her wellbeing after the prison guards strip-searched her in a dark room. When he said *you and me* on the edge of the slums, it had sealed things in her heart. "If there's a chance he might ever feel the same, I want to take that chance."

"You've spoken at length about desiring a family."

"And you've proven to me a family doesn't only come from blood."

"You're nineteen years old."

"Almost twenty now. And?"

"You have your entire life—"

"This won't change. My dedication to the Accord reform and his freedom should be proof to you that I'm not some flighty child who doesn't know her own heart."

"Audrey." He rested his hands on both her shoulders, giving a gentle squeeze. "Gunnar may never give you what you desire. He might not be capable."

"And he might."

"He might," Theodore conceded, his expression stern, his hands warm through the sweatshirt. "But if he doesn't, you may move on. You may find another. Maybe the family you once dreamed about when your parents gave you away?"

He really did like to pull out the low blows, didn't he? Audrey hadn't cried about her parents for a decade. She certainly wouldn't now.

But the weight of the past two days, the last six months, the years preparing for the Accord hearing? And the long years before, knowing a good man had been thrown into a hole so she could live?

She was so, so tired and threadbare. She needed a good night's sleep, and the insurance that her heart's true dream—Jonathan viewing her as more than debt, maybe even more than a friend—wasn't impossible. Audrey must have been silent long enough for him to pick up on her emotions, because he tucked a thumb under her chin, tipped her gaze up to his.

"A compromise then," Theodore said, and she recognized his amusement now. Audrey narrowed her eyes at him, wondering what exactly he found funny. Maybe it was the absurdity of a human making demands from an Aperien descended from gods and dragons. "I will give you protection from *undesired* pregnancy, so if the day comes when fate changes your path, you will still have power over this choice."

She launched herself into him, hugging him for all she was worth. "Thank you."

Chapter 9

Present

Despite Virtue's offer to accompany her, Audrey walked home alone. It was broad daylight now, the trek to her and Jonathan's homestead a straight shot up the unused portion of the old Trans-Siberian railway, the same that brought the weekly trains to town. She pulled her jacket tighter, the sky clear and the air crisp and cold, the snow crunching under her heels. Jonathan promised to be back from his early morning hunt in time for lunch.

Not long to decide how to tell him she was pregnant.

Pregnant with his child, and with the curse from his blood, she would die before this was over.

She ran over her discussion with Theodore the night they left the ESC. *Undesired.* The word beat around in her skull, and she couldn't help how her chest tightened. Her eyes stayed strangely dry as she trudged boot over boot.

Undesired.

Was she that foolish?

There wasn't a moment Audrey could pinpoint where she'd decided *I desire a child.* But they'd been spending their mornings with the chuchuna family. Luybava was hunting again, so she'd watched the triplets more than a few times to give the parents a break. They were murder, the three of them together. Trouble on a primal level, and most times she came home exhausted and definitely *not* desiring three of her own.

But there were other moments which came mostly when she watched Jonathan interact with the cubs. It was absurd how easy he was with them and how he could snap them into behaving faster than their father. The kindness he showed them, and how he watched after them innately because his instincts to protect those weaker than himself didn't just apply to Audrey. There was no denying that part of him at this point. He could have easily killed Tomas when he'd been afflicted with blood madness. Instead, Jonathan found a solution and supported his recovery. He'd taken the younger vileblood under his wing, helping him manage his parcel, his hunt quotas, even teaching him to process his kills and make the most trade. Jonathan treated Tomas like a brother, or maybe a son.

So yes, there were moments when she watched the man she loved and thought he'd make a great father.

Audrey could picture how overprotective he'd be. She could imagine how it would feel to be a child of his, faced with such fierce devotion and love, given the chance. At times it made her sad, this one thing among many that made his vileblood unfair. A curse he never asked for, yet made the best of, to be among the most incredible people she'd ever known.

And Audrey knew she'd love a child of his own, with the same black eyes and broody moods, as much as she loved him.

But they were fleeting thoughts, not anything Audrey dwelled on. Jonathan was more than enough for her. Her life was full and happy, and she found ways to keep busy. She didn't long for a baby; she didn't feel incomplete without one in her life. Family, like she'd told Theodore, was all around her, and she'd never felt more at home or loved in her entire life.

Yet somehow, despite the rune on her skin, she was pregnant.

Audrey reached their home and blinked a few times, still lost in her thoughts, trying to unbraid the situation as if it were a puzzle she could solve or a law that wasn't fair. As if, with enough willpower and determination, she could change the outcome.

She laughed, a sharp sound in the quiet winter around her.

Because she was pregnant, and it would kill her.

If the baby survived being born, a boy might live, but a girl would be doomed, as Audrey. And then Jonathan would be either left alone or with the son who'd killed his lover. He'd suffocate in the guilt, the very thing he'd fought himself over for months when he already cared for her but wouldn't let himself touch her, want her, or love her. Because he was a monster, because his blood made him this monster, because his blood was a curse to end humanity.

She'd told him she was safe from his cursed blood, and he'd believed her. And then, deep down, she'd desired a child with him, hadn't she? A dream, maybe, an impossible dream, a passing thought, but that was enough to thwart a demigod's tailored spell work.

How was she going to tell Jonathan?

A thump on the deck made her jump. She'd been standing there, staring at the front door, for gods knew how long. And there he was, covered in snow, frozen mud, and blood. Behind him, a bukavac was laid out, the many-legged beast tangled, bright blue eyes wide and dead as they stared her down. It had an excellent set of horns—good for trade, her mind idly supplied as she stared at the carcass.

Jonathan dusted his hands off as he leaped down from the deck. "Zhadan needs to get his ass in gear. This thing was squatting between our parcels, and he's supposed to be watching the west side while I'm helping Tomas." He frowned as he got closer, nostrils flaring when he pulled down his scarf. "What's wrong?"

Audrey closed her eyes, squeezing so hard she saw flashing lights. Of course, he'd know right away she was distressed. No chance to warm up to the conversation, try to find a way to do what, exactly? How do you tell the person you love you're going to die and they're going to blame themselves for it?

"I'm pregnant."

Apparently, you just blurt it out.

Birds chittered in the far trees. That was how heavy the silence fell after her words, and she opened her eyes to find Jonathan stock-still. It might have been comical, the bald-faced shock on a man who was almost impossible to surprise, if the situation was anything besides dire.

He didn't move at all. She wasn't sure he breathed.

"I'm pregnant," she said again, a whisper this time. When she reached out a hand, suddenly needing to be closer to him, to touch him, she trembled. Head to toe and not from the cold.

"No."

The single word was so sharp and cruel, Audrey jerked her hand back. And his expression, gods. Her heart hurt. In all the time she'd known him, she'd never seen his expression this cold. Venomous almost, in the way he stared into the space beyond her shoulder.

"Jona—"

"This some kind of fucking joke?"

That drew a broken laugh from her. "You think I would joke about this?"

She blinked, and he was on her, right in her face, snarling so close his breath warmed her cheeks. "Theo then? What? Needed fucking proof or some shit?" Gods, he bit the words out, and he still wasn't looking at her, despite growling in her face, falling immediately back to his baser instincts of anger and intimidation in the face of a threat.

"Of what I really am? He fucking lied about that rune?"

"*Stop it!*"

They both stalled at the fury in her voice, how her shout cut through the narrow gap between them, enough that it made Jonathan retreat a step. He finally looked at her, but for all she knew him, his eyes were blank black pools that told her nothing.

"Good thing the fucker's in town, huh?" When he laughed, the sound made her cringe. He checked his belt, the blade on his thigh, and then turned around and walked north.

"Jonathan." He ignored her, his boots crunching hard on the snowpack, his motions jerky. "Jonathan, where are you going?"

"To fucking kill something." Then he laughed again, not looking back, a sneer in his voice as he added, "What I'm good at."

Audrey couldn't find her voice, staring at him until he vanished over the ridge. She watched the shadows, the slow-moving clouds, the wind shifting through the far tree line. She wasn't sure how long she stood there, but now her hands hurt, and her toes were numb. She turned from their home, crossing the flat area between their cabin and where Tomas lived now.

When she knocked, she heard both Tomas and Innocence inside, arguing about whatever they were arguing about today, because it seemed to be part of how they expressed affection. A few seconds later, Tomas swung open the door, shirtless with his trousers hanging half undone on his narrow hips. He ginned from ear to ear, his cheeks flushed despite his tanned skin, and his curly, short hair thoroughly mussed. They'd clearly been busy, but Tomas seemed delighted to see her.

"It's Audrey!" he called over his shoulder, earning some grumbling from the incubus. When Tomas looked back at her, his brow creased. "Hey, is everything okay?"

Innocence appeared at Tomas's side a second later, sighing dramatically as he draped himself over the shorter man's shoulders, his eyes the same sea-green glow as his sister's. "You better have a good reason to interrupt, I was just . . ." Innocence brushed a flop of blond hair from his forehead as his nostrils flared. Then he muttered, "Oh, shit."

Audrey burst into tears.

Chapter 10

"And that motherfucker just," Rina made a flippant hand gesture, fingers dancing around in the air violently, "decided to go for a walk in the woods, did he?"

Audrey held her tea in both hands, a gift from Virtue when Innocence and Tomas brought her to the station. They all crowded Rina's office now, along with Theodore. Tomas had been sent on a fetch quest for Jonathan on Rina's uncompromising order. It had been a few hours, and Rina was losing what little patience she had since they'd come to her.

Tomas and Innocence let Audrey settle after her outburst of emotion, full-body sobs that left her wrung out and empty. Relaying the situation two more times to Theodore, then Rina, had left her numb.

"The taiga is a big place," Innocence offered, picking at his nails from his leaning spot on the far wall. Audrey was thankful he'd stayed around; anything felt better than Jonathan turning his back to her.

Virtue tsked. "My advice, brother, is that you make yourself scarce before they return. I can't imagine Gunnar will want your input on this situation." She sat in Rina's chair because Rina had been pacing for the last thirty minutes.

Theodore remained silent. Not a word since they arrived, found him, and told him. Nothing said when he confirmed what Virtue sensed. Not a whisper when Tomas set off to find Jonathan.

"Hmmm, well, he better find his manners," Innocence muttered. He pushed off the wall and ran gentle fingers over Audrey's hair in a soothing motion. "Steady on, darling," he added, and she managed a wan smile up at him. She'd never seen his expression so grim. She'd only ever known Innocence as carefree. He shut the door behind him without a sound.

"You all really don't have to sit here with me," Audrey mumbled after he left.

"Please," Rina snapped. Since it wasn't train day, she'd dressed down in casual leathers, her bright blond hair loose instead of in a tight, single braid.

"Sit, love," Virtue cooed, vacating her seat. "Drink some tea."

"I hate tea," Rina snarled, but took the invitation, the chair creaking with the force she put into simply sitting. "If he really thinks he can hoist this off on you, as if his dick didn't play a part in this gods-damned mess?" She ended with another growling noise, which reminded Audrey so much of Jonathan she might have laughed if she wasn't struggling to keep herself together.

"I imagine shock overrode logic," Theodore offered quietly, which was the first time he'd spoken. Audrey tightened the blanket around her shoulders. He was as closed off as Jonathan, but she knew his mind was working.

But about what, she wondered? Could he have done the magic differently? Maybe he'd never believed Jonathan would love her, or maybe that she wouldn't have been so stupid . . .

Rina's office door slammed open, rattling on the hinges, and Jonathan filled the doorway. "You got a fucking reason for dragging my ass in like this?"

For all his fury, it didn't compare to the chill that settled on the room as Rina rose from her seat. Audrey swore she heard her molars grinding from across the room.

"Are you serious?" Rina asked. Virtue put a restraining hand on her forearm.

Jonathan's attention danced around the room. "Your problem ain't with me." He motioned to where Audrey sat beside Theodore on the leather couch. "Ask these two what the fuck all this is about."

"This is her problem, is it? You have nothing to do with the child in her?" Rina sneered each word, and Audrey honestly wondered if Virtue was restraining her through magic. She looked ready to hurdle her desk and throttle him.

"All feels like a fucking joke to you, too, huh? How I'm told she's safe, she believes she's safe, and then this? You know about the fucking runes." Jonathan's tone became more vicious by the second. "I would have never fucking touched her!"

Audrey blinked a few times, wondering if screaming at Rina was an easier way for him to have this conversation. He still wouldn't so much as look at her, and it . . . gods, it hurt.

"Jonathan . . ."

"No, this is bullshit." His gaze lanced to her, the full weight of it, the beast in his blood ready to tear the entire world apart and she knew why; he'd promised to keep her safe, and he couldn't, not from this. "What is it? Bad magic?" he snapped at Theodore now, teeth bared. "A trap? Undesired. You told her it would protect her if she didn't want it, so what is it? Your spell work shit?" And then Jonathan's disdain hit her again. "Or are you that fucking stupid?"

"You watch your fucking mouth," Rina bellowed.

When Theodore cleared his throat, the texture of the air shifted.

Audrey flinched because Theodore rarely flexed in the way many Aperiens flaunted their strength. All he did was clear his throat and it was as if time itself paused. An unnatural sort of calm held the world in place, and the gathering could do nothing but stare at Theodore.

When he spoke, his voice was quiet but firm. "The magic I wove is a protection against undesired pregnancy. In order to supersede the spell work, both parties involved must want the child as a true, deep-seated desire of the heart."

Audrey's breath caught hard, the tea mug crashing to the floor from her limp fingers the only sound in the room. And she stared at Jonathan, just stared.

She never seen him confused. Utterly, entirely unmoored as he processed Theodore's words, no doubt retracing his own thoughts, his own desires, and the realization that, however impossible, part of him, a big enough part of him, desired a family with her.

The understanding that it wasn't some kind of trick or trap, at least not in the way he might have thought. Oh, he probably thought it was a trap, Audrey knew, as his expression flickered from confusion to almost annoyance that he'd been caught desiring more than he was allowed to want in his life, believing himself safe from idle thoughts he'd considered inconsequential.

But then the anger flushed from Jonathan, leaving him bone white instead of his normal pale complexion. He swayed as his expression shifted again, to what she could only describe as horror, then pain. And then he looked at her, really looked at her for the first time since he'd stormed into Rina's office.

The first time since she told him she was pregnant.

Audrey saw the moment this man, the man she loved, one of the strongest people she'd ever known, broke.

The life went out of him. The fight, the confidence. It all abandoned him in a single heartbeat, and Jonathan Gunnar *crumbled*.

And then he turned and left her again, but this time it didn't hurt.

Because it wasn't him struggling with feeling an unfounded betrayal, but fear and grief and guilt. She recognized those emotions, but Jonathan didn't know them. He'd never known them. She'd just watched his heart break in front of her, the unspoken words right there as if he'd screamed them: *I killed you.*

Rina shouted after him, Virtue doing her best to calm her. Audrey felt Theodore's attention on her, but she didn't care about any of it. She stood, avoiding the broken mug. She'd apologize later and replace it. Audrey folded the borrowed blanket and set it on the couch, everything a dull hum as she took her coat from the hook and put her arms in the sleeves. She pulled on her hat and gloves and almost had her scarf on before Rina grabbed her arm. It forced her attention back to the room.

Audrey patted Rina's hand. "It's okay."

"It is *not*," Rina snapped back.

"It will be," Audrey said. "I need a little time with him first, then we'll come back, and we can figure out what to do." She turned her gaze on Theodore. He offered her that fatherly, proud smile she knew. "We have an esquire and an archivist right here. If we can change an Accord, we can cure a curse, right?"

Virtue gave a soft laugh. Rina ramped down as she watched Audrey curiously, as if unsure if she'd lost her entire mind.

Audrey tucked her scarf tight and blew out a long exhale. She'd been holding her breath since Virtue told her she was pregnant, frozen by shock and overwhelmed by the fear she'd made a terrible mistake. But no, she and Jonathan had simply longed for more, unknowingly and together.

That mattered. If they could hope for an impossible child and make it happen, then she would damn well believe they'd find a solution. And if they didn't, Audrey would go down fighting with everything she had. She knew in her heart that Jonathan would too. He just needed her to help him pick up the pieces first, before they could put them back together.

Chapter 11

The cabin was dark inside when Audrey arrived. The fact that Jonathan let her walk home from the station alone this close to sunset told her what she already knew about his mental state. But he'd be at their home this time, not running off to hunt and kill and try to burn off his aggression.

This wasn't about anger or fear anymore. Jonathan had never known grief or guilt like she'd seen in his eyes at Rina's office. She might not be an expert, but she'd dealt with it over her brief life enough to at least recognize the feeling. And he was always the stronger one.

Well, she could be the strong one too. It was remarkably easy. At least right now, because finding a cure for a hundred-year-old blood curse? Not exactly an easy task, but what was the alternative? Lie down and die?

No. She had far too much to live for.

She said nothing when she came in and quietly shut the door behind her. Audrey stripped off her outdoor gear, her boots, and put them all away where they belonged. She rubbed her hands on her thighs to warm them up as she stepped into their main room, Jonathan's breathing an uneven rasp coming from the dark kitchen, the cabin otherwise silent.

He sat on the floor where the counter butted up against the wood-burning stove, tucked in the shadows. He sat like a child, with his knees curled to his chest and his head buried in his arms and retreating as far into himself as possible.

When she toed onto the floor near him, he flinched. "Don't."

She ignored him, sinking to her knees in front of him. He trembled; no, he quaked, his entire body hitching with violent shudders. When she rested her hand on his forearm, his head jerked up and he tried to scramble away, but he'd backed himself into a corner.

"Don't touch me," he rasped.

"Hush," she whispered, crawling over his knees, ignoring the pained whine he let loose as she settled herself into his lap and curled against his chest. He leaned away when she pushed his tangled hair back from his sweat-soaked skin and fevered cheeks. "Jonathan, don't push me away."

"Didn't know."

"I know."

"Didn't try to want."

"Me either." She pressed her cheek against his. He didn't hold her, his arms stiff at his sides. "It was just passing thoughts now and then for me, always about how happy we are together and seeing you with the cubs. How kind you are, how protective. I never had a family, so imagining what one might be like with you just happened sometimes."

Jonathan swallowed, the sound painful. "Yeah."

She took his face in her hands, but his gaze stayed unfocused on her chin. His chest heaved, and he said it: "I killed you."

"No, you haven't. Because we're not letting that happen. We're going to find an answer."

"Don't do that."

"Do what?"

"Try to make this anything but a fucking mess."

"Oh, it is a mess," Audrey agreed. "But I changed an Accorded Law through research and hard work. And I got the first vileblood ever paroled, which was also very difficult. If I fought that hard for you, I should at least fight that hard for myself. And for our child."

He tried to shake his head no, but she didn't let him.

"Don't argue. Tell me yes. Tell me you'll fight for us. You know how to fight. You told me you'd give me anything you have, so give me this."

The silence was deafening, but his arms slipped around her, pulling her closer, and then he finally whispered, "Yes."

She rocked him while he sobbed in her arms.

"It's not like blood madness?" Tomas asked as he chewed on his thumbnail.

"No," Innocence murmured as a few others shook their heads.

"Blood madness is a roll of the dice, so to speak," Virtue offered. "Any duster risks turning up a poor result. It comes from the conflict of human and Aperien blood, which I imagine were never intended to coexist."

"That would have been too easy." Audrey tried to keep her tone light, and the strained smile in place, but she knew it looked more like a grimace.

Despite it being train day, her friends gathered in this back room to discuss options. The station building was massive, parts of it still dusty and unused, but Rina had set up a few places like this down dark halls for private conversations. There was nothing inside but an oval table and a few mismatched chairs. The company was what mattered.

Jonathan stood behind her, leaning against the wall with his arms crossed over his broad chest, outwardly stone. Audrey knew better; his turmoil was an inward storm he wouldn't show anyone but her, and she might never see him so raw again. He'd wept in her arms last night between begging her to forgive him, while she soothed him and coaxed him to bed. Eventually, they'd fallen into dreamless sleep as they held each other.

This morning he'd woken collected and calm, a predator on the hunt.

Rina was frustrated that she couldn't join them, but she needed to oversee train day. The chuchuna family stayed away from the town proper on train days, but they didn't really possess helpful insight into this sort of thing to begin with. Aster ran the tavern, Celaeno kept her scouting detail, and the Clan handled the rest. Tomas wanted to help, Innocence had come without a word. Virtue, E, and Theodore already awaited their arrival.

"What we know is that a human woman impregnated by a vileblood will gradually transition from human to duster over the course of the pregnancy," Theodore offered, his fingers steepled and his expression calm. Audrey knew he was their best option for information and guidance, not to mention hope. "The curse is designed as a slow transition, giving the best chance for an outcome of two new vilebloods. Near the end of the nine months, the mother will become entirely corrupted by Lamashtu's hand in the curse.

"Female vilebloods are twisted and dangerous, possessing no remnants of their former humanity. And that's if they aren't malformed and dying by the time the childbirth is upon them. If the baby is female, it is born monstrous, and will . . ." Theodore hesitated, glancing across the table at Audrey with a wince.

"We need to know," Audrey said, her hands in tight fists under the table. "All of it."

He cleared this throat. "Often, the female offspring will tear or eat their way out of the mother."

"Gods," Tomas muttered.

"A male child is much more likely to be born normally if the mother hasn't twisted in such a way to physically prevent the birth. Or doesn't kill the child as soon as it leaves her body." Theodore tapped his thumb a few times on the desk. "All of which is what we seek to avoid, yes?"

Audrey laughed, covering her mouth after the sound escaped because it was entirely inappropriate. The entire room tensed at the sound. Jonathan's hand came to her nape and squeezed.

"That'd be ideal," Jonathan drawled, and she heard the smirk in his voice. She leaned back into him. He kept his hand on her neck, his thumb moving up and down in a soothing gesture.

Everything seemed better this morning with a goal in mind, trying her best to look at her situation in an almost removed way. As a problem and puzzle to solve.

Not a matter of her impending malformation and possibly murdering her own child.

When she shivered, Jonathan's palm squeezed again, warm and heavy against her skin.

E grunted, his beard in a neat braid today, as if treating this gathering with a certain formality. "There wasn't much known about all this during the war, which is why the vileblood got so far spread."

"With the first children of the Vilestars, yes," Theodore confirmed. "We were fighting a widespread war on bloody battlefields, in a time with much more frequent calamities. Attentions were divided, the Icelandic Citadel was new, and the Accorded Territories weren't officially bound. No one realized the impact on humankind before vileblood dusters had infiltrated in staggering numbers."

"And no one was looking for a solution beyond stopping the spread and ending the war," Virtue added, her smile wry as she glanced at Jonathan, then Tomas. "No offense, gentlemen, but after the Accords founded, containing your kind in place of genocide was the only priority for years."

"Humanity teetered on extinction, and it drove fear into Aperiens, as we still don't know if our existence can continue if the source of our existence vanishes. The consensus was to protect those humans who remained and contain the fallout. That may seem like bad news," Theo added, "but it really means there are opportunities. This side of the curse, the pregnancy itself, hasn't been studied in terms of a cure, a treatment, anything really. Preventing the source of such pregnancies was the goal instead."

"Am I the only one willing to address the unsavory?" For all that Innocence was normally biting wit, Audrey couldn't help but notice his clear unhappiness when he said, "There are abortive measures, quite a few different options. Many are harmless to the mother if implemented early enough."

Audrey's stomach did a slow roll. Jonathan's hand tightened around her nape, not a tender soothing but a jerk reaction.

Her chest tightened and her lungs emptied, because . . . well, it was foolish that it hadn't even crossed her mind. This wasn't a flippant conversation or a simple inconvenience. It was likely both her and the child would die, or she would be a dangerous monster if she survived. Someone would have to put her down, worse if it was Jonathan at the end. Worse yet if he had to then kill his daughter as well.

How had neither of them considered this as an option?

"That has been tested extensively, perhaps the only proper area pursued. No matter the method, ending the pregnancy killed the mother, likely an intentional facet of the curse." Theodore rubbed his face as he spoke. He looked exhausted. She wondered if he'd been involved with such testing and how much of a toll it had taken on him.

And how much a fool was she for feeling an odd sense of relief that the best option wasn't to kill the child she and Jonathan had created from their mutual longing. She shivered then, Jonathan's thumb stroking along her anxious pulse.

She wondered if he felt the same, but decided it wasn't a question worth asking. If the road was set, dwelling on impossibilities did no favors for anyone.

"You said it's not blood madness," Tomas offered after silence stretched a few heartbeats too long for anyone's comfort. "But it still has to do with blood if it's changing hers. What about the blood mage who helped me? Could they come and take a look?"

"A good suggestion," Virtue said, smiling warmly at Tomas, who blushed under her praise. Innocence shifted closer to Tomas, the glare he gave his sister half-hearted. "At the very least, a blood worker, magical or otherwise, can help us monitor the curse as it progresses."

Theodore nodded. "Although calling one out here again so soon may draw unwanted attention from prying Dominion eyes. It might not be something we can avoid. Audrey, what do you think?"

"It sounds smart to me," Audrey said. "I don't think any of us want more attention from Moscow, but they're always watching, considering their vested interest in Nizhny." She paused, because Theodore grinned as the rest of the room stared at her like she'd grown a second head. Jonathan's hand stilled. "What?"

E chuckled. "He asked you in Old Norse, lass, and you answered the same. I'm speaking it now, and I wager you understand?"

"I . . ." Audrey's brain stuttered as she thought backwards a few steps and realized she'd transitioned languages without even thinking about it. She rolled E's words over in her mind, and they were clear and crisp, the meaning entirely coherent as if he'd spoken English.

Then she remembered visiting Aspen and his compliments on her improved Russian, but it wasn't from studying, wasn't it?

"Angels are polyglots." She spoke English for everyone in the room, knowing very well how uncomfortable it was to be excluded from conversations. "Any amount of angel blood, however thin."

"So, it's already taking hold," Jonathan grumbled.

"As soon as Audrey conceived," Virtue corrected. "My kind can sense such a change in a woman's pheromones within days. How far along?"

"Oh, um, maybe five or six weeks?" Gods, for all the other more important matters at hand, life and death and all, it didn't make it less awkward to share her cycle with an entire room full of people, more of them men than women. "The baby will be due in November."

"Plenty of time then, right?" Tomas said. The naked, desperate hope in his expression made Audrey's heart ache.

"We can send a request on tomorrow's train for a blood mage," Theodore said, writing notes. "I'll need to depart soon to monitor the situation around a certain unaccounted-for individual and pursue countermeasures; I have a few ideas in mind. As for this," he motioned toward Audrey as he spoke, "the Citadel is the best place to search for more information."

"Should she go with you?"

When Jonathan asked, Audrey spun her in her chair, but his expression was a void. She couldn't tell if he hated the idea, if he wanted her to go, or if he planned to travel with her if it seemed to be the best call.

"I wouldn't advise it at this point. If I show up with Audrey at the Citadel, I'm not sure if they'll want her confined for safety—yours and theirs—which would cripple your ability to search for answers elsewhere. And I'm not sure if we have a blood worker in residence currently, as Citadel restrictions throttle them when it comes to research. Non-interference, and all that."

E snorted. "Knowledge, but not the pursuit of wisdom, is it?"

"Preservation over learning, yes," Theodore said, his tone dry. "Not news to you, I'd wager."

"Not," E said, arms crossed as he leaned deep in his chair, one of Odin's smiths but clearly at odds with the stance his patron god had taken as a member of the Citadel pantheon.

"My library is limited," Audrey said, "but I have a contact with the head bookkeeper in Moscow. I trade the ink I distill from Jonathan's quota kills for books. I can tailor my requests."

"The Dominion is a vast resource, like it or no," Virtue added. "The ESC brokers in technology and digital archiving, and while the MD uses some for the upper cast, their physical archives are unmatched. They are one of the few parts of Europe the Storm Belt didn't destroy. More mythos, more old architecture left standing, more fondness for ancient ways, and Koschei the Deathless will deal in anything that gives him a firmer hold on his power."

"No doubt influenced by his charming bride," Innocence sneered, meaning Rina's aunt, one of the Baba Yaga sisters, Jaga Baba.

The pair were a powerful and efficient combination, one of the unofficial four superpowers of the current world order: the Citadel at the head, with the ESC, MD, and the Coalition of Creatures of the old American continents the most dominate of the Accorded Territories, each for their own reasons.

Audrey rubbed her forehead; as much as she delighted in research, none of this was going to be easy.

The door swung open, Rina entering like she owned the place—which she did. Nizhny's leader scowled at the room as she tossed a missive on the middle of the table, the wax seal already broken.

"I wouldn't interrupt if this wasn't important." Her gaze flicked to Audrey in apology, but then she gestured at the parchment. "But I need advisement. Now."

Chapter 12

No one responded to Rina's dramatic entrance. Everyone looked between the letter, the table, and Nizhny's fearless leader with her expression of complete exasperation. Audrey had no idea what the formal missive might contain, but if Rina was asking for help, it couldn't be good.

"Tomas, dearest, that would be our cue to depart. What comes next is far beyond our paygrade." Innocence rose with his usual grace, tugging a bewildered Tomas by the elbow.

"Are you sure?"

"Entirely."

The pair left and shut the door behind them, silence heavy again. Audrey rolled her eyes and grabbed the paper. Rina wasn't so scary, not really, not once Audrey understood her motivations. And if she needed help, Nizhny needed help, and sitting here gawking wouldn't do anything.

The paper was silken, high quality, and she recognized the Moscow Dominion's symbol on the letterhead of sorts—a silhouette of the Kremlin, which still served as the head of state, along with St. Basil's Cathedral, which now acted as the familial home to Koschei the Deathless rather than a place of worship. The area was still called the Red Square, which Audrey only knew from reading the *History and Policy of the Moscow Dominion, Ver. VII.*, the gilded tome a gift from the Dominion's head bookkeeper as payment for her shipment of inks. A red ribbon dangled from the broken wax seal.

As Audrey unrolled it, her throat caught; it was penned in Russian. She not only recognized the script, but she could also read it. Apparently, as long as one had a basic ability to read and write, the polyglot nature of angel blood took care of the rest.

Rina moved closer, arms crossed as she leaned in to read the letter again. There was a second, smaller folded note, which Audrey set aside to read the main letter first.

"This is a summons for all provincial leaders for the Symposium of Trade, Welfare, and Law of the Moscow Dominion, to begin on the summer solstice and conclude on the autumnal equinox. Housing will be provided for the duration in the Red Square, limited to two servants on site. Additional entourage may be arranged at personal expense. Confirmation of attendance is required upon receipt, to be returned via the designated messenger."

When Audrey glanced up, Rina jerked her head at the door. "In my office for now, didn't want him wandering around. Some fat official, but the magic snapped as soon as I took the letter."

"A common assurance," Theodore offered, his expression curious. "We use it with Citadel missives, as it avoids false claims of missing mail when one doesn't wish to reply."

Rina snorted.

"The rest is a schedule of meetings during the event, other attendees, topics of import, and then signed off by Koschei the Deathless," Audrey frowned up at Rina. "Everyone else on this list carries a title within the Dominion, all the dukes and duchesses that he's appointed over the years. Nizhny is listed as a Dominion province, with you as the head."

"He thinks to claim us?" Virtue laughed. "A letter and we belong to the Dominion?"

"He can think whatever he fucking likes. That doesn't make it a fact," Rina bit out. "But he's already sent this to all his people. They'll see me listed as if I've bent."

"And?" Virtue tsked. "Even being the Deathless doesn't make his wishes true by simple want."

"No, but the game is clear," Theodore said. "The Deathless likely views this as a generous offer, extended without directly threatening you. He's offering you, and Nizhny by proxy, his best offer with this letter. Accept his oversight, and you'll keep your position and control of Nizhny. A flat out a refusal to acknowledge this . . . *invitation* would be akin to spitting on his olive branch."

"We're not at war," Rina snapped. Audrey knew by the way she paced that this was more than annoyance.

"Not now, no. But this is an official mark of his desire to fold Nizhny into the Dominion," Theodore replied. "You cannot ignore this, Rina. To do so is inviting him to attack you, and Nizhny will never stand against a true onslaught from the MD."

"Just like that, huh?" Jonathan grumbled from beside Audrey. He'd shifted, arms crossed over his wide chest. "Waited until we got some value, good trade going out, then it's time to move in with the big stick."

"More or less," E agreed. "He's got more than enough weight to do so." His attention shifted to Rina. "You knew it was risk when we set up trade with them. This was always waiting down line if we didn't keep ourselves dark."

"You'd rather have kept on in the woods, living off scraps? No, we all agreed. I didn't make this call without the rest of you ready for more than campfires and mud."

"And the second letter?" Audrey asked as she unfolded it, scanning the contents as Rina spoke.

"Fucking Dimitri offering to house me personally. To welcome me properly to the Dominion." Then she laughed, scrubbing her face.

"Along with an intention to court you," Audrey said, huffing. "He's hoping to arrange a mutually beneficial engagement by the equinox."

"I've known he was a fool for a long time, but this?" Virtue chuckled. "This is what comes of desperate boys ignored by their fathers."

"He also offers to act as your guide and tutor," Audrey added, her nose wrinkling. "How can he possibly think you'd agree to any of this?"

"He's been after Nizhny since my first time back to the Dominion to negotiate the train lines. Dimitri's an ass and an idiot, but he's also an opportunist who wants nothing more than to prove his worth." Rina shook her head, hands on her hips as she stared at the ceiling. "And it's not the first time he's sought an alliance between us through marriage. He idolized my father, who gave him more time than his own ever has. And my mother was warmer to him than my aunt, who only cares for his sister as her witch heir."

"Dimitri likely views this as a way to smooth the sting, paint himself as the gift-giver and helper, rather than the one orchestrated this entire thing," Theodore said.

"Well, they call all go fuck themselves," Rina said.

"And the alternatives?" Theodore prompted. "Because unless you have a way to summon an army out of thin air to challenge the second strongest Accorded Territory on the world stage, that will not end in your favor."

"She can't go," Virtue said. "Not even to attend the Symposium and dispute this farce." Her eyes were fiery with anger. "She denies this status, they simply assassinate her, if that isn't the intention to begin with. And if not, this peacock of a boy will surely make a move once he's rejected yet again. And with Rina locked in his estate, Dimitri would hold a dangerous advantage."

"And leaving Nizhny without its leader just makes us an outright target," E added. "Accorded Leaders never step foot outside their territory, save for those pocket planes the Citadel conjures up for all your big important Accorded meetings."

"Yes," Theodore agreed. "It's not just political either. Even as an Independent Territory, Nizhny is already developing new ley lines under Rina's ownership. Names and intentions have power. The Aperien Brites De Almeida, the baker in Portugal, proved this decades ago. The protector of a realm, no matter how small, cannot leave it unguarded without suffering for it. And if Nizhny were ever attacked, simply having Rina present in the town would align fate and luck in your favor. The opposite is true without her. Seven years is more than enough time for that kind of natural magic to begin taking root."

"Says you have to answer the message, not go to Moscow," Jonathan said. "So write back and tell them to eat shit. Or is that a cause for war too?"

"An official summons from an Accorded Territory leader is not answered by missive," Theodore said. "It is simply not done. Aperiens don't take well to being snubbed, especially in a manner this public. This move is intended to back you into a corner. At the very least, Rina would need to send a representative in her stead."

Of course. The answer was obvious.

Audrey folded up the letter. "Send me."

Chapter 13

Everyone's attention snapped to Audrey, including Jonathan's, though his expression was more curious than surprised.

"Send me," Audrey repeated, "as your representative. It's a respectful and accepted alternative to attending yourself. I can treat it as a misunderstanding we wish to reconcile and attend the meetings in your place as a concession. Maybe I negotiate more trade taxes or something like that, to show you're taking the situation seriously." She stood, her mind racing. "It's all about wording when it comes to magical contracts, but there isn't one in place, at least not beyond the summons and our current agreement with the trains.

"And I'm human. They're bound by Accorded Law to protect me, even if you aren't," she said to Rina with a grin, then turned to Theodore. "They would lose too much face if they didn't go with it, at least for this symposium, right? Both the Deathless and Dimitri wouldn't push publicly because it would suggest they don't have control over their provinces."

Audrey could see the wheels turning as Rina considered the implications and possibilities.

"It's possible there aren't magically binding contracts between the Dominion and its provinces if the Deathless appointed them as he desired?" When Rina shrugged, Audrey went on, "That alone would tie up some time. You have a contract for the trains running between an Accorded Territory and an Independent. Treating you as a province leader instead of a trade partner is a violation of the existing agreement between Nizhny and the MD." She tapped her lips once. "It's magically sealed, right? It would need to be dissolved to change your status."

"Drown them in paperwork, is it?" Theodore asked, his expression amused.

"Legitimate concerns and questions, if this is all to be taken seriously," Audrey corrected.

"You're expecting the Deathless to adhere to rules he can easily break with little consequence," Virtue said.

"Don't downplay matters of pride," E said. "Delaying is a viable tactic. And the Dominion won't march to war when its leaders are tied up in this symposium, or before the autumnal equinox passes."

"The day holds too much power," Rina confirmed. "It's not just a celebration, it's a blessing. Most of the Dominion population subscribes to some form of belief or superstition around nature's cycles. Bad omen to spit in the face of those traditions."

"You could send me with an offer?" Audrey suggested. "What can you give that might turn his attention from subjugation? We pay a trivial taxation on all goods moved across the rails for the use of the trains. What about an additional lumber tax? It's a high-demand item we ship every week. Or a tribute of some sort of rarer alchemy items?"

"If I'm paying a fucking tribute, I'm not an Independent," Rina bit out, her tone carrying an icy edge that startled Audrey from her pacing.

It was far too direct of an ask. They wouldn't get anywhere with Rina putting up a wall. "You're right. I misspoke."

"No, you didn't," Rina said, rubbing her face with both hands again. "These bullshit games are why I left the Dominion in the first gods-damned place."

"You've never been immune," Virtue offered, her voice soft now. "I'm surprised it took this long for the Dominion to make a move like this."

"Waited until it was a better investment," Jonathan said. "No gain to war over a pile of sticks."

"This also would eliminate the need to call a blood mage," Theodore added. "In fact, it offers many avenues for other pressing matters." To Audrey, he said, "The Dominion archives are housed in the Red Corner, with a large portion open to the public. Anyone who visited Moscow would be interested in the library; Audrey also has a preexisting connection related to trade affairs."

"Yes, with the head bookkeeper. We trade weekly, ever since he sent a letter complimenting my ink quality. He pays me in books. It would be helpful, really," Audrey said, settling back into her chair, her mind drifting back to her own very real and very pressing matter. "And we'd probably be able to talk to more than one blood mage, given their prestigious clinic. Maybe even gain access to their research?"

"Said two people would go with you," Jonathan said. "We do this, who else comes along?"

Audrey glanced at Rina in question, who stood now with her arms crossed, staring at the parchment roll as if she could burn it to ash with her gaze.

"Virtue and Innocence are out," E said. "Too much history there with the Accorded for worse." Virtue inclined her head in agreement. "Much as I want to help on both fronts, sending an old dvergar as a young woman's escort? Only draw questions we don't want to answer."

"Aster," Rina mumbled. "She the one. Cornflower maidens are associated with the seasons. Sending her would be seen as a gesture of good intentions, as would having her partake in the capital celebrations." Rina's lip curled in disgust. "Not that I have good intentions."

"You have neutral intentions," Audrey offered. "To correct a misunderstanding in the most respectful manner possible."

Rina scoffed.

"A bodyguard and a handmaiden are perfectly acceptable to act as a human envoy's company," Virtue said, her head canted at Audrey in renewed interest. She blushed under the assessment, more so when Virtue hummed. "We'll need to arrange for a proper wardrobe."

Audrey frowned. "What's wrong with my clothes?"

"The Dominion is not the ESC, Audrey," Theodore offered, his tone gentle. "Moscow is steeped in old traditions, with an almost medieval view on matters including hospitality, aesthetics, and presentation. You will need gowns this time, not business casual suits."

"Good thing, those suits of hers were awful." Audrey elbowed Jonathan hard in the gut, and he chuckled down at her.

"They were perfectly professional."

Rina shifted on her heels, frowning still, but her posture read looser, less furious despite her obvious frustration. "I'll cover any expenses." She looked at Audrey then, her stormy gaze gentler. "You're sure about this? All things considered?" She nodded pointedly toward Audrey's middle.

She couldn't help folding her hands on her stomach. "The curse's complications won't come until later." Audrey winced and straightened her spine. "But there are risks if anyone found out about my pregnancy. At the very least, they'd arrest Jonathan."

Jonathan shrugged. "They'd try."

"Hiding your belly could be difficult," Virtue said. "And even normal pregnancies can have unexpected complications. Perhaps illusions?"

"They'll sniff that out, easy. Or ban such magics entirely," Rina said.

"Something more direct?" Theodore asked.

"Not on her fucking skin again, that's for damn sure."

The room went utterly quiet because everyone present knew what Jonathan meant. His tone was brutally cold, his posture almost threatening as he leaned forward to press his knuckles to the table, leaning toward Theodore.

A vileblood openly threatening a Citadel representative, and a demigod no less.

Audrey rested a hand on his forearm, but Jonathan didn't back down. If Theodore suggested another rune, Jonathan might leap across the table and try to break his neck.

Theodore, for all the implied insults—that Jonathan might attack him, the not-so-veiled accusation that his magic had failed Audrey once already—didn't so much as blink. He stared Jonathan down, calm and collected, inhumanly so, but he didn't flex his power or posture other than refusing to cower.

"I had no intentions of suggesting as much," Theodore said, his deep voice steady, his tone carrying finality. He also had no intention of indulging Jonathan's anger, misplaced or not.

"Other options then?" Audrey asked, squeezing Jonathan's arm.

"A token with bigger magic on the surface level, let it overwhelm the illusion," E said then, the smith thoughtful as he ignored the power struggle across the table. "Something they'd expect a human envoy to have protection-wise." E gestured at Rina. "Another way to show you're serious. You send in your diplomat unprotected, you show her throat and yours."

"She won't be unprotected," Jonathan all but growled.

"Keep your pissing where it belongs, lad," E said. "Those runes of hers," he asked Theodore, and Audrey bristled a bit at not being asked directly—it was on her skin after all—but she didn't want to ruffle any more feathers, not when everyone wanted to help her and Nizhny. "What are the other magics?"

"Protections from hellfire, persuasion and possession."

A grunt from the smith. "Big stuff, good. If they have anyone checking deep for magic, they'll pick up hints of your work, no matter how subtle. I'll work something up with persuasion and possession wards. That'd be well within rights, especially with a human girl. An illusion to cover pheromones and a little tummy'll get lost in the mix."

Virtue stood when E did, the smith already mumbling to himself about heat and kindling and something about metal thread. "Can you work all that magic yourself?"

"You wound me, lass," E said with a snide grin, but then he shrugged. "Illusions aren't my best suit, and if you're offering, I'll let you take a pass."

"My, such confidence," Virtue purred, then turned to Rina with a small nod. "You'll need all the proper paperwork and contracts done today, before the return missive."

"More fucking paperwork," Rina grumbled.

"I'll help you, whatever you need," Audrey said. And to the rest, she said, "Thank you, everyone. For your help, your support." She offered a wry smile. "Your magic."

E waved a hand. "Don't undersell yourself, lass. We're sending you into the lion's den for Nizhny matters, not just that babe in your belly." Toward Rina, his expression was sterner. "This is the first step in the next fight, Katerina." Audrey swallowed at his use of her full name. Rina stiffened, but she didn't seem offended. "This isn't the battlefield you'd choose, but we'll fight nonetheless."

"Alright, *Afi*," Rina groused. The dvergar only smirked, departing with Virtue close behind him. She turned on the rest of the group, blowing out a loud exhale. "Well, you heard the old man. Let's get to work, then."

Later that evening, with Jonathan out to clear his quotas, Audrey had been about to turn when a soft knock came at the cabin door. She pulled a shawl over her shoulders and answered, surprised to find Theodore on her stoop.

"Is everything alright?"

"I feel like I should ask you that question." Theodore said, asking to come in with a head tilt.

"Sorry, come in, of course." She shut the door behind him. "I can make some tea?"

"No need. I won't be staying long. In fact, I'll be flying out when I'm done here."

"Oh," Audrey said. Her shoulders sagged as she clutched her shawl in tight fingers. "You haven't been here very long." She'd imagined at least a few more days with his company, maybe going through her small library together like old times in the ESC. Really, just having her friend nearby in any capacity. It wasn't like she didn't have support from other quarters, and plenty of it, but she'd known Theodore the longest and . . .

"Chin up," he whispered, coming over to rub her arms.

"Do you really have to leave so soon?" She hated sounding like a child, but she felt a bit like one in the moment. They'd gone from quiet repose with a problem on the horizon to drowning in crisis.

What if she never saw him again?

Her breathing hitched, and she didn't have to ask for comfort. Theodore folded her into a tight hug, and she clung to him. There'd been moments not unlike these during the fight for the Accord revision and Jonathan's freedom, where everything felt overwhelming, even helpless, but Theodore never let her dwell in uncertainty. He'd let her feel what she needed to feel, and they'd brainstormed next steps.

Audrey swallowed a few times. "Do you think the Dominion will really push for Nizhny?"

Theodore laughed softly, and when she pushed back from him, he held her shoulders. "This is why you succeed, you know."

"I don't."

"Because of how much you care, Audrey."

She shook her head. "It would be nice if it was so simple."

"It would, wouldn't it? Good thing we have other tools at our disposal." Theodore pulled a neat envelope from his robe pocket. She took it; it wasn't sealed. "A contact of mine in Moscow. I've known him my entire life. I trust him with my life." Theodore paused, then added quietly. "And with my secrets."

An Archivist was a servant of Citadel Pantheon, dedicated to the preservation of knowledge above all. He wasn't supposed to have any secrets, and yet he'd kept her and Jonathan's escape a secret. He'd held back what he knew about Kushiel's death to give them time to find a solution.

"He'll know I sent you to him. You can trust him."

She turned the envelope in her fingers. "When you say he'll help, you mean . . ." Audrey flattened a palm over her stomach. It was still so new. So strange to touch her body, knowing she wasn't alone in her own skin anymore.

"Yes. He won't get involved with Accorded affairs, but he may have access to less widely known information about the vileblood curse.

That's my hope, at least."

"Who is he?"

Theodore's grin, when it was mischievous, always made him seem so much younger. It made her wonder what he was like as a boy, before he'd come into his blood as a hybrid Aperien demigod.

"He's a defector from the Citadel Pantheon."

Audrey sucked in a breath as she pulled out the simple card stock and the firm, sure handwriting she'd recognize anywhere. All it contained was an address and specific instructions on how to knock at the door.

"Alright," she said as she read it over once more before folding the card back into the envelope. She cleared her throat. "Won't you stay a few more minutes?"

Theodore smiled, his eyes kind and warm as always. "Of course."

Chapter 14

Six Weeks Later

Audrey was incredibly thankful that while much human technology had been lost or discarded after the Aperien event, indoor plumbing made the cut. When mythos became reality, so did bodily functions, and Aperiens valued a working toilet as much as any human.

Audrey flushed, then shut the lid. She rested her forehead on the cool porcelain seat, her eyes closed. She had a hundred more important things she needed to be doing than sitting on the bathroom floor like an invalid.

Another minute, though, that would be fine.

When a knock came, Audrey stifled a groan. "Just a second."

"Shall I brew another draught before we board the train?"

Audrey considered telling Aster no, because she didn't need her to act like her servant before they reached the Dominion, and how Audrey was perfectly capable of making her own morning sickness tea.

Morning sickness, bah. More like all the time sickness.

Instead, she said, "Yes, please."

She peeled herself from the floor a few minutes later, stopping to rinse out her mouth and wash her face. She stole a glance at her reflection. It had been almost six weeks since she found out she was pregnant and they'd made plans for her to represent Rina against the Dominion's power grab after Nizhny. The train left in just a few hours.

The young woman who stared back in the mirror looked terrible. Not like anyone ready to go toe to toe with the Dominion nobility. She smoothed her sweaty hair, tucking the loose strands of brown back into her fancy braids. Her skin was wan, dark smudges under her eyes, her brow sweating again already. Audrey forced herself to stand taller.

Time to drink more tea to fight her constant nausea, weakness, and headaches so she could be the diplomat Nizhny needed.

Theodore had sent a few missives since departing Nizhny, updating them on Kushiel's status within the Accorded Territories. He also worked to ensure when the news of Kushiel death broke, the truth of what happened would also come out. He had little news on either front, and less about vileblood pregnancies. All sources collaborated that the worst changes to her body—becoming an inhumane monstrosity—happened right before the birth. Not that she'd expected the rest of the pregnancy to be a breeze, but . . .

She was violently ill daily, multiple times. Keeping anything in her stomach was a challenge at best, and projectile vomit at worst. She was often weak or dizzy, and feverish when she woke from dark, oppressive dreams she couldn't remember. The nightmares about Jonathan dying had retreated, but she was so exhausted from lack of sleep that it wasn't much of a relief.

Without Aster, they would have needed to call this whole thing off. Herbal teas, draughts, balms, lotions, scented oils, the cornflower wraith had earthly remedies for everything that ailed Audrey. The effects were limited, a few hours of relief before her symptoms came roaring back, but at least she could sneak a nap or eat some toast. Aster was also skilled with cosmetics, which helped Audrey appear less like a walking plague.

But her eyes and veins weren't black yet. Outwardly, she seemed human as ever, and aside from her newly discovered talents as a polyglot and vomit expert, not much had changed. Audrey pressed a palm low on her stomach, still flat despite being nearly four months along. Prepping for the trip to Moscow kept her mind busy, but the truth was, she avoided thinking about being pregnant more often than not.

Inside her was a tiny life. A life both she and Jonathan desired deep in their hearts. Guilt warred with fear on a daily basis. How could she focus on joy with so much at stake? How could she not?

"We'll figure this out," she whispered toward her belly.

The train yard was busy, trade being piled onto the cargo cars. Audrey watched the bustle from inside the station's tavern, Jonathan lugging their excessive baggage toward the gilded passenger cars closer to the steam engine.

"I still don't see why we need so much," Audrey muttered.

"You will."

Aster wore a modest blue smock, her white-blond hair drawn back in a tight bun. If it wasn't for her ethereal gaze, she'd have easily passed for a simple human woman waiting for a train ride. It only made Audrey feel more ridiculous.

She wore one of the three dozen new dresses Virtue had crafted or commissioned for her wardrobe, all with adjustable corsets for her growing stomach. Layered skirts, petticoats, stockings, jewelry, hairnets. The list went on forever. They'd arranged new clothes for Aster and Jonathan as well, but they were plain by comparison, with Aster in blue and Jonathan insisting on black.

Audrey avoided touching her hair or face. Aster had fixed her up after giving her tea and toast once her stomach settled. She didn't want to ruin her hard work.

Aster made a few final adjustments to Audrey's handbag for their three-day trip across the rails. "The draughts should taste well enough without being warmed. Remember the sachets for under your pillow and the lozenges if the train's motion bothers you. Plenty of water, small bites whenever you can, and windows open for fresh air. I went over it all with Gunnar."

"While I was throwing up again?"

Aster patted her arm. "Many women have trouble with pregnancies when they are not infusing angel and god magic into their blood."

"I still don't like putting you with . . ." She trailed off, not sure exactly what to say.

Aster tsked. "The labor?" She wrinkled her pert nose when Audrey nodded. "For this journey, I am a servant. We must go through the motions. What is the saying? When in Rome?"

Audrey grinned. "I'm surprised you know that phrase."

Another tsk. "And you humans forget how old the things around you actually are." Aster wasn't a particularly powerful Aperien, but she was an original. She'd manifested with all the other mythos nearly a quarter century ago.

"Sorry," Audrey mumbled. "I didn't forget. You've just never seemed very interested in human culture beyond your mythos."

"That is a fair assessment. However, humanisms infiltrate everything."

"A feat, considering your kind is almost extinct," E said as he joined them at the window.

Audrey's throat went dry. "You finished, then?"

"You doubt me?" The old man smirked as he held out a simple silver chain with a wooden ring hanging on it. Rina's favor to her envoy, carved from the first tree felled when they founded Nizhny.

"Of course not, I just . . . well, without your magic this whole thing could fall apart."

The smith grunted, motioning for her to take the chain. E chuckled at her hesitation. "It won't bite ya, lass."

"There's no clasp?" The silver metal was cool to the touch and feather light.

"Hold it to your neck, speak *hulða* to set it in place. To release it, *ógǫrr*—although that I wouldn't recommend taking it off until you're back here, safe and sound." When she didn't move, E shooed at her. "Go on, then."

"Alright." Audrey cleared her throat and held the chain to her skin, whispering, "*Hulða.*" A chill blossomed against her throat, then the enchanted metal warmed to her skin temperature. Both Aster and E studied her; Audrey shifted in her fancy, polished boots. "Well?"

"I sense nothing," Aster said.

E snorted. "If a cornflower wraith sniffed out my work, we'd have more than trouble on our hands." Aster didn't rise to the jab. "It blends nicely with the archivist's magic. Should keep all the attention on the necklace, away from your skin, and away from the underlying charm." He studied her for a moment, his expression softening. "Moscow is a den, and for all Dimitri is a smug shit, he's not without means. You and Rina finished all those papers?"

Audrey nodded, her palms sweating now. "All the contracts are in place and sealed. Unless the Deathless openly disregards the customs he's put in place, we're covered. What comes after, we'll see, but we're following their rules."

"Good." E nodded, his gaze drifting to her throat, and Audrey couldn't help but palm the thin thread, another wonder crafted by one of Odin's forgotten smiths. Her life was decidedly strange. "Anyone who asks you to remove it is threatening you outright, and you tell them you know it."

The train whistle sounded, signaling fifteen minutes until departure. She'd already said the rest of her goodbyes, except for Rina.

E rested a warm, heavy palm on her wrist. "We'll be waiting for ya, mead at the ready." He nodded to Aster.

The cornflower wraith tsked down at him. "If you damage my tavern, I will send the bees away for fifty years and all of you will starve for mead."

E grumbled something about rude curses as he left them. Audrey pulled on her coat. Not a minute later, Jonathan strode in, giving her a cursory once-over that happened every time they reunited, no matter how little time they'd been apart.

There she is, she's not a monster yet.

His black gaze drifted over E's necklace, his nostrils flaring, but all he said was, "Almost time to go."

"Indeed." Aster handed Audrey's travel bag to Jonathan. She almost argued she could carry it herself, but she had a role to play, and Jonathan wouldn't let her, anyway. "I will see you both when we arrive." To Audrey, she inclined her head, her expression impish when she added, "Miss."

Audrey groaned, but miss as a formality was better than the alternatives. She was no ma'am, madam, or mistress.

Aster breezed out the door, and Jonathan caught and held it, his expression unreadable. Her heart squeezed a little. They'd barely had any time together with all the preparations, and she'd been so tired she collapsed next to him every night, but she knew preparing for this trip was as much a distraction for him as it was her.

Well, they'd have three days on the train together, just the two of them in their private cabin. She smiled up at him, looking forward to it. His stoic expression warmed, and he canted his head out the door in silent question.

Ready?

Guess they'd find out.

Chapter 15

T he rails ran directly outside the station, leading to the rebuilt platforms for the passenger trains. Rina maintained very strict rules around where visitors disembarked. She didn't like people wandering beyond the pop-up market, the station tavern, brothel, and guest rooms.

Rina stood by the Moscow train, chatting with a finely dressed gentleman. As Audrey and Jonathan approached, his fine features pinched. His skin had a sheen to it, opalescent almost, curved ears under his velvet top hat and auburn curls. Fae blood, Audrey guessed. Not that she would ask as most dusters were private about their blood and being unique meant documentation by the Citadel.

Rina spoke in Russian. "Here they are. Audrey Doe and her bodyguard, Jonathan Gunnar. All the paperwork is in order for her to serve as my envoy until the Symposium concludes." She motioned to Audrey for said paperwork. As she fished it from the pocket inside her billowed sleeve, Rina added, "This is Cornelius Venn, the maître d' of the Moscow railway."

"I must reiterate, this is very unusual." His frown deepened, attention flitting to Jonathan before settling back on Rina.

Audrey barely kept herself from crushing the scroll in her fist as she handed it over. "What exactly is unusual?"

Rina didn't seem bothered by the interjection, and she practically felt Jonathan's smirk behind her, knowing she used what he called her 'esquire voice.' She accompanied the tone with a lifted chin, a habit she'd developed because almost everyone she'd ever had to debate with was miles taller.

Cornelius carefully unrolled the scroll, recognizing the parchment for what it was: a binding, magical contract. He snapped his fingers, and a pair of tin reading glasses appeared on his pointy nose. His Russian lilted with an Irish accent. "It is unusual to be escorting a vileblood into Moscow."

Audrey pursed her lips. "Into an Accorded Territory."

Cornelius flicked his gaze to hers, his expression dull, like he was speaking to a slow-witted child. "Obviously."

Audrey hummed. "Into an Accorded Territory, which no doubt adheres unerringly to all Accorded Laws."

He paused his reading this time, his regard more serious, maybe uneasy. "Obviously," he repeated, but Audrey heard the underlying question in his tone. This duster knew he didn't speak for the Dominion, no matter how important his position on this train.

Audrey smiled sweetly at him. "Not all Dominion citizens are up to date on every nuance within the Accorded Laws, especially those policies that don't affect them daily." Jonathan chuffed behind her. Rina watched the exchange with a stoic exterior, but Audrey saw her lip twitch. "Are you aware the Vilestars Accord was amended just over a year ago?"

The maître d' cleared his throat. "Yes."

"Meaning that vileblood are no longer imprisoned for existing and are free to move around through Accorded Territories the same as any other duster."

"We have passenger cars for staff." He gestured further down the train, where Aster would travel. Simple cars with minimal amenities.

It still irritated her that Aster had to stay there instead of with them in the gilded car.

"Can't bodyguard without the body," Jonathan drawled.

Audrey raised a palm before Cornelius threw out some other inane argument, and the man's cheeks reddened at her interruption. "Which is clearly stated on the contract in your hand. Jonathan Gunnar is bound by Katerina Yaga to maintain my safety during my time as Nizhny's envoy to the Moscow Dominion. He can't do that from ten train cars away from me just because you're uncomfortable with his blood."

The maître d' blinked a few times, a reminder that Dominion social maneuvering wasn't normally so blunt, but she wasn't about to let this duster treat Jonathan like anything less than he deserved. Cornelius glared down at the contract, clearly hoping he'd find an argument there, but he did not.

The duster gave a stiff, formal bow she recognized as reluctant acceptance, and Audrey curtsied in return.

"Your items have already been delivered to your quarters. No one else of note for this journey and no stops along the way, so you'll have the gilded cabin car to yourselves. A few others for the sterling, however, whom you'll encounter during meals and evening indulgences, should you partake."

"Thank you," Audrey said.

Cornelius studied her for a beat, his honey-colored eyes surprised she'd thank him following their conversation, before he bowed again. He turned his attention to Rina. "The return reservations are set for the day after the autumnal equinox. I don't foresee any issues."

"Let's keep it that way," Rina returned, arms crossed, her father's sword slung over her back as usual. The weather had turned, chilled and windy with a lingering winter bite, but Nizhny's leader stood tall as if the cold was nothing. As if the taiga was hers. "That's all."

Cornelius took the dismissal for what it was, ducking inside the train.

"Don't cause problems, Gunnar," Rina muttered. "This will be enough of a pain as it is."

"Not sure what you mean," he drawled, and Audrey elbowed him. He grinned down at her, but then his expression shifted to serious as he and Rina regarded each other. "I know what my part is."

"Don't forget it." Rina said, her expression grim as she turned on Audrey. "Be careful, Little. From what I know about the ESC, they're pretty open about their bullshit. Moscow likes the game itself, all smiling faces with teeth at your back."

It was no secret Rina hated the Dominion. Audrey wasn't exactly looking forward to this adventure, as much as it was necessary to help Nizhny and find a cure to her cursed pregnancy. Despite that, she was glad to go in Rina's place, and not only because if Rina went to Moscow, it would probably end in war.

"We'll be careful," Audrey said. She'd never seen Rina hesitant, but there was a reluctance in her posture now that made Audrey a little nervous. She asked in English, quietly, "Are you . . . is there anything else?"

Rina grunted, waving a hand before she shouldered past them both. "Come back, that's all." She stomped down off the platform toward the station.

Jonathan chuckled beside her. "Pretty sure she was just talking to you."

"Ostentatious is a good word," Audrey mumbled as they stepped into their cabin, which took up almost the entire passenger car.

"I was gonna go with ugly."

She didn't find it ugly as much as ridiculous. Thick brocade fabric covered the walls, bright crimson threaded with gold. The carpet was plush, so thick she felt unsteady on her fancy, heeled boots. Heavy curtains were pinned open with braided golden ropes, the Dominion icons emblazoned on the fabric. Even the lamps were gilded with shiny tassels and beads, and they'd somehow wrangled a beautiful hand-carved bedframe into the narrow space. Their luggage waited on racks attached to the wall opposite the window. Audrey wandered through the space—narrow, despite being otherwise spacious, for a train car of all things—and opened a folding door to reveal a comparatively modest bathroom.

Jonathan prowled the space, checking all the nooks and crannies. Doing his job, of course. While he did, she set about unpacking her handbag, the one with Aster's draughts. Maybe she wouldn't need them for the few days' travel between Nizhny and Moscow? They could eat in the room, she could rest, and they could spend some quiet time together, just the two of them.

Since discovering she was pregnant, followed closely by the summons from Moscow, Audrey felt like she'd barely had time to even talk to Jonathan, let alone spend any real time with him. Between the dress fittings, studying up on Dominion culture, reviewing contracts and Accorded expectations, and then being sick all the time, she was lucky to see him at all some days. Most times not until they went to sleep for the night, if she hadn't already passed out from sheer exhaustion or the teas to help her sleep through her fitful, feverish nights by the time he came to bed.

They'd barely touched, let alone made love. They'd shared passing embraces, brushing hands. A kiss on the forehead if she was lucky, while Jonathan stared down at her with a barely concealed wince.

As she leaned against the built-in armoire as he paced, she realized any physical contact between them since finding out she was pregnant, she'd been the one to initiate. He'd almost seem startled by it, then would reciprocate hesitantly before the next interruption.

Was he avoiding her? Had *she* been neglecting him, neglecting them, in all the chaos? Gods, she missed Jonathan so much, and he was standing right in front of her. How could he feel so far away while they stood in the same room?

"What's wrong?"

Audrey startled. His deep voice was laced with a low growl, his black eyes searching the room for a threat. Normally, he would have closed the space, maybe pinched her chin, soothed her with soft touches before helping her calm while he hunted down answers. His arms would have already been around her, keeping her close and safe. Now, he didn't move a step in her direction, instead watching her like she was some sort of deadly trap he didn't know how to disarm.

"Why won't you touch me?" she blurted out.

Jonathan frowned but came closer, reaching out to smooth a hand down her arm, then squeeze her elbow. His hesitance was crystal clear, but she pressed into him anyway, tightening her fists on his shirt. A heartbeat later and his arms went around her, a hand coming up to cup the back of her neck, avoiding the fancy braids Aster had done that morning.

"I am," he mumbled, but he knew. She heard the hesitance in his voice, the recognition of what she'd just realized. His heart was a drum under her ear. "Been a lot happening."

"That's not all it is. We haven't kissed. We haven't had sex, not since we realized I'm pregnant."

He stiffened at the word pregnant. Audrey pulled away from him, and he didn't stop her. They stared at each other.

"Jonathan."

He rubbed his jaw. "You've been sick."

"The draughts are helping."

"And tired. And all this shit to get ready."

"Don't make excuses. And don't pull away, please. I will fight for us, like we said we would, but Jonathan, I can't do this alone."

He held her tighter this time. "I'm not going anywhere, sweetheart."

"I need you with me," she whispered against his shirt.

"I am." She could feel the tension in every inch of him, crawling under his skin like a living, breathing disease. Jonathan let out a little growl. "You need to focus on you. Can't be worried about me and what I need."

She pinched his side, hard as she could.

"The fuck was that for?"

"I'm not worried about you, silly." That only made him glower more, and she huffed out a little laugh, but then she sobered. "I'm worried about us."

"We're fine."

"We're not."

"Not fucking for a bit ain't gonna kill me, Audrey. It's fine."

"No, it's not." When he tried to protest again, she pressed her fingers to his lips. "Stop. It's not about fucking, and you know it." He smirked under her fingers. She rolled her eyes because he couldn't seem to get enough of her cursing. "It's about intimacy. Being together. Loving each other. We can't just brush that aside."

Jonathan took her wrist and kissed her palm, his expression softer and darker at the same time. She could tell he understood. He'd told her that sex was different for him with her, because their hearts were as important as their bodies. But he was a demanding, hungry lover, and she knew part of him worried he was at times too much, despite her reassurances otherwise. Any time their lovemaking was rougher, or longer, or more desperate and animal, he'd always soothe her afterwards.

Audrey couldn't help a small grin as a realization hit her. "You know you can't get me more pregnant, right?"

Oh, his scowl. She laughed—she couldn't help it—and then his hands found her waist and squeezed, pushing her until her back hit the closed door to their train cabin.

"You done, smartass?"

Audrey shook her head. "Jonathan, you didn't do this. We did."

His expression faltered; he still didn't believe that, either. She threw her arms around his neck, pulling him close, and he sank into her embrace, burying his face in her neck with a shaky breath. She ran her fingers through his hair, savoring having him close. He wasn't pushing her away, she understood then; he was holding himself back.

"What did you think about? When you wanted this?"

He was silent for so long. Audrey wasn't sure if Jonathan would answer. When he did, she felt his words against her skin in tiny exhales and trembling, delicate words.

"How you were with the cubs, with Tomas. With everyone, really, just . . . loving people. That warmth and kindness you have that never seems to end. Made me . . ." He swallowed, the sound scraping. "Made me think, if I'd had someone like you, instead of being thrown away, who I might have been."

Audrey squeezed him tighter, her eyes stinging. "Oh, Jonathan."

"Yeah, well, you can guess the rest."

"Tell me," she whispered.

He exhaled, nuzzling her neck. Hiding, almost, in the way he clung to her and whispered. "A son," he murmured, his lips whisper soft. "So I could watch you with the boy I didn't get to be."

Chapter 16

Later in the night, the train well underway and the entire room thrumming with the momentum of the rails under wheels, Audrey felt content. Tangled in the absurd silken sheets, buried in pillows, and wrapped in Jonathan's arms. They'd pulled back the shades on the picture window, the landscape rolling by under melting snow and cold moonlight.

Audrey leaned against Jonathan's chest, his hand resting heavy on her stomach, keeping her close, insistent almost in how he held her. She sighed. She needed to get up and brew a fresh batch of tea. Nights were worse than mornings for her body all around, nausea creeping up as the train rolled, sweat already collecting at the back of her neck, but she didn't want to move, not yet.

"It's so empty," she said. Aside from a smattering of trees and brush, rocks and muddy hills, there really wasn't much for miles in any direction.

"Was empty out here even before the Aperien event, didn't you say? Long stretches between cities."

She hummed and snuggled back into him; he kissed the top of her head, and she sighed again when she heard him inhale deeply.

"Alright?"

Audrey grimaced at the acrid taste building in her throat. "For a few more minutes." When he started to get up, she tightened her grip on his forearm. Not like she could keep him anywhere he didn't want to go, given how strong he was, but he stayed with a displeased grunt.

"We might not have much more quiet time like this once we reach Moscow."

"Contract means I stay in your room."

"That's true, so maybe private nights, but the rest . . ."

"Professionalism," Jonathan drawled, his tone almost nasally, and she knew he was giving an intentionally poor impression of Rina. She laughed. "Contract or not, we don't need other problems, like a vileblood with his hands all over a human woman. And before you argue with me, because you want to, I know you do." She did. "People are gonna treat me like shit, not want me around because of what I am, Accorded change or not."

"You have the same rights as any other duster now," Audrey insisted, turning in his arms.

His expression said he couldn't care less. "We're not here to fight for vileblood rights. Lots of humans in Moscow, all under contracts like the one you drew up with Rina. That means dusters and Aperiens are accountable if shit goes sideways and a human under their care gets hurt."

When she pursed her lips, he canted his head, a smirk tugging at his mouth. Her cheeks warmed, distracted by thoughts of everything those lips and that mouth had been doing less than an hour earlier. Audrey cleared her throat, but his smirk stretched into a feral smile, because he smelled the thoughts all over her skin.

"That's not the point," she insisted.

"Kinda is," he drawled, tugging on a loose strand of her hair before tucking it away behind her ear, fingertips lingering on her jaw. "You're not here to change the Dominion's views. You're here to represent Rina and save yourself."

Audrey let him go this time, watching his bare body in the moonlit cabin as he meandered around prepping her nightly teas—a sleeping draught, and another dosing to keep her persistent nausea at bay. If it wasn't for the other factor—the curse from Jonathan's blood—they might have sought a doctor who focused on modern human medicines, but going back to the ESC wasn't an option.

Maybe after this trip was done. She'd be near seven months along by the autumnal equinox, which was impossible to imagine right now, as she sat in bed feeling utterly weak and horrible with nothing to show for it. Everything ached, her head hurt constantly, and food was flavorless when she could keep it down at all. Bile tainted her tongue, and her breasts were so uncomfortable.

And she'd only lost weight so far, and it was still too early to feel the baby move. If it wasn't for her new abilities as a polyglot, she might have thought she had some weird illness. The thought made her feel even worse about everything.

She drew a shaky breath as Jonathan mixed the draughts into one barely palatable drink so she could forget feeling terrible until the morning. Audrey rubbed her forehead, not for the first time wondering how in the hells she was going to manage this.

Sure, taking on the Accords had been a challenge, but the Vilestars Accord had been wrong. Jonathan more than proved that when he saved her life at the cost of his all those years ago. And yes, she still had Theodore in her corner and on her side, along with everyone in Nizhny.

It had to be enough. She gave Jonathan a tired smile as the mattress sank under his weight, and he handed her the drink. She took it but didn't drink right away

He frowned. "Don't it get worse the later it gets?"

"Maybe I'd rather be a little sick and spend more time with you," she said with a flippant shrug.

"Audrey."

"Just a few minutes," she said, ignoring how she already felt shaky from head to toes. Aster had stronger remedies in her repertoire, but they'd agreed to use them sparingly and only when necessary, being that magic and babies and folk medicine, well. They were playing alchemy roulette with her and her child's future health, but if they couldn't find a solution to the curse, side effects would be the least of their problems.

She squeezed her eyes shut against the sudden sting. "This is supposed to be something wonderful."

Jonathan snorted. When she glared at him, he shrugged. "This," he gestured between them, "isn't supposed to *be* at all. If it was easy? That'd be some kind of weird-ass magic."

Audrey huffed. "I guess that's true." She nibbled her lip, looking down at the cup, inhaling the faint scent of ginger and Aster's magic. "It's childish, but I want there to be just one minute of this we can enjoy, you know? Not have all of it be . . ."

"A fucking shit show?"

"Jonathan!"

"Drink, sweetheart. I'll be here when you wake up. We've got a shit show for days coming up, so rest while you can."

She rolled her eyes but obliged him, drinking it down in a few gulps, the cool chill settling in her stomach and already easing some of the discomfort. She handed back the empty glass, and he set it on the armoire before slipping back under the sheets and pulling her close. Audrey tucked in beside him, warm and safe, already yawning.

She felt his lips, warm and soft on her forehead, when he whispered, "We'll find that moment for you, sweetheart."

Chapter 17

Maybe it was her time in the Eastern Seaboard Conjunct slums, followed by the York hub proper, which had left Audrey numb to the fanciful side of magic. Silly, considering the entire world was inundated with it, but for all that humans dreamed, magic didn't hold the same wonder it did as when she was a child.

In the factory where she worked during her brief indenture, the human and duster children performed simple tasks like packaging, moving boxes, and sorting. It was a tool factory, smelting things like screws, nails, and washers. Very little magic day to day, but the factory owner, a duster smith who never shared his name, let her and the other kids watch from the rafters whenever they brought in a drake to ignite the forges. They didn't burn forever, but enchanted ceramic cylinders could stoke drake fire for a few months at a time under the right conditions.

Like so much of the underbelly of the ESC, the right conditions were pretty terrible. The drakes fought, whipped until they breathed blue-hot fire, and the forges lit up like fireworks. Floating motes crackled and practically sang as the enchantments settled in, the smoke itself filled with sparkles in a dozen different colors as the kiln resettled.

And for all it had been fantastical to witness as a child, it was all magical byproducts of practicality. The York hub was a more refined replica of the cities that existed in the early 21st century, just before the

Aperien event. More neon lighting, more flashing digital billboards, but very little that said 'magic.' Nearly everything in the ESC hubs was powered by an electrical grid fueled by repurposed power plants infused with various enchantments for efficiency.

In Nizhny, magic was rarely for beauty or show, instead focused on survival. The eerie blue souls of the berserkers in battle, E's runes to keep the settlement warm, or even Aspen's forest. They lived on the taiga in the middle of nowhere, a frontier town on the fringes. No one spent effort on making things fanciful, with Aster's cornflower gift bouquet a rare exception.

Audrey should have known from the Moscow train things would be different in the Dominion capital. That wasn't true; she had *known*, but there was a stark difference in reading about the capital city and stepping into the Aperien era version of Moscow.

"Oh," Audrey whispered as Cornelius ushered them through the train station, up a series of stairs, and outside. Jonathan stayed close to her side with their luggage. The view wouldn't distract him, but she couldn't help herself once they were outside.

Everything was *magical*.

Despite it being late spring, the air swirled with glittering snowflakes, dancing and flickering even though there was no wind, no hint of cold despite the heavy clouds blotting out the late afternoon sun. The open plaza was well lit, but they weren't ordinary streetlights. Glass bells with a flickering flame inside, red at the heart and wicked in gold. The area directly in front of the station doors was a vast mosaic that stretched as far as she could see. A phoenix, she'd read, all crimson and gold and orange, each tile painstakingly placed by the artisans after the Accords were founded. She wondered what it looked like from above; she bet it shimmered at sunrise and sunset. The foliage and gardens framing the pathways were styled to match, the air heavy with the scent of chamomile.

Audrey almost laughed; she'd read the *History and Policy of the Moscow Dominion, Ver. VII.* cover to cover, multiple times as part of her preparation for this trip, and she'd have to thank the head bookkeeper when she met him. It added something to the experience, knowing things like how chamomile had been the national flower of old Russia, a tradition that withstood their world's transition. The scent eased her nerves a little too. Maybe there was more to the placement than nostalgia.

But the glorious plaza was strangely empty. Cornelius kept them at a fast pace.

"People don't gather here?" Audrey asked.

The duster sniffed. "Rare is the person who has use for a train. The loading docks are on the lower levels. And rarer is the person who has reason to leave Moscow once they've come."

Or they had no choice, Audrey mused. Jonathan said, "Seems like a waste, all fancy like this for nothing."

"First impressions are paramount," Cornelius replied as they stepped across the beautiful stonework. "Our world was in chaos. Not only did the Deathless save our city, he returned art and beauty to us as well. Ah, there is your carriage now."

Audrey blinked a few times, because sure enough, there was a carriage, velvet set with gilded wheels, drawn by a pair of stark white pegasi.

"Oh," she whispered again, transfixed as the magical creatures pulled the carriage effortlessly into place, prancing when they stopped, golden tassels complementing their manes and wing feathers. They watched her just as curiously, as if they were unused to the attention. But their wings . . .

They were trussed with ribbons and fine chains to keep them from flying.

Audrey was here to act as a well-educated envoy, but she couldn't stop herself from extending a palm.

"They bite," Cornelius said, the duster perpetually annoyed.

Audrey really didn't care. Being bit by a pegasus for the chance to touch one? She must be grinning like an idiot. The closer pegasus flicked his ears and snorted, tossing his head as Jonathan's hand touched her elbow.

Audrey glanced back at him and asked, "Are they scared?"

He chuckled, black eyes studying the creatures as his nostrils flared. Jonathan shook his head. "More like confused. And I don't think they like how I smell."

"Can you back up?"

"He just said they bite."

"They probably bite people who are rude," Audrey mumbled. To the pegasi, she asked, "May I pet you, please?"

The closer one, the stallion, blinked at her with liquid eyes. One ear flicked, and that didn't seem like a *no*, so Audrey stepped closer. She didn't push more, and after a few seconds, the pegasus huffed and stretched in her direction. Her fingers twitched, but she waited and was rewarded with a soft muzzle on her palm, puffs of warm air across her skin.

Audrey smiled as she gently stroked his mane, fascinated by the silken hair. "So handsome," she murmured. "What's his name?"

Cornelius didn't reply. When she turned, she found the duster bent at the waist as the carriage door swung open.

Dimitri syn Koschei stepped down with a creak from the carriage, and the pegasus jerked away from Audrey with a snort. Audrey kept herself tall as Dimitri glanced around, aware of how close Jonathan stood to her now.

The nobleman was exactly as she remembered from their first meeting in Nizhny, when he tried to buy her: overdressed, arrogant, and otherwise unremarkable.

He dressed even more fancifully here in the Dominion capital. She didn't doubt he preferred the polished mosaic under his polished heels over the mud and snow of Nizhny. He noticed Audrey then, glancing between her and Jonathan, his expression flitting to confusion before he smirked and tapped his golden cane against the curb.

He wasn't an unattractive man, blond hair and blue-eyed, by all appearances human if one didn't know his Aperien heritage. Average height, which still put him a half foot taller than Audrey even with her heeled boots, more so with the top hat fitted with literal peacock feathers.

Audrey curtsied because it was polite and expected as an envoy greeting her escort. Jonathan gave a stiff, barely-there bow beside her.

Dimitri chuckled, his voice nasally when he ignored her completely to address Jonathan in Russian. She wondered if it was deliberate, if he recalled from their first encounter she hadn't been fluent.

"With all the riffraff in her little town, you're what Rina picks for her two hands? A vileblood and a human girl?"

Audrey kept her chin up, folding her hands neatly at her waist and answering in perfect Russian. "You misunderstand, sir."

He blinked but covered his surprise otherwise. "Oh?" His smirk, unlike Jonathan's, made her wish he'd go away. No luck there; they were staying in his residence. "Are you a gift, then?"

Jonathan kept quiet, the tension radiating off him; she felt it in her bones.

"Rina sent me as her envoy to act in her stead for the Symposium." She offered her hand, an expected gesture. "I don't believe we've ever been formally introduced. My name is Audrey Doe. I think you and

Jonathan Gunnar are already acquainted." Audrey lowered her hand when he didn't take it. Dimitri observed her warily now, all the snide pretense replaced by calculating intelligence. "My handmaiden Aster, a cornflower wraith, is coming from the other train car."

Dimitri ran his finely manicured fingers across his chin. "My cousin thought the best answer for a summons from the Dominion was to send an uncontracted human to Moscow?"

"Not at all," she answered as she gestured to Jonathan, who already had her travel bag open.

She withdrew the scroll bundle and pulled the icy blue ribbon until the bow released. A quick flip through a few pages, and she found two papers: her personal contract with Rina and a letter from Rina to Dimitri directly. She handed him the latter first.

"This is for you, a personal reply from Rina." Dimitri took the parchment, nose wrinkling as he no doubt felt the subtle magic used as proof of who penned the document. He didn't look down yet, so she held out her contract, touching the 'marker' they'd selected to show Rina's ownership, the simple wood ring looped on E's enchanted chain. "This is the contract between myself and Katerina Yaga, formalized in the Dominion fashion, meeting the Accorded obligations for human protections, sealed by intention and three witnesses proving no coercion was involved."

Dimitri scoffed, his expression edged with annoyance as he took the second paper.

"I also have Jonathan's documentation."

"Oh? And that would be what, exactly? A magical muzzle set in place by my cousin?"

"Not quite," Jonathan drawled.

"Jonathan is bound by an archivist's seal to serve as my bodyguard for the duration of my stay in Moscow," Audrey answered. "Perhaps you've heard of Theodore Avialian?" Dimitri's gaze shot up, brows at his golden hairline. Of course he had. Anyone involved in the upper echelon of Accorded Territory politics would know of him. "He bound the contract himself, to ensure Jonathan's duties to protect me wouldn't run in conflict with Rina's contract."

Dimitri rolled the parchment up with a snap. "And all that fuss last time I came to Nizhny? Pretending not to understand Russian when you speak it just fine?"

They were here, by all implications, to fight off a direct bid for Nizhny's independence by the Deathless himself, and Dimitri wanted to discuss a perceived slight from months ago? Right, spoiled Aperiens really didn't like being told no.

"I increased my studies after meeting you," Audrey offered, which was not entirely untrue. "You made me realize how important it was to learn the local language as fast as possible."

"And this contract with Rina? When you supposedly already had one in place with this?" He gestured at Jonathan, dismissive, and she bristled at him being so rude.

"A necessary change when she decided I would take the role of her envoy. I needed to serve her first." She shifted her feet; she really hated these fancy shoes, and standing here in this ridiculous dress, but this was only the beginning. "The contract is legitimate."

She wasn't lying, because while contracts over human protections could be broken and reassigned, she had no reason to tell him there'd never been one between her and Jonathan.

Dimitri was annoyed now. She could particularly see the wheels turning behind his eyes as he ran through his possible recourse at this moment and realized he had none. He'd volunteered his hospitality to Rina's entourage for the Symposium. He couldn't leave them here at the curb.

"Then I suppose we should carry on," he muttered, his expression almost amused now. Almost. None of the emotion reached his cold, pale eyes.

"Of course," Audrey said, trying to focus on her genuine excitement at seeing Moscow instead of Dimitri's wounded pride. If just the train plaza was this magical . . . She stole another glance at the pegasi, who watched Dimitri with their ears flattened. "The pegasi are beautiful. What are their names?"

"Names?" Dimitri arched a brow, then hummed. "Ah, yes. I forgot the human predilection to anthropomorphize everything they encounter. The beasts are for transport, not pets, and you should know they bite."

Audrey pressed her lips into a thin line, but then forced her expression to relax, granting him another forced sunny smile. "Of course," she repeated, trying to keep a dry monotone from sneaking into her voice.

She'd need to work at it, because they'd been here all of ten minutes and she already wanted to strangle Dimitri with the fancy ribbons he used to keep the pegasi from flying.

Audrey ducked her head, covering her bitter expression with another curtsy. She was tired from the train ride. And everything else. She glanced over her shoulder, a few more train patrons milling out from the station now, but she didn't see Aster yet.

When Dimitri offered a gloved hand, she took it, focusing on how nice the leather felt against her bare fingers instead of the fact that she had to touch this man at all. Inside, the carriage was as ornate as the elite train car, with cushions of embroidered satin. Dimitri slid in beside her and smacked his cane across the doorway, preventing Jonathan from climbing in even though there was room for at least six more people inside.

"Your role is a servant's, is it not?"

Jonathan grinned at him, showing teeth, and Dimitri leaned away. He smelled like expensive cigars—the kind other esquires celebrated with when they won their cases in the ESC —and a musky cologne that might have been pleasant if he wore less. Her stomach rolled.

"Can't bodyguard without the body."

"Are you implying I can't see to the security of my guests?"

Audrey placed a hand on Dimitri's forearm. Both men looked down at the touch, both gazes narrowing. "Of course not, but his contract stipulations are very strict. He has to be in the same room as me or an adjoining one. If he rides in the second carriage, he won't be meeting his obligations." Audrey left her hand on his arm, a request in the gesture. She didn't want to fight him about everything. The idea was exhausting and they'd only just arrived.

"Servants do not sit in stride with the nobility," Dimitri said simply, as if there was nothing in the world that would make him shift, not even the possibility of magically enforced punishments on Jonathan for breaking his binding obligations. Granted, they hadn't woven any such repercussions into the magic, but Dimitri didn't know that.

"A compromise? He could ride with the coachman?" Another glare from both men. "Please," she added quietly, trying her best to sound as if Dimitri was doing her a big favor. "I don't want him to be in discomfort on my behalf."

Dimitri sighed. The look Jonathan shot her over his shoulder might have curdled milk.

"Fine, go on," Dimitri said, once again dismissing Jonathan as if he was nothing. Audrey took her hand from his arm, putting both in her lap so she could clench her fists until her palms ached from her nails digging into her skin. "The cornflower wraith will follow separately."

"Of course," Audrey said again, demure, and the carriage door slammed shut in Jonathan's face. She looked out the carriage window, summoning the patience that had rewarded her in the past. Watching Jonathan treated like trash and unable to speak against it was going to be harder than she'd expected.

But she couldn't dwell. As Jonathan reminded her on the train—and would likely need to continue reminding her—her job wasn't to defend his honor, nor to fight any other injustices she found within the Dominion. They'd come here to protect their home and find a way to break the vileblood curse before it killed her.

She took a deep breath, taking in the ethereal beauty of Moscow again, drumming up genuine excitement before she asked Dimitri questions about Moscow's architecture. Within a few minutes, the Aperien preened as if he'd created the entire Dominion himself.

Chapter 18

"The Moskva River," Dimitri said as the carriage wheels hit the bridge. Audrey couldn't help but plaster herself to the window, palms pressed against the glass. The crossing wasn't overly wide or long, but the mosaic tile from the train station plaza continued like a red and gold carpet, guiding them along toward Red Square. Apparently, this path was reserved for people of import, with everyone else forced to cross at some less fancy bridge about a mile to the east.

Her mind moved away from the absurdity as they passed over the Moskva, with the wealth, magic, and prosperity of Moscow blooming around their carriage. She held her breath as she looked back and forth between the windows, the surrounding buildings gorgeous.

"Amazing," she whispered. "Imagine all the places like this lost to calamities."

To the west, the Kremlin itself, with Ivan the Bell Tower and the Annunciation Cathedral shining with their golden caps. They weren't cathedrals anymore—not places of human worship, at least—but that did nothing to diminish their beauty and historical significance. Of course, the syn Koschei home, once known as Saint Basil's Cathedral, stood proud and wonderful, a kaleidoscope of color and shapes and just . . . it was breathtaking.

Audrey grinned. Humans were the dreamers, after all. And what a dream this architecture must have been. To stand as long as it had, well-loved in all its iterations. The carriage swung around the syn Koschei estate, only a small portion of the ruling family's personal holdings. She craned her neck to take in the details, mouth hanging open as they pulled deeper into Red Square.

Monumental buildings flanked them on the right; she didn't remember their original human purposes, but now they made up guest quarters and business suites. And there, to the north, what was once a museum was now the Moscow Dominion's vast, amazing library. She bit her lip, barely able to keep in her excitement. She'd be able to go *in* there, maybe even today. To be surrounded by books, shelves and shelves of books, along with other relics from world history, magical and human, all carefully kept by the head bookkeeper, who she hoped really liked his inks because she'd probably talk his ear off if he let her. Maybe he'd give her a tour. Maybe she would just get lost in there for days. Maybe . . .

"They don't let you out much, do they?"

Audrey stiffened, schooling her expression as she turned toward Dimitri. She'd almost forgotten about him for a minute.

That had been nice.

He smirked at her, twirling the cane he didn't need, like he'd said something incredibly clever. Audrey forced a smile. She'd spent so long among friends, among people who didn't pretend they were so devastatingly important, she'd almost forgotten how to perform.

"You know nothing in Nizhny is this extraordinary," Audrey answered, unable to help peeking out his side of the carriage. "Does the library have certain visiting hours?"

Dimitri chuckled at her; gods, he even made that condescending. She kept the smile plastered on, doing her best to seem like a naïve human girl. Let him underestimate her, just like others had in the ESC when she'd worked for Jonathan's release.

"My dear, you're an official envoy on summons for the Symposium. The library will create hours around your desires."

She bit back her knee-jerk reaction to deny preferential treatment, to say that normal visiting hours would be totally fine. She needed to play their game.

"Of course," Audrey said. "I'd like to meet with the head book-keeper. He was kind enough to send me *History and Policy of the Moscow Dominion, Ver. VII.* and I'd like to thank him personally. It's already proving invaluable."

"As I said, your time will be prioritized." He waved a gloved hand. "You'll have a secretary assigned from my household staff once we arrive. They'll keep you apprised of the Symposium schedule and arrange any travel, meals, and other requirements. You'll also have access to your own carriage.

"You are my guest," Dimitri added, a glint in his gaze telling her exactly what he thought about that. He'd expected to court Rina, and he'd believed he'd win her over with this pomp? Audrey was truly baffled. "My estate is yours for the duration of your stay. My staff will serve any need of yours that arises." Another snide little smirk, his expression thoughtful. "Why not fully experience everything a life here in Moscow has to offer a human? Perhaps by the equinox, you'll understand all you're missing out on, wallowing out in the mud."

"I'm sure," Audrey replied, her smile genuine, because she imagined Jonathan's scowl from the driver's seat, where he'd no doubt overheard the entire conversation.

They stopped in front of another former cathedral, this one red and white and capped in gold. The building looked almost exactly the same as the old photographs in the *History and Policy of the Moscow Dominion, Ver. VII.*, aside from missing the crosses. Kazan Cathedral, she recalled, which wasn't an original but a reconstruction. It still charmed.

Audrey noticed Dimitri syn Koschei's personal home stood detached from the larger family holdings across Red Square. What did that say, she wondered, as the door swung open on her side. Before she could move, Dimitri stepped over her legs and down the carriage steps. Jonathan waited just outside, glaring as Dimitri exited before her, then stood directly in Jonathan's way to offer Audrey his hand down.

She took it like a good envoy, gathering her skirts in one hand and nodding her thanks. The air swirled with always active magic, shimmering snow painting the sky with subtle swirls and the aroma of a perfect winter morning. At least two dozen people flanked the walkup to Dimitri's home, framing the approach like knights for their king, all bent at the waist and dressed in crisp uniforms. Behind the rows of what must have been his household staff—who were all humans or dusters with very thin magic in their blood—a handful of soldiers watched on, armed with rifles and swords.

"Bring the bags," Dimitri called over his shoulder to Jonathan, who ignored him and took his place at her side. When Dimitri frowned, receiving a blank expression from Jonathan in return, he snapped his fingers toward his staff. Two young men bowed deeper before darting off to their luggage. "This way."

And so they walked into the lion's very fancy den.

Chapter 19

Thankfully, Dimitri seemed eager to get away from them once they moved inside, citing personal business needing his attention before the Symposium began the next day. Audrey thanked him, claiming fatigue and appreciating the evening to rest. They studied each other for a few seconds. Audrey inclined her head to acknowledge without words that they both knew the excuses for what they were and accepted them, no harm, no foul.

Dimitri introduced his head of house—an older human gentleman named Mikhali, with the Koschei crest emblazoned on his golden brooch—before leaving in a flourish. The difference between the brooch representing Syn Koschei and the wooden ring for Rina was a testament to the gaping wealth divide between Moscow's leadership and Nizhny's.

Mikhali was a stern man who'd obviously held his post for years. He guided them to their quarters without fanfare, on the ground floor only a few paces from the main entryway. Their private receiving room was as fancy as everything else, and three human women curtsied when Audrey and Jonathan stepped inside. Like Mikhali, they all wore the same brooch over their hearts on high-collared, modest gowns. Beside them stood a man who was very much not human. His skin was bright blue.

"This is Envoy Audrey Doe from Nizhny and her bodyguard,

Jonathan Gunnar." Mikhali spoke in heavily accented English. Audrey wondered if Dimitri had told them she didn't speak Russian. "This is Yulia, second head of house; Varavara, primary housekeeper; and Ulyana, your personal secretary for the Symposium's duration."

Each woman curtsied again in turn. Audrey noted they all looked Russian. They were all taller than her, fair-skinned and light-haired. Yulia was the eldest by decades, her expression stern and capable, her hands wrinkled and strong from years of work. Varavara was similar, down to the greenish-gray gaze, but her hair was blonder than gray, so alike, Varavara could have been Yulia's daughter. She probably was, considering Dominion contracts for humans covered any children produced during their association.

Ulyana was younger than the other women, a touch of kindness in her expression that made Audrey glad she was the secretary, probably the one she'd have the most contact with during the next three months. Her hair was darker blond, streaked with just a hint of auburn in her braids, and she had less piercing brown eyes. None of the women wore makeup or embellishments aside from their gilded brooches.

"Pleased to meet you all," Audrey said in Russian, offering her own partial curtsy.

"And?" Jonathan asked, with a pointed look at the unintroduced duster.

Mikhali motioned the man forward with a tight hand gesture. This duster was shorter than the Russian women, wearing a black suit with a heavy leather overcoat. The Dominion emblem adorned his left shoulder. He kept his bare hands folded, his nails abnormally long and black, which stood out against his skin. Not just pale blue, but jewel-toned. His eyes were a vacant, milky white. His hair fell to his shoulders in white-gray coils.

"Ingqondo comes from the Deathless's inner circle. As a magic reader, his duty is to assess you and your belongings for threats," Mikhali said, his tone ambivalent as the duster approached, but Jonathan blocked his path to Audrey.

"You can start here," Jonathan rumbled, arms crossed. No one seemed bothered, and Audrey assumed they accepted that he was just doing his job guarding her, but she was pretty sure Jonathan wanted to bite his head off.

Ingqondo lifted a clawed hand, held it level with Jonathan's chest, and stood there for about fifteen seconds.

She wondered what he checked for—and how? Was he reading auras? Minds? Did he sense things with a magical ability? Was it a trainable skill, or was it innate?

"Vileblood," Ingqondo rasped. "Enchanted metal within the chest cavity, aiding in heart and lung function."

Audrey's own heart fluttered at the reminder of how close Jonathan came to death, but she forced herself to ignore how her fingers tingled, phantom scents of burnt skin and pine tickling her senses and making her stomach roil.

Focus, here and now. She couldn't faint five minutes after they arrived.

A nod and Ingqondo motioned for Jonathan to move. He did, with a little growl of warning, which was enough to anchor Audrey in the present.

She found herself eye level with this strange duster. Wouldn't it have been nice to smell things like Jonathan did, instead of being assaulted by fickle memories? On impulse, she inhaled as Ingqondo lifted his palm level with her heart, and she couldn't help but wrinkle her nose when she caught a strange scent. Cool, almost, and clean, like . . . glacier water?

"You are warded," Ingqondo said, not a question, his words English but his accent wasn't Russian. It wasn't anything she'd ever heard before.

"I am." She touched the necklace. "The ring is only wood from the taiga near Nizhny, a visual token for my contract with Katerina Yaga. But the chain is a ward against persuasion and possession."

That strange, watery scent grew stronger as the duster studied her, his hand utterly still between them. The scent definitely came from Ingqondo. Was it his magic? She'd have to ask Jonathan later. If she smelled it, he definitely did.

"The wards are within the allowed magics," Ingqondo said in his gravelly voice, then moved on to their bags, much quicker in his assessment. "Draughts, salves, teas, all benign and permissible. The third?"

"Aster, a cornflower wraith," Audrey offered. "She's following on the second carriage."

"To arrive in short order," Mikhali confirmed. "I can escort you to her now."

"Yes," Ingqondo replied. He left the way they'd come in without any further acknowledgment. Mikhali followed.

"Dinner will be brought to your suites this evening, miss," Varavara said after the pair departed.

"That's perfect, thank you. For all three of us, please."

That gave the woman pause, but she curtsied and left.

Yulia motioned for Ulyana to join her as they moved toward the door, and the older woman said, "There are two bells on the doorframe. One for the house in gold, and the silver will summon Ulyana for Symposium matters and personal needs outside the household proper. She will return in the morning, two hours before the opening brunch at ten o'clock, unless you have urgent needs now?"

"No, we're fine. And Aster?"

"Once Master Ingqondo appraises her and any other baggage, she will be brought here." The old woman gestured behind them. "The sitting room connects to the hall. To the right, the main suite with a private bath. The left hall houses the bunk room for your company, a second bath, and the dining room."

Yulia pressed her palms together, bent at the waist, less formal but still subservient. Ulyana mirrored her posture, both of them looking down.

Oh, right. They waited for a dismissal. "Thank you, um, that's all then?"

"Miss," they both said and left her and Jonathan alone in the receiving room, easily twice the size of their entire cabin, with polished marble floor and walls carpeted in tapestries and fine artwork. A shimmering crystal chandelier hung over the hand-carved iron table and velvet-finished couches. An untouched tea service waited on the coffee table, along with a bowl of fresh fruit, a platter of cheeses, nuts, and breads, and a winding silver dish covered in tiny, colorful cake squares—even though the housekeeper told them dinner was coming soon.

Audrey stared down at her dress boots; they were new, but she'd already scuffed the toes, and they were dappled with mud from Nizhny. They looked kind of sad against the pretty marble floor, and when she tapped her toe, dirt chafed off.

"There." Audrey lifted her head like a queen as she fought down a giggle. "Now it's just like home, isn't it?"

Jonathan's lip twitched. "Can't even tell the difference." He canted his head down the hall. "Gonna check the rooms, make sure nothing's off."

She toed off her dirty boots and followed him, not ready to be alone in the vast apartment. Jonathan paced their borrowed space with relentless efficiency.

"Did that man smell strange to you? The duster who checked us for magic."

"Everything here smells strange compared to home." Jonathan pulled back the curtains in the bedroom, his expression stern as he swept the outside before dropping the red fabric, apparently satisfied with whatever he saw. She couldn't help a small smile at hearing him call Nizhny home. "Why you asking? Something about him bother you?"

"No, I was just curious." She sat on the bed, another ornate piece of furniture, complete with four posts and a sheer canopy. The down-filled comforter puffed up around her. "He smelled cold to me when he came close." Jonathan stilled for a beat, but it was enough to break his prowling. "What?"

He seemed almost uneasy. Not a normal look on him. "What do you mean, smelled cold?"

She shrugged. "I don't know, but when he lifted his hand, it reminded me of maybe melted snow? And the scent lingered?"

Jonathan hummed, taking her chin. "You smelled him working his magic. That sort of prying bites a bit." His thumb traced her jaw. "No way a human would pick up on that."

She realized what he was doing then; he was checking her eyes to see if they'd turned black.

Audrey swallowed, both hands grabbing his forearm, needing an anchor. "Lamashtu's blood." Jonathan nodded, his lips a thin line. She leaned into his palm. "Okay, well, that's not unexpected, I guess."

"Gotta watch how you react," Jonathan said. "Speaking English and Russian, that's expected. You can tell them apart now?"

"Yes." She needed to pay attention, but Russian and English were already becoming almost interchangeable in her thoughts.

"Good." He paused, one last gentle sweep of his thumb on her cheek before he let his hand fall. "Only a matter of time before the rest kicks on."

Of course. All of Jonathan's senses were extremely heightened. To her, one duster's scent had been distracting when he used his magic. If she suddenly had a full influx of enhanced senses, from all directions? She rubbed her face with both hands. One problem at a time, she mused, though the problem pile only seemed to get bigger.

Jonathan said, "Wait here," and headed for the receiving room. A few seconds later, the outside door opened, and he called, "It's Aster."

Audrey ran to greet her. Aster looked the same as when they'd boarded in Nizhny, with her perfect blue dress and carefully coiffed hair, and Audrey couldn't stop herself from throwing her arms around the woman. Aster tsked but returned the hug.

"Was the train alright? Did they treat you okay?"

Jonathan chuckled, hefting the bags as he headed down the hall to put them in the right rooms.

Aster shrugged. "The train was boring. A box on wheels, no open windows." Another tsk. "I see no appeal to it."

"Maybe you would if you'd been in our fancy room."

"I doubt it. Now, tell me, what is next?"

Audrey smiled, so thankful Aster was here with them. She'd be the perfect counterpart. Jonathan would protect her, but he wouldn't be much help navigating Dominion politics.

"The opening brunch is tomorrow." She took Aster's hand, which earned her a questioning look as Audrey tugged. "I'll show you your room, and then we can all eat dinner together. I want to hear more about your boring train ride."

Another tsk, but Aster let herself be pulled along.

Chapter 20

Ulyana, Audrey's assigned secretary for the Symposium, arrived early the next morning as expected. The knock came as Aster put the final touches on her hair, a tight crown of intricate braids woven with blue ribbon. Her ribbon matched her dress, the billowy fabric trimmed in sculpted gray velvet, with a coordinated fur shawl. The top half was a boned corset, laced tight. With what little food Audrey had kept down since becoming pregnant, her belly didn't poke out yet, even though she was four months along. Rina's ring hung heavy on the chain against her sternum, in plain view on E's enchanted chain.

Jonathan strode across the room, admitting Ulyana without a word. The woman smiled brightly, curtsying before she entered, a leather binder clutched in her hands along with a brilliant crimson quill.

"Good morning, miss," she said in clear Russian. Audrey wondered if Ulyana's family line went all the way back to those who'd survived the Aperien Event here in Russia, bunkered down tight when the world around burned with magic and calamities.

"Good morning," Audrey said. Ulyana was easy to smile at, the young woman pleased with her post. She sat on the chaise across from Audrey. Behind her, Jonathan's nostrils flared, and he gave a nearly imperceptible nod. Nothing amiss, not on the surface at least. Aster continued with her hair.

For a breath, everything seemed absurd, with all of them treating her like some kind of royalty.

Audrey cleared her throat. "How long do we have?"

Ulyana opened her leather binder, the penmanship inside perfect. Rows of times, names, places, and a few empty slots scattered on the schedule. "We'll be leaving for the carriage at the front gates in around forty-five minutes, miss."

"Ulyana, right?"

The woman paused, confused at the question. "Yes?"

"You can call me Audrey. We're going to be spending hours together, and I'll be drowning in formality as it is."

She smiled. "Of course, Miss Audrey."

It was all she could do not to wince. Audrey didn't push. She also ignored Jonathan's grin from behind Ulyana. "Thank you. Tell me about the rest of the day, please?"

"The brunch will run into the afternoon, with two meals served along with an afternoon tea. Introductions to those attending, followed by a presentation on the state of the Dominion at large, to be given by Dimitri Syn Koschei. The rest of the day and evening will be at your leisure, though I can recommend activities."

"Dimitri said I can make appointments with you?"

"Yes, Miss Audrey."

"I'd like to visit the Moscow Library during my free time this afternoon. The head bookkeeper is a personal trade partner. Can you find out if he's available?"

"Oh, he will be, Miss Audrey," Ulyana said, taking notes, the quill waving as she scribed. Enchanted then, no ink pot in sight. It made sense for mobility, but it still made Audrey grin. Modern pens and pencils were probably more efficient and less expensive, but only the best for the Deathless, his family, and their contracts.

"It's alright if he's not free. I'll still visit the library, but I'd like to see him as soon as he has time."

"He will see you today, Miss Audrey."

Audrey frowned. She hadn't written ahead and didn't want to impose. He wouldn't know she was in Moscow, and she didn't want to make the wrong impression.

Aster laid a gentle hand on her arm. "Those gathered for the Symposium are given priority when in the capital. It is a manner of respect to accommodate you. Host honor demands it. Miss," Aster added with the barest smirk, Ulyana still scribbling away.

Audrey sighed inwardly and didn't even look at Jonathan this time; she could feel his snarky smile from across the room. "Thank you," she murmured. "Can we look ahead a few days while we have a minute?"

The Symposium matters were being hosted in the Kremlin, much to Audrey's excitement, but nothing could have prepared her for stepping into the Faceted Chamber for the morning's brunch.

The red outer walls and the stark white of the main building had been breathtaking. Walking through the cultivated gardens, far more lavish and expansive than during the human era, had been exhilarating. But walking up the grand entry on the plush carpet? That was astounding.

This room though? Gods above, below, anywhere and everywhere . The photographs and drawings in the *History and Policy of the Moscow Dominion, Ver. VII.* did nothing to prepare her.

The room itself wasn't so large, but the ornate and exquisite décor, the weight of the chamber's history, and the fact it still existed, given how much of the human world had been lost since the Aperien event? Audrey stopped dead in the doorway, the air leaving her lungs in a rush, a hand pressed against her heart.

The Faceted Chamber gleamed from floor to ceiling, golden paint and carved trim, glittering chandeliers accented with red and gold fairy fire. Every wall and every section of the ceiling bore sweeping murals between the gilded arches. A central pillar anchored the entire room, intricately woven carpet covering the floor.

"Oh," Audrey whispered, taking in the mural scenes of humanity in different times. She basked in the warm glow, wanting to linger for just a moment and not think about all the expectations that came with standing in this room at all.

She let herself be just a human girl, soaking up the wonder.

She didn't get long. Ulyana politely cleared her throat and whispered, "This way, Miss Audrey," after only a few seconds.

Audrey tore her gaze away from the art—not that she'd be able to ignore it, it covered the entire room—and toward the banquet table set up on the central pillar's far side, already laden with decadent pastries, bread and butter sandwiches, fresh fruits in all colors of the rainbow, and a variety of prepared eggs. Porridges with a spread of jams, nuts, and syrups and a few dishes she didn't recognize but assumed were made from cottage cheese—a popular choice in Moscow both before and after the Aperien Event. Beyond the main table, the wall recessed, an inlaid table set up on a platform with a seat nothing short of a throne. Empty, because of course Dimitri Syn Koschei would enter with fanfare.

Audrey kept her spine tall as Ulyana led them toward the table, acutely aware of Jonathan and Aster behind her. She kept her hands folded at her waist, doing her best not to squeeze her fingers together.

And to breathe through her mouth.

Her sense of smell continued to improve, but it wasn't doing her any favors this morning. Even with two draughts—one for nausea and one for the headache already blooming behind her eyes—every inhale made her stomach twist and turn. All the foods on their own probably smelled amazing, but the mixture was a mess, not to mention whiffs of what must have been magic, which she wasn't used to at all. Aster had painted extra color on her cheeks this morning so she didn't look as sick as she felt.

The main table was shaped like a compass, the province leadership positioned according to their locations within the Dominion. A small, secondary table was set with four chairs, the only empty seats aside from the elevated throne.

It could be worse, Audrey supposed. They could have made them stand.

She swallowed down the sticky taste on her tongue. They were last to arrive aside from Dimitri, and Audrey wasn't sure what that meant. All eyes followed their entrance with interest. She tried to ignore her nerves and focus on the information in her arsenal instead. It always helped her during her time as an esquire in the ESC. And she'd worked hard to be ready for this moment, hours and hours spent learning everything she could about the people in this room. The province heads of the Dominion, all appointed to their positions by the Deathless himself.

There were no chairs on the table's western side, a nod to the territory lost to the Storm Belt. Perun, the Slavic god of thunder, had perished with the rest of his equivalents. The statement was obvious: the Dominion would have been larger and grander had that one calamity played out a little differently.

Of course, they wouldn't have seated a human envoy and her company in *that* space.

Ded Moroz kept the direct north. He appeared much like Audrey had expected, given his counterparts included Father Christmas and Santa Claus. A tall man dressed in fur-lined blue robes far too warm for spring and the heated indoors, with a thick white beard that reached down to his waist. He wasn't overly plump, more wizened than whimsical.

Maxim Syn Sadko occupied the next spot at the northeast, a duster who came from the line of Sadko the Rich Merchant, a human legend, which was an Aperien who'd manifested with immortality and little else in the way of magic. Sadko was known for catching a gold-finned fish. Like many seated around the table, the Dominion strove to keep tradition and mythos anchored in local Russian and Slavic culture. Audrey had no idea how many generations came between Maxim and the original Sadko, but Maxim certainly dressed the part of a wealthy merchant. A portly man well into his sixties, with a shimmering copper cast to his skin that suggested other Aperien blood in his lineage. He was already eating, uninterested in her group's arrival.

Nikita the Tanner manned the eastern territory, and by his look of surprise, he'd expected Rina. Unlike Maxim, he dressed in simple leathers, his calloused hands folded in front of an empty plate. A shrewd expression sat behind a thick black beard and heavy brow, and Audrey knew why. As Nizhny expanded, it was Nikita who held the ground that might one day border an Independent. From what she'd learned about him, Nikita was well-liked by those who lived under his supervision and was considered fair. Of everyone gathered at the table, he was Nizhny's best chance at an ally—or their biggest hurdle.

To the southeast sat a duster descended from the Aperien human legend Vasilisa the Wise. He was beautiful, of course, but reminded Audrey of Kushiel just enough she had to suppress a shiver. Jacob Syn

Vasilisa, angelic in all appearances save for his lack of wings. His mother, Vasilisa's granddaughter, died less than a year ago. The circumstances were not made public, though it had caused strain between Moscow and the Dominion's Southeast quarter. Vasilisa, the original Aperien, shared many mythos with Koschei the Deathless, most often as his victim. Her post had been reparations to that mythos, offered as proof that the Deathless of reality was not the same as the man of myth. The ramifications of her descendant's demise were yet unclear. If Jacob's ascension troubled him, he didn't show it now. All smiles, golden curls, and warm blue eyes.

The south marked the only woman at the table as a province head, her seat replaced by a spread of cushions on which the sphinx lounged, her lion tail swaying as she studied Audrey and her company. Grecian in nature, with a woman's head, lion's body, and great, billowing eagle wings, she cut an impressive silhouette reclining among the gathered men. This sphinx had taken the name Ophelia, and there wasn't much known about her beyond having the Deathless's ear since shortly after the Aperien Event. Her expression as she watched Audrey was indecipherable.

Audrey barely suppressed a gag at the platter of raw, bloody meat in front of the sphinx.

Dobryana Nikitichi, another well-known Aperien human legend from Russian mythos, occupied the southwestern seat. He wore full traditional bogatyr's armor from his era, including the pointed helm. A dragon breeder, the Aperien had held his position since Koschei the Deathless founded the Dominion prior to the Accords, and his dragon children, as he called them, comprised a very dangerous portion of the Moscow army. Dobryana himself reflected his humble mythos origins, human by all appearances, and relaxed at these proceedings.

Lastly, to the northwest sat Poloz, and for all he appeared human, his gleaming green eyes hinted his true nature. The Great Serpent from Siberian myth, the Lord of All That is Gold. Dimitri might run the symposium formalities, but it was Poloz who acted as Koschei's left hand to accompany his wife, Jaga Baba, at his right. Audrey hoped the kindness from Poloz's mythos carried over into reality. She had to fight back a smile, because the Aperien was truly yellow from head to toe.

Each had three companions. First, a human bearing the Koschei brooch and carrying a quill and leather binder, the same as Ulyana, their assigned secretaries for the Symposium. The other two varied widely between each province leader, though none seemed to serve as a bodyguard like Jonathan. In fact, everyone gathered seemed relaxed, which made sense; they all knew each other, probably having done this same thing in the same room many times.

Then the casual mood shifted as Dobryana Nikitichi stood, armor clanging, his hand reaching for a weapon that hadn't made it into the chambers. "A vileblood?"

Audrey didn't hesitate. "Katerina Yaga of Nizhny contracted Jonathan Gunnar as my bodyguard. An acceptable position given the recent reforms to the Vilestars Accord."

"And Katerina Yaga is where, exactly?" asked Ophelia, her voice deep and low, a resonant purr to her words.

Before Audrey could respond, heavy heels sounded behind her, the entire gathering's attention shifting as Dimitri entered the chamber. All the of the human secretaries stood and bowed, Ulyana dropping to a deep curtsy beside Audrey.

"That is the question of the hour, isn't it?" Dimitri shot Audrey a knowing smile, the gleam in his expression nothing short of predatory as he brushed by her, past the banquet table, and up to his elevated seat. Two human women waited for him, one pulling out his chair, the other offering him the leather binder, which he dismissed before sitting down.

Once he did, the other secretaries took their seats, but Dobryana remained standing. Everyone was silent, watching Dimitri watch Audrey as he drank from a golden chalice, then motioned to Audrey and her company.

"Well, go on then. We thought Katerina Yaga would be here to discuss matters on behalf the Dominion province of Nizhny. Yet," Dimitri drank again, then set down his cup as he leaned forward on his elbows. "We're graced with a human, a vileblood, and a cornflower wraith instead."

Audrey lifted her chin, because she wouldn't have dared to come into this room without preparing for exactly this scenario. Granted, she'd thought Dimitri might weave his own version, that he'd perform for the gathering with whatever he wanted them to believe. Either he wanted her to stick her foot in her mouth, or he enjoyed being a pompous ass.

She wagered it was a mix of the two.

"I'd like to begin with my most sincere apologies," Audrey said. She curtsied as low as she could manage, ignoring the way the room wobbled and rose once the dizziness passed. "I've been assisting Katerina Yaga with contract matters for nearly a year now. However, as Dimitri knows from our first encounter, my Russian was lacking." She held his gaze as she spoke, wondering if he had any means in place to detect lies, but it didn't really matter either way. This wasn't about the truth; it was about the performance. "It was my responsibility to draft Nizhny's acceptance to the symposium, a great honor. I didn't realize I'd made an atrocious error until the formal summons arrived. You see, my translation was incorrect, mistaking the word province for territory, not realizing the implications and the formal status of provinces in the Dominion."

Audrey inclined her head again. "And while Nizhny remains an Independent Territory, we would never diminish the importance of our trade relations with the Moscow Dominion on Nizhny's success. It is my greatest honor to attend the Symposium on Katerina Yaga's behalf as her envoy. My name is Audrey Doe."

Dimitri's gaze never left her, a few mumbles coming from those gathered, Dobryana Nikitichi sitting down with another rattle of silver armor.

Jacob Syn Vasilisa was the first to respond, his expression curious. "You're the human girl who worked with Theodore Avialian, aren't you? The one who proposed the Vilestars Accord change."

This wasn't unexpected. They'd decided it was a fool's errand to try and hide her identity. Kushiel had been the one who tried to kill her, and he was dead now. And if she was alive, all the speculation that Jonathan killed her didn't really matter any longer.

"That's me, yes." Her palms were sweating. For whatever reason, she didn't think *she* would be the focus of the conversation. Audrey set her jaw, trying to ignore how Jacob smelled like feathers even without wings, the reminder of Kushiel creeping like acid in her veins.

"We've been graced with a celebrity of sorts, friends, although the ESC claimed you're dead?" Jacob lifted a brow.

Audrey offered a smile. "Even the most powerful can find themselves misinformed."

Poloz barked out a laugh, the golden man shining, mirth in his golden gaze. "Mmm, cheers to that." No one else at the table seemed amused.

"Have a seat, envoy," Dimitri said, smirking down at her from his pedestal as she curtsied one more time. "I think we've had enough delays." He clapped his hands once, and said, "Shall we begin?"

Jonathan helped her sit at the secondary table, with Aster on her left and Ulyana on her right. The table setting was the same as the main table as far as she could tell, but everything was empty except a single glass and a water pitcher. Gods, she was so thirsty, but when she reached, Jonathan was faster. He grabbed the cup from her hand, sniffed it, then licked the rim. Audrey balked at first, then realized what he was doing.

Not everyone knew vilebloods were immune to poisons, only that they were fast healers. He tested the water in the pitcher next, before pouring a glass and passing it to her with a nod.

All of that for water.

He'd done the same thing last night when their dinner service arrived, Audrey realized. She'd thought he'd just been hungry—they'd gone all afternoon without a proper meal and the dinner came very late—but he'd tasted everything first, then served both her and Aster.

She flattened a hand on her stomach, willing it to calm. Being a human protected by the Accords didn't mean the entire world was unwilling to take what might be seen as an acceptable risk. And no one in the room batted an eye at the blatant suspicion; did they all have tasters?

While Dimitri rattled off formal introductions, Jonathan went to the main table and reached over one secratary to grab them breakfast. Her cheeks warmed—another slight. Fortunately, he returned with a light, bland meal she'd probably be able to stomach and sampled each item on the plate before setting it in front of her. Audrey would wait to eat anything until their formal introduction so she wouldn't be caught chewing.

She realized belatedly Dimitri had launched right into his own merits and the state of the Dominion's trade affairs, the beginning of what was clearly an extended presentation. She slumped back into the seat, warring with relief and irritation. He'd bypassed them entirely.

Hours dragged on. Beside each of the provincial leadership, their assigned sectaries dutifully took notes. Upon request, they produced statistics and numbers from the relevant regions. More than once, they would subtly draw the attention of their pairing and whisper in their ear. Maybe show them what they'd written.

Ulynana had yet to open her leather-bound journal, the quill across the cover. She hadn't even looked at Audrey since they'd seated.

No one had.

Since their arrival and Audrey's explanation of Rina's absence, no one spared any of them a second glace. Not even when Jonathan went to the table to fetch her refreshments a second time when the wait staff changed over the banquet table to a tea and coffee service, along with sweet cakes and savory sandwich bites.

Audrey held her skirts in tight fists as the extent of this farce really sunk in.

She'd spent weeks pouring over everything she could learn about Moscow, the Dominion, the Deathless and his trusted leaders before leaving Nizhny. Hours upon hours diving into contract laws, trade values, exports, and imports. Train details, province weather and how it affected feeding the Dominion population at large. Gods, she'd even learned the province leaders' favorite meals and activities when they stayed in the capital at length, and she'd memorized every version ever written about their various mythos.

All the while imagining she might do some good here, accomplish something for her home, perhaps not unlike she'd managed during her time as an esquire.

But no, that wasn't the case at all, was it?

Dimitri had gambled, come up short, and now she would sit here for weeks, ignored and belittled, as a stark reminder that the Dominion didn't give a damn about Nizhny except for subjugating Rina.

Chapter 21

"D id you both know?" Audrey asked as she tugged off her shawl and tossed it at the coat rack by the apartment's front door. After six hours of in-depth Dominion trade discussion while being stuffed in a corner and roundly ignored, they'd only now returned to their rooms.

Jonathan's lip twitched as he looked in Aster's direction. The corn-flower wraith canted her head, as if finding Audrey's frustration curious.

"It's not funny," Audrey snapped, brushing by him as she struggled out of her boots.

These corsets were unbearable now that they seemed entirely pointless, like this entire gods-be-damned trip to Moscow. Aster tsked, a sound Audrey used to find endearing and now found condescending.

"I spent weeks studying trade manifests, histories, and personal preferences. Hours poring over documents, books, letters, all so I could be useful when we arrived, so I could contribute on Nizhny's behalf, and for what? Nothing? And you knew, both of you, didn't you? You knew that as soon as we showed up here as an envoy, and not Rina bending to Dominion oversight, we'd be . . . we'd be . . ." She threw up her hands. "Decoration? I might as well be a potted plant!" Her voice rose into a shriek at the end.

Aster tsked again. Audrey glared at her.

"Come, did you really believe you would sit at that Aperien table and negotiate trade relations within the Dominion proper?" Aster took her hands, squeezing before she could muster any sort of protest. "No, you did not. You knew much of this would be performative. And perform you did. Your preparation allowed you to handle Dimitri Syn Koschei's childish posturing with grace, in a way that neither diminished him nor the Deathless, nor those gathered for the symposium."

"But that's really it?" Audrey said, not sure why it all stung so much, not when Aster was right. She hadn't expected to be an equal, but she also hadn't expected to feel so utterly pointless. "We come all the way here, to stay for three months, to just . . . sit there and look pretty?"

"Got the pretty part covered," Jonathan drawled.

"Jonathan Gunnar!"

Aster grinned now, and Jonathan made no attempt to hide his own amusement at her expense, but he held up his hands and headed down the hall. "Let me run you a bath, relax you some."

"I am relaxed!"

But he was already gone. She huffed. Aster tugged at her arm, leading her to the bedroom and helping her undress, peeling away the layers of costume.

"You did very well, Audrey. Dimitri is a petty man and will do whatever he can to ease his stinging pride. Now you shall sit at his petty table, smile with grace, and remind them all Nizhny is not theirs to do with as they please."

"Play the game," Audrey said with a sigh.

"Indeed, but do not diminish the importance of your role in the game. Being here buys valuable time. Rina does not want to admit it yet, but she will have to face the Dominion's power, one way or another."

Audrey shivered, stripped down to her chemise. "You think that will be soon?"

Aster busied herself folding clothing and laying out more casual attire for her trip to the library in an hour. "I think it will be sooner than any of us would like. Rina is . . ." Aster paused, then shook her head. "Rina is many things, but as you know, being unwilling to bend in the wind can cause more damage than good."

She meant Aspen. At first, Rina had wanted to deal with the problem of a leshy on her border as she would any potential threat: with brute force. When Audrey went against Rina's wishes to treat with the leshy instead of killing it, she thought Rina was going to exile her from Nizhny, and Jonathan by proxy. Rina had ultimately accepted the better, peaceful approach. She wasn't so stubborn as to throw away a solution because she'd been wrong, but for weeks afterward, Audrey worried she'd irreparably damaged her relationship with Nizhny's leader, who was also her good friend.

Things worked out, but accepting a leshy as a citizen of Nizhny under Rina's authority was mild compared to what they faced now. If the Deathless claimed Nizhny through force, they wouldn't survive the onslaught. But asking Rina to bow to Dominion authority over the Independent Territory she'd built from nothing?

They might as well set the town on fire and start over somewhere else.

Audrey rubbed her face.

"This is not your problem alone to solve," Aster said as she set to undoing her pins and braids.

"Nizhny is my home. Of course this is my problem."

"Mmm, and the esquire seeks to right the world."

"You don't have to make it sound so trite," Audrey said, stepping away so she could work on the braids herself, her frustration simmering with a fresh wave of nausea. Her draughts were wearing off sooner than yesterday. "Can you make me some fresh tea, please?"

"It is not a dismissal but a reminder," Aster replied, but left her side to start a fresh batch. "Your stomach?"

"Yes. I don't want to risk being sick in public."

Audrey sat on the bed's edge and ran her fingers through her loose hair. Running water sounded from the adjoining bathroom, and she had to admit, a bath sounded nice. When Aster handed her a cup, the porcelain warm against her palms, the cornflower wraith offered a gentle smile.

"Take the boon for what it is." Her gaze flitted purposefully to Audrey's middle. "This gives you more time to focus on other matters, which are far more pressing."

"I'm one person, Aster. An entire town is a little more important."

"I did not say you were more important. I said your matter is more pressing." Aster arched a brow, because she was mincing words and she knew it. "Play the part; learn what you can. We may find whispers helpful, or tongues may dance when they should rest. In the meantime, find *your* answers." Her mirth dropped off, her tone stern when she added, "A dead esquire can help no one."

Audrey flinched. She couldn't help it, even though she knew Aster didn't mean to be cruel. She was on borrowed time, and helping herself—saving herself—was going to take a lot of work, starting with the first trip to the library this evening. Research was one of her strengths, after all.

Aster excused herself, off to play her own role. She'd mingle with the house staff and introduce herself to those arranging the upcoming equinox festivities. Maybe Aster would stumble upon some sort of miraculous solution while she eavesdropped? Wouldn't that be easy?

The water shut off and Jonathan emerged. "Alright?" he asked, his expression the measured neutral he so often wore, but she knew he smelled her frustration, her fatigue, her looming worry.

"Alright enough," she answered honestly and wandered into his arms. He grunted when she did.

"Still pissed I called you pretty?"

She pinched at his side, laughing when he growled at her. Well, loving him was easy, and Audrey decided that was enough for today.

Nothing could have readied Audrey for taking that first step into the Moscow Library. The building was so much more than just keeping books and a place for citizens to visit and partake of the Dominion's wealth. The library itself was the central hub of a bigger network of buildings, all interconnected and all dedicated to the preservation of the past and future.

Audrey ran up the marble staircase as soon as their carriage arrived, Jonathan's chuckle floating up after her. Like everywhere in Moscow, the way was lit by gilded lanterns and edged in crimson and golden filigree. The main windows were stained glass, a different motif on either side of the grand entryway, re-creations of different scenes from of Russian mythos. At sunset hour everything glittered and glowed, and she grinned like a fool.

Thank goodness for Aster's draughts, her nausea and fatigue were at bay for the next hour at least, and she smoothed her pleated skirt when she reached the archway. Beyond, the grand entryway opened like a flower, the petals hundreds of shelves, floor to ceiling, filled with thousands and thousands and *thousands* of books of all kinds.

"It smells like paper," Audrey said with a giggle, hands on her cheeks.

Three stories tall with winding balconies, rolling ladders, and an enormous tree growing up tall enough to frame the glass ceiling with rich leaves and the last of spring flowers. The reception desk wrapped around the entire trunk, a dozen workers speaking with clients, the room carrying the low hum of whispered conversations. People who could fly buzzed around on their hunt for stories and literature, or perhaps histories. Guides and law books, maybe cookbooks too. Encyclopedias and rescued journals. Holy books from bygone eras, and technical manuals for early twentieth-century machinery.

Audrey could get lost in here for her entire life. It was nothing like the sterile knowledge repositories within the ESC borders. Sure, there were bookstores as corner shops, and stands with gossip prints and news pamphlets, but this was something else entirely. This was an adoration of the written word. Whoever maintained this place cared about it. They loved it.

And while the main chamber was a vast library, each wing was its own dedicated archive—relics of the past, historical and magical. Artwork and statuary. Say what one liked about the Dominion's iron fist, but they appreciated beauty in the arts and magic.

"Don't drool," Jonathan drawled as he stepped up beside her. She elbowed him in the ribs, and he gave her an amused grunt. "We're a bit early."

"We should let someone know we're here, then we can wander until our appointment."

Another human greeted them, this one wearing a contract marker Audrey didn't recognize. The young man was cordial, happy to welcome them, but then nose-dived into a panic over a Symposium member being here—*here, now, early.* He was blabbering, with no idea how to handle the situation. Audrey just smiled, reassured him she'd arrived early to see the paintings, and he frantically directed them down the hall. After she thanked him, he *ran,* and she couldn't help but sigh because he was probably going to disrupt the head bookkeeper ahead of the set time.

"Do you think Symposium members are rude to everyone? Threatening to impale the staff if their water isn't cold enough?" Audrey muttered as they headed away from the vast shelving toward an archway leading into a more formal museum layout. There were no windows and the hall appeared empty.

Jonathan followed close, his stride lazy and loose. He didn't seem threatened here, so she took that as a sign she could relax and enjoy the sights for a few minutes.

"Dunno. Seems people expect things a certain way around here. All about appearances and shit."

Audrey considered that for a moment; so many humans served under contract. Maybe it was a matter of pride to serve their patrons. She imagined if one contracted well, they wouldn't want to risk losing their positions. So far, most of the humans she'd encountered seemed a little uptight but not unhappy. Ulyana seemed overjoyed by the opportunity to be Audrey's secretary, despite it involving little more than being a walking calendar. Everyone in Dimitri's household that they'd met appeared content, comfortable, and well cared for.

She hated the indenture system in the Eastern Seaboard Conduct. The standards for providing care in the industry sector adhered to the bare minimum of the Human Protection Accord. She'd expected the Dominion's contract system to be the same sort of terrible, but it wasn't, at least not in the Red Corner. Although the rich in the ESC—as Audrey had discovered once she started working with Theodore in the York hub—treated their human indentures better than in the slums. They'd barely seen beyond the gilded nobility here in Moscow. Who knew what waited outside all the concentrated wealth?

"All that thinking," Jonathan said. "Why don't you give that big brain of yours a break for a minute, enjoy the art."

"I took a bath."

"Yeah, you lasted a whole ten minutes before you were asking when the carriage would come."

"I didn't want to be late," she grumbled, gaze wandering as they moved through the dimly lit connecting hall and into the gallery proper. "Oh."

First the sheer volume of books and now this: a winding marble theater, papered floor to low ceiling with paintings upon paintings upon paintings.

"It's the largest surviving collection," Audrey whispered, her voice carrying in the space between history and art, her eyes darting this way and that, too many masterpieces to pick from. "I read you can arrange a private tour guide who'll shuffle the paintings around if you want to see one closer."

She stopped in front of a piece on the lowest level. A table of fruit, cloth, and a vase of flowers, but she saw the texture of the oil paints, with tiny cracks in a few places. Just above it, a sweeping black and white line drawing of a nude woman. And up one more, a man in what must have been a military uniform, riding a horse, sword pointed to lead a charge. She wrinkled her nose at another piece—squares and circles and lines that didn't really make much sense—and then grinned at a landscape painting, rolling hills with snowcapped mountains and a river bisecting the verdant valley.

The gallery went on and on and on and on. Audrey glanced back, wondering if Jonathan was bored, and smiled when she found him taking in the vast array of paintings. She wondered what he was thinking, which ones he liked best, but stopped herself from asking. They could talk about what they saw later, she decided, because at this moment, well. Maybe they'd come back again before they returned to Nizhny, or maybe they'd never find themselves in a place quite like this again.

The minutes ran slowly, and she didn't rush, but she didn't linger too long looking at any single piece. There was too much to see, and she didn't want to miss anything.

Jonathan's hand brushed her lower back, right as she heard footsteps coming from deeper in the gallery. He'd avoided touching her in familiar ways in public since they arrived, and the touch was gone as soon as it came. A warning. They both faced deeper into the gallery, and as they waited, Audrey realized she could hear Jonathan's heartbeat.

She rubbed her arms, suddenly chilled. More changes, more shifts in her blood and her senses.

Audrey focused instead on the approaching figure. As the painting gallery seemed deserted, maybe even closed for the day aside from letting in envoys they needed to entertain, this man approached from a different access. Either that, or he'd been wandering through the collection before they arrived.

It felt rude to stare, so she let Jonathan play his part and look intimidating. She offered a nod in greeting and went back to viewing the nearest artwork. This time the subject was a park beside a river, filled with people. A different art style, almost like little dots instead of brush strokes.

"*Sunday on La Grande Jatte,*" the man said as he drew closer. "Georges Seurat, a French painter from the post-Impressionist era. Did you know he was only thirty-one years old when he died?"

Audrey smiled. "I didn't know any of that. Thank you for sharing."

He inclined his head, his smile crinkling around his eyes, which were a plain brown. Balding and graying, clean-shaven, with skinny arms and a portly middle, the stranger looked nothing more or less like a middle-aged human man. Nothing about his features was remarkable, yet Audrey sensed a weight to him. He was Aperien; she felt it under her skin. Despite his expensive yet simple clothing—a crimson tunic and a pair of leather slacks, his shoes finely polished—he kept his hands folded neatly behind his back as he returned his attention to the painting he'd described. Even his voice was unremarkable, calm and low, and scratchy as if from lack of use.

This was a being who either enjoyed hiding in plain sight or couldn't be bothered with the show. Audrey found the latter unlikely, especially with the way Jonathan stood, spine stiff and his jaw grinding.

Well, there wasn't any reason to be rude. "Do you visit the gallery often?"

The man gave a single, sharp nod. "I do. I find it a pleasant reprieve from my duties. A quiet place. Despite the beauty, few seem to have the patience to be still and admire things simply for being."

Audrey smiled again, unable to keep the warmth from her expression. "I wish I had more time. Or a place like this closer to home."

"You are Katerina's envoy."

It wasn't a question. He kept his gaze fixed on the park, the scene captured in bright colors, stolen from the past. She knew they were done with pretending they were just looking at the art, and Audrey bit back a sigh. She would have loved to hear more about the paintings.

"I am." She turned on him, giving her full attention and a half curtsy. Not entirely formal, but respectful.

But as she opened her mouth to introduce herself and Jonathan properly, the man fixed her with a shrewd gaze. "Esquire Audrey Doe and the liberated vileblood Jonathan Gunnar, no less."

Audrey couldn't help catching her hands together, squeezing her fingers, as Jonathan shifted closer. She was getting sick of 'Audrey Doe' all the time. She felt less and less human by the minute. And she wasn't some castoff, not anymore.

Audrey forced another smile, knowing it was thin. Not enough to seem rude, she hoped. "Yes. Seems you have me at a disadvantage, sir?"

He chuckled, but he no longer seemed as cordial. Not threatening, but cautious. Interested. It made her skin prickle, head to toes.

"A tactic I admit enjoying," he offered, giving her back the same forced smile. "When you oversee an Accorded Territory, it's nice to wander undeterred from time to time."

Audrey blinked once, then repeated her curtsy, deeper this time. She felt Jonathan's stiff bow beside her.

Koschei the Deathless waved a hand, dismissing the attempt at formality. "If I'd expected worship, I'd have dressed for it."

Audrey huffed out a small laugh. "Sorry, this is the first time I've met an Accorded leader. I'd rather err on the side of caution."

"Is that true? You've attended tribunals twice—first for the changes in the Vilestars Accord, second for this man's parole. You're closely acquainted with an archivist—Avialian, yes? —and you must spend time at Katerina's table for her to send you in her stead." The Deathless quirked an unkempt brow, a few wild gray hairs poking out. "You're not unaccustomed to Aperien company by any means."

It took everything she had not to fidget. "No, but only a fool forgets respect where it's due, especially when you're only a human."

"Only a human, is it?" His gaze flicked over her shoulder to Jonathan. She hoped he wasn't glaring at the leader of the Moscow Dominion. He probably was. "Now, being so modest is verging on dishonest."

"She's got a meeting with the head bookkeeper," Jonathan said. "Wouldn't want to keep him waiting, being he rearranged his schedule."

"Jonathan, I'm sure he will understand." She rested a hand on his arm as he shifted forward, enough to put a shoulder in front of her—not a threat but getting dangerously close.

"No matter," the Deathless said, his attention back on Audrey in full. "I won't keep you, though I would ask before you depart. Are you here to challenge more Accords? Perhaps vet the Dominion's regard for humanity?"

She blinked a few times, tightening her hand on Jonathan's bicep. "Of course not, no." Her cheeks warmed because her next words skirted a lie. "I'm here on Rina—Katerina's behalf, as her envoy for the Symposium. To address the confusion I unintentionally created in the reply to the Symposium summons."

Another hand wave. "A clever diffusion in reply to my son's gambit, yes, I am aware. That doesn't interest me." Audrey filed that away for later as the Deathless continued. "You have appointments with the head bookkeeper, with whom you've requested several resources about Dominion policies leading up to your arrival. You've made requests for time in my archives, with no topics specified. Tomorrow you're visiting the Dominion Blood Clinic. And so I ask again, Esquire Audrey Doe, 'only a human' who overturned an Accord and is supposed to be dead, do you have aims to disrupt my Dominion?"

Jonathan practically vibrated beside her, as if her nails digging into his arm were the only thing holding him back from . . . from what? Trying to kill an Aperien who couldn't die?

"No, sir. I have no intentions of being a disruption." She blushed more, her own foolishness honest and bared, and it made her sound like an idiot, but she admitted, "I thought I would play a larger role in the Symposium, so I studied. For the rest, I've traded with the head bookkeeper for months. It seemed rude not to at least introduce myself in person. I didn't mean to be inconvenient to him, I . . ." She cleared her throat, straightened herself tall, remembering she'd earned her place as an esquire and envoy. "I wanted to learn anything and everything I can while I'm here." She gestured around them. "When will I ever have the chance to be here again? Maybe never. I don't know what I'll read. Everything I can, until my eyes hurt and I fall asleep at the table."

Jonathan snorted.

The last was the trickiest, and again, a lie through omission with as close to the truth as possible. It would be best if Koschei the Deathless walked away from this conversation and never spared her another thought.

"I want to learn more about blood madness," she said. "And about the vileblood and their curse. No one has cared beyond locking them away. I care. Curses are broken all the time. Maybe someone needs to care enough to try for them." She lifted her chin at the last part. It was all true, every word, even if she didn't specify her own changing blood and borrowed time. Audrey's head swam a bit, her mouth sticky again, but she kept her head high.

The Deathless looked between her and Jonathan, his expression less fierce, as if he listened—really listened—unlike his son who'd been as eager for her silence as answers about Rina and Nizhny. A weighted observation, a calculated consideration of every word. The reason this man, this unassuming Aperien, had held an Accorded Territory for well over a century with little internal strife or outside conflicts.

A smart, dangerous, and powerful man.

After the silence between them stretched long enough to become uncomfortable, the Deathless inclined his balding head, hands still in a basket at his lower back and his expression entirely unknowable. "In that case, enjoy your time in Moscow."

She curtsied again and whispered, "Thank you," as he turned and walked back the way he'd come.

Audrey realized then she'd never heard his heartbeat.

Chapter 22

"**Y**ou can just cancel, you know," Jonathan grumbled as they made their way back to the main entry and the reception desk.

"That would be rude."

"Yeah, so? People are rude all the fucking time. You're exhausted. That's a good enough reason."

"My exhaustion is the reason we're here," she snapped, a little harshly, but she *was* exhausted, more than a little annoyed, and entirely unnerved from their unexpected encounter with the Dominion's master. "Do you think he's really worried I'm here to cause trouble?"

Jonathan shrugged; how very typical of him and not at all helpful. "Yeah, sweetheart, I'm pretty sure he wouldn't waste his time if he didn't think you might stir up some shit."

She huffed. "Maybe we shouldn't have used our real names."

"Maybe you shouldn't have gotten your face plastered all over the ESC for changing an Accorded Law."

Audrey didn't bother arguing further, not when they were both agitated.

The same human receptionist greeted them, relaxed now that it was the correct time, and escorted them up two flights of winding staircases. After a landing overlooking the library proper—gods, the sight! It was almost enough to make her forget everything else in favor of just standing here and basking in the staggering, beautiful collection. They were ushered down a narrow hall flanked by polished steel filing cabinets. A few more steps on the marble floor, and they reached a modest office. It was so mundane after everything since arriving in Moscow, Audrey wondered if it was some sort of joke.

Then again, Audrey hadn't expected to come to the Symposium and do nothing. She hadn't expected to meet Koschei the Deathless while looking at paintings and be casually interrogated. And she certainly hadn't expected the head bookkeeper of the Moscow Dominion—a territory which so heavily focused on the preservation of Russian and Slavic mythos—to be an elderly Chinese man.

The short man didn't look up from his unpolished desk when the receptionist knocked on the open door. He used a ballpoint pen in a spiral notebook and wrote with tight penmanship, the desktop otherwise bare. The room itself was empty aside from the bookkeeper himself, his desk, and the wooden stool he perched upon.

"I can only imagine what you're thinking. 'A ballpoint pen after I sent him so much quality ink? What madness is this?'" He continued writing. "To which I reply: One doesn't need the finest cerulean distillation from bukavac horn dust that I have ever encountered when one is addressing the drudgery of uninspired paperwork." A flourishing wave of his free hand toward a locked cupboard fastened to the far wall, as unassuming as the rest of the office. "Quality when needed, not quality for quality's sake."

Audrey grinned. She couldn't help herself, waiting until the bookkeeper finished his note, closed his notebook, and shoved the very human pen into the spiral. He stood, dusting off his hands and shuffling around the desk, a slight hunch in his squat shoulders.

He smiled in return, his attention warm and kind. Audrey caught a faint aroma of chrysanthemum flowers, a spicy, almost earthy scent.

She resisted inhaling deeper because there were no flowers in the room. Was it his magic she smelled? Best to ask Jonathan later, she thought as she curtsied.

"Bah," he tutted at her, taking her hand and patting it. "I deal with bloated formalities from stuffy aristocrats day in and day out. You are the same eager learner and curious girl I've exchanged letters, books, and ink with, are you not?"

Audrey laughed. "Of course, yes."

"Good, good." He patted her hand again, his skin leathery and cool, before letting it drop to give Jonathan a once-over. "And this would be?"

"Jonathan Gunnar," he answered. They didn't shake hands.

"I'm realizing now I don't know your name. I'm sorry," Audrey said. He'd always signed their letters with his formal title despite their wandering conversations on history, myth, and other fancy texts he kept under his thumb.

"Because I never gave it, yes." The bookkeeper seemed amused by this. "Keeps things simple by having the lower scribes answering less important correspondence, then everyone thinks they are getting the most personal touch on every frivolous request. We do like to be important here in Moscow. You, however, may call me Zhang."

"Thank you." Maybe it was human nature, but she felt better addressing him like a person instead of some kind of magical fixture.

Zhang idly scratched at his stomach. "Now, to what do I owe the pleasure, Miss Audrey, that you've taken time from your extensive duties as envoy during the Symposium to visit my door?"

Jonathan snorted. Audrey shot a glare at him, and she turned back to find Zhang's silver mustache twitching in amusement. She sighed.

"I wanted to meet you. And it seemed rude to be here and not pay you a visit. I'm sorry that they made you rearrange things for me. I could have waited."

"You're too polite, child. I would have told them to piss off had I wanted. The Symposium members are important, true, but my role isn't their amusement." Another smile from Zhang, mischievous almost, and Audrey decided she liked him even more in person. She assumed Jonathan wasn't concerned; he leaned against the doorframe now, arms crossed and his posture loose. "And I wanted to meet you as well. That said, I know a mind seeking when I encounter it. You flatter me, but you're here for more than social idling."

She blushed; gods, was she so obvious about everything? "Yes, I have a few questions. And I wanted to do some research while I was here, but it can wait."

Zhang peered at her from under his pale, bushy eyebrows. He actually had to look up at her standing this close, a novelty for her. "Too polite. No, these questions of yours are important or you wouldn't come to me, worried you'd bother me. You'd have said your hellos and rushed away so I could get back to my endless work, itching out of your skin for believing you might inconvenience me." To Jonathan, Zhang added, "One thing for a human to minimize themselves around powerful beings, but this girl, an esquire no less, should learn to be a touch less altruistic."

"Preaching to the choir," Jonathan drawled.

The teasing was good natured, but it still stung a little. Audrey managed a strained smile, unwilling to ruin the moment.

Which was exactly what they implied, wasn't it?

Audrey sighed.

"I'm planning to visit the blood workers at the Clinic, but I want to learn more about blood curses and blood madness, particularly concerning vilebloods beforehand." She fought the urge to touch her stomach or glance back at Jonathan as she danced around the exact truth. "There are bound to be pregnancies with the Accord changing. We need a better understanding of how the curse works. Who knows, maybe we can even help female vilebloods. Or stop the curse from spreading to begin with. We'll never know until someone tries."

"And the Esquire vileblood liberator, with her trusty edge case and willing test subject at her side, well, who better to try," Zhang said, but nothing in his tone was patronizing.

While it left out her very urgent, personal stake in the matter, he wasn't wrong. And maybe Audrey would have chased these answers, anyway. Fate had simply pushed their hand. She nodded. "Who else. I figured you might streamline my research, or at least direct me toward more obscure resources."

Zhang nodded, his gaze focused in the middle distance now, his deceptively human eyes twitching as if reading. "Of course, yes. A few things come to mind immediately, and I can have them delivered to your guest quarters at Dimitri's manor. I'll delve deeper over the next few days, but please send a missive if you find yourself at the end of my suggestions before new documents arrive."

Audrey exhaled, relief sinking into her bones. Finally, taking a step *in* a direction. Research, she was good at that, and she desperately needed to do more for the future of her family than vomiting between headaches. "I really can't thank you enough."

"It is my job, child." When she opened her mouth to protest, Zhang tutted again. "Please, this will be much more intellectual than the latest duster on the fringes of the nobility scourging the archives from any sign of their importance. Or the endless sea of paperwork regarding trade numbers, tallies, histories, bah! If I have to look at one more list of movements for yarn and spices between the provinces this week, I might fall asleep at this desk."

"Don't you have people for shit like that?" Jonathan asked.

Audrey almost scolded him, but that would be overly polite, she thought with a private smirk. Zhang noticed, because he tossed her a wink before shooing at them both.

"Oh, I do, but being best at your work, and magically inclined, you can decipher the rest. Now go rest, because I know you didn't wish to slight me by delaying introducing yourself, so consider me not slighted. Now you can start your research, and come to with me interesting queries, I am most certain."

He shuffled back behind his desk, settling in on the stool and reclaiming his simple pen, already back at work.

"Good night," Audrey offered. Zhang didn't reply, so she and Jonathan left quietly and shut the door behind them.

By the time they arrived back at the apartment, there was already a stack of scrolls, two books, and a three-ring binder filled to bursting on the sitting room table.

"Not tonight," Jonathan said as he helped Audrey out of her jacket, holding her elbow while she slipped off her shoes. "You're about to fall over."

She didn't argue, but she gave the pile a longing gaze as she headed down the hall to the bedroom. Aster wasn't back, but she'd left Audrey's nighttime draughts on the bedside table, along with a glass of milk on a warming plate. There was a folded letter, which turned out to be the Symposium schedule for the following day. Mostly the same as today; they had to cover five years' worth of upkeep since the last Symposium, after all. At the bottom, Ulyana had penned in an appointment with the Clinic's director. She handed the schedule to Jonathan as she padded across the plush carpet to pull her nightclothes from the wardrobe.

"I don't think we'll get as warm of a reception tomorrow," she said. Jonathan chuckled, then tossed the letter on the comforter. He still had his shoes on. "Everything okay?"

"Yeah, just gonna get you settled and walk the grounds once."

"I thought you can't let me out of your sight."

He squeezed a squeak out of her as he pulled her against him. "Hmm, it's a problem, but you know we left the contract language with wiggle room for shit like this. But if you don't want me leaving, all you gotta do is say so." Jonathan pressed a kiss on her jaw, then a nibble that made her laugh.

"No, it's fine. I'm sure I'm going to fall asleep fast, anyway."

"Feeling alright?"

"For now, but the draughts are wearing off." He moved to let her go, but she held his forearm, keeping him close. "I'm fine, really, but . . . in a minute?"

He held her, indulged her want for his touch, for closeness, waiting while she went to the bathroom and cleaned up for sleep, but she paused when she crossed by the enormous mirror over the double sink.

What had Zhang really thought of the excited girl who wrote all those letters? He probably hadn't expected to meet someone who looked so entirely spent. No wonder he'd sent them away. The dark circles under her eyes were awful without concealer, her cheeks sunken, her normally bright hazel eyes dull.

Wasn't she supposed to glow or something? She almost laughed, but tears stung instead. Having a child, being pregnant, it was supposed to be a joy. A gift, not a curse. A change and a demand on a woman's body, of course, and more so in a world of magical half-human creatures born every day, but . . .

Audrey rubbed her eyes. She wanted just one moment where this could be a joy for them, the life inside her, the family they'd created, but so much hung in the balance. It was so much more complicated than it was supposed to be.

Supposed to be . . . This time Audrey let herself laugh. Her being pregnant wasn't *supposed to be* at all.

A rap sounded at the door. Jonathan. "Alright?"

She wiped her face; he'd know, he already did. She wasn't hiding from him, but she also couldn't wallow. Audrey would find joy; they'd find it, because she would not give up, so that was that, wasn't it?

"I will be."

Audrey woke deep in the night, startling upright against the silken sheets. Sweating, confused, until Jonathan's warm hand brushed her arm and squeezed.

"Bad dream?" His voice was thick with sleep.

"Maybe, I don't know. Don't get up; I'm okay. I just need a drink of water."

"You sure?"

"Yes." Audrey patted his hand, then brushed her lips against his. He let out a grumble, trying to pull her closer, but she slipped away. "I'll be right back."

The room was dim, light peeking through from the closed brocade curtains, sliver hued from the always illuminated streets outside. Yawning, she made her way to the washroom, shivering when her bare feet hit the transition between carpet and cold tile. A quick drink, and hopefully she'd be right back to sleep. She left the door open.

As she drank, she tried to remember her dreams, but there was only an empty, uncomfortable fog. Just as well. Her dreams weren't anything good, not for a long time now. The glass clinked when she set it on the granite countertop, and she paused, catching her reflection in the mirror again. Audrey squinted; something was off, but it was too dark. Likely nothing, she thought as she rubbed her face, but the reflective surface tugged at her. Sighing, she shut the door before she flicked on the electric lighting, not wanting to wake Jonathan again if he'd already drifted.

Yes, there was her tired face in the mirror, she thought with a smirk. She touched her cheek just below her bottom eyelid, leaning forward. Her pupils were large. Expanding.

And then they kept going, flooding the whites of her eyes with black.

Her throat caught as she tried to call out to Jonathan, but his name wouldn't come. The black kept on, swelling, inky night, before it overfilled, running down her cheeks in rivers. She couldn't move, couldn't breathe. Pain lanced across her forehead, horns spiraling out from her skull in bloodied ivory. Audrey opened her mouth to scream, her teeth serrated, tongue lolling and pronged.

More pain, in her middle this time.

Burning, tearing, chewing.

She stumbled away from the mirror, fumbling for the doorhandle. Locked from outside.

A cold, wet sensation between her thighs, and she looked down, black coating her legs, puddling on the floor, dark and spreading.

Audrey let out a muffled howl, slipped, crashed to her knees into the mess, another wash of pain making her bend in half, her stomach bared and naked and huge and rippling.

A pair of clawed hands, like little bird feet, separated her skin from the inside, peeling back her belly.

Audrey screamed, thrashing and tangled in sheets and sweat and Jonathan's arms, his voice a booming growl in her ear.

"Wake up, Audrey. Sweetheart, it's a dream."

She pushed at him with a whimper, pulling at her nightgown. Then she stilled, panting, "The lights, the lights," and patting at her wet face. Jonathan kept her tight to his body as he leaned to flick on the nightstand lamp, warm light washing over them.

She checked her hands, no black. Lifted the gown, nothing underneath but her still flat belly.

"Hey," Jonathan mumbled against her neck and her hair, then cupped her face to make her look at him.

"My eyes," she gasped out, searching his.

"Same as they've always been, sweetheart." He wiped at her cheeks; his brow furrowed. "You had a nightmare."

She nodded, closing her eyes and slumping against him, homing in on the steady, ever-present drum of his heart as she tried to settle hers down from a racing gallop. He kept her close, hands soothing her back and her arms, brushing the sweaty hair back from her neck.

"Need to talk about it?"

"No," she whispered, just wanting it to go away, to go far, far away from her mind and memory.

A soft knock sounded. Jonathan inhaled. "Aster."

"I'm okay," Audrey said, sinking back into the downy pillows. "Was I screaming?"

"Yeah." Jonathan rubbed his face, his posture reluctant as he slipped from the bed and pulled on a loose pair of pants. "Worse than other times," he added with a grimace.

"Sorry," Audrey whispered, but he only shook his head and answered the door.

The pair exchanged quiet words as Audrey stared at the canopy, unwilling to close her eyes again just yet. Her fingers pressed into the warm, unbroken skin of her stomach. It felt the same as always, maybe a little softer? Maybe a swell was just starting? Nothing moving though, and as desperately as she wanted to feel the baby quicken—for that . . . *tangible* thing to show her there was a life inside her growing—she was pretty sure if it happened right this second, she'd faint.

She groaned, pressing the heels of her palms against her eyes, chasing dots of light behind the darkness, repeating, *just a dream, just a dream.*

For now, just a dream.

Audrey sat up, about ready to leap out of her skin when Jonathan shut the door. She folded her hands in her lap as he walked over and sat on the bed's edge.

"She said you can have another draught. If you double up the sleeping one, it should put you too deep for more dreams. Not something to do every night, though, or it could get addictive." Jonathan nodded toward her middle. "And long term, not great for the kid."

She exhaled through her nose, once, sharp, then lifted her chin. "It's fine. I just need a minute."

"The fuck you're fine," Jonathan growled, his expression downright hostile. "I've never heard you scream like that before."

"Sorry, I'm just—"

"Stop fucking apologizing," he snapped, and when she winced, he cursed under his breath and stared up at the ceiling as if someone had painted all the answers right up there, just out of reach. In a softer tone, he said, "You don't need to apologize to me for any of this shit, ever, Audrey." When he looked at her again, he was as helpless as that night on their kitchen floor in Nizhny. She grabbed his hand, and he brought it up to kiss her knuckles. "Just tell me what you need."

Audrey considered Aster's advice, glancing sidelong at the nightstand, which was covered in tiny vials. All the things to keep her held together and functional. She should probably give up being upset about the Symposium, because she could barely handle sleeping, and apparently couldn't even be pregnant correctly.

What was worse? Drugging herself to sleep through the night and putting their child at even more risk that he or she was simply for being conceived in the first place? Or maybe just never sleeping again. That sounded nice.

She huffed a bitter laugh, a small, fleeting sound that evaporated as it passed her lips.

"You're spiraling, sweetheart," Jonathan said. "One fight at a time, remember?"

"Yeah," she whispered.

"You done sleeping?"

"Yes. No? I don't know."

Jonathan grunted. "Get dressed. I'll show you the grounds. Lights are pretty at night. Give it an hour, you might be tired enough to pass right out."

She smiled, nuzzling against his skin with a sigh, agreeing to the distraction.

Chapter 23

They never did get back to sleep, instead wandering the manor grounds and exploring a flowering hedge maze, later enjoying a splendid sunrise. Audrey was paying for it now. They were back in the Faceted Chamber, the brunch much the same, the conversation a continuing catalog of statistics. Ulyana had fetched them right on time, presented her with the day's schedule, and escorted them over. She sat on Audrey's left, content with her closed binder while the other secretaries studiously took notes at the main table.

It took everything she had not to doze off. Aster was a blessing this morning with a nudge on her elbow, a refill of her tea, offering her small bites, and handing her papers. Maybe it was meaningless to the meeting, but made sure Audrey was engaged instead of falling asleep in her poached eggs. Jonathan might as well have been a statue behind them, if he felt any fatigue from missing sleep at all.

Probably not, Audrey thought as she picked at the tablecloth near her knee, out of sight, but the idle motion helped keep her awake. He'd never needed as much sleep as she did anyway, which was good, because someone needed to pay attention.

So far, the most interesting topic had been when they discussed a new cultivation of silk-producing moths. Apparently, this was a big deal. After two years of negotiating, the cost had included a breeding pair of cockatrices. The eggs were not only a delicacy but had alchemy qualities when exposed to brine and a type of talc only found in the most northern parts of the Dominion. That recipe hadn't made the trading table, which had the entire group chortling at the success.

Audrey poked at her egg, wondering what animal it came from. Aster's hand touched her wrist, and she set down the fork. *Right, don't act like the low-bred human you are when you're sitting at the fancy table, even if it's the* small *fancy table.*

The cornflower wraith leaned close. "Remember, this is truly riveting and you are blessed on high to be among such esteemed company."

Audrey snorted, covering it with a cough into her napkin.

The hours droned on. Audrey miraculously stayed awake, and Dimitri hurried himself out the doors before anyone else without a glance at her table. In fact, she hadn't seen him once in his own home since they arrived, but just as well. The less she had to perform today, the better. Audrey sighed as she stood, her lower back aching, her seat cushion more decorative than functional.

"Miss Audrey," Ulyana said, the young woman chipper and delighted as always, and Audrey couldn't help a genuine smile. "Vrach Ueman, the director of the Dominion Blood Clinic, has made time for you this afternoon, though he stressed it would be a short meeting."

"Alright, when?" Audrey asked.

"Now, miss."

"No rest for the wicked then," Jonathan drawled from behind them.

"An hour at most, he insisted," Ulyana offered, apologetic. "I'm sure we can arrange a longer visit tomorrow."

Audrey touched her arm. "It's fine, really."

"Yes, Miss Audrey." Ulyana nodded, leading her toward the exit. "When you return from your appointment, the groundskeeper has arranged for the tour of the menagerie."

"The what?" Audrey frowned, trying to remember what else she'd asked Ulyana to look into.

"The Syn Koschei Menagerie is Sir Dimitri's personal collection on the manor grounds."

"Oh, but . . ."

"You'd asked about seeing the carriage pegasi."

She had. Tired as she was, Audrey felt a brief twinge of excitement. "You didn't have to do that, but thank you. That sounds wonderful."

Ulyana inclined her head, clearly pleased. "Anything else for today, miss?"

"No, that's fine for now."

"Yes, miss."

From there, Ulyana ushered them back to their carriage, the pegasi pair watching her from Dimitri's. She waved at them, wondering if they liked apples.

The Dominion Blood Clinic was just outside the Red Corner, housed in what was once a state-of-the-art 21st century hospital from the pre-Aperien era. It had been repurposed to support magical healers, alchemists, and doctors, but what had once been modern medicine still existed in the Dominion, albeit less popular than in the Eastern Seaboard Conjunct. Symposium discussion today had included the ongoing exchange of medical technology and magical healing resources between the ESC and MD. And like everything in Moscow, the building itself was grand and gilded.

As they left the carriage and climbed the steps, Audrey wondered which branch might be most helpful. Approaching her situation as a blood curse was most accurate, but she couldn't come out and say: *'I'm pregnant with a vileblood child, please save us.'*

While blood madness was most often treated by a branch of alchemy—uniquely tailored potions got results efficiently and quickly, if caught early enough—curses tended toward magical or divine solutions, and neither leaned into medicine.

Whistelae, the druid who'd cared for Audrey all those years ago in the ESC and later fostered her, practiced earth-based healing as a natural skill. She'd been at the ESC to expand her knowledge into human medicine, so Audrey learned a few things during her time living with her. DNA and genome mapping were rarely used, as most of the equipment and technology had been lost. Magic solved many diseases quicker and cleaner than 20th century medicine, though not all. There were pockets, however, including in the ESC and Dominion, who still turned to such methods when magic didn't garner the expected results.

Unlike the library, the Clinic was cold, the entry way little more than a white rectangle. It smelled clean, unnaturally so, and the dry air made her nose hurt. Three partitions separated as many desks. No art, no magical frills, only a plain waiting room with plain chairs. By far the coldest place they'd encountered since arriving in the Dominion.

"Emergency?" The woman behind the first desk was human, her sigil a plain silver circle with a blue shield inside.

"No," Ulyana answered. "We have an appointment with the director. We're about five minutes early."

The receptionist nodded, and she wasn't unfriendly as much as in a rush. The woman used a digital tablet. Audrey had used similar technology in the ESC, mostly in place of accessing physical books and documents. The ESC didn't keep the kind of library the Dominion did.

"You can have a seat," the receptionist offered. "He will come to you."

Ulyana curtsied, then ushered her and Jonathan to their seats. Their steps echoed. Once they settled, Audrey said to Ulyana, "You can go if you have other obligations."

"I'm expected to escort you, Miss Audrey."

"Escorts are required to the hospital?"

"If you were ill, then no," Ulyana corrected. She sat prim and proper, ankles folded, and the chronically underused binder on her knees. "Since we're here for an official consultation and you're a guest in the Dominion, it would be dismissive if you were without your attendant."

"But not for Zh . . ." She caught herself. "Not for the head book-keeper?"

"He specifically declined, being that you were previously acquaint-ed."

Audrey couldn't help a small smile. That was kind of him, and he seemed to peg her right away for being uncomfortable with all the formalities. It made her feel guilty she hadn't looked at the literature he'd sent over yet.

She rubbed her neck, then her shoulder. A mild headache had settled behind her eyes about two hours into the Symposium today. And they'd head to the menagerie after this meeting, and Audrey honestly didn't know how she'd find the power to sit up on the couch, let alone read, by the time they got home tonight. Gods, she was so tired, going off barely half a night's sleep. At least her empty stomach wasn't complaining. Eating had been a challenge today. The draught might mask the worst of the nausea, but every bite had tasted like ashes on her tongue.

Her head felt heavy now that they sat down again, exhaustion poking and prodding. She exhaled hard and blinked a few times. Maybe she'd walk the room; there wasn't much space, but it would be better than falling asleep sitting up. Audrey was about to stand when the air crackled, swelling with a burst of heat and static as a figure manifested from thin air right in front of their seats.

Jonathan leaped up, bodily between Audrey and the potential threat, and she struggled to stand as Ulyana stood beside her, immediately dropping into a deep curtsy.

"Vrach Ueman," Ulyana said smoothly, keeping her head lowered.

The air smelled like summer heat, old stone, and a deep scent of blood Audrey somehow knew came from organs. But it already faded. His magic?

Thank the gods, because the brief whiff sent her stomach into a tailspin. She half-held her breath, hoping she kept a neutral expression.

The director stared down a hawkish nose, though he wasn't a particularly tall individual, and Jonathan towered head and shoulders over him. He was the most powerful in the room, but Audrey had known that before they arrived. He wore a crisp white jacket, dark suit pants, and starched crimson button-up shift underneath. His hair was swept back in a neat knot, silken black with rich auburn highlights, his complexion a deep warm brown common in the humans from what had once been Mesoamerica.

Ueman was a descendent of Tezcatlipoca, one of the Aztec gods, which was where he sourced his particular skills as a blood mage. Grandson, she'd read, though any information about Ueman specifically excluded references to his other heritage. Her natural curiosity might have wandered more if the director wasn't glaring at her like she'd offended his entire pantheon.

Maybe she was being rude? Audrey curtsied. He wasn't considered Dominion nobility, but he was a powerful figure. "Thank you for making time to see us, Vrach Ueman."

"Director will do," was his reply, curt and chilled, crimson gaze studying her like she was some sort of vermin crossing his toes. Audrey straightened.

"I'm Audr—"

He waved a hand. "I know who you are. And while I respect the demands placed upon everyone in Moscow while you and yours gather for the Symposium, my time is not so free that I can spend weeks on entitled chatter. What do you need that is so urgent?"

Ah, so that explained his annoyance. She tried to imagine anyone at the Symposium not being entitled after listening to them talk for two days, particularly Dimitri, and found it impossible.

"If this isn't a good time, we can find another—"

Ueman cut her off again, and she barely heard Jonathan's low rumble of annoyance. "No, I'd rather have this over with."

The sooner this was over, the better for everyone, so Audrey moved on. "A blood mage recently came to Nizhny and saved a friend of mine. I wanted to start by expressing my thanks."

"Easily accomplished by a missive."

Her fists tightened. "I wanted to discuss vileblood with you, particularly their blood curse. I hoped the clinic have insight on where we might begin, or perhaps previous research?" The director's glare flicked to Jonathan, then back to her, a scowl slowly turning up his mouth. "With the recent changes to the Vilestars Accord, I wanted—"

"To pull me away from my work saving lives to have a casual chat about a two-hundred-year-old curse?" He scoffed. "What is it you think I do all day, girl?" Another hand wave, another sneer. "Wander around contemplating magic that has no bearing on our day-to-day lives? That's the work of apprentices, at best."

"This curse isn't—"

"Relevant? No, it is not. A subsect of the population, mostly contained, as one does with a violent, infectious disease vector, magic or otherwise. The curse is only spread between human and vileblood as a sexual transmission accompanying pregnancy, which I dare say has a simple, elegant solution already.

"As for the vileblood themselves." Ueman canted his head at Jonathan. "The simplest solution to curses is to snuff out the source. As the Vilestars and their sires are dead, and the curse remains, the options are obvious, are they not? Which the Accords handled efficiently until recent meddling."

He didn't know who they were. And it was painfully obvious revealing their identities wouldn't do anything. She took comfort in Jonathan's warm palm as it pressed against her lower back. Audrey knew what he said without words. They'd already talked about her picking fights on his behalf, and the director's stance was clear.

"I'm sorry for wasting your time," Audrey said.

For the first time, Ueman seemed to consider her seriously, the apology not expected. He squinted down at her, but then his interest evaporated quickly as it came.

"See that you keep that in mind as you schedule other appointments." And then he was gone in the same burst of magic, the air shivering around them as he vanished, the same scent stinging her nose.

She turned away from Ulyana, gagging. Jonathan was outright growling now.

"Shall we depart, Miss Audrey?"

"Go ahead," Jonathan answered for her. "We'll figure it out."

Ulyana didn't argue. As kind and polite as the young woman was toward them, she always left as soon as she could, showing no interest beyond her assigned responsibilities. Just as well; she served Dimitri's house. Anything Audrey said or did went directly to Dimitri's ears. They'd worked too hard to cover her pregnancy and morning sickness to have it used against them.

She squeezed her eyes shut as the nausea faded, gripping Jonathan's forearm as an anchor. If anyone found out she was pregnant, Jonathan being the father wasn't exactly a tremendous leap in logic. And then what? Accorded Law protected humans. By definition, Jonathan endangered her through the pregnancy. It certainly violated his parole. And the Human Protection Accord.

They could take him from her. Lock him away, maybe in the Ireland Pen this time, and she'd never see him again.

"Breathe," Jonathan said quietly, his thumb brushing her elbow. Then he tensed, his attention snapping to their left. A young woman approached them, but she stalled when they both looked at her.

She wore a simple black cloak, the hood down, and a plain gray dress. Shorter than Audrey, the girl was obscenely pale, her skin almost translucent, an obvious marker she wasn't entirely human, if she was human at all. White skin, white hair, pink eyes. Albino, Audrey's brain supplied, if there wasn't an unnatural grace to how she moved, even when she gave them an awkward wave. Jonathan's tension spoke volumes; then she realized why. The girl had gotten very close before he noticed.

"I overheard your conversation with the director," she offered in greeting. Her pert nose wrinkled slightly, and she spoke in a hush. "He is very busy, but also very rude."

"What do you want?" Jonathan's tone was colder than the Ueman's. Audrey squeezed his arm and let go, trying to let him know she was okay.

"He mentioned your requests are better suited for an apprentice." She gestured to herself. "That's me."

"You want to help us?" Audrey asked.

The girl smiled. "Yes. I don't get as much opportunity to work as I'd like." She hesitated but then shrugged. "Being that he's vileblood and obviously your friend, and you want to help vileblood, I figured you might be a bit more open-minded than most."

"I don't mind that you're an apprentice," Audrey said. "Are you a mage or alchemist?"

"Mage," she said, licking her lips. "But it's how I access my skills that's a concern to most people."

Jonathan inhaled deeply, leaning closer to the stranger, but she didn't flinch. "Vampire?"

"Dhampir, actually. Part vampire. I inherited little from that side of the family beyond needing blood to survive and being able to read the blood I drink." Another shrug; she seemed young to Audrey, but vampires were immortal. She had no idea how that translated to duster lifespans.

"My mother was fae, which enhances my abilities to work blood magic, but . . ." The girl lifted her chin. "I can obviously drink out of a container. I'm not a savage. And I'm in my apprenticeship still because I don't get the chance to work, and not because I'm not trying my hardest to help people. Most request a different blood worker when it becomes clear what I am."

Audrey was grinning by the time she finished her huffy rant, the dhampir's pale cheeks flushed now. Jonathan chuckled. "What's your name?"

"Oh." The duster blinked a few times, then thrust out her hand. "May. Maythorne is my full name, but I go by May."

Audrey shook her hand, her skin chill to the touch and strangely soft. "I would love to work with you, May. I'm Audrey, and this is Jonathan. Are you free now?"

May's smile lit up the entire room.

Chapter 24

May led them down a plain hallway, a few turns, but since Jonathan showed no signs of unease, Audrey kept up with the duster's brisk pace. She chattered the entire way, mundane questions about things like their travels into Moscow and the weather. The conversation seemed a bit at odds with May's excitement. They hadn't crossed paths with anyone else since they left reception.

They reached her office a few minutes later. "Sorry, one second," May mumbled, patting her robes until she came up with a copper key on a single ring, then she swung the door inward. "Here we are then."

It wasn't much more than a closet. No windows, tucked at the end of a hall for storage. The room itself was stuffed to the brim with two chairs, a plain desk, and a bookshelf bursting with papers, books, pens, and loose literal leaves. An alchemical set and rows of dried flowers and herbs filled the bottom shelf.

"Sorry, bit of a mess, isn't it? I don't have many patients. Er, requests? Visitors?" May winced as she cleared the seats, shoving the armful of paperwork onto an already full shelf. "Please, sit. And shut the door?"

Jonathan motioned Audrey inside, and she took the offered seat even though the idea of sitting any more today was agonizing. Door shut, he leaned beside it with his arms crossed as May buzzed around. "You take people here so you can hide the bodies in this mess?"

May jerked up tall, nearly dropping her folders and books. "What?"

"He's joking," Audrey offered. "He's just not as funny as he thinks he is."

"I'm hilarious," Jonathan deadpanned, and Audrey rolled her eyes.

May seemed a bit stricken though, and Audrey felt of strum of sympathy for her. It reminded her of her first few days working with Theodore. He'd been patient with her nerves, and it had made all the difference in the world.

Audrey motioned to the alembic, trying to distract her. "You said you were a blood mage. Are you can alchemist as well?"

May resumed her tidying. "Oh, well, I'm a mage, yes, but I've been studying alchemy in my spare time, which turns out to be most of my time." She cleared her throat. "Sometimes a potion is the simpler solution, or even human medicine. There's a lot of high-handedness around what's better or ideal, or stronger, or blah blah blah. It's all hogwash, really, because each school has its own applications, and trying to use a complicated ritual when all you need is an antibiotic is really quite daft in my opinion."

Jonathan chuckled at that, and Audrey found herself liking May more and more by the minute. "I've listened to Aperiens argue when a very simple human solution would save a whole mess of headaches more time than I can count."

"Exactly. Humans might be weak and squishy, but they aren't entirely without good ideas." May paused as she sat behind her desk. "No offense."

"None taken."

"Great, good. Now, before I chatter your ears off, can you tell me more about what you need?" May shuffled around in a drawer, gave up, and turned over a page of scribbled notes to use the blank back. "I wasn't meaning to eavesdrop in the lobby, but I did hear enough about theories and 'go bother someone else, I'm too important and busy' to pull my attention. Like I said, I rarely get to work with anyone, so." She paused then, her brow furrowed, her expression earnest. "I'm sorry. Theory or not, people rarely need a blood mage unless there's a problem. I don't mean to make light."

"You're fine." Audrey considered her next words, resisting the urge to touch her middle. She liked May already, and Jonathan seemed very relaxed for being around a stranger, but despite her evolving senses, she didn't know exactly what lies and truth smelled like. "You know Jonathan is a vileblood. I'm not sure how much you know about his kind's origins?"

"Enough," May said. "Men are that." She pointed her pen in Jonathan's direction. "Women, if there are any alive now at all, are abominations. And then there's the matter of their purpose: to eradicate mankind."

"About right," Jonathan said.

"With the changes in the Vilestars Accord, vilebloods are being released from the pens. It would be foolish not to expect pregnancies, through ill intent or, more likely, ignorance," Audrey said. "Most vilebloods have been imprisoned since they were children. I'd wager most of the Wardens who released them didn't spend time on education."

"Why would they?" May said with a little snort. "No offense, again, but that Accord change isn't exactly popular."

"Still not offended."

"Jonathan," Audrey chided, but he only grinned at her. May grinned, too, the two of them getting along just fine. It was a fight to keep a straight expression.

"I just mean a vileblood screws up, mistake or not, and knocks up a human woman? They've violated the Human Protection Accord and womp," May swirled her pen in the air, "back they go into the hole."

Audrey stiffened at the phrasing, at the invading memory of the first time she saw Jonathan chained to that table in the ESC, filthy, malnourished. Half-dead.

A hand closed around her nape, warm and heavy. "Easy," Jonathan soothed. To May, he said, "Hits a little close to home, being she got me out of a hole."

"Yeah, I . . ." May paused again, canting her head like a cat. "Oh, shit." She pointed at him first. "Jonathan." Then at her. "Audrey. Oh, fuck me, you're the one who changed the Accord." Then she frowned. "I thought you were both dead?" And then May burst out laughing.

"That's funny?" Jonathan drawled, but Audrey could tell by his tone he found it just as amusing.

"Oh, nothing, just of course they'd frame you for killing her, even though vilebloods can't even use hellfire." May made a face, stuck her tongue out. "Just like how anyone with even a drop of vampire blood needs to suck a human bone dry every time they feed, because once we get a taste, we can't stop ourselves."

"I'm surprised they let you work as a blood mage at all," Audrey said. She wanted to find it funny, but she couldn't. Maybe that was the difference between being a duster with dangerous blood and not. Maybe they laughed so they didn't go mad, because Audrey felt like she might lose her mind entirely

But May watched them a little closer now, and for all her youthful demeanor, she was a sharp mind. "It wasn't easy," May confirmed. "But I've proven myself through the proper channels." Her expression shadowed, but then she smiled. "Enough about me, though. So, you want to see if there's some way to . . ." She considered for a moment. "Well, there's negating the 'curse' itself, at the very basic level. Curing being vileblood."

"Oh," Audrey said. Jonathan snorted. "I didn't even think that was possible?"

"It's probably not," May said. "Most dusters who've tried to cure or remove the magical side of their blood have either died trying or flat out failed. Can't really remove what you are, right? There are a few exceptions, but that's for an imparted curse rather than a birthright.

"Take me. Vampirism has a few means of reversal if a human, or human-enough duster, gets treatment within a certain amount of time, provided the sire comes from three lines that have been extensively researched. But being that I was born the way I am, the treatments would do nothing. They're designed to halt the process, not reverse the end result.

"Given the work Lamashtu and Lucifer put into creating their offspring? There's no way they'd leave a back door so wide open you could just remove god and angel blood, and the combined results, and leave the human behind."

May studied Jonathan then, her expression curious. "I mean . . . maybe if the vileblood was so far removed, they were almost entirely human. But it's only been what? A hundred and thirty years since that war started? Six or seven generations out is pushing it. And that doesn't even account for mixing in other Aperien magic along the way." She hesitated, licking her lips. "I could read you. Tell you."

Jonathan didn't react outwardly, but Audrey felt the slight tightening of his hand before he dropped it from her neck. "You gonna need some vileblood either way, right?"

"Oh," May leaned back and wiped her mouth. "It would help. I've never . . ." Her cheeks were pink again. "I've never, uh, sampled it before, so yes, it would help to have a benchmark for how the magical lines interact. That's how most blood magic works, you know, it's all about untangling the knots. Where and how they get caught up. At least for blood madness."

"Yeah," Jonathan drawled. "We had a blood worker out in Nizhny for a vileblood a few months back."

"I remember hearing about it. A straightforward case, far as I understood?" May said. "They're okay now?"

"Yes, he's fine," Audrey said, unable to help a smile, thinking of Tomas.

She wondered how everyone was doing, going about the days in Nizhny like they always did. It made her chest ache.

"How much you need?" Jonathan asked, pulling the eversharp blade from its sheath on his thigh. She'd never seen him without it, not since the night she gave it to him, hours before Kushiel tried to kill them both.

"Just like that?" May asked. For the first time, she seemed uneasy. "I ask to drink your blood, and you just say go ahead?"

"Pretty sure you asked to sample it so you can help us, so yeah, I'm not seeing a problem."

"We wouldn't have come here if we weren't willing to explore options," Audrey said. "We're not expecting to cure for being a vileblood. But there's inevitably going to be pregnancies between vileblood and humans, which hasn't happened for a very long time." *Except right now.* "And there's little research on saving the woman and the child, aside from the fact that abortive measures kill both.

"We shouldn't wait until it's too late," Audrey went on, trying to ignore how her stomach rolled, how her mouth dried, how her skin felt flushed. "We should see if we can find an answer now, maybe save lives in the future."

Save my life. Our lives. Our future.

May nodded as Audrey spoke, the wistful duster pondering research and possibilities replaced by a serious researcher. "I won't lie to you. Curses don't always have backdoors, or the backdoors don't have keys within our reach. There might not be an answer. But if there is, I need to you know me helping you isn't entirely altruistic. If we can find a cure, or some way to keep the mother from transforming, permanently or temporarily, or maybe some way to shield the child?" May waved a hand, impatient suddenly. "I just need you to understand that this kind of research, if successful? That's exactly what I need to have an actual career here and not just shoved in a closet where everyone can forget I exist. As long as you're okay with that, then yeah, let's give it a go."

Before Audrey could reply, Jonathan rolled his eyes. "That's it?"

"Jonathan," she sighed, doing her best not to laugh.

"What? People do shit so they can get something out of it. I'm supposed to be surprised?" To May, he said, "You got a cup or something?"

May smirked right back at him, leaning her elbows on the desk. "That knife clean?"

"I always clean my blades, yeah."

"That's good enough."

These two, Audrey decided, were going to be trouble. Jonathan didn't hesitate, a quick, shallow cut on his forearm, a press to catch a few drops of black blood on the blade's edge. Audrey looked away; she'd seen him bleed enough for a lifetime.

"Oh wow, it really is black."

"Yup," Jonathan drawled. He passed the knife over, and May sniffed once, licked, and passed it back.

May leaned back in her seat as Jonathan tucked the weapon away, and Audrey shivered as the duster licked her lips a few more times than necessary. Her stark white cheeks flushed, pupils dilating. She looked between them, unfocused, her expression distant. Silence stretched, her hand twitching once, and then she shook her head.

"Damn, alright. Angel and god, and a lot of it." She licked her lips again. "Powerful. And yeah, the curse. The combination of the two lines. It's deliberate and violent and hungry. Intricate. Angry."

Audrey leaned forward a bit in her seat. "You can tell all of that? Just from a taste of his blood?"

"It helps I know what I'm dealing with, makes it easier to mark things," May offered, but then she gave Jonathan a curious look. "How old are you, exactly?"

"Not sure, best guess is mid-thirties."

May frowned. "You don't know? Because far as I can read, you're half-human, clean down the middle."

"That can't be right," Audrey said. "That would make Jonathan a direct offspring of a Vilestar. They've been dead for a hundred years."

"Maybe he's older than he looks," May offered with a shrug.

"Nah," Jonathan said. "At least not that far off the mark. I've got memories, and there's documentation of being in the pens back as early as five. No way I'm missing seventy plus years."

"Hm, well, might just be a potency thing then. I can take more time with it, see what I can tease out." May glanced between them. "Studying the curse is going to take more of your blood, anyway. You didn't bring any blood from the other vileblood, the one they helped with blood madness? A few other benchmarks won't hurt."

"No, but there's this," Audrey said, shuffling in her bag. Jonathan tensed beside her as she pulled up a small glass vial, this blood red.

Her blood.

It was a risk, but her gut told her May was trustworthy. If Jonathan read their interactions differently, he would have stopped her from handing her blood over.

May took the vial, swirling it around. "Not vileblood, obviously." Audrey bit back the thought: not yet. When neither she nor Jonathan spoke, May hummed. Undeterred, she popped the cork and sniffed. "Is this a test or something?"

"No," Audrey said. "Just . . ."

"We're protecting someone," Jonathan said flatly. Flat as in murderous.

May nodded. "Sure, got it." She took a quick sip, closed the vial, and passed it back without question. Then paused, canting her head. "Mostly human, but traces of angel and god." Her crimson gaze flicked to Jonathan, then back to the blood vial as Audrey tucked it away. "Clean, though." Audrey watched May's sharp mind ticking away. "No curse." Then May quietly added, "Not yet."

"No, not yet." Audrey said.

Was she a complete idiot? They'd met this duster less than an hour ago, and she'd let her taste her blood, knowing it was changing with her pregnancy. Protecting someone, Jonathan said; it was almost laughable. What intelligent person wouldn't put two and two together?

"Well," May said, her smile kind. "Good thing my schedule is wide open."

Chapter 25

"**W**as that a mistake?" Audrey asked as they walked toward the Syn Koschei Menagerie entrance.

"It's a risk," Jonathan offered. They'd both been quiet, processing their encounter with May in their own ways on the carriage ride back. "But she never lied. Self-interest is a hells of a motivator."

"She's not treated well," Audrey added. "I think it made me trust her more? Maybe that's silly, but I'm not sure how telling someone whatever she figures out about us will help her."

"Yeah, her boss doesn't seem like he'd be big on rewards."

"I like her," Audrey added, unable to keep a bit of hopefulness from her tone.

"I could tell."

She poked Jonathan in the side. He grunted, like it bothered him, when she knew it didn't. "You liked her too. I could tell."

"I don't like anyone but you."

"You're such a liar," she laughed, then sobered up as they reached the gilded gate.

Like all of the Red Corner, the enchanted snow made the air glitter, sunset casting the city in crimson and gold, as if the sun itself performed for the Dominion's magic. Mikhali, Dimitri's head of house, waited for them at the gates in a crisp uniform. He greeted them with a half-bow, a basket tucked in one elbow.

"I trust your stay has been acceptable so far."

"Yes, thank you. The rooms are lovely."

A small smile graced his serious veneer. She wondered if any Aperiens in Moscow bothered to compliment the people who worked so hard under them to make this place prosper.

"And thank you for arranging the tour."

"It is no trouble." Mikhali turned then, swinging the entrance open for them, which was apparently kept unlocked. Beyond waited lush greenery, more glittering lights, and an ancient cobblestone path. Tiny flowers and bright moss crept between the stones. Once they passed, the gate shut silently behind them. "Would you like to tour the entire grounds or only visit the pegasi this evening?"

Audrey was exhausted. And once again, feeling guilty for how the world rearranged for her when she probably could have walked around the gardens herself and left Mikhali free for more important work. She kept in her sigh. "Just the pegasi today, please. Could we come back another time, maybe without bothering you?"

"No bother," Mikhali corrected, his stride long and purposeful. "But an escort is required on the grounds."

Of course. She imagined Dimitri didn't want anyone enjoying his things without supervision and permission, but it didn't really matter. Any desire Audrey had to return to this place evaporated as the trees parted.

Menagerie, he'd called it. This was little more than a prison disguised as a private zoo.

It wasn't uncommon for magical creatures to serve beasts of burden, as they were far more efficient in most cases. Intelligent creatures were often more than happy to partake in mutually beneficial arrangements. For all the wealth Dimitri had to offer, bars were still bars. And these were cages, lining the walkway in neat rows, all with expensive, beautifully constructed habitats. There was no reason for a dryad to be locked away; she watched them curiously with luminous eyes from the branches of her oak tree. In the next cage beside her, a nesting phoenix, its flaming plumes subdued as it slept.

On and on it went.

A manticore, which chilled her, the human face watching with hungry intelligence and hatred. Several creatures she recognized from the Siberian taiga, some mundane, others dangerous, all displayed as a fanciful collection. She doubted Dimitri had caught a single creature in the terrible place. A striking griffin with snow-white feathers and sharp yellow eyes. A sleeping chimera, the snake tail watching them pass by, hissing softly.

"Here we are," Mikhali said, stepping up to the pegasi's fence, more of a traditional pasture than a cage. A flat space with a wildflower lawn, and both of the pegasi were awake, watching them, their wings still bound.

"Are they always tied?" Audrey asked, knowing she wouldn't like the answer.

"Yes," Mikhali said. "It takes far too much time to prep them for the carriage so they don't fly away. It would be dangerous, as the carriage is not stabilized for flight, and the pegasi have not been properly broken for such travel."

Jonathan's hand touched her lower back, that soft brush of comfort he always offered, and she forced a smile. "And they don't have names?"

"No," Mikhali replied, and his expression turned curious. "They are work beasts, miss."

She bit back further comment. This man had no control over what made her ever fiber itch with this cruelty and disregard for the creatures around her. Arguing wouldn't do anything but frustrate her.

The pegasi trotted over, the stallion huffing and shaking his head. Did they recognize her?

"If you would like." Mikhali offered her the basket. The old man's expression had softened a fraction, a flash of kindness in his otherwise stern exterior. "The children like to feed them."

Audrey pulled back the cloth, four bright red apples nestled inside. She smiled up at Mikhali. "Thank you."

Another half-bow, then a sideways glance at Jonathan, who stood beside her with his arms crossed. Mikhali cleared his throat. "I will complete my rounds, then return in about twenty minutes."

The pegasi waited a few feet back, nostrils flaring, their attention on the basket with ears perked high. Their ivory coats shimmered in the sinking light, golden feathers bright among the white. Jonathan smirked beside her, then backed away a few steps.

"Don't get bit."

She wasn't worried. Audrey walked right up to the fence, held out an apple, and the stallion strode up. "You're both beautiful," she mumbled. "I'm sorry you're treated like this." He took the apple, crunching loudly, and the mare came over for the fruit. Audrey let them eat in peace, giddy despite her exhaustion and appreciating the gift for what it was. "I wish you could fly."

At the word fly, both pegasi perked up, watching her with attentive expressions. She winced.

"Sorry, I can't let you out. I wish I could." She offered the second apple to each, content to watch despite wanting desperately to touch them again. She already felt like she was taking too much. The stallion nibbled on her sleeve, and she laughed. "That's all I have." Audrey almost offered to come back again with more, but she wasn't sure if she would.

A soft muzzle interrupted her thinking, snuffing at her hands, so she petted him, and the stallion leaned in to her touch. Smiling, she scratched at his neck, laughing when the mare came over and nudged for attention as well. Both went still when Jonathan came a step closer.

"He's nice," Audrey offered. "He just stinks."

"So damn rude all the time," Jonathan drawled. The stallion nickered, stomping one foot. "Yeah, you're a good-looking animal, but don't get any ideas." He jerked a thumb at Audrey. "That one's mine." Jonathan offered his hand, and the mare shifted away. The stallion stood his ground, eyeing Jonathan like he might bite him. "Watch out though, she'd drag all you back to Nizhny if she could, and the house ain't big enough for a damn zoo."

"They shouldn't be in a zoo," Audrey grumbled. Jonathan grunted in agreement, leaving his palm up. The stallion craned his neck, sniffing but not touching Jonathan before trotting off. The mare followed.

They watched the pegasi, ribbons and manes trailing. They really were beautiful. Jonathan looked down at her, his expression soft for him. "Right now, gotta save you."

"I know. But I would." She huffed. "I would take them all back with us to Nizhny."

Audrey turned, ready to be done with this place, Mikhali's footsteps echoing up the garden path, and she froze. Just across from the pegasi sat another golden cage, this one thick with winter trees. A wolf watched her, but Audrey knew at a glance it wasn't a mundane animal. Its fur was glossy white, pure as fresh snow, a black iron collar anchored around its throat. Runes electrified the surface, pulsing, as if the wolf struggled against whatever magic kept it imprisoned. Audrey's skin prickled under the weight of that ancient ice blue stare.

"Jonathan?"

"No idea."

She heard the frown in his voice following a deep inhale, probably because the wolf didn't even glance in Jonathan's direction. It was entirely focused on Audrey, ears up, as if it heard their entire conversation. Intelligence radiated from the heavy gaze, a question hanging between them. The air nearly hummed.

"Nothing we can do, Audrey."

"I know, I just . . ."

"Ready then?" Mikhali asked, and as soon as he spoke, the wolf darted into the underbrush of its enclosure.

"Yeah," Jonathan answered, no doubt to deter her from opening another door they couldn't walk through.

The next two days were quieter. Audrey went through the motions of the Symposium, bringing the bookkeeper's reader as she dutifully sat like a table decoration. If anything in the trade discussion needed her attention, Aster touched her arm. Ulyana still hadn't opened her binder once during their time in the Faceted Chamber. Dimitri continued to ignore them, to Audrey's relief. Pretending to enjoy his company was a chore, at best.

After the day was done, they'd returned to the rooms. Jonathan prowled, Aster mingled with the staff or met with the equinox committee, and Audrey drank her teas and read. Each afternoon, a new pile of documents and books awaited her, even though she hadn't spoken to Zhang since their first meeting. May sent a missive; she'd dig into the blood workers' archives for any related information on their request and would contact them within the week.

Audrey turned a page, this tome a deep dive into effective cures on various forms of lycanthropy. May's comment about cures being implemented *before* transformations completed stuck with her. And May seemed to think Audrey's blood was clean, thus far, even though her senses continued getting stronger. Although being a polyglot from angel blood had been a switch flipped more than a transition.

Audrey had to stop herself from reading further about the werewolves; there was a very interesting subsection documenting the known clans living within the Coalition of Creatures' borders. The Greek goddess Artemis birthed a new werewolf line from moon magic and her legendary hunting hounds. Was Artemis able to weed out the inherent weakness of silver? It sounded like she created them anew; she didn't piggyback on an existing bloodline.

Audrey shut the book. "Focus," she mumbled to herself. But she set it aside for later reading, maybe on a day when she needed to get lost in anything that wasn't tied to her life and death. She leaned on an elbow, glancing at the clock. Not so late yet, but Jonathan liked to run the grounds right after nightfall. Audrey smiled to herself; habit, she wondered? He hunted most nights in Nizhny.

She sunk back to the couch, staring at the ceiling. They hadn't been gone so long yet, but she wondered how everyone was doing. Tomas and the chuchunas could handle all three parcels. Innocence was probably annoyed the extra work took away from his time with Tomas. Rina probably yelled more than normal, since it must be driving her crazy wondering what was happening in Moscow. Virtue would keep her calm, Audrey knew, and E would keep the tavern running smoothly with Aster away. The Clan, well, nothing ever seemed to ruffle them. They'd keep on doing whatever was needed. And by the time they got home, there would be a fresh round of dire wolf pups in the dens.

She missed home.

Audrey missed their simple cabin, the routine days, the private nights. She missed her friends and the comfort she'd found in belonging somewhere. And she missed seeing Jonathan thrive in their community. He'd found home as much as her in Nizhny, as much as they'd found it in each other. She didn't know how Theodore traveled all time, never home for more than a few days at a time before flying off to his next goal.

Audrey stood, mind snapping back to her last conversation with Theodore before they'd left Nizhny. Gods, how had she forgotten? She jogged to the bedroom, shuffling around her belongings in the largest luggage piece until she found a hideaway compartment where she'd tucked his note.

She traced a finger over Theodore's perfect penmanship.

The outer door to the apartment opened and shut, and Audrey tensed but immediately relaxed. Her ears were good enough now she recognized Jonathan's stride because he wasn't making any effort to be stealthy. "In the bedroom," she called, even though he'd find her easily.

He leaned against the doorframe, striking as always in all black. The fine cut trousers and loose dress shirts were a pleasant look on him. Jonathan grinned at her, crossing his arms.

"Enjoying the view?"

"Yes," she said, lifting her chin. It only made him grin wider as he pushed off and walked to her side.

"What's that?" he asked as Audrey handed it to him, watching his nostrils flare as he read it. "Theo?"

"He gave it to me before we left," she said, searching through the wardrobe for a pair of slacks and clean socks. "It's a contact he suggested we visit."

"Off the books then?"

"Yes." Audrey hesitated, because Symposium guests weren't supposed to be under surveillance, magical or otherwise, in private chambers. They'd found no evidence otherwise, but still . . . "A friend," she offered, and Jonathan only nodded, reading over the note again as she changed her clothes.

"Sounds like a pain in the ass, just like Theo. But I think I know where this is."

"Should we go now? He said to go at night."

He handed her the card. "You feeling up for it?"

"You mean after sitting on my butt all day?"

"Sure," he said, not rising to the bait.

Audrey shrugged. "I'm tired, grumpy, uncomfortable, and I have a headache, and my mouth tastes like vomit. So I'm normal."

"Cute. You gonna answer me now?"

"I'm fine, for now. I'll bring my bag in case it changes."

"Or we'll head back and try tomorrow."

Audrey gave him a stiff nod. He didn't push for now, but he knew better than anyone how terribly she'd been sleeping. After that last nightmare, she'd taken to leaving the bathroom light on at all times, and he didn't ask her why. But for all his protectiveness, the fierce core of him she loved so entirely, he rarely stepped in and insisted she rest.

Probably because they really didn't have much time, now did they?

Chapter 26

Jonathan found the location from Theodore's note easily, thanks to his evening prowling through the Red Corner. The building was part of a townhome row at the Red Corner's western edge, nestled up with a river view. The doors were carbon copies, a dozen homes built at the same time with the same materials, but the fourth door from the end bore a door knocker that perfectly matched Theodore's sketch.

"Thought it looked familiar," Jonathan said as Audrey studied the door. The knocker was painted red, the face a Chinese dragon, a golden ring between sharp teeth. "Not a damn thing around here isn't decorated Russian, aside from this thing."

Audrey pulled note from her pocket, reading a complicated series of directions for knocking aloud, wrinkling her nose. It definitely wasn't the kind of sequence that could happen by chance.

Jonathan smirked. "Overkill much?"

"I guess it depends on what's inside," Audrey mumbled. "Ready?"

Jonathan did the honors, and Audrey read each step again, holding her breath as he completed the sequence with six rapid taps on the knocker.

The world swirled, shifted, and her nose burned with live magic, a current swarming her senses before dissipating with a faint pop. And they were suddenly somewhere else, somewhere warm.

A simple foyer, to match the simple townhouse façade. Well lit, with bookshelves lining the walls, a single armchair, and a potted plant that looked more like a miniature landscape, complete with tiny trees that reminded her of bonsai.

Jonathan growled beside her. "Alright?"

"Just a little dizzy for a second. A fixed portal?" She glanced over her shoulder at what seemed to be the same front door, just the other side. It even had the same doorknocker.

"Seems like," he muttered, but he didn't seem as much concerned about the situation as annoyed. Audrey hid her grin because as much as Jonathan and Theodore chafed, she knew they trusted each other—when it came to her safety.

A voice boomed down from the floor above them. "Theodore Maximilian Avialian, I know for a fact your mother taught you better manners than dropping in unannounced, and well after evening tea, to boot."

Audrey blinked. Theodore had a middle name. And she recognized the voice.

Grumbling, dressed in red and blue flannel matching pajamas and pink bunny slippers, the head bookkeeper Zhang all but stomped down the stairs to the first landing, where he startled when he saw her and Jonathan standing in his foyer.

The silence stretched.

Audrey gave a nervous little wave.

Zhang smoothed his beard with a little humph before he said, "I'm going to box that boy's scaly ears next time I see him." Then he turned and headed back up the stairs, waving them after him. "Come on, then. No sense standing around gawking at each other, not when we're already acquainted, anyway. Watch the fourth stair, it's loose." And then he was gone around the bend, up into the space above.

"Maximilian, huh?" Jonathan said. Audrey grinned. "Don't even try to tell me I can't give him shit for that."

"I wouldn't dream of it." Audrey laughed, and they climbed up after Zhang.

The stairwell opened up into a surprisingly cozy sitting room, fireplace blazing warm, more bookshelves covering every wall. No windows, Audrey noticed, but given this place seemed to exist inside and outside of Moscow at the same time, it didn't surprise her. A low coffee table sat between two well-worn but mismatched couches. The room smelled woody, warm and cinnamon, incense embers curling on the table's corner in a dish shaped like a swan. Zhang shuffled around in his slippers—Audrey covered her lips to hide her grin—coming from the connecting kitchen carrying a plate piled high with bite-sized flower cakes.

The room felt homey, well-loved. A place where this Aperien had spent countless years removed from Accorded affairs via the Citadel. And yet he worked as the head bookkeeper for one of the most powerful Accorded territories.

"Theodore didn't . . ." Audrey gestured helplessly.

"He sure didn't. Go ahead, sit. I'm guessing he told you who I am, and that's why you're suddenly skittish?" Zhang flopped down on the farther couch, folding his hands on his middle once he got comfortable.

"Not exactly, just . . ."

"Citadel defector?"

Audrey nodded as she sank down on the couch, Jonathan joining her, though he didn't lean back, instead sitting forward with his elbows on his knees. "He mentioned that, but not your name." Audrey glanced at Jonathan, who only shrugged. She sighed, rubbing her face. "He said you might be able to help us."

"With more than your library request?"

"It's related," Audrey said, unable to stop fidgeting. No one outside of Nizhny knew about her pregnancy. She trusted Theodore, but for all she'd known Zhang through letters, he was a stranger. And he was an Aperien, and powerful considering his position in the Dominion and his desire to remain hidden regarding his past with the Citadel.

"Child," Zhang said, his voice gentle, the tart annoyance for Theodore's manners evaporating. "I've known that boy since he was born, and he's one of the few who knows I still exist." The Aperien god lifted both bushy brows. "He would not have sent you here if I were a threat to you." Zhang's expression shifted, almost wistful. "He does quite adore those mortals who surprise him, and he is a fiercely protective sort of those he believes deserving."

"I'm pregnant," she blurted. "Jonathan is the father."

She reached out, fumbling for his hand and gripping it tightly. She needed Zhang to know this wasn't . . .

"Theodore gave me protection against it, but the magic was . . . In case things changed, but we . . ." She swallowed a few times, her eyes stinging as she stared at Jonathan's profile, the tension in him a hard edge. His expression remained tightly controlled, unwilling to show any belly to a dangerous Aperien he didn't know. "We didn't realize just thinking about it . . ."

"Theodore wouldn't have been careless," Zhang mused. "A heart's true desire, then, and shared? And it bypassed his magic when you both thought you were safe."

"Yes," Audrey said, using her free hand to wipe the tears. Gods, why was she crying? Jonathan squeezed her other hand.

"This is no mere exercise, then. You need a solution to one of the most powerful curses created since the Aperiens manifested, and in what?"

"Less than five months," Jonathan offered, his voice steady. Calm. Everything she didn't feel right then, hearing the dwindling timeframe said aloud. Hearing the clear, undiluted concern in Zhang's gentle words.

She might throw up. Or pass out? Or both?

"Can you help or what?" Jonathan ground out. Audrey winced at his poor manners, but Zhang was unmoved.

"Never let gods who draw their magic from knowledge convince you they are unerringly omniscient," he said. "We might be powerful. We may never forget any moment, but we're still tied to our origin mythos, like any other Aperien. Some of us are focused, others generalized, and I've never met a god of knowledge, wisdom or learning, or the like, who isn't able to access their memories to perfection given a few moments and proper meditation."

Zhang leaned back. "But can I help? I don't know. What you want is a magic bullet, and I know don't have one of those. Give me a few days, I can comb my experiences, but what you're asking is for is a solution that, as far as I am aware, doesn't exist." He stroked his silvery beard, his expression wistful almost as he considered. "What Lamashtu and Lucifer created in their children was more than a curse. It was an act of war on creation—our creation—and the desire to unmake the fabric of magic and reality alike. An act of hatred, from an Aperien dreamed up to be the unredeemable villain for humanity's grace and a true, unadulterated monster who hated for hatred's sake, but even Lamashtu was made as she was by human dreams."

Audrey only nodded; nothing he said was a shock.

"That said, power alone doesn't weave what they wrought. They undoubtedly built in a release—doing so buoys the power of a curse if the magic knows it can be undone. But how do you pinpoint the answer to such a riddle when the progenitors are long gone?"

Zhang regarded them both, as if expecting an answer. Audrey managed a helpless shrug, Jonathan's growing anger the only thing keeping her from collapsing inward.

"Plainly speaking? Dumb, blind luck." Zhang held up a hand when Jonathan snarled and surged to his feet. "Not that the effort isn't worthy. I will help however I am able, but I will not lie to either of you. I won't promise you answers we may never uncover. At least not in time."

"Then what's the fucking point?" Jonathan's voice stained. "What fucking good is magic if it can let her feel safe enough to love something like me, only to have it kill her?"

"Jonathan . . ."

"No, fuck this shit. What good is any of this shit? Tell me that. Theo's not a fucking idiot, much as I like to pretend. He knew she wanted me, knew where this might go, that we might fuck, and his magic . . . Why? Gods fucking damn it, why didn't the magic fucking know? Why did this fucking happen?"

He yelled now, the burst of emotion so unlike him, pain radiating off him in waves. The agony in the way his voice cracked. And she couldn't fault him, not when she felt the same. Not when her heart, for all she'd tried to find hope, to believe, desperately wanted to the same answer.

How could they love so, so much, and the cost be this high?

Why?

Zhang weathered the outburst, his expression sympathetic, which almost made it worse. "I don't know, son," he said gently.

Jonathan sank back into the seat beside her. Audrey buried herself against him, his arm steel and warm. His heart, gods, it beat so fast and loud.

"Sometimes hatred is stronger than all the love in the world. Now, that doesn't stop any of us from trying, hmm? Humans, gods, or otherwise. So, please, have some cakes and rest your hearts. Understand the odds, and then tomorrow? Fight on."

They made their way back to their apartment in silence; what was there to say when a god of knowledge told them to get their affairs in order because this probably wouldn't work out? Audrey slipped off her boots, watching Jonathan's back as he tore out of his coat and threw it at the rack.

They'd been working on her scenting emotions, mostly regarding Jonathan since Audrey was most familiar with him. His anger and frustration gave his natural scent, masculine and musky with hints of what reminded her of open forest and dark nights, a sharp heat and spice, enough it cloyed on her tongue.

"Bathroom," she mumbled, needing a moment alone.

Audrey's own emotions about drowned her, and she needed a few seconds without getting buried by his emotions as well. The bathroom was cooler than the rest of the apartment, easing the feverish cling on her skin. Flushed cheeks, sweaty brow, she mused as she washed her hands and splashed cold water on her face. At least she wasn't so pale she looked like a corpse.

The mirror gave her pause, though. It always did since that nightmare. She studied her reflection, but her hazel eyes reminded clear and light. The fine veins on her throat were still blue, not black. She touched her cheek, skin clammy, but that was normal. A little less nauseous right now, but that was probably just because she hadn't eaten since brunch.

They needed to talk.

It was a conversation they'd both been avoiding, about what happens at the nine-month mark.

She needed to know if Jonathan could handle killing her or if they'd need to ask for help. Same was true with a daughter. Audrey knew their friends in Nizhny wouldn't let Jonathan deal with that alone.

She almost worried more about a son; how would Jonathan face being a father, alone, if they had a baby boy who needed him when Audrey was gone? A baby boy that was indirectly responsible for his mother's death?

She swallowed, her throat a vice.

Tonight wasn't the right time for the conversation, was it? Not with everything so raw, with his burst of fury at the injustice of their situation, but it had to happen soon.

She needed his promise that he would love their child without her. She needed to hear the words from him. What the grief of her death might do to him terrified her. After almost losing Jonathan twice, Audrey was completely unmoored. Nightmares, triggering sensations—sounds or smells or even words.

How would she ever go on without him and take care of the child that wasn't even supposed to exist?

Audrey lifted her chin and flattened a palm against the very minimal swell low on her belly. No matter how much it hurt, she would love this child. *Their* child. Even if it was with the battered remains of her heart, she would. And Jonathan would too.

If he gave her his word, she knew he would keep it.

Then she felt it.

A flutter, just there, just under her hand.

Her heart skipped, then tripled, and she held her breath.

The lights were on. The door was open. She could hear Jonathan moving around in the hallway, headed toward their room, likely to check on her and get her bedtime draughts ready since Aster wasn't back yet.

It came again, a tickle, a gentle rub inside her body.

No pain, no blood, no tearing and clawing.

Audrey exhaled in a rush, then pinched her forearm hard enough to bruise.

Not a dream or a nightmare.

She looked down, tentative, placing both hands back on her belly, and whispered, "It's you?"

The flutter came again, a bit more insistent, and Audrey laughed. The timing was right, a little behind maybe, but Aster said the quickening came later in first pregnancies, not to mention that magical pregnancies played by their own rules. This was unlike any sensation she'd felt before, and yet so distinct. Unique.

"It *is* you."

And she grinned, a smile so wide her cheeks hurt. She dashed from the bathroom as Jonathan came into the master bedroom and slammed the door behind him, his expression still stormy.

"Jonathan!" She gasped and shouted at him at the same time.

"What? What's wrong?" He had her by the shoulders, his handsome face twisted, scowling, checking her over.

"I'm sorry; I'm okay." She grabbed his forearm, his huge hand, pressed it to her stomach over the skirt and blouse. "I felt the baby move."

He stilled for an entirely different reason, and Audrey inhaled at the same time he did, a deep draw, trying to guess what he felt at the same time he tried to measure her scent. His cooled dramatically, as if the anger drained out of him, but otherwise was a jumble to her nose. She couldn't really pick out details, but she didn't expect him to snarl at her. He reached up to tug at the chain around her throat.

E's chain, the magic which concealed her condition. All aspects, giving her a visual illusion to cover her middle and markers such as scent.

Jonathan's expression looked like murder as he bit out, "Take this fucking thing off."

He'd been cut off from her true scent since E sealed the chain, Audrey realized as her heart did a little swoop. Her scent must have shifted as her hormones and pheromones and her blood chemistry changed with the baby growing. She hadn't even considered that part when they planned to come to Moscow, how much it would take away from Jonathan, from the experience of her pregnancy.

She touched the chain and whispering, "*<<ógǫrr >>*," as E instructed.

The thin silver chain separated without a sound, and Jonathan caught it and the wooden ring from Nizhny, throwing them roughly to the nightstand before crushing her against him. His face buried in her throat, inhaling against her skin like it hurt him to breathe. She shivered, clinging back to him, smoothing her hands through his hair.

"Fuck," he mumbled, his lips soft and warm at her pulse. "You smell different. Like us. Like mine." Another growl, another inhale, and then he was pulling at her clothes. "Let me see you."

She helped him tear off her blouse, kicking out of the skirt as he unhooked her bra and threw it aside. Nothing about this was a seduction, just him wanting, *needing*, to *know* her again without illusions. Her breathing hitched as he sank to his knees, a huge palm covering her entire stomach, cradling the tiny life growing inside her. His chest heaved las if he'd ran for miles, his brow furrowed as he waited, intense now as when he hunted. Audrey waited, too, silently willing the baby to show him, to show their father.

A second later Jonathan blinked, his hand squeezing, pressing in, his other at the small of her back to keep her steady. She held on to his broad shoulders and bit her lip when he huffed, then went still, waiting for it to happen again. Needing to be certain. And then he looked up at her, wonder etched on that handsome face.

This was the moment Audrey's heart needed so desperately.

The love all over his expression, entirely lost in possibility. Without the risks, the curse, the uncertainty. Just the three of them, for just a moment.

Jonathan grinned, that rare, boyish expression of his, and Audrey laughed. Then he did, too, and pressed his face to her bare skin, nuzzling her belly. Kissing, running his fingers along the curve. She ran a hand through his dark hair again, holding him while he held them both.

He surged to his feet a second later, both hands taking her face, searching her eyes for what, she didn't know. Jonathan leaned down, his forehead against hers, and they breathed into each other.

"You smell like us," he murmured again.

"I do?"

"Yeah, like my scent is part of you." Then he chuckled. "Guess it is."

"Jonathan?" Her heart raced. She wanted to . . . They needed to . . .

"Not now," he said, speaking against her lips. "I need to love you, sweetheart."

What could she say besides, ". . . *yes*."

He muscled her into the bedpost, and then he was on his knees, her underwear torn off her skin, a thigh over his massive shoulder, and her head fell back with a cry as he buried his mouth between her legs. It was a focused assault, his impatience was an animal of its own.

He knew exactly how to get her wet and rile her up; he did it now, quick, meticulous, every stroke of his tongue sending a hot spike through her entire body. She ached already, twinges between her legs as her body answered, as her arousal rushed to meet his tongue and lips and oh-so-careful teeth. He sucked until she keened and left off when her legs shook so hard she almost collapsed, but he held her up with a firm hand on her hip as the other delved inside her. One finger first, seeking, testing, before he buried two inside her and started pumping them in a lewd rhythm.

"Jonathan, gods," she gasped out, fisting his hair, nails digging into his scalp as she tried to stay standing, pressure and tension and pleasure curling and spiraling, higher and higher, fast and slick and desperate. "I . . . please . . . you . . ."

She wasn't even making sense, just babbling, and he growled against her, whispering about her pretty cunt, how she tasted like his, and how he was going to fuck her until she couldn't tell them apart anymore.

Audrey came with a near shriek, her entire body quaking and stuttering, clenching around his fingers as they continued to work her through the high, and she wasn't even finished coming when she found herself tossed on the bed, Jonathan tearing off his clothes, her desperate, apex predator fixated on his very captive prey.

Seconds and he was on her, his body over hers, and she had to close her eyes, everything about the moment overwhelming. The way he tangled himself around her, a hand in her hair, the other angling her hips. Her body reeled with aftershocks as he muscled his cock inside her, and she wailed, clawing at his back and shoulders, because it didn't hurt, but he felt huge and hungry and then he was buried so, so deep inside her she felt like her entire body was being reformed.

And gods, his grunts in her ear, his teeth on her throat, bruising and claiming. Each thrust jarring both of them further up the bed, the sheets sliding against her skin, sweat-damp already. Her eyes rolled back, her orgasm swelling again and dragging her under, her vision whiting out. She thrashed under him, but there was nowhere to go, nowhere to move, nothing to do but spasm around and under him, drowning in cascading bliss.

The sounds would have made her blush if Audrey wasn't so lost in the sensations of his body inside her, how each thrust ended on a sharp snap. Gods his scent. She let out a long, pitiful whine as her high faded back from shattering and unbearable to floating lost at sea.

Jonathan didn't relent, but she felt the tension building in his massive frame, the faint tremble where his hand moved down to squeeze at her ass and thighs, the desperate pants in her ear between nonsense strings of words.

Mine, love, us, ours, love, love, I fucking love you.

When he came, he groaned out her name, *Audrey*, in a long, plaintive moan that made her entire body shudder as his warmth flooded inside her. He all but collapsed on top of her; she'd never seen him so entirely spent, so utterly lost as she was in that moment, and she cradled him against her, clinging to him with everything she had, refusing to let him move.

Eventually, he shifted so his weight wasn't fully on her, but he didn't leave her body, making a point of muscling his softening cock deeper inside her when it slipped, anchoring their thighs to hold them close as possible, as long as possible.

She fell asleep to his lips on her throat, his breath on her skin, his scent covering her in a warm, perfect blanket.

Chapter 27

They didn't have that conversation about the future and promises the next day, or the day after. The days bled into weeks, and Audrey kept telling herself they would, just not right now.

The Symposium went on, the days all the same. No one ever invited Audrey to after-hours visits or private dinners, and she didn't feel any overwhelming urge to push the farce of her presence in Moscow any further than necessary. She'd taken to studying openly in the Faceted Chamber while everyone ignored her. Business as usual.

Aster spent more time out in the evenings socializing with locals. Being a cornflower wraith made her essentially a native, and she was welcome in most quarters, but there really wasn't anything for her to uncover, at least not about Nizhny or Audrey's pregnancy.

Zhang, while helpful both as the head bookkeeper and a sneaky deity, had yet to hand them a magic bullet. He'd pulled up his memories regarding female vilebloods, but most were from during the Vilestars War. All of them had already transformed, none of them pregnant. No research on the latter. When dealing with curses so powerful, Zhang explained, mitigating fallout came first, which wasn't news. He sent new books and tomes daily, and Audrey read as much as she could, but so far, nothing.

Jonathan hardly left her side.

She hadn't removed E's protective necklace since the night they felt the baby move, but that shared moment eased Jonathan somewhat. For now, he had proof Audrey was stable. She enjoyed the evenings most, when he'd sit behind her on the couch or bed, her personal pillow as she researched.

May became a frequent visitor in the late evenings. Each visit, she'd take more of Jonathan's blood for her research. May prodded him about his Wolfstar lineage, making cracks about him being an older man than he thought.

Audrey enjoyed May's company. She was honest and endearing. A sharp mind and wit, and May got lost in the borrowed books as much as Audrey did. They'd get off on some topic barely related to their research until a drawling remark from Jonathan reeled them back in.

She wondered if May might want to come back with them when they returned to Nizhny, but it would mean leaving her position at the clinic. Her apprenticeship wasn't an ideal situation, but she'd clearly gone through a lot to secure her place. That alone held Audrey back; she didn't want to be selfish by asking her new friend to give up so much, but Audrey really did worry if May would ever find true belonging here in the Dominion.

Despite May's efforts, her research was nothing but dead ends. Every day, Audrey considered coming clean to May, but Jonathan didn't like the idea. There was too much risk. They never knew who might catch on, and he was pretty sure May had already guessed and was smart enough not to point it out. Instead, they kept giving May vials of Audrey's blood and May took them without comment.

Audrey's blood remained mostly unchanged. Less human as the weeks went on, but still red, still clean, and still tasting nothing like vileblood to May.

Thankfully, her pregnancy symptoms got milder as time crept by. Aster thought her blood was balancing out, that maybe the sickness had to do with all the changes in her body and not just the growing child, but Audrey didn't care either way. Less vomit, fewer headaches and fevers, and not as many foul-tasting draughts? She'd take it.

The illusions tied to E's chain hid the other changes, but her stomach grew, and the baby moved more and more. The tiny flutters that felt like butterfly wings made the circumstances feel less like unraveling a curse and more like fighting for a miracle.

Still, the weeks dragged. Audrey and her companions had been in Moscow for eight weeks. Another month until the equinox, and after, they would head back to Nizhny. Four weeks before they'd leave with or without an answer to the vileblood curse inside her.

Audrey would return home for a future or to say her goodbyes.

Aster touched her thigh. Brunch started about an hour earlier, the Faceted Chamber no less glorious despite the tedious Symposium matters. Her mind had been wandering, but Aster wouldn't prod her without reason, so she turned her attention to the current conversation.

"How extensive is the damage?" Dimitri asked from his head table, lording over the gathering like usual. Today, he wore a floppy velvet hat to match his red and gold doublet.

"Extensive," Nikita the Tanner answered. He held the easternmost province, the closest to Nizhny, and was heavily involved in all ventures related to the Trans-Siberian railway. The Aperien was not pleased. "Enough to be considered a minor calamity."

Maxim, the gilded merchant, scoffed. "If we treated every incident as a calamity, we'd be forever in crisis."

"What begs a crisis, then? How far your profits fall only second to loss of life?" Nikita replied. Maxim only shrugged, and Nikita turned his attention back to Dimitri. Audrey sat up taller. "Namazu, who escaped its prison when Takemikazuchi fell during the Storm Belt

Calamity, went missing after ravaging the Enlightened Sun for almost a decade. It was driven deep into the sea, later chased under the land shelves."

Audrey knew both names. Takemikazuchi was the fallen Japanese thunder god and Namazu a giant catfish responsible for terrible earthquakes. The Enlightened Sun was an Accorded Territory that occupied what was Japan before the Aperien Event.

"Well, we found it," Nikita went on, "hiding and hibernating in the Angara-Lena basins. Our recent expansions on the eastern borders disturbed it two days ago. The quakes have stopped for now, but the damage is done."

"And the big fish?" the sphinx asked, tail slapping at the marble floor beside her cushions.

"It fled north through the stone, and the quakes followed it to the shore. It was keen to avoid us; they must have come close to killing it last time, because it didn't attack. It simply wanted to escape, but its movements left the entire region in shambles. We need relief."

The debates went on: what kind of relief, how many lives lost, how many lives were still in danger. Audrey took studious notes. Moscow had sent initial aid the evening before along the railway. Rebuilding, however, seemed to be a sticking point.

No matter Nikita's suggestions, delegating resources beyond the initial recovery were roundly denied. For all the Dominion was a unified Accorded Territory, no one seemed willing to risk their own province's profitability. Audrey's stomach soured the longer she listened. The excuses went on and on, no help in sight for rebuilding efforts.

Audrey touched Ulyana's elbow. "Can you let them know I'd like to speak?"

The woman hesitated but made her way over to the main table.

She waited ten minutes before anyone bothered to look her way, but Ulyana stood there until one of the other secretaries quietly spoke with her, then moved down the table to speak to Nikita's secretary, who discreetly passed him a note.

Audrey waited with her hands folded in her lap until the Aperien read the note and glanced at her curiously. When a lull in conversation came naturally, he gestured at her table. To her surprise, he wasn't dismissive. He was annoyed, but not at her interruption. "Nizhny wishes to offer something to this discussion?"

"Yes, please," Audrey said as she stood. When he nodded, she cleared her throat. "It seems lumber is going to be one of the largest challenges for you, being that the area around the border was clear-cut and never replanted. Nizhny already exports lumber weekly for the capital. We can adjust our exports for a few weeks, focus entirely on lumber. We should be able to export at least five times the current amount for the rebuilding efforts. We might be able to push those numbers higher if the local leshy assists. He should be willing, given the efforts are to repair and not expand. Our alchemical exports will need to be put on hold temporarily, but none of Nizhny's exports are survival critical."

Nikita's secretary wrote as she spoke, and they whispered back and forth before he regarded Audrey with a stern expression. "There's no way we can pay for that volume of imports given our current situation, even if it would meet our needs."

"Oh, no." Audrey frowned. "I would need to get approval from Rina and verify logistics, but this is an offer of help, not a trade negotiation."

The room went oddly quiet, every Aperien and duster at the gathered table shocked. Audrey's cheeks warmed under the intense attention. Her heart thrummed; had she violated customs or policy by offering to help?

Dimitri snorted. Audrey had to crane her neck up to see Dimitri on his elevated platform. "Katerina Yaga, our fierce Independent neighbor, will aid the Dominion for nothing?"

Would Rina help? Audrey believed she would, that she'd understand offering an olive branch strengthened her position, being that it was for the right reasons, for people who needed it and not for a power struggle. She wouldn't like it, but, "She will, but these initial numbers are an estimate. Please keep that in mind," Audrey went on, turning back to Nikita. "It might take more shipments. Or there might be another contract in place that we can't delay. I need to send a messenger, but I should have confirmation in a day, maybe two?"

Nikita might be only a human legend, but he was still an Aperien. She felt the weight of his stare, the power behind his mythos, and the shrewd expression of an experienced barterer who'd fought time and time again for his prestigious seat at the Dominion's table.

But as he studied her, the edge to his features eased. "I will send my secretary to your lodgings after the Symposium today. She can arrange for whatever communications you need and see them expedited."

"Thank you," Audrey said, bowing before taking her seat.

"Thank *you*," Nikita replied, his nod a bit more than a casual head dip. For the rest of the meeting, the Aperien seemed thoughtful, almost distracted, his attention wandering to their table. The meeting moved on to other matters, with lunch served shortly after.

Aster gave her knee a squeeze under the table, and when she glanced at her friend, the cornflower wraith's approval was obvious. She gave her a little shrug. She'd like to hope if her home needed help, someone would offer if they could.

Now she just had to convince Rina.

Swiftwren messengers, magical versions of carrier pigeons, were notoriously expensive, but province leaders, even ones in crisis, had extensive resources.

Rina, true to her nature, complained a lot but came around quickly and shifted Nizhny's production priorities. She made it clear how much she enjoyed the idea of sticking it to the Dominion at the same time she was helping the Dominion, and was oh so very sorry to tell the Dominion nobility their frivolous exports must be delayed for the greater good.

"It would be nice if she was a little less smug about," Audry said as she passed the latest exchange to Aster, who only laughed.

"Let her be." Aster folded the letter and set it next to the fresh fruit always waiting on their foyer table. "Much better for her to gleefully cooperate than begrudgingly acquiesce."

Jonathan reached over her shoulder and grabbed an apple; today they were golden yellow, accompanied by dates, plums, and starfruit. He talked with his mouth full when he said, "I thought she was going to shit her pants." Audrey smacked his arm as he leaned back, which got her one of those all too handsome grins of his when he mouthed *What?* at her. She rolled her eyes, shooing him away as someone knocked at the door.

Aster let in May. Audrey grinned, happy to see their regular visitor.

"Hello!" May called with a wave. It was just after sunset now, five days after she'd offered Nizhny's support to the Dominion border. Nikita had greeted them every morning since, and even visited their table once during a break to ask questions about the leshy. He'd seemed genuinely curious, as they avoided the Dominion border, and wondered what, if anything, he might do to change that for the better.

Otherwise, things stayed the same.

Which meant no progress. And less and less time on their side.

May plopped down on the couch with a small oof, taking out her tablet. She poked and swiped a few times, at ease around the rare piece of human technology.

"Not much new, but," May paused and hummed, then, "Oh, here it is." She passed the tablet over.

Audrey took it, and Jonathan leaned over the back of the couch to see. A report about a rare type of blood infection from about five years back that only affected dusters with traces of angel blood. Its cause was exposure to a certain type of brimstone, from a specific version of hell, brought in during a surge in illegal hellhound breeding. The closest analog for humans was rabies. They'd discovered a successful alchemical treatment, with the only recorded side effect being itchy skin.

"I know," May said with a sigh. "It's barely related, but I figured might as well track it down, see what the composition looks like. I have a friend, a witch focused on alchemical injections like these, so I'm going to ask her tomorrow about mixing up a dose."

"Do you think it would do anything?"

May swung her feet back and forth a few times, then thumped them down on the fancy carpet. "No," she said. Audrey appreciated May's honesty. "But I can see how it interacts with duster-angel blood." She watched Audrey for a moment, her red eyes a bit too knowing. Jonathan shifted; May immediately looked away. "Worst case, I get to taste weird blood. Still more fun than my normal days."

Audrey laughed as another knock sounded. All four of them stilled. Aster glanced between them to confirm no, they weren't expecting anyone. Jonathan strode over to open the door with her. May moved to sit closer to Audrey.

Mikhali, head of the house, greeted Jonathan and Aster with a curt bow, and they let him inside. He walked stiff-backed, the bit of warmth he'd shown Audrey when he gave her the apples nowhere to be found, and she realized why. He made no move to hide his blatant disgust toward May before addressing Audrey. May, for her part, appeared bored by it all.

"The master of the house has requested you join him for a late supper."

Audrey gripped her skirt; they'd been home for hours. Dimitri had as well. It was impossible to miss the show every time he came or went. He was well aware Audrey had a guest, and that May had only just arrived.

"Right now?" Audrey asked.

"Yes, miss. The first course is ready, waiting at your leisure."

If she was Jonathan, she might have said "leisure my ass," but May tapped off the tablet and tucked it under her arm.

"I was on my way out." May patted Audrey's shoulder, and when she leaned in close to her throat and whispered, "Have dessert for me, you know, since I can't," Audrey thought Mikhali might burst at the seams. May saw herself out. Mikhali didn't even look at her.

Being cruel to dusters based on their blood had never been reserved for vileblood, after all.

Audrey wanted to smack Mikhali in his smug face.

Then she winced at her sudden burst of violent temper. It wasn't like her.

But it had been another in a series of long days, she was tired, and Mikhali and Dimitri were both incredibly rude. She could feel annoyed; it didn't mean she was going to hit him.

A part of her still kind of wanted to, though.

The last thing Audrey expected, walking into Dimitri dining hall for an impromptu meal, was to be confronted with his entire family.

Audrey stalled in the doorway, Mikhali striding far enough head to bow formally to the gathering. Jonathan's hand rested briefly on her lower back, hidden from view. Had she been told, she would have dressed more formally for dining with the Dominion's leader.

Dimitri knew this and had told Mikhali not to mention the fact. His smug expression confirmed it.

Audrey dropped into a deep curtsy, Jonathan a crisp bow, and held, waiting for an acknowledgement. This wasn't the unexpected encounter with Koschei the Deathless in the back hall of the art wing. Well, unexpected for her maybe, but protocol stood.

"Join us," Koschei said almost immediately, his expression kind when she rose. He looked exactly like she remembered. An unassuming, middle-aged man. Dimitri looked more like an Aperien than his father did.

"Thank you," Audrey said, making her way to the empty seat between Koschei at the head and Dimitri on the other side, which put her directly across from Jaga Baba, the witch-queen and Rina's estranged aunt.

Koschei held the Accorded Territory, as the Moscow Dominion was bound and tied to his magic and he'd named no successor, but it was common knowledge he ruled with his wife. Many speculated if their marriage carried any love, but they were deadly efficient as partners. Where Koschei dressed as casual as their encounter among the paintings, Yaga Baba wore finery, head to toe, draped in as much as her son. She also reeked of old, powerful magic and mythos, so much so Audrey's newly attuned senses burned.

She smelled like peat moss and heavy bog water, but it wasn't an unpleasant scent. Not rot or decay, but rather the underpinnings of an entire ecosystem. As if the very fabric of her Aperien nature lived and breathed by the lands under heel. Fierce, wise, and unrelenting. The woman wore her power on her skin, the matriarch but not the crone, and she didn't hide behind false youth or beauty. That said, she was striking, a remarkable visage with carefully coifed silver hair, deep lines in her pale skin, and eyes the color of yellowed, rotten fruit.

The part of Audrey that was newly unburied screamed at her to run, flee, bury herself somewhere safe from the monstrous Aperien drinking from fine silver. Yaga Baba's expression read mostly bored.

Their daughter, Lisliria Syn Koschei, was her mother's child in near every sense of the world. She smelled of the same deep-rooted witch magic, her eyes the same eerie pale glow, her silver hair long and loose over her bare shoulders. Her dress was gorgeous, a youthful copy of Yaga Baba, and she would have been breathtakingly beautiful if she didn't glare like she hated the entire world. She glanced Audrey over once, then Jonathan, and yawned.

Audrey didn't expect a chair for Jonathan, but she still hated sinking into the plush, cushioned seat while he stood at the wall with the servants. They'd decided before coming into the dining room he wouldn't taste her food. Too likely to offend. Besides, if Dimitri wanted to get rid of them, it was unlikely he'd dirty his hands at his own dining table.

As soon as she sat, Dimitri snapped and the servants swept into motion, topping her glass with fine wine. Within seconds, they filled the table with a breathtaking feast. Thankfully, her stomach stayed quiet despite the cacophony of rich scents.

"I appreciate the invitation," she said. Once the Koschei family served themselves, she took a modest portion. Enough she could move it around, eat a few bites, and not be rude. If pressed, she'd just tell them she'd already eaten. And it would be a lie; she'd had an apple earlier.

"The very least I could do is host Nizhny's envoy after your heroic efforts on Nikita's behalf," Dimitri said, his tone dry, with just enough to lift to the words to pretend he meant it as a compliment instead of an annoyance.

"After I insisted on this meal," Koschei said, winking at her as he ate. "My niece might be stubborn as her cousins, but she's always had a good head on her shoulders."

Lisliria rolled her eyes. "Please, she only did it to get your attention."

"That doesn't change the Dominion benefited." Koschei tipped his glass in Audrey's direction. "But it was your suggestion that got the lumber moving to where it needed to go. Seems your esquire title was well-earned, yes?"

Audrey smiled under the praise, which felt genuine. "I'm glad we could help."

It was strange, though, with how powerful he was and the vast Dominion he ruled over, that he was the least assuming at the table.

"I wondered if it was all a game on the Citadel's part, putting a human at the face of Accorded change." Yaga Baba's voice was low, a deep and scratchy timbre that made Audrey's nerves itch. She'd filled her plate, but the Aperien witch didn't eat a bite. "Control always erodes over time, dwindling like the stones beat to sand on the shore. Adjustments to Accorded Laws, no matter how seemingly insignificant, allow for a redistribution of magic." Yaga Baba perked a thin brow. "Your work, girl, allowed them to rebound a law entirely. Now, it is strong as new."

Audrey knew bindings decayed, the speed of which depended on the power behind them, but she hadn't considered the amount of magic the Citadel Pantheon invested in the Accorded Laws that held the current world in a state of balance. Any erosion of that power threatened . . . well, everything.

"*Dorogaya*," Koschei said, wiping his mouth. "I'm fairly certain Miss Doe's motivations aren't driven by Accorded magical checks and balances. Her taste in art is far too good for all that." To Audrey, he asked, "Have you found your way back to the gallery?"

They chatted casually from there, and Audrey found herself a bit lost in the fasciation of speaking with the immortal of immortals about his art collection, the foremost of what remained across the globe. Dimitri joined in after being aloof for a few minutes, luxury an appreciation father and son shared in earnest. Even Lisliria indulged, although she never engaged with Audrey directly, and had very strong opinions about the different sculpture techniques of the ancient Greeks, Romans, and Egyptians. Talking about Egypt bridged into a lively conversation about the resurrection of the Library of Alexander and what was saved before the iconic building burned down a second time.

Yaga Baba didn't speak again.

Before Audrey knew it, the table was cleared, dessert course set out, and the conversation quieted with the coffee and tea service.

"There is a matter I've been meaning to address," Dimitri said, reclining now, his jacket tossed over the back of his seat. He'd relaxed into the meal, apparently putting aside his petty behavior in favor of pleasant conversation. She should have guessed it wouldn't last. He smirked already. "You've been having evening company."

"Yes, Maythorne is a research assistant with the clinic," Audrey said, folding her napkin next to her plate. "I'll probably never have the chance to study at the Moscow library again, so I welcome any help while I'm here." She shot Koschei a smile, genuine, hoping he recognized her appreciation for the chance. "I'm hoping to find a way to protect humans from the vileblood curse."

"Yes, yes, so very noble and all that. But she is a dhampir, did you know that?"

"Yes."

Dimitri hummed, resting his chin on his knuckles. "Given Nizhny's loose protocol with less savory dusters, I'm not surprised you're unaware that vampiric bloodlines are not given free rein to wander where ever they please. As per the Human Protection Accord, you understand."

Audrey inhaled, then let it out slowly; she had to tread carefully. "May is an employee of the clinic. I wasn't aware she was under any restrictions because of her blood?"

"She isn't, but I must consider the personal obligations to my household. Having a dhampir coming and going as they please is making my staff uneasy. This is also their home. As their benefactor, I strive to give them more than the barest accommodations the Accords demand. Dominion contracts are nothing like the ESC indentures, you understand."

"Of course," Audrey said, forcing a smile. She felt sick now for entirely different reasons. "What would you suggest?"

"Perhaps it is best you keep your visitations to the clinic? Or another, more public venue, where there is proper security. For your own protection as well."

She wanted to argue, but given Dimitri's smirk, both the witches' grimaces, and the Deathless's silence, she knew it was pointless. "The last thing I want is to make your staff uncomfortable. We'll meet at the clinic from now on."

Dimitri bowed his head. "Excellent, thank you. And here I feared this would be a problem, maybe a fresh crusade for an aimless esquire?"

Audrey smiled; it made her lips hurt. "My role as an envoy is perfectly fulfilling."

"Well," Koschei said, his tone bored, the warm, lively man who'd spent the last hour talking about paintings replaced by the cold, Deathless leader of the Dominion. Yaga Baba and Lisliria stood as he did. Audrey and Dimitri both followed suit. "Seems this evening's pleasantries have run their course." To his son, he added, "Thank you for hosting."

"At your pleasure, Father, always." Dimitri gave a stiff bow.

When Koschei motioned for Audrey to proceed with them, she didn't hesitate. Jonathan followed her out, and they didn't speak until they were back in the apartment.

Audrey rubbed her face a few times, kicked her shoes off, and flopped on the couch. Jonathan chuckled, sinking down beside her and pulling her feet into his lap. He rubbed them, then her calves, and she sighed.

"I really hate him."

"Hmm, yeah, I'd probably be an asshole, too, if I was the little prick at the big boy table."

"Jonathan." She nudged him with her other foot, but he just grabbed it and rubbed that one instead.

"What?"

She giggled. "Nothing." Then she sighed. "May will . . ."

"She's probably used to shit like this. She'll be fine."

"I know, but—"

"Shit's not fair."

She prodded him with her toes again and squirmed when he tickled her foot. Audrey chewed her bottom lip. "Do you think May would want to come to Nizhny when we leave?"

He considered for a minute. "Not sure. It's nice, living somewhere where everyone ain't shitting on you, but she's fought to get where she is. She might not what to give that up, even if it'd be easier to leave."

Audrey sighed again, staring at the ceiling. "Should I offer? I know Rina would welcome her. I'm sure she'd love having a blood mage in Nizhny."

"Can't hurt. What's the worst that happens? She says fuck off, no skin off your nose."

"She wouldn't say that."

"Nah, probably not."

Chapter 28

They left a message at the clinic informing May of her ban from Syn Koschei manor, along with a promise Audrey would come to visit her as soon as possible. It didn't help her sour mood; she'd woken up annoyed, disheartened, and uncomfortable.

Her stomach pressed against the corsets now, no matter how much Aster loosened the ties. The boning pinched her skin, left red marks, and she always felt short of breath. And since the first wiggling about a month back, the baby had decided to never, ever stop moving, usually with a foot or hand or head pushed into one of her organs.

The discomfort would be less frustrating if she wasn't under the illusion charms. Audrey had to avoid touching her stomach, and the impulse was getting harder to ignore. Aside from the urge to rub away discomfort, she wanted to rest a hand over the little person inside her body just *because*. And she couldn't. It would look really weird if she walked around with her hand hovering a few inches away from her belly.

She slept poorly the night before. No more dreams about black blood and tearing flesh, but the heavy, cloying dark behind her eyes felt like something waited in that darkness, ready to strike as soon as she dropped her guard.

Zhang also dropped off a new item, a procurement from the defected god, not the Dominion bookkeeper. A dusty and battered journal with yellowed pages that smelled forgotten, but it contained a firsthand account of a human woman's vileblood pregnancy.

Reading the first few pages this morning was enough to ruin Audrey's mood. The woman's lover had been executed for violating the Human Protection Accord, though his death didn't bother her much. They'd locked the woman deep down in the Sri Lanka Pen, and she knew neither she nor her child would ever see the sky again.

Now, sitting in the Faceted Chamber with said journal in her lap, listening to the symposium drone on about clothing manufacturing in Moscow while all these fancy, rich dusters and Aperiens ate their fancy, rich food, and Jonathan stood in the corner like a dog, Audrey really wanted to stab someone with her pretty silver fork.

"You're scowling," Aster said quietly in Audrey's ear, and she immediately schooled her expression.

"Sorry," she mumbled.

"Did you need a fresh drink, miss?" Aster asked, code for if she needed a draught for any of her pregnancy symptoms.

Audrey shook her head. No, her current nausea had nothing to do with the state of her body.

The meeting droned on, and when it finally ended, they waited as usual for the "more important" people to leave before they gathered themselves.

"Alright?" Jonathan asked as she stood on wobbly legs. Audrey fisted her hands to keep from soothing her stomach. She was pretty sure the baby didn't like her breakfast. She didn't like her breakfast much either at this point.

Audrey shrugged. Aster chuckled next to her, Ulyana already a few paces ahead, waiting for them so she could get on with her day. Audrey wanted to lean into Jonathan, feel his arms around her, close her eyes and breathe him in, but she couldn't, not with eyes and ears everywhere, not until they were safely back at the apartment.

Audrey rubbed her forehead.

No, first they needed to visit May and apologize properly for Dimitri being unreasonable. And she really needed to read this journal, a brick in her fist, because so far it was the only source of firsthand information on a vileblood pregnancy they'd uncovered. And any direction, any hint, would be better than the vast sea of nothing they'd been drowning in for weeks. The equinox crept ever closer. After that, they'd go home to Nizhny. They'd lose May and Zhang's help.

They'd be less than two months away from her due date.

Less than three months away as of today.

Audrey's eyes stung.

"Hey," Jonathan said, his voice gentle as he rubbed her arm once. "Let's get back, take a breather."

She offered him a smile she knew was weak. "Okay."

They left the Faceted Chamber, headed out down the vast carpeted hall and all Moscow's finery, and out to the entryway plaza. A sunny day at least, and the enchanted snowflakes swirled around the magical lights. Audrey hummed, letting herself appreciate the uncomplicated beauty as they headed toward the carriages, the glittering motes against the blue sky no less wondrous than the day they'd arrived.

Until a new scent found her.

Feathers and holy steel. The touch of heavens, of sunlit halos and ethereal, deadly Aperien power.

There, not a hundred paces away. Dimitri spoke with a man whose back was to them, but Audrey knew what he was. White wings tucked neatly against a white suit, hands folded at his back, golden-blond curls tied with a cerulean ribbon.

Her throat tightened.

Dimitri saw her, gestured her direction, all casual smiles.

Her chest ached, a lancing pain in her lungs.

The angel turned, his wings shifting, opening . . .

. . . smelled boiling, black blood, tasted it in the back of her throat. Heart blood, as it pumped and evaporated from chest rent open. The heat of hellfire, the scent of brimstone. It couldn't burn her, but the heat was oppressive, crushing, like the weight of Jonathan's limp body. Ringing in her ears, echoing, the sound of her love dying in her arms, louder, louder as the world tunneled, her vision blackening to nothing at all . . .

"Audrey."

A cool palm touched her face as the world came back into focus. Blue sky, motes of silver snowflakes, and Aster's face, her expression tight, but there was an urgency to her voice.

Why was she on the ground?

"You fainted," Aster said. "You are alright, but this situation is not. Can you sit?"

She swallowed a few times. She felt like she was underwater, but the white noise in her ears died down. Her skin felt damp, head to toes, but she was okay. Maybe. "I think so?"

Aster helped her sit, and she tried to make sense of the chaos in front of her.

Dimitri watched her down his nose, his expression smug. Beside him stood the angel, who watched her with genuine concern, his hand bleeding.

Not Kushiel. Audrey processed this on a sharp exhale.

He looked similar, of course, as all angels did, but this was not the same Aperien, because Kushiel was dead and buried on the taiga outside Nizhny. He couldn't hurt Jonathan again.

Jonathan.

She blinked a few more times and found him, there, just out of reach. Pinned to the ground under six duster guards wearing Dominion colors. He panted, his black hair mussed, his face pressed against the plaza stone. Jonathan's lip was split, black blood pooling around his snarl. His eyes were wild, but they held hers, and he visibly relaxed when they made eye contact. His eversharp knife rested near her feet, bloodied.

Audrey tried to stand; the world shifted violently. "Let him go." No one moved. "Get off of him!" Her voice came out shrill, almost a shriek. Aster restrained her, keeping her from trying to get up again.

"Audrey—" Aster tried, but new panic was settling in, fresh off the dreaming memories of him dying against that burning pine tree, and she could *smell his blood*.

"Let him go, now!" Audrey all but snarled.

Dimitri scoffed. "I will do no such thing. He just assaulted an Accorded Warden."

"What?" Audrey glanced between the angel, his bloody hand, the knife on the cobblestone. No . . . he . . . "What?"

"You fainted," Aster said, speaking loud enough for the gathering crowd. The Symposium members. Their staff. Moscow citizens with straining necks. Two dozen onlookers, maybe more. "Both Dimitri and the Warden Pyriel were quick to come to the aid of a woman in clear distress."

Warden Pyriel. Kushiel's second.

Audrey's heart lurched. Oh gods . . .

"In a moment of confusion, and out of concern for your well-being, well within the demands of his contractual obligation as your bodyguard, Gunnar reacted to what he misinterpreted as a threat." For all the calm she sounded, Audrey now knew what fear smelled like coming off Aster's skin.

Jonathan wisely said nothing, watching only her with an unblinking, unwavering stare.

"I'm okay," she whispered, for him more than anything, but then spoke louder, returning her attention to Dimitri and the angel. The angel Jonathan had attacked. "I'm okay," she repeated, louder, making sure her voice carried.

Pyriel held his injured hand, the wound already healing. A few ruby drops staining his suit cuff and the stones near his feet.

"Good," the angel said, his voice remarkably gentle. She'd only ever known Kushiel's disdain; this angel's kindness was disarming. And terrifying, because he could only be here in Moscow for one reason. Pyriel studied her, but it didn't feel oppressive. He seemed concerned, almost a bit confused, as he added, "I'm not used humans being frightened of me, to be honest."

He must have meant it as a joke, maybe as an attempt to lighten the dangerous mood. It was everything Audrey could do to keep her voice steady.

She didn't. The words poured out in a trembling mess. "I'm sorry," she said, hands clenched on her skirt. "I didn't sleep well, or eat enough this morning I think, please, I just . . ." She squeezed her eyes shut, licked her lips a few times. "He didn't . . . He . . ."

"What exactly?" Dimitri hummed. "This vileblood didn't *mean* to resort to violence at a simple gesture of aid to fainting woman?"

When Audrey met Dimitri's stare, he didn't hide his satisfaction, his slimy smile as he motioned to the guards, who roughly hauled Jonathan to his feet. He didn't fight; he knew there was no point. He'd reacted on instinct, probably his own trauma from an angel tearing him apart, threatening everything he loved, coming after her again.

None of which they could explain.

Jonathan looked like the mad monster they all expected from a vileblood.

Gods, if they took him away . . . now . . . if she never . . .

If she lost him . . .

Audrey gripped Aster's arm; she couldn't breathe, she couldn't . . .

She couldn't do this without him.

"Come now, Dimitri," Pyriel said, his tone soft for the deep baritone of his voice, and without force or malice. "This was clearly a misunderstanding."

Audrey dared to look at the angel directly, dared to look at him with all her hopes and fears. He looked back, calm and curious.

"Warden, I can't have it said that guests of import are unprotected within the Dominion capital of all places. This vileblood—"

"Responded under the compulsions of contracted magic, by whom?" Pyriel spoke to her and Aster, a hand held up to stall an increasingly furious Dimitri Syn Koschei, who was being put in his place in front of the entire Symposium.

"Under service of Katerina Yaga," Aster answered, "Aperien Independent leader of Nizhny."

"No magic a simple duster can overcome, vileblood or otherwise. And as there is no lasting damage." Pyriel flexed his palm, the wound healed clean. He didn't move any closer to Audrey or the guards holding Jonathan. "I trust you examined the contract for authenticity upon the Envoy Doe's arrival?"

"Of course," Dimitri answered, his tone clipped.

"Then the matter is settled."

Pyriel and Dimitri stood there for a heartbeat too long. And Audrey saw the second Dimitri realized he'd lost control of the moment.

And she also learned what the scent of hatred tasted like on Dimitri's skin.

There'd be a price later, but Audrey didn't give a damn.

"Release him," Dimitri said, and the guards did.

She wanted to run into his arms; Aster's ironclad grip on both her arms was the only thing that kept her from doing just that.

Jonathan wiped his nose, his mouth. He bent down to pick up the knife, making a point to wipe it off on the sleeve of the guard closest to him, which got him a glare, but the gesture was obvious. No attempts to capture the angel's blood for some nefarious purpose. He sheathed the knife and gave Pyriel a full, formal bow, which she hadn't seen from him since Virtue taught him how. Dimitri stiffened, recognizing that the vileblood did, in fact, know how to show proper respect by the Dominion's standards.

"Sorry about that," Jonathan said, no drawl, no growl, only careful, simple words. "I take protecting her seriously. She saved my life. I'd never let a damn thing happen to her if I'm still breathing." He stated this as a fact, nothing more. No threat or posturing, just a brutal kind of honesty as he lifted himself from the bow.

Pyriel nodded once, those eternal blue eyes far, far too knowing.

Audrey drew a shuddering breath, her scattered mind racing back through the conversation. Pyriel had called her by name. He knew exactly who they were.

"I'd like to get her back to the apartment now, have Aster make sure she's alright."

Pyriel didn't answer, instead deferring to Dimitri. It was obvious the angel had no desire to cause more of a scene or to demean Dimitri. He'd simply disagreed with Dimitri's interpretation of the situation and stood for justice instead of pride.

Audrey barely heard Dimitri's agreement, then she was in Jonathan's arms. They all three got into the carriage, and the plaza fell away behind them. She closed her eyes and let him hold her.

Chapter 29

Thankfully, the next day was the weekly day off from Symposium matters. When they'd come back to the apartment yesterday, Aster insisted Audrey take a bath. None of them spoke otherwise. After, she'd gone to bed in Jonathan's arms, under a double dose of sleeping draught.

She slept in, exhausted, Jonathan at her side, and eventually they joined Aster in the common room for a light meal. Nothing was planned for the day, and Audrey was more than happy to keep it that way. She lay on the couch, her head in Jonathan's lap. She felt the tension in him, as if every muscle was a second away from snapping, and when they did, it probably wouldn't end in just a scratch.

They spoke briefly about Pyriel and what the angel's presence in Moscow might or might not mean right now, and the very real possibility they'd be called to meet with him. There was also a good chance they wouldn't be able to get word to Rina or Theodore before such a meeting took place.

"I miss home," Audrey mumbled.

Jonathan ran a hand through her loose hair, working his fingers through the tangles. "Yeah."

"I do as well. This might still be native soil, but this is not where my roots belong." Aster poured a cup of green tea for Audrey, adding honey, and slid it across the coffee table. Audrey didn't move yet, content to stay under this blanket and snuggled with Jonathan, with Aster here safe with them, and never get off this couch again until it was time to return to Nizhny.

Of course, there was a knock at the door.

Jonathan growled at the sound, and Aster perked a brow at him. "No mauling," she said primly and held up a hand for him to stay put. "I will answer, for everyone's safety."

"You're funny," Jonathan drawled, and Aster smirked at him.

Audrey didn't care for the joke.

Aster spoke quietly with whoever was at the door, not anyone who was an immediate threat, because Jonathan relaxed a fraction. Audrey inhaled, but she didn't smell anything strange, at least nothing she'd learned to notice yet.

Aster returned with a sealed missive and held it out to Audrey. "From Nikita the Tanner, but delivered by his personal steward. Not the Moscow secretary."

Audrey frowned as she ran her hand over the wax seal, but delaying opening a letter wouldn't change anything. She unrolled it, summarizing as she read.

"It's a very warm thank you for Nizhny's help with the Namazu incident. We exceeded what they needed, and he plans to arrange a purchase of any excess after the Symposium completes, unless we need payment sooner." She scanned over the numbers, the offered amount generous. "I'm not sure why this didn't go directly to Rina," she wondered aloud. "There are descriptions of how they used the wood. I don't . . ."

Audrey paused, studying the numbers more closely, because they weren't just about the lumber. In fact, very little was about the wood itself; the details focused on the personnel, most notably soldiers sent from Moscow proper to facilitate the repairs. Nikita listed how long they'd been in the area, how big the camps were . . .

How they planned to depart the day after the equinox, by train, with arrangements underway to secure extra train cars from the capital for moving such a very large compliment, also accounting for beasts of burden, unspecified "metal implements," and food for a prolonged journey.

This wasn't an inventory of relief efforts.

This was an army preparing to mobilize.

"Gods," she whispered, hands dropping to her lap with the parchment. "Dimitri plans to attack Nizhny as soon as the equinox passes."

"What?" Aster swept to her feet as Jonathan took the letter from her, both of them reading through it. The cornflower wraith cursed, her archaic Russian dialect taking Audrey a few seconds to process. "This is Nikita returning your efforts on his behalf the only way he is able."

Jonathan tossed the paper on the table. "Let me guess. Anything else is treason?"

"Undoubtedly," Aster said. "We need to burn this. And figure out how to get this information to Rina."

They had barely two and a half weeks of warning before an army they had no chance of standing against descended on their home.

"All our correspondences are routed through Ulyana. I don't think anyone is pretending Dimitri doesn't read all of our mail, incoming and outgoing. At the very least, its being screened for him." Audrey waved the letter. "There's nothing we can send that would be convert enough."

"Something off the grid?" Jonathan asked Aster.

"It is possible, but I have my doubts Rina will take this news seriously enough as a mere piece of paper." Aster's expression was grim, and her scent had soured. No, that wasn't quite right. She smelled like burning grass. The cornflower wraith was furious, but that sour note, it was something else.

It was fear.

"What is seriously enough?" Audrey asked, but the answer was already pretty clear.

"These numbers? Dimitri's going to roll Nizhny, no question. Sure, E's got the hammer, maybe a few other tricks locked up in his vault, but the town has what? Maybe thirty fighters, the the wolf pack and the leshy." Jonathan held out his hand, and Audrey passed him the letter. He scanned over it again and scoffed. The noise had a dark edge, and Jonathan bared his teeth when he spoke next. "He's not aiming for a fair fight. This will be a slaughter."

"He may believe he can intimidate Rina into submission," Aster said, "but he is wrong. Yet he is also intelligent enough to bring the necessary force to make his threat a reality."

"Why?" Audrey dragged her hands over her face, pressing her palms against her cheeks. "This is all, what? A childhood rivalry? A chance to prove his worth to his father? At the cost of murdering an entire village?"

Jonathan laughed, the sound grating. She had no doubt he wanted to be there in the trenches, bloodied, when the battle came. It warmed her, that he'd come to care so much for their home, at the same time it chilled her down to her bones. "If you think anyone else in Nizhny entered this equation, that'd be a mistake, sweetheart."

Audrey closed her eyes. "If Rina won't bend and they can't win the fight, where does that leave us?"

Aster's smile was brittle. "No letter will be enough to convince Rina to flee."

"Nothing is going to convince Rina to run," Jonathan corrected, and Audrey' heart ached because she felt the truth in his words. "She might drive the rest out, get them to save themselves, but there's no way Virtue leaves her. And the leshy is bound to the fight, so, yeah."

"That would be the best-case scenario," Aster agreed.

Audrey's breath caught, the crisp calm in Aster posture making the unspoken clear. If they didn't find an alternative, Aster would stand with Rina. Aster would die on the fields of her home before she became a slave to the likes of Dimitri syn Koschei.

She felt like the gilded walls, the flashy curtains, the ridiculous chandelier, all closed in around her, crushing and relentless.

"No," she managed, rubbing her chest; it felt like her heart was going to burst from her chest. Jonathan's entire mood shifted from an edged blade to concern as he stepped toward her. She held out a hand. "No, this can't be the only answer. Nizhny is a place. It might be our place, but the people are what matter. Not the railway, not the station. We can rebuild somewhere else with everyone alive."

"Audrey," Aster said, her smile sad.

"No." She lifted her chin. "You don't have to die on those fields, Aster. And no one else called Nizhny home before you did. We can rebuild. Maybe Aspen can't follow us, but if the transition is peaceful, the leshy won't attack."

"The magic grows roots; ideas take hold. Rina has been an Independent power there for nearly a decade. For her, cutting those threads may cost more than she is willing to give."

"Worse than death?" Audrey asked.

"Some are, yes," Aster said, unflinching. "Such as having your body enslaved under a man with no regard, used as a tool, slashed and burned when it refuses to bloom. All while the soul withers away elsewhere."

Jonathan moved closer, a warm hand on her shoulder. "Then we talk to Zhang, find out how to move your soil." That was a goal, at least, a direction. And one that didn't seem entirely hopeless.

Aster smiled again, slightly warmer, but, "That does not solve our larger problem."

"We leave?" Jonathan asked. "Get home, talk with the town. Maybe E will have some ideas how to cut Rina's connection to Nizhny and negate the damage. Shit, maybe we knock her ass out, drag her away. She'd be pissed, but she'd be alive."

"She would be diminished, and not only in magic. Trust betrayed, dream taken, purpose destroyed. To her, a failure on the oath she swore to protect, both to those under her care and her parents' legacy." Aster canted her head. "And she would likely kill any involved."

"Whoever she could, yeah," Jonathan said as he rubbed his jaw.

"Leaving would arouse suspicion as well," Aster added. "We are expected here until the equinox festival, and we have performed our part. A change now brings suspicion. It could make him march early, before any warning reaches them."

"Is there nothing we can do?" Audrey whispered.

"Nothing?" Aster arched a brow. "I think not. We move forward. And you think, little esquire, not succumb."

Audrey shook her head, shrugging Jonathan away, leaving the room behind, not sure where she was going, what the hells she was doing, but for that moment, that breath, it was too much. Everything was too much.

"Better thinking in here?" Jonathan asked without levity; his expression was as grim as she felt as he followed her into their bedroom.

She walked in circles, meaningless motions that kept the walls themselves from coming down around her.

"Was this all for nothing?" She hugged her middle, the air leaving her lungs in a frustrated huff. Under fabric and illusion, the baby kicked against her stomach.

She needed to see herself. The truth, not some pretty illusion that none of this was happening. Her stomach rounded out without the magical concealment. Seven months pregnant and no closer to a solution.

And now, an army coming for Nizhny.

Audrey grabbed the necklace, muttered, "*ógǫrr*," and tossed it on the bed. "I've done nothing. And how can I?" She scoffed. "I can't even save myself." She pressed her hands to her stomach, to the life they'd made of love, to the possibility, all of which was weeks away from getting crushed. "I can't save us."

"Audrey."

She looked up at him as he crossed the room, but then he stopped, his expression wary, and Audrey knew why. She knew he saw the sudden, fierce determination she felt rising inside. Because she saw the worst future now, clear as it was dark, with Nizhny dismantled, their family and community scattered to the winds. Jonathan, alone.

Or alone with their son.

With no one to help him with his grief, to manage those dark thoughts, the guilt she knew came for him in the deepest parts of the night when he thought she slept. With nothing to hold back the monster he believed lived deep inside his blood.

"You have to promise me something, Jonathan."

He paled, despite how light his skin always was, and he opened his mouth to argue, but then someone was banging on the bedroom window. Audrey barely had time to register the sound before Jonathan had his knife out, pulling her away from the window and putting his body between her and the threat.

He jerked back the curtain. "It's May."

May? But it was the middle of the day, and she never came except during the evenings. And why was she at the bedroom window?

Audrey peeked around Jonathan as he flipped the latch, and sure enough, there was their blood mage, half buried in the hedges, a dark hood drawn tight around her face. May didn't hesitate once Jonathan opened the window, vaulting through with ease. She shut the window behind her, didn't even greet them as she pulled the curtains.

"May?" Audrey frowned as the dhampir pushed by.

Her hood fell back as she checked the bedroom door, down the hall. "Is anyone else here?"

"Just Aster," Jonathan said, a snarl in his voice. "The fuck is it?"

May turned, her crimson eyes struck wide, a thread of panic in her jerky movements. The lower half of her face was an angry red along with both hands, in what had to be horribly painful burns.

"You're hurt," Audrey said, right as May blurted, "They know."

May ignored her concern, gesturing between her and Jonathan. "About this." She didn't so much as flinch when Jonathan pressed the knife to her throat, her burned hands raised in surrender as he pressed her roughly to the wall. "I'm staring at her belly right now, so whatever you've been using to hide it isn't working. And this isn't really the time for a song and fucking dance." She hissed out the last words, flashing white, pointed canines.

"Careful there," Jonathan drawled.

"Jonathan, let her go." Audrey tugged at his arm; he trembled under her touch, but for a few desperate heartbeats, he didn't back down. May glared at him like she wanted to rip out his throat with her teeth. Audrey squeezed his forearm, the wrist holding the knife, coaxing him back. He might as well have been made of steel for all she could move him. Audrey swallowed and changed her request to a demand. "Jonathan, that's enough."

A grunt and he moved away, pacing the room like a caged animal as May talked, faster and faster.

"I got your note about Dimitri being a shithead, but that's just how things are around here, so I didn't think anything about it. But then I came in to work this morning, and he was there with some angel in my closet. My office." She waved both hands, then flinched. "They had all my shit out, my tablet. And look, I swear I didn't write anything you away even though I figured this might be what was going on—that it was you pregnant, right now, not someone someday—but I never, never wrote anything down. I tried to hide it, best I could, even though no one gives a shit about my research. They just want me to go away really, but every once and awhile someone gets a stick up their ass."

She huffed, went on, "They were there, and they were talking, and Dimitri was going on about how this proves you," May said, pointing at Jonathan, "aren't protecting shit. And how you," May pointed to Audrey this time, "are a liar if you're claiming to be human and using that to do gods know what in threat of the security of the Dominion people.'"

"Fuck," Jonathan said.

"Yeah," May agreed. "The angel didn't seem all that interested, but Dimitri is going to daddy. And I can tell you one thing about the Deathless. He might not seem so scary, but he does not like being made to look stupid. And you are definitely not human anymore, Audrey, if that's your blood I've been tasting. You need to leave. Get the fuck out of Moscow, and now, because the way Dimitri was talking? They're going to ship you both to the Ireland Pen."

"She's right," Jonathan said. "Change your clothes, pack whatever shit you need."

"Jonathan," Audrey tried to protest, but he brushed by her, yelled down the hall for Aster, who came running with a few seconds, looking between them and May with wide eyes. Jonathan filled her in, and Aster's lips set in a firm line. She nodded and said to give her five minutes, and she disappeared.

This was it, Audrey realized. They'd run out of time, of options, of chances besides running—and hopefully running fast enough to find some way to save Nizhny. May touched her shoulder, her expression crestfallen.

"I'm so sorry," she whispered. "I mean, I knew they could break my encryptions on that tablet if they really wanted to get in. It's all tied to the Moscow network, which comes from ESC tech, but I just didn't think anyone would even notice me. They never do, I thought . . . I just wanted to help."

Audrey grabbed her hand, and May yelped in obvious pain. She frowned, realization hitting. "You only came at night to meet with us because the sun hurts you."

"Well, yeah. Dhampir," May said, shrugging.

Yet she hadn't even hesitated. She'd run right to them, not bothering to take a few seconds to spare herself injury, worried what those few extra minutes might have cost them.

Audrey hated this city.

For all the beauty and glittering magic, for all the books and art and wonder, she'd take her dirty, muddy, cold taiga town any day, without question. A place with a heart, a place where people cared even if they pretended they didn't. Not here, where no matter how good a person was, or how much they deserved to be free, they'd be forever shackled shallow cruelty.

"You're right. We need to leave." Audrey lifted her chin, tone firm as she said to May, "And you're coming with us."

"I'm what?"

Audrey pulled out her smaller bag and started stuffing things inside, including the journal from Zhang. She felt a pang of guilt and sadness that she couldn't say goodbye to her new friend in person. Maybe one day, they could share letters again.

Her vision blurred; she didn't have very many days left.

She sniffed, wiped her face.

Not now. She couldn't break now.

Over her shoulder to May, who still stood dumbfounded in the middle of her borrowed bedroom, Audrey said, "Nizhny is lovely this time of year. You'll like it, I promise."

"You . . . you want me to come with you?"

She sounded so unsure that Audrey stopped packing, stomped over to her, and pulled her into a tight hug. After only a second's hesitation, May returned the embrace with a shaking inhale.

"You risked everything to come warn us. I'm not leaving you behind. I've been wanting to ask you to come with us since you started helping us, because Moscow is awful and you deserve better than how you're treated here."

May's grip tightened, her fingernails digging in a little before she let Audrey go and stepped back. She blinked a few times, her eyes redder than normal, then cleared her throat.

"Okay, bitchin'. I hate this place anyway. What's the plan?"

Jonathan came back into the room then, tossing Audrey's travel boots—the well-worn pair from home, not the stupid, fancy, uncomfortable ones she'd been forced to wear since they arrived in Moscow. Aster came after, holding the missive from Nikita and a satchel stuffed with all her draughts and teas.

Audrey frowned when Aster placed them inside her travel bag. "Aster?"

"I will interfere," the cornflower wraith said. "They will still attempt to maintain the veneer, so if I claim you are indisposed, even ill considering yesterday, they may even wait a few days to attempt a maneuver. I imagine the spoiled boy will want all his pieces in place before he attempts another gambit that might embarrass him as the encounter in the plaza did. During that time, I will also get a letter to Nizhny. They will know, at the very least, what comes."

"What will Pyriel think?" Audrey wondered aloud. They'd barely had time to consider those consequences. "I act so terrified of him and Jonathan attacked him when he came near me. He's going to assume we're guilty when we vanish. And that we have something to do with Kushiel."

"Well, we do." Jonathan drawled, and Audrey sighed at his positively feral, proud expression. "What?"

"He is right," Aster said. "We cannot control the path of that angel any more than the one who came before him."

"Okay, fine, but what about you?" Audrey crossed her arms. "You really think I'm going to leave you here? I'm not leaving May here; I'm certainly not leaving you."

Aster regarded the dhampir, made a thoughtful little sound in the back of her throat. May grinned at her.

"Aster, you—"

"I am of the Earth, Audrey." Aster stepped forward, taking Audrey's face in both hands. "They cannot hold me here without well beyond the power they would wish to expend or have time to prepare before I slip away. I will see you again before the fate of our home is decided." Aster kissed her forehead, and Audrey felt a tingle on her skin—a blessing, she realized, and almost protested, but Aster tsked. "You have more than made yourself a child of the taiga, Audrey Doe. As you pass, so will that be known." She let her go, smiling, the bright gleam in her eyes dimming back their to normal, almost eerie glow. "Now," Aster asked, "how do we get you three out of this place?"

That was when Audrey noticed Jonathan shoving apples in his pack, along with the other food Aster had brought in from the sitting room.

She couldn't help a tiny smile.

"I have an idea."

Chapter 30

"**I** love this idea," May whispered as they walked through the Syn Koschei gardens. After getting May a pair of gloves, they'd packed everything they could reasonably carry. Audrey put E's enchanted chain back in place, and then they'd left through the window from the master bedroom, which put them about a hundred yards from the menagerie's entrance.

The gilded portcullis slid right open; the ruling family didn't expect to be defied.

From there they moved fast, but not too fast. Running drew the attention of magical beings, and the menagerie was filled to the gills. Audrey kept her head down because they needed to escape with their lives. She couldn't release all the creatures held hostage in this atrocious zoo, and if they lingered, she'd tried to find away.

When they arrived at the pegasi corral, May let out a soft whistle.

"Oh, wow. I've only seen them from across the plaza." She grinned at Audrey, the childlike wonder in her expression only firming up Audrey's feelings toward May since their first meeting. This was a good person with a good heart, destined to become a good friend.

Audrey's mind muddled with conflicting futures.

One where Audrey was alive to be May's friend, another where Nizhny wasn't crushed under Dimitri's wounded pride and cruelty. A future of any kind, she just . . .

She needed to focus.

Audrey handed Jonathan her backpack while she fished out two apples. The pegasi wandered over to the fence edge, ears perked under her attention. "You two should stay back."

"Yeah, we stink," Jonathan said to May, who snorted.

"Let me have the knife?" Audrey asked, her smile trembling.

Maybe Jonathan and May would be friends, if all else failed. If she had a son, would May stay? Would she help Jonathan, if Nizhny was gone, if she was gone, if Jonathan didn't lose himself entirely . . .

"Steady," he murmured, pressing the knife into her palm hilt first. She tucked it in her belt, so glad to be back in pants, even though she had to unbutton them and roll them down so her pregnant stomach hung over.

The baby chose then to kick, and hard, into her lungs. She let out a huff; right, if they didn't get out of this damned city, none of these futures would be possible for any of them. Back straight, spine tall, she approached the fence.

"Hi," she whispered. The stallion huffed, flapping his lips at her. He smelled the apples. "Yes, I have snacks for you both, but we need your help, please."

Both beasts stilled, and Audrey really hoped the pair were as intelligent as they seemed.

"We're in danger. We need to escape." Audrey offered the apples, and the pegasi accepted, watching her closely with liquid eyes. She pulled the knife out to show them and gestured at their bound wings. "Can you fly if I cut your binds?" That word—fly—got a reaction. Agitation, flattened ears and snorts. "And if you do, will you please take all three of us with you?"

She reached for E's necklace and commanded it to release, then tucked the chain and wooden ring in her pocket. The pegasi's nostrils flared at her new scent. Audrey put a hand on her belly.

"My child is in danger. My home is in danger. My friends," she gestured to May and Jonathan as she spoke, "are in danger. Please, can we help each other? Can we fly away from here together?"

The pegasi pranced in place now, the stallion huffing a few times, digging at the dirt.

"Doesn't seem like a no," Jonathan said as he stepped up, holding out his hand. The stallion sniffed his palm this time. That done, he helped Audrey over the fence and followed her. May joined them. Both the pegasi skirted away when she moved closer.

May winced. "Sorry."

"No, it's okay," Audrey insisted. They'd find another way if the pegasi rejected May. She took May's wrist and tugged her forward to the stallion. He reminded her a bit of Jonathan, with how protective he was of his lady. Audrey brought May's gloved hand to her own nose, then held it out. "She's a friend."

The stallion flattened his ears but stretched his neck until his nose touched May's fingertips. Another huff, and he tossed his head.

"We need to go," Jonathan said, motioning to the knife. "Other shit is paying attention."

Audrey couldn't help but look across from the pegasi enclosure, meeting the cold, intelligent gaze of that strange wolf bound and tied and caged. It watched from between the trees in its prison, white fur stark against dark green.

"We can't, sweetheart," Jonathan said, his lips against her temple. "Another ten minutes, we're going to have the wrong kind of company."

"I know," she exhaled and forced herself to turn away, tears stinging as she started cutting at the beautiful ribbons and glittered ropes woven between the stallion's wing feathers. He danced nervously at first, then stilled when the first tension released, as if he tasted freedom by inches. She kept sawing and cutting, wincing when a feather floated free, yet marveling at how they glittered in the late morning sunshine breaking between high clouds.

"Jonathan, you'll be faster," she said, hoping she'd done enough to earn the stallion's trust. He tensed when Jonathan took over, but two more snaps, and one wing was free. The flap battered them all. The mare trotted around in impatient circles.

"I can help?" May offered, peeling off the gloves to show thick white fingernails closer to claws. The mare lowered her head as she stepped nervously forward.

Audrey went first, gently petting her muzzle, her mane, then her neck. "You're very brave," she whispered as May stepped around to her wings. "I know this must be terrifying, but I promise, we'll all go someplace better. It's called Nizhny. Our home. It's a small place, and not as warm, but there are good people there."

Good people waiting for them to help save them. Somehow.

"Lots of wolves, too," she added, glancing again at the caged, strange wolf, who still stared at them. Did it understand? Would it find them, someday, if it managed to escape? "But they won't eat pegasi. They're very well behaved. And we have horses, too, furry ones that are stubborn and rude, but you can run with them, if you like."

May finished the first wing, and Jonathan came over to help with the second. The stallion darted around now, flapping wildly and jumping off the ground in higher and higher spiraling leaps.

"We take good care of each other in Nizhny," Audrey went on when the mare's muscles tensed under her petting, the whites of her eyes flashing toward the freed stallion. "And we would never, ever tie your wings like this. I swear it."

The last bindings came free. Jonathan and May stepped back, and

Jonathan caught Audrey's elbow, pulling her with them.

This was it. They'd fly, with or without riders on their backs, and Audrey clutched at Jonathan's shirt as the pegasi ran in a few circles, then launched themselves into the air, then came back down on the paddock, nudging each other and trotting pressed together.

She held her breath; she couldn't help it. She hadn't been able to think beyond this moment.

How would they get out of the city?

How much time could Aster buy them? Would it be enough?

Audrey squeezed her eyes shut, her forehead resting on Jonathan's shoulder, fatigue hitting her in a fresh rush; she was so tired, and they had so far left to go.

Warmth brushed her skin, the nuzzle at her cheek silken soft. Audrey opened her eyes as the stallion lowered one wing to make space for her to climb up.

They flew out of Moscow undetected, the pegasi soaring above the cloud layer in seconds that felt like eternity, and then they glided northeast and out over the open, wild continent.

But after only a few hours, the flying horses lathered, adrenaline and the thrill of freedom only carrying them so far. Audrey clung to the stallion's mane as they spiraled down toward a meadow with a winding stream, wondering how long these poor beasts had been bound. Jonathan jumped down and helped her off the stallion's back as soon as they landed, May dismounting easily from the mare. The pair nuzzled and circled each other before settling to drink greedily at the water.

Gods, her thighs and hips ached. Audrey rubbed her legs, grunting as her boots sank into the marshy soil. With the equinox only a few weeks out, melt and damp pretty much summed up the Siberian wilds. The tree line was only a few feet away, and Audrey frowned as May all but ran toward it and vanished into the shadows. She followed, her boots sucking with each step. Jonathan prowled nearby, both bags slung across his chest, assessing the area for threats and checking on the pegasi.

"Are you alright?" Audrey called as she reached cooler, darker space under the canopy, the soil a bit firmer here. May sat on the ground, back rested against a shaded trunk, still wearing her gloves and her hood pulled tight.

"Yeah," came the raspy answer.

"Yeah?" Audrey sat beside her. When she peeked forward, May sighed and tipped her head back against the bark with a soft thump. Her face, gods. Skin peeled across her nose and cheeks, her lips blistered and bloody. Now that Audrey was close to the dhampir, she smelled burnt hair. "Oh, May."

She waved a gloved hand. "I'll live."

"That doesn't mean you need to suffer." When Jonathan joined them in the shade, Audrey said, "We need to travel at night from now on."

"It's fine, really—" May went quiet when Audrey glared at her.

Jonathan chuckled. "Don't bother arguing with her when she's like this; you'll never win." To Audrey, he asked, "How you feeling?"

"Sore, but fine. How are the pegasi?"

"Exhausted. We'll probably need to walk them between flights and give them lots of down time. They smell happy though."

"That's good at least."

"How far is . . ." May trailed off, gesturing east.

"Nizhny," Audrey said, her smile widening, then falling.

"Far," Jonathan answered, tone flat. "Three days by train from Moscow. We'll make good time in the air, but these animals have no endurance in their wings. We're better than walking, and hopefully they can let us ride on the ground some, but it's going to be tight."

He meant getting back in time to try and advert all of the terrible outcomes for Nizhny. She still didn't know how they'd do any of that, but if they couldn't even make it before Dimitri's army . . .

"And you can get us there? Across the entire taiga?" May asked, the question directed to Jonathan, who considered and then shrugged.

"Think so. We'll have some clear markers once we get closer, and better getting eyes from up above. But we'll have to deal with at least one major river crossing, so hopefully they'll still be able to fly when we get to that point."

"At least it's not winter," Audrey muttered.

Jonathan grunted, slipping off the two packs and hanging them on a broken branch to keep dry. "Would be easier, aside from the cold. Gonna be all mire and moor and fucking swamp."

"Lovely," May grumbled.

Jonathan stood, dusting his hands. To May, he said, "How bad is daylight for you?"

"Dawn and dusk are fine, but even with the clouds, it's not great," she admitted. "But I can push through until we're farther out from Moscow."

"Nah, we're ahead for now. We got out clean far as I could tell, but if anyone is searching wide, they might already be looking for flying horses. Better to wait for night, fly low and fast as far as we can in one shot, then walk until morning. If you collapse, won't do any of us any good." That settled, he turned his attention deeper into the trees and brush. "I'm gonna scout around a bit. Seems quiet here, but not taking any chances. If they'll let you, try to rub down the horses. Hands or maybe a piece of cloth. It'll help some."

"Pegasi," Audrey corrected, and he smirked down at her. "What? I'd be annoyed if I was magical creature and someone called me a horse. They can hear you."

"Hmm." Jonathan's expression shifted, serious now, calculating. She took his hand and squeezed. "Anything goes sideways, you scream." To May, he said, "And anything looks like a threat? Kill first, ask questions later."

May gave him a salute.

Chapter 31

They quickly fell into a pattern. Jonathan scouted when they camped, hunted for food, and tried to keep the pegasi at ease. They'd warmed to him, probably because he rubbed them down after every flight and scavenged tasty snacks. May spent most of the time buried under moss and dirt to keep from burning.

Which left Audrey alone for hours at a time.

She was supposed to be resting, but it was hard to sleep during the day. The exertion of flying, riding and walking for hours and hours won over eventually, but it took Audrey hours before exhaustion won out over racing worries and anxious energy. She read before she slept most days, the journal Zhang gave her the only item in their bags not strictly survival related. And while reading passed the time while May stayed in cover and Jonathan prowled the taiga, it also served as a very uncomfortable reminder.

Not that she needed one. Her body might not be twisting into a monster yet, but everything ached. The baby had a knack for making her breathing difficult, and her feet barely fit in her shoes anymore they were so swollen. She rubbed at her belly a few times, but their child was stubborn. Hardly a surprise, was it? Audrey smiled, gazing wandering to where Jonathan had vanished into the tree line.

She sighed and opened the journal. The pegasi napped nearby under the bowers, May safely hidden away from the sun. She rubbed her face a few times, but she knew at this point she wouldn't sleep yet.

They'd been at this a week now. A grueling pace as the days fell away, and Nizhny seemed further and further out of reach. She traced the yellowed paper and tight, neat penmanship. Watermarks stained the edges, the pages wrinkled from age and damp.

The first page stuck with her.

Dearest Diary,

As it seems you will be the only the thing I ever see again, we might as well be friends. Lucky me, since these four walls and metal bars are my reward for an ill-advised and unremarkable fuck.

They tell me I can do a good thing by recording my spiraling descent into monsterhood and motherhood. Why? Who could possibly want to read this sad story? Poor Candice Steward, brothel whore, who spread her legs to the wrong duster. I'm sure my story isn't even original. But whoever reads this, I'll try to be entertaining at least?

There are two rats that must live nearby. I only know there's two of them because one is missing an ear. Also, the food here is terrible.

My advice? Do yourself a favor and don't get knocked up by a vile-blood.

-CS

Audrey paged to where she'd left off the day before. She was fast reader, and there wasn't much left in the journal, but she wasn't ready to read the ending. Instead, she shuffled through places she'd already read in the off chance she'd missed some crucial piece of information.

Dear boring paper friend,

I hate being pregnant. It's not enjoyable in the least, and I'm really, really not sure why anyone bothers. I'm fat, I pee all the time, and everything is uncomfortable. Not to mention being imprisoned.

It's been four months, which I only know because I'm writing the dates down, so thanks for that, I suppose. It's strange to document one's doom. My veins look darker, like his were, and I can definitely see in the dark now. I can hear better, too, which is not a gift because whoever they've locked down the hall is a mouth breather. Another one talks in their sleep.

I know it's not English, but I know what the words mean.

I have no idea what's happening to me.

Meals come from a metal armor suit that moves like a person but has nothing inside. Yesterday, it stepped on one of the rats. Tate, not Molly. And now Molly hasn't come back.

Gods, I want to go home.

Actually, I don't care where I go, I just don't want to be here anymore.

-CS

Audrey closed her eyes, resting her head against the bags, which made for poor pillows but probably better than CS had in her cell. She tried to imagine being told she would turn into a monster and then left alone in a prison cell waiting for it to happen.

Things could be worse, after all, Audrey thought with a huff.

The pegasi snorted, both shuffling to their feet with tails thrashing. Audrey tensed, trying to use her expanded senses, but everything smelled like mud and rotting plants, and she couldn't hear anything else besides pegasi. She pushed herself up with a hand on her stomach as she tossed the journal back into the satchel.

"Everything okay?" she called, making soothing noises as she approached them. Both pegasi twitched, wings snapping, ears back. Audrey gave them space; a misplaced kick wouldn't be good. The whites of their eyes flashed, both prancing nervously. Warm, thick air washed over Audrey from the trees, moist and earthy and foul. The stallion whinnied, the sound shrill, and both pegasi shot into the air in a flurry of feathers.

The troll burst through the trees, all three heads watching them fly away. It roared as they soared out of reach.

Gods, it was huge. Well over ten feet tall, drenched in mud, uprooted swamp matter and plants tangled around its thick legs and arms. Its hands were as big around as boulders, bumpy, molded skin slick with algae, brown and green and gray.

Audrey kept stone still, instinct thrumming at her to wait, that the creature might pass her over. Trolls weren't very smart and tended to be easily distracted. If she was lucky, it would chase after the pegasi, then Audrey could wake May so they could run.

The troll stomped, mud flying, snorting and gargling and spitting in rage. Two heads knocked together, then bit at each other. Wet, stringy hair tangled all the way down its back. An arm swung wide, reminding her of a child throwing a tantrum, and its fist split the nearest tree in half.

She had no choice but to move, the log hitting the ground hard, spraying muddy black water and pine needles in all directions. Audrey barely stayed on her feet, but the third head, which wasn't bickering with its mates, saw her movement. Murky yellow eyes stared her down, plump lips smacking over broken, uneven teeth. It clunked skulls with its neighbor, and six eyes found her.

Audrey screamed, "May!" as she fled for cover.

The ground quaked as the troll chased her, but it was massive and had to shoulder through the forest with the swamp land sucking at its feet. It was slow, but she wasn't much faster, her legs and feet so sore from riding and endless walking, her belly heavy, but she kept going, kept running, and screamed Jonathan's name.

A roar of pain echoed after her.

Audrey dared to look over her shoulder, her breath catching.

A flash of black and white in the gray-green landscape, flickering around like some sort of misty ghost, and the troll bled bright red.

May.

It held one face with a meaty palm as May materialized, claws and teeth bared, hissing as she slashed through the middle head's throat. Blood rushed, pouring down its massive body, and May wicked out of sight.

Something grabbed her, rough and fast enough to lift her off her feet, and Audrey thrashed, but then Jonathan's scent filled her nostrils as he put her behind him.

"We need fire," he barked before he sprinted forward with his blade drawn.

Of course. Trolls healed absurdly fast. Even if they took it down, it would recover in minutes. She hadn't gotten very far, and they had a lighter in their bag. Gritting her teeth, Audrey ran wide but back the way she'd come, her heart in her throat.

The sounds were awful. Rending flesh, May's ethereal hissing, the troll's roars of frustration. Branches snapping and breaking and shattering, birds shrieking and scattering to the air. Audrey barely dodged another felled tree, splinters stabbing into her arm and shoulder and scratching at her face, but she finally got around the fray and stumbled into the clearing.

There, just a few feet away. Their bags. She fell on them, breathing ragged, lungs burning, pulling out clothes, food, draughts, everything until she found the lighter. She ripped the sleeve off a spare shirt.

Gods, everything was so damp. She wrapped the cloth around a stick that wasn't soaked, hoping it would catch. She flicked the metal lighter open, struck it once, twice, and nearly cried at the small orange flame.

"Please, please," she whispered.

Both Jonathan and May were filthy, covered in troll blood and muck as they harried the giant creature, working in tandem to keep it off balance and furious.

The cloth caught, and Audrey cupped her hands around the tiny fire until it spread, and she'd done it; she'd made a makeshift torch. She felt like her heart was going to burst it raced so face, her entire body shaking, but Jonathan and May were in danger, and they needed her.

Jaw set, she gripped the wood in both hands and charged forward.

Jonathan saw her first, and his expression might have been terrifying if she didn't know him. Black eyes gleaming and teeth bared, the beast in his blood up and fighting. May was worse, her almost innocent features twisted into gleaming red smoke and fangs as long as Audrey's fingers.

But she didn't hesitate, struggling forward at Jonathan's signal. The troll turned as May scaled up its shoulders and dug her claws in deep. He grabbed the torch from Audrey and smacked the troll's leg.

The monster went up in a rush, and Audrey had never been more relieved for an Aperien to adhere to the legends it sprang from.

May vanished in a pulse of white mist as Jonathan grabbed Audrey and pulled her away.

And gods, its *screams*.

The reek of burning flesh.

Her head swam, holding tight to Jonathan's arms as darkness dotted the edge of her vision, consciousness dangerously close to slipping through her fingertips.

"I got you," Jonathan growled, his voice a harsh rasp. Audrey buried her face in his chest, focusing on his heartbeat and his scent, his arms a vice around her. Her belly, their child, tucked safely between them. She knew it didn't burn as long as it seemed, but silence eventually descended on the battered stretch of forest.

Jonathan's lips pressed against her hair when he mumbled, "It's over. It's dead."

Audrey nodded but didn't open her eyes, letting him hold her. The scent of burned flesh and pine made her stomach roil, but Jonathan was alive; he wasn't the one burning. In fact, he seemed to have made it out without a scratch. She double-checked him for injuries as he did the same for her. Her shirt was torn, her arm and neck and cheek scratched up, but it was all superficial.

"Is May alright?" When Audrey tried to turn toward the dead troll, Jonathan shifted into her view. She frowned up at him, he shrugged and let her see. The gasp came out before she could stop it.

May crouched over the dead troll, her mouth fixed on a throat. Her face and neck, the only part of her pale skin exposed, were blistered and weeping, her white hair all but seared away by the sunlight. But as Audrey watched her drink in hungry, desperate swallows, May's wounds patched themselves, with pale, fresh skin growing over the sunburns, and her hair coming back in curls. Her eyes stayed closed.

She drank like she'd die if she stopped.

"She's okay?" Audrey whispered.

"Think so, just give her a few minutes." Jonathan turned her away. Audrey let him this time. She didn't need to watch; it felt like prying somehow. "That thing get the pegasi?"

"No," Audrey said on a sharp exhale. "But they're gone."

"Yeah, figured as much." He caught her chin, made her look at him, open in his concern. "Are you okay?"

She squeezed his forearm. "Yes."

His eyes flicked to her belly. "The kid good?"

The kid in question decided this was the right time to wiggle, probably mad about being jostled around so much. She took his hand

and pressed it to her belly. "Seems like it."

Jonathan nodded, fixated on his palm against her swollen stomach. "Got a brave mom, kid."

Her breath caught; it was the first time he'd spoken to the baby, or about the baby in a way that wasn't just "the pregnancy" as a nebulous, looming threat. And they still hadn't talked about the end of this road. She touched his cheek, and those black eyes flashed to meet hers, and she knew he was still riled up from the fight, but . . .

"Jonathan, we need to talk about this."

"Is everyone okay?" May's voice was timid and strained, and they both turned to find her leaning on a tree in shadow, her hood pulled up but unable to hide her uncertain expression.

Jonathan pulled Audrey close, an arm slung around her shoulders. "Yeah, we're good. You?"

May licked her lips. They seemed redder than normal. "Uh, yeah, I mean I am now. Sorry you had to, uhm." She trailed off, not really looking at either of them now. "See all that mess."

Oh. May thought they were going to reject her after witnessing her feeding, the violence of the fight, or maybe how she looked when the dhampir let out those darker edges. Audrey leaned her head against Jonathan's chest.

If she only knew.

May had protected Audrey until Jonathan could, at risk to herself and suffering under the sunlight, without hesitation. And then she fought by his side, violent and deadly and seamlessly. Audrey smiled; she couldn't quite help it.

May would learn, though, and figuring it out on her own would have much more impact than Audrey interrupting now to tell her if Jonathan didn't trust her before, didn't consider her part of those he considered worth his time before this moment? He did now.

Jonathan waved a hand at May and grunted. Audrey's grin widened. He still hated admitting the world was bigger than the two of them sometimes, but she heard the undercurrent of his words even if May didn't yet. "Nice fighting back there. Rina's going to put you to work, just so you know."

Thank you. You're one of us now, Audrey wagered was what he was actually trying to say, in the best way Jonathan knew how. Praise and acceptance weren't things he'd had much of in his life before her and Nizhny; it warmed her how quickly he'd hand out what he'd lacked in his life when he felt it was earned. She wondered if *he* realized it.

She buried her face in his chest; she didn't want to ruin the moment by drawing attention to the two of them. Audrey figured they might be a little more alike than either of them realized quite yet.

"Oh," May said, then gave a little smile. "Yeah?"

"Yeah." Jonathan grunted again. "If we get back to more than ash."

"Right. Cool."

"You good if we stick to the shade?" Jonathan asked he packed up the mess Audrey'd made of the bags. She was too tired to help, or argue about helping. "Need to get away from here. Anyone comes across this mess, they'll know."

"I can handle it," May said. "After, uh, a meal that big, I should be good for a bit."

"Good, let's get moving then. From here, we're walking."

Chapter 32

I smell rust on the magical armor suit. If it falls apart, will I starve before I die?

The nightmares are getting worse. And pressure, inside me. Sometimes I imagine it chewing.

I tried to escape last night. Silly, I know, but I climbed the bars, and when I fell, I busted my lip open and the blood was black as sin. Black as his eyes. When I tried to spit more, I'd already healed.

I don't remember much of my mother. I was her third mistake, and unless I wanted to be like her, I need to find a way out. I didn't.

There are ridges under my scalp. They feel like bone, maybe, or scales? My ears are bigger. My fingers are longer. Last night, I broke through the stone wall, but it only led to another cell, and there was a man inside who smelled like soot and hells, and when he tried to touch me, I ripped out his throat and drank his blood and laughed. It felt good, I felt good, and when they came for the body, it was three metal suits, and my hands still smell like steel. But now the walls are all bars that smell like magic and danger, and I don't think I'll get that close to freedom again. But killing, now, that was a freedom I've never enjoyed, and I think it's quite unfair I might never get to do that again.

How can you give me wings and I don't get to fly. This place is too fucking small.

I think this is the last time I'm going to write. I look back sometimes, read what I've written, and I feel lucid. Like me. And those moments are coming less and less. I spent two days obsessed with the dirt under my fingernails because I could smell the prisoner I killed and I wanted to turn him inside out so I could eat his organs again. Thoughts like those come up and I lose myself. For days maybe, I don't know. I just wake up sometimes, and I feel like me for a few minutes before I start slipping away into whatever this is. I don't want to write some of the other thoughts, the deeper, darker ones that echo in my dreams. The ones that aren't mine, gods damn it. So, goodbye, diary, goodbye sad reader, and goodbye me. I hope when the end comes, there's none of me left at all. I'm throwing you outside of the bars so I can't reach you again. -CS

Audrey shut the journal. She should have waited to finish it, but it felt like a disservice to the woman—to CS, to Candice—to never finish the woman's story. She put it away now, wondering if anyone else ever read these pages. If Zhang absorbed this knowledge or passed it along to her without ever knowing what waited inside.

Did whichever Warden locked her away and handed her pen and the notebook even bother to read it after she died? Had it been Kushiel? Probably not, she decided. She couldn't see him bothering to give her pen and paper, caring nothing for her fate or others like her in the future.

And Audrey had learned nothing new about vileblood pregnancy, aside from the fact that she should have already started changing.

CS's shift to a polyglot and her heightened senses matched Audrey's experience. But around six and a half months into the pregnancy, the journal mentioned physical changes, like darkening blood. She wondered how much variance there was between different pregnancies.

Audrey rolled up her sleeve, but her veins were the same as they'd always been. Her eyes, she knew, were the same, because she asked Jonathan every day, and every day he answered, "Looks clear."

She leaned her head back and closed her eyes, trying to ignore how bad she smelled, how dirty she was, how far away they were from Nizhny while the equinox crept closer and closer. Ignoring the persistent ache in her hips. The discomfort between her legs. How her belly felt so, so heavy, and the baby . . .

At least she'd been too exhausted for more nightmares.

All three of them walked all night, every night, at least until Audrey flagged. Then Jonathan handed May their bags and carried Audrey for the last hours until dawn. They didn't talk about how there was no way in all the hells or heavens combined they were going to reach home in time.

Whenever they reached Nizhny, it would be to the aftermath. But they still walked every day, foot over foot across the taiga.

May did her best to stay positive, and it helped. "What's this town of yours like anyway? I've never been outside Moscow."

"Nothing like Moscow, that's for fucking sure," Jonathan grumbled as they picked their way over a particularly wet stretch of marshland.

"It's much smaller and not as fancy. No one uses magic for decoration. It's not an easy life, not really, but," Audrey considered for a moment. "It's honest. I think I like that the best. And as long as you're willing to work, and fight for your home and your neighbors, Rina will fight for you."

"Just don't piss her off."

Audrey rolled her eyes at Jonathan. "Well, if you can avoid it," she agreed. "Unless it's important."

Jonathan snorted as he lifted her over a fallen log. He jerked his head to another patch of forest in the distance. "That's the goal for tonight."

"Little early yet?" May asked, but she almost sounded hopeful.

"Yeah," was all Jonathan said, and Audrey knew it was because of her. She'd barely been able to peel herself to her feet this morning. Having a campsite in mind was Jonathan's signal he'd pick up pace to scout, and within a few minutes, Audrey walked alone with May. She kept close and caught her elbow when she stumbled a little bit.

"Sorry," Audrey mumbled. She wiped her forehead, sweating despite the cool night air.

"Don't be. Being you right now must be really shitty."

"It's been better," Audrey admitted, sharing a grin with her new friend before she sighed and turned away.

"You really don't think this Rina will find some sort of peace, huh?"

"I want to think so. She's a strong leader, but . . ."

"Pride? Lots of Aperiens have that problem."

Audrey considered, but shook her head. "Not exactly. I think she truly believes that giving Nizhny to Dimitri will ruin everything it stands for. And I don't think she's wrong, but I find it hard to believe the idea of Nizhny can only exist in that one spot. Maybe she'd rather break than bend, if she sees it as losing everything. I do believe she'll try to save as many as she can, if Aster was able to get her enough warning. But there's a lot of people—Aperiens and dusters—who feel they have nowhere else to go."

May waved hand and said, "That's pride," with a little snort. "There's always *something*. Sure, it might be shit, but dying is dead and done. And choosing to die because you lost? Isn't that just giving up?" May wrinkled her nose. "I'd been in that closet for years and I showed up every day. Honed my magic, learned other things. I mean, yeah, sucked being treated like shit, and I thought about fucking off more than once, but look right here."

May gestured between them. "I couldn't have helped you, couldn't've had a chance at something better, if I'd pissed it away because I had to do what the bigger, stronger assholes told me for a while. Can't beat them, join them or whatever, right? At least until you find something else to try."

It did sound much better than being dead, Audrey mused as she kept a hand on her stomach. She might not have much longer herself, but she wasn't going to give up either.

They'd only been camped a few hours when a peeping noise drew Audrey's attention. Lots of monsters liked to lure humans to their demise in the Siberian wilds. It was Audrey's turn to watch camp while May took a quick nap and Jonathan scouted.

The peep sounded again, like a baby bird.

Audrey inhaled and opened her mouth slightly, tasting as much as a smelling, with the technique Jonathan had taught her. Despite the fact that everything around here smelled wet and gross, she'd learned to scent both Jonathan and May's moods fairly well. It wasn't so hard since their moods didn't vary much beyond tired, frustrated, and ignoring everything else.

She didn't smell anything remarkable or unusual now, and the sound wasn't far. May slept close by, buried under a foot of loose dirt, and the dhampir's senses were almost as good as Jonathan's. And she didn't sleep, not really, more like a trance that left her sensitive to danger. May hadn't moved yet, so Audrey got to her feet and dusted off her pants.

This forest swung north, their camp at the very edge because the next stretch of miles they'd conquer was a desolate stretch of rolling moor. Audrey shivered; at least it wasn't raining again. She'd never take being dry for granted ever again. And she was thankful she wasn't entirely human anymore. Her feet might have fallen off by now. Every morning when they settled for camp, she had fresh blisters, her feet wrinkled and peeling, and by the time they picked up again in at sunset, it had all healed.

Audrey considered her wet boots, soaked socks, and her still recovering feet—it was only about ten in the morning—and decided she'd rather cut off her own feet than stuff them back in her boots before nightfall.

The pine needles were thick here, not too uncomfortable, but she still winced as she stepped barefoot into the forest, a hand pressed to her lower back and her stomach heavy against her hips. Gods, the ache in her groin got worse daily, and she swore the baby rested more on her bladder now than ever.

It didn't take long to find the source of the sound, a pair of baby birds fallen from their nest. She wanted to run right to them, but she imagined Jonathan's crossed arms and glare if got herself chewed up in a trap. She inhaled again and listened, but she smelled nothing besides the forest and damp soil. As far as she could tell, the baby birds were just baby birds.

The forest itself carried a tang of old magic, but it had for days. Jonathan had been on edge since they crossed into this area, irritated whatever lived here purposefully avoided them instead of coming out for a fight. May was less bothered, and said it felt uninterested more than anything else—and then she made fun of Jonathan for not feeling important.

It was the first time they'd laughed since they lost the pegasi.

Well, she hoped whatever lingered in this wood wasn't waiting until right now to lure her to her death with distressed baby animals, Audrey thought, because of course she'd fall for it. She sighed at herself, watched the struggling chicks for another minute or two, then decided whatever it was could very well deal with May's claws and Jonathan's knife if it decided to be so cruel.

Besides, the lingering feeling of these woods didn't bother her. She didn't know why, but the magic felt old, but never dangerous. Then again, her senses weren't entirely refined yet, but she swore it felt familiar. And not disinterested, like May and Jonathan expressed. She'd gotten the distinct impression they were being observed, and closely, yet not in a threatening manner.

"Alright, alright," she whispered and almost stomped on her way over to the crying babies. Gods, as if she could resist with her hormones, anyway. She felt a second away from tears listening to the poor, sad things and scooped them up from the damp ground, wrapping them in her shirt. "Sorry, I'm not very dry. Nothing here is dry, ever, I don't think." A quick once over showed they were both fine, and they quieted as she held them, their feathers downy soft, their eyes still closed. "How did you fall?"

Audrey squinted up, hoping to see the nest in the branches. Maybe Jonathan could climb up.

She didn't expect to find a face in the tree, with a trailing beard, and a crooked nose, and glowing green eyes.

She screamed. Really screamed, and tumbled backwards onto the dirt, still clutching the birds in the shirt.

May was at her side a second later, pulling her away, muttering,

"Shitshitshit*shit.*"

"Wait, wait," Audrey breathed, her heart racing. Gods, had she just had a heart attack? She grabbed May's arm to steady herself, the duster completely covered in dirt. "It's okay, I think."

She looked to the tree—the face in the tree—which blinked down at her as the branches quivered and bent into long, reaching arms. It crouched, the bowers groaning as they shifted and pine needles sprinkled down.

"Hello," Audrey offered, speaking Russian. "Thank you for letting us travel through your forest. We mean no harm and have only taken what we need to eat and drink, nothing more."

May swallowed. "Is that a leshy?"

Audrey nodded but kept her focus on the leshy. Treeman, she recalled Zhadan yelling about Aspen, and she'd never felt more homesick in her life. Audrey held the birds out, cupped in both palms.

The tree creaked as a third branch—arm?—extended, and she grinned, she couldn't help it. It held a nest in the cradle of twiggy fingers, a raven perched on the edge. When it saw the chicks, it cawed and cawed, absolutely furious. Audrey put the chicks in the nest and got her fingers pecked as a reward. The branched lifted, nest and birds disappearing into the canopy.

"Thanks," Audrey said.

The leshy blinked, the motion slow, deliberate, before it finally spoke, a voice that carried on the wind, deep and resonant and wise, the Russian dialect so old it was almost difficult to understand. "You are Audrey Doe of Nizhny."

May's hand tightened on her arm, and Audrey smelled her worry. She patted the dhampir's hand, hoping she'd relax, while also hoping Jonathan didn't arrive attacking; he'd be here any second with his blade out.

"I am."

"You brought safety to Aspen in place of axes. You forged a peace between the warriors and the trees."

"I helped," she offered. "Katerina Yaga is a good leader, a strong Independent, and Nizhny is better for having Aspen as part of our home."

"You are modest," the leshy said, what sounded like a chuckle echoing around them. "You came with nothing, risked yourself, and eased a peace."

"I did what I could," Audrey said with a shrug. "As much as I hope anyone would have been willing to try."

The leshy rustled. "You are far afield."

She laughed at the understatement. She couldn't help it. "We're trying to get home," she whispered, wiping her eyes. Why was she crying now? "Nizhny is in danger. The Dominion is planning to attack after the equinox. We just need to get home." She pressed the heels of her palms into her eyes, leaning into May when she tightened an arm around her shoulder. "I don't know what to do."

Silence stretched, the wind whistling through the forest, the crow still yelling at them, the leshy ancient and calm, and for the first time since leaving Moscow, Audrey took a deep, long breath, heather and lavender and wild chamomile fresh and heavy on the air.

"I am Larch."

Audrey blinked up at the leshy. She hadn't known until after the fact that Aspen sharing its name with her—a human girl, outside its mythos, hardly worthy of being considered a friend mere moments after meeting it for the first time—was significant. Most leshys never named themselves, and when they did, it was the tree most prominent to their magic. They didn't even name themselves to each other, not really, but when they used names, it was a way to honor those who walked their woods and earned their boons.

"Oh," she whispered. The larches were amazing trees, flashing golden for a few weeks in the year and making the cold forest bright. "That's a beautiful name. Thank you for sharing it with me."

"You wish to return to Nizhny?"

"Yes, please. We do."

"We will help."

Jonathan burst upon them, knife out just as she expected, slowing when he saw the leshy, then Audrey, before he shook his head and put away his weapon. He nodded to the leshy, moving slower now as he came to her side, kneeling down to help her to her feet with May. Jonathan smirked at her, then pressed his lips to her forehead.

"Can't leave you alone for five minutes, can I?" he mumbled, but she scented amusement and relief in his scent. She nuzzled into him, exhaustion and relief bone deep.

Maybe they'd make it after all.

Chapter 33

T hey knew from their interactions with Aspen that the leshys possessed vast power over the stretch of forest they called home, with eyes and ears everywhere within the trees and nurturing the animals and plants that lived in their borders. They could bar passage to those unwanted, or twist and turn the brambles and leave trespassers lost until they died.

They could also make a path through their territory, one that didn't abide by rules like miles and time. And that was how they closed the distance to Nizhny by leaps instead of inches.

There were so many leshys spread out over the Siberian taiga. Aster's words echoed back to Audrey, when she'd scolded Rina for wanting to fight Aspen for an easy solution. If the leshy were willing to help them because they were Aspen's friends, an army of angry treemen would have spelled the end of Nizhny months ago.

Audrey was also reminded that she absolutely *hated* her name.

Every time they crossed into another leshy's range, she'd call out her name, Audrey Doe of Nizhny, and ask if they would please help them get home. The trees would part. Sometimes they would meet a new leshy. Sometimes the way would simply open, and they'd hop-step their way across another stretch of Siberia.

But Doe was a name for a human with no family, no ties, and in some case, no identity or life at all. Every time she called out into the woods asking for passage, it grated, because she wasn't that girl anymore.

That was another problem for another time, because they were making up ground and fast. By Jonathan's best guess, they might hit Nizhny before the equinox.

But even as they gained time, Audrey knew hers was running out.

She was barely seven months along, but Audrey *knew*.

This, she wagered, must be when the vileblood curse settled over her. It matched the journal's story with when Candice lost her humanity and never picked up her pen again.

It started with a shift in the way her stomach sat, the weight in her belly dropping even lower into her hips. She had to stop more to relieve herself, to rest, constantly rubbing against the discomfort. Audrey didn't say anything, just kept walking. They had to keep moving. They didn't have time to change clothes, didn't have many extra clothes anyway, and she avoided looking at her own skin. For all she knew, she was sprouting wings or scales where her spine throbbed and ached with every step.

That was two days ago.

They still traveled by night and rested under leshy protected trees during the daylight. Stretches between enchanted woods were few and narrow, so they didn't spend much time knee deep in bog and swamp, which was good. Audrey felt two seconds away from falling asleep on her feet all of the time now. She probably would have tripped if they weren't walking on smooth dirt paths laid with ancient magic.

She couldn't seem to cool down, though the weather remained mild, especially under the canopy. Every once and a while she felt a twinge, or a sharper stab of pain, and those she decidedly ignored.

But the pain happened more often.

Maybe she needed a little more rest. She could steal a few more hours next time they stopped. She couldn't catch her breath today.

"Hey, you alright?" Jonathan had stopped walking, May coming up behind her. They always made her walk in the middle.

"I need to pee again, but otherwise . . ." She shrugged. She wouldn't ask to stop early, at least not yet. Audrey could push herself another hour at least. But when Jonathan studied her longer than normal, his concern and doubt blatant across those handsome, dirty features, she stuck out her chin. "My feet hurt, I'm grumpy, I'm tired, and I want to be home."

Before I'm not me anymore.

Or dead.

When Jonathan frowned, something in her snapped.

"Of course I'm not *alright*, nothing is *alright*, but we have to keep walking! So let me pee in peace, then we'll keep going."

With a huff, she headed off into the brush, grumbling, because grumbling was about all she could do at this point, because she was pretty sure she'd just peed herself in her little angry fit.

Out of view, she wrestled down her pants, but then froze.

No, it wasn't . . .

She checked her garments, which were soaked.

And streaked with red.

Audrey closed her eyes, breathing through her nose.

She'd read the midwife books, and she knew all the signs of pre-labor and false labor had been creeping around for at least two days, if not longer.

She just . . .

This could not happen.

Not now. Not this close to home.

Nizhny needed them; this couldn't happen now.

"Audrey?" Jonathan's voice snapped through the branches, startling her, and in another second, both he and May knelt beside her.

His nostrils flared, but May was faster. "I smell blood," she said, immediately scanning her for injuries.

Audrey shook her head, pulling at Jonathan's sleeve. Was it now? Was this the moment? She needed to know, she needed . . . "My eyes, Jonathan, are they? Is it?"

"No, sweetheart, they're fine."

"Okay." She exhaled, harder. "Okay. I'm bleeding, but just a tiny bit and . . . and I think . . ." She squeezed her eyes shut, whispering, "It's too soon."

No one spoke, the three of them kneeling in the underbrush off the perfect path the most recent leshy, a silent observer, had carved through the forest. A bird took flight nearby, disturbing the leaves, but then it went quiet again. She pressed her face into her palms, trying to blot out the entire world.

Then Audrey was being lifted, tucked close to Jonathan's chest. "We push, fast and hard. You'll need to deal with the sun."

May said, "Of course," before Audrey could form any argument, and the dhampir led the way back to the path. "How fast?"

"However fast you can pace and not burn out."

"How long do we have?"

That question was for Audrey. She looked to Jonathan first, his expression a grimace, then May. Her expression was almost comical, her red eyes were so wide.

"I don't know."

"Alright, well." May shifted the bags and gave a stiff nod. "Do me a favor and let me know if that changes."

She set a grueling pace. Jonathan kept up easily.

They made it about ten hours before the contractions truly started. Audrey closed her eyes and tried to breathe, clutching at Jonathan's shirt as they jogged along. Another leshy greeting, another stretch of magically shortened forest as they jump-stepped across more taiga. Jonathan squeezed her tight every time the pain spiked.

"I need a few minutes," Audrey finally begged. Every motion hurt, each step jolting her body. "Please, I need to stop." Jonathan did, but before he could set her down, she asked again, for at least the twentieth time in the last hour, "My eyes?"

"The same."

But he moved back a step and frowned, nostrils flaring. She smelled it too. Her water had broken, the fluid soaking through her pants and his shirt, thick with the scent of blood.

Audrey ran her hands over the veins in her wrist and forearms, still a pale blue.

"We're almost out of this stretch," May called as she jogged back toward them. She grimaced when she looked between them, setting the bags down. Audrey didn't miss the way May's gaze followed her fingers tracing her veins.

"May," Audrey grabbed for her, the idea barely formed as she blurted, "Check my blood."

"What?" May recoiled, but Audrey didn't let go.

"The curse, check it, please. Maybe you can . . ." She looked to Jonathan, who knelt at her other side. The fact that he didn't protest spoke volumes. "Please, I need to know."

May looked like she might be sick, but at Jonathan's weary nod, she lifted Audrey's wrist toward her mouth, pausing with a little head shake and a mutter. "Never fed from a person."

Before Audrey could process the guilt at hearing those words, it was done. Barely a pinch, barely a sip, and then May licked her skin and pulled back, no mark left in her wake.

She swallowed, then huffed. "You don't taste anything like a vile-blood, Audrey."

None of this made sense. "How?"

"I don't know, but your blood is a very powerful mix of god and angel, with almost no human." May squinted. "I mean, it's not so far off Gunnar's blood, but it's not tainted." She shrugged at him. "Sorry."

Jonathan waved a hand, his "How," more of a demand than a question.

"If I had any idea, maybe we wouldn't be running our asses off across this fucking swamp forest?" May stood. "I'm going to scout ahead. I think I heard water." And she darted off, her speed startling, her form mist-like as she faded into the distance.

"Check my hair," Audrey said, remembering the journal, grabbing at Jonanthan's arm again. "Check my ears and my hair. My back." She tried to move, but a contraction lanced through her, this one so sharp it made her yelp.

After it passed, Jonathan brushed her sweaty hair from her face. "Take a breath, sweetheart. You're still you."

"Okay, but, even if that's, even if? But it's too soon."

"Yeah."

"And w-we didn't talk about—"

"We don't need—"

She all but screamed at him, clutching his shirt, shivering on her knees on the muddy path. "Jonathan, if our child lives, you have to love him."

He went utterly still in that way he had when he turned inward. He didn't look at her, not directly, his gaze unfocused. She couldn't breathe through another stab of pain, gripping his forearm as the wave rippled through her, leaving a dull, persistent ache behind.

The contractions were still spaced out, and there had only been a few truly strong ones. Maybe they had more time. False labors weren't uncommon. Audrey read all about them, but there was something deeply instinctual, perhaps in the unintentional gifts the mother of monsters gave her blood, because Audrey knew . . .

This was happening.

Their child.

And she had no idea what it would mean.

Where it would end.

"Jonathan," she whispered. He pressed his forehead hers. His hand cupped her nape. He didn't speak. She wasn't sure he was breathing. "You told me you'd give me anything. If this child lives, love it for us both."

Nothing.

Her body shook harder; she had no control over it. Her hands were so cold. "Please, Jonathan . . ."

"Don't." He bit out. "Don't leave me, how about that? Don't leave *us*." There was a growl to the words now, a fierceness that made her chest ache. "You hear me?"

She wanted to say yes. She wanted to believe she could say yes to him, promise him, but if it ended up being a lie . . .

"Hey guys," May called, running back toward them full tilt, glancing back over her shoulder ever a few steps. "We have . . . uh . . ." The dhampir gave a helpless shrug. "I don't even fucking know, seriously."

Behind her, the path had opened, the trees unfolded like an accordion into a clearing that was not there when they stopped a few minutes ago. And just beyond where the tree line ended waited a cabin, overgrown with moss, neatly tucked beside a willow tree and an iridescent, green pond. A few raised garden beds framed a cobble-stone path, lush with out of season vegetables and herbs. There was a crooked weather vane, off center from the roof's high point. A toad croaked, a loud bark into the otherwise silent woods.

The hut had chicken feet.

And the door was open.

Chapter 34

“That’s . . .” May swallowed a few times. “That’s the crazy one’s hut. The sister who went nuts and ran off years ago. The big sister. *The* Baba Yaga.” She shook her head. “Do you guys just have the worst fucking luck or something?”

Jonathan smirked. “Or something.”

Audrey huffed. “This might not be bad. Baba Yaga is . . . ah . . .” She cut off as another contraction hit, closing her eyes and focusing on breathing. Gods, they were lasting longer and becoming more painful. “She’s Rina’s mother.”

“Fucking shitballs,” May muttered, watching the hut like it might walk on over and eat her.

Not really that outlandish, but . . . “There’s no way this is an accident.”

As if the hut itself had ears, or a very powerful Aperien inside listening to their conversation, the door opened further. The glow inside was warm, tinted green, and Audrey smelled a warm hearth.

“Can I stay outside?” May whimpered.

Audrey couldn’t help a little laugh. “That would probably be rude.”

They had nothing to offer for any hospitality customs. And she had no idea how they were supposed to act around an Aperien this powerful who had gone mad, but Jonathan scooped her up, his expression grim.

"You're bleeding. It's getting worse. We don't have time to fuck around."

There really wasn't a better option. May followed close, so close she stepped on Jonathan's heels twice by the time they scaled the creaking stairs and stepped onto the porch. The door remained open, the light from inside warm, the smells coming from within homey and pleasant. A stark contrast to the swampy forest they'd been trudging through for days. Inside was a simple room, with a wood burning stove lit under a black steel cauldron. Steam wisped, smoke winding up and out the chimney. Dried herbs, an abandoned knitting project, and an old rocking chair, paint worn away on the arm rests.

In the chair sat Baba Yaga, rocking as they peered into her home.

She looked nothing like Rina.

And very unlike her sister in Moscow, as she made no effort to mask what she was: Swamp Witch. Bog Hag. Ancient with one foot in the grave. One of the many, many monsters who prowled the Siberian dark.

But like many monsters, Baba Yaga was one who'd shed her myth's mantle for a better life, at least until the man she loved died.

Baba Yaga wore a plain frock over her wrinkled, greenish-grey skin, folded hands ending in black fingernails. Her hair dripped with moisture, unkempt and sticking to her cheeks and neck. Her nose was huge, her most prominent feature, curved so far it nearly touched her thin, cracked lips. She watched them with the same yellowed-rotten gaze as her sister, a color far too unique to forget, but she only had one eye.

The witch didn't move besides rocking, back and forth, back and forth, as Audrey tried to wrangle her newly developing instincts.

Her hindbrain screamed at her to run.

This was by far one of the most dangerous Aperiens she'd ever encountered.

Theodore was part god and part dragon, and he paled. Zhang, a god himself, was either really good at holding himself diminished, or the defected god of knowledge simply didn't wield danger in his every cell like this woman did. And Jaga Baba had done nothing to mask her own power—she'd openly flaunted it at dinner simply because she could—and it was clear, hands over fists, this Baba Yaga was more powerful than her sister counterpart.

Audrey gritted her teeth, patting Jonathan's arm so he'd set her down. He did, but he kept an arm tight around her chest. She wasn't going to be rude just because Baba Yaga was strong and dangerous. That sounded like the perfect way to get them all killed.

Instead, she offered a shaky smile. "Your daughter is doing very well. And she's happy."

The witch stopped rocking and returned her smile, and it felt like spiders skittering across Audrey's skin. Blackened, broken teeth with gray salvia stringing along her tongue when she finally spoke, her voice remarkably clean and clear by comparison.

"The trees whisper about you, you know," she mused, never blinking. "That's how I found you in all this forest. Chatter from the leshy, and they rarely make a sound, all about trying to get a girl home." Baba Yaga canted her head. "You are Audrey Doe of Rina's Nizhny."

Gods, the name again. She opened her mouth to—what, she wasn't sure. Ask the powerful witch to call her just Audrey?—when another contraction nearly drove her to her knees. Jonathan kept her on her feet until it passed, fresh sweat breaking out across her entire body, head to toes, in the warm humidity of Baba Yaga's den.

When Audrey blinked up, Baba Yaga watched with eternal patience, then hummed before she peeled herself from her rocking chair. Her bones crisped and crackled as if she hadn't moved her body in years.

"And you're kind as they chatter," Baba Yaga said, though she seemed to be talking to herself as she shuffled toward a rusty pump-sink in the room's corner. Audrey realized then the room didn't seem to go anywhere else. No stairs, no other doors. "Most would walk in with threats, or big fancy introductions, or desperate pleas for wishes. Not you." A dry chuckle. "You come in clinging by a thread and first you tell me my daughter is well."

Baba Yaga worked the pump, which whined at first, then garbled before murky water poured into the basin. "I know my daughter is well, but your kindness is not unappreciated. There hasn't been a day I haven't kept an eye on that girl, mad or not." She tapped under the missing eye.

"You watch over Nizhny?" Audrey couldn't help but ask.

"I watch over nothing, no. I *observe* my daughter for my own piece of mind. All she's done, she's done herself." She stopped the water, setting the full bowl on the counter. Audrey blinked a few times; it was clean now.

"Rina misses you," Audrey said, desperate to keep the conversation going. The Aperien seemed wistful almost, talking about her daughter. And she had no idea why Baba Yaga had found them on the taiga.

"She misses her family still, an open wound, the life the three of us shared before Ilyes died," Baba Yaga answered. The bowl steamed, the water hot, and the witch laid out towels and clean cloth strips as she spoke. "That is gone."

"She worries about you. She doesn't talk about you often, but part of what she does, why she works so hard, it's for you." Jonathan's arm tightened in warning, but Audrey ignored him. "She doesn't want your name to be shamed. Or forgotten."

The witch hummed again, pinching out herbs here and there, then wrapping and tossing them into the bowl.

"If you visited, even once, to let her know," Audrey trailed off, because the witch in front of her didn't seem crazy, but maybe she made a dangerous assumption.

"To know I'm not an old loon, eating paint and mushrooms in the dark?" Baba Yaga flashed a grin, both terrifying and almost charming.

"Pretty much," Jonathan drawled.

The witch laughed this time, the sound nails on broken glass. Another contraction came, and by the time it passed, Audrey found herself carried over and set in the witch's rocking chair, which now had a very comfortable cushion. May remained at the open door, paler than normal.

"My madness is not what you think. Grief runs different insanity, and I'm better off out here in the dark where I can't cause problems. Besides," she said as she waved a hand, "Rina's claim is still new. Ley lines draw, new mythos write, and magic learns. If I came to Nizhny, I'd push and pull by existing, and knowing my daughter, she'd try to give me her dream if she thought it might recapture our past.

"No. I won't take from that girl, not when she works so hard for a dream worth fighting over. Maybe in another fifty, a hundred years? Maybe then I can walk in her fledgling myth and not threaten it with my own. All of which is neither here nor there, girl." The witch pointed at her. "I can smell that child reaching for the world. It comes now. And as the equinox begins, no less."

Audrey shook her head, but Jonathan barely had to push a gentle hand on her shoulder from where he knelt beside the chair. "We need to get to Nizhny and warn them."

"Yes, about my little nephew and his army. Hm. There's time. He's not brave enough to harness the power of a day like today; he'll march on the next dawn."

"But," Audrey gasped out, clenching her fists. "We don't have time. Nizhny doesn't have time."

Deflection and they all knew it.

She wasn't ready to have this baby.

To face . . .

She couldn't stop the sob.

Gods, she didn't want to die. She didn't want to leave her family. She couldn't.

Baba Yaga rolled up her sleeves. She dipped the cloth in the water, then wrung it out. "I might not be able to step into Nizhny, but I can bring you beside it with a wave. Now, this baby."

"Not yet," Audrey gasped, gritting her teeth, the pressure growing low between her legs. "Not yet, please. I'm not ready . . ." She looked to Jonathan, his expression a stone wall. Tears slipped, another sob.

She wasn't ready to say goodbye.

"Your fear won't keep this baby in your body, girl. It comes and soon. So you need to tell me, Audrey Doe of Nizhny, if—"

"Don't call me that," she gasped out, ignoring the danger of interrupting *Baba Yaga*. She squeezed her eyes shut and shook her head, then turned on Jonathan. "Will you marry me, please?"

He blinked once. "What?"

"I'm not a Doe, not anymore. You don't have to bind yourself to me or make me your mate, or whatever. No magic, just the human way, just so I can have your name. I want to be Audrey Gunnar of Nizhny, because I'm yours, and I'm not . . . I'm not *no one* anymore, with no family, and nothing, and I—"

He grabbed her face, his forehead pressed against hers. "Whatever you want, sweetheart. You gave me a name, seems fair I give you one back. Yeah, I'll marry you."

"Okay, okay," she whispered out between hiccups, then let out a sharp cry at the next contraction. Gods, they were getting closer, faster. And they *hurt*. And she knew it was just going to get worse.

And . . . more fluid leaked down her thighs.

Blood.

Aside from being early, something was wrong. With her body. She whimpered, glancing desperately between Jonathan, Baba Yaga, her stomach. His lips pressed her temple.

"Still hazel. Still you."

"Well, if that's settled, Audrey *Gunnar* of Nizhny," Baba Yaga said, her tone amused of all things, "do you permit me to be your midwife?"

Audrey felt Jonathan's hackles rise, and although he did his best to cover it, his voice was a snarl when he said, "Anything you take in trade, you take it from me, not her, you hear me? I did this to her, so I'll pay."

The witch snorted. "The pair of you, tooth rotting, truly. What I *ask* is that you let me first deliver this child, so I can then deliver your Audrey to my daughter in time to influence the fates. A simple, uncomplicated exchange of services. As I swear it upon the blood of my sisters, my ties to the deepest witch blood, and my Rina's soul." Baba Yaga smirked. "Good enough for your honor, vileblood?"

"I can't," Audrey blurted before Jonathan could argue, or agree, or whatever came next. "The curse . . . we . . . I . . ."

"Ah." The witch gathered her bowl, the clean towels, and a pair of shears—the last making Audrey's head swim—and set them on the rug a few feet from where Audrey sat in the rocking chair. "Look at me, Audrey Gunnar of Nizhny."

Jonathan retreated far enough for Baba Yaga to close the gap and take Audrey's jaw in her palm.

"Seven months and a handful of days," the witch said as she inhaled. "And your eyes aren't black, the blood in you as red as roses still." She canted her head, not looking at May when she asked, "And what did you taste in her veins, scared little dhampir?"

May's voice was barely a whisper. "Angel, god, and human, but the human is fading. No vileblood."

"You don't trust her tongue? Your own eyes? Your body?" Baba Yaga's skin was cold and clammy, yet somehow comforting.

"I don't know," Audrey whispered. "We searched everything. I read a journal written by a woman up until days before she lost her mind. We . . . there's nothing to tell us how to break the curse."

"The dhampir gave you the answer, because fewer things are more reliable than how blood tastes. You're not cursed, you never were, because you broke it from the start. And isn't it quaint that a curse steeped so deep in hate could only be overcome by love?"

Audrey opened her mouth, shut it again.

"Lucifer and Lamashtu were incredibly powerful, together near unstoppable, but a curse becomes even stronger when it can be bro-ken—especially the further afield the solution lies. The more unlikely for it come to fruition. Feeds the roots, twist them deeper, the longer the curse persists and the longer it goes uncompromised.

"And true love is a deep, old mythos, so it anchors and sings when woven into magic. Few things are quite so eternal. And a human to love a vileblood? The threat to their humanity? And a vileblood to love a human? When one with a good heart would never risk the curse to begin with? Unlikely, to say the least. Yet, here you sit. Alive and well and untainted, because of that love."

"That's really it?" Jonathan asked, his tone utter disbelief. "After all this shit, that's really it? She's not gonna die?" He swallowed. Audrey grabbed his hand. "Seems a little too easy."

"It is, in a sense, but not the ease you imagine." Baba Yaga chuckled again, and there was a certain malice, a cold appreciation in her what she said next that made Audrey shudder. "You didn't kill this human girl. Whatever the babe, it will not propagate the vileblood curse. And yet, *they* have still won."

"What do you mean?" Audrey whispered.

"You are not human anymore, girl, and by the time this babe leaves your body, you'll not have a drop of humanity in your veins. And this child will not be a human either. Even if love saves every vileblood pregnancy, it still removes two more humans from the world. Bringing Lucifer and Lamashtu's desire to see the dreamers die, to see humanity end, that much closer to fruition." Babg Yaga shrugged. "Truly brilliant, I must say. And of course, utter madness, as we still have no way of knowing what happens to magic if the dreamers that created it cease to exist."

Baba Yaga patted her cheek. "Now, are you ready then?"

Probably not, Audrey knew, turning to Jonathan, who watched her with an expression she knew she mirrored. Hope. She didn't look away from him, those black eyes, as she said to Baba Yaga, "I, Audrey Gunnar of Nizhny, accept your terms as my midwife."

She didn't have much to go on, but the labor . . .

It was the worst pain she'd experienced in her life. And it went on for hours.

Hours.

Jonathan supported her now, her back against his bare chest, both of them drenched in sweat. She'd left indents in his skin where her nails dug in, holding on for dear life as the contractions got worse, and faster, and assaulted her over and over and over again.

She bled. Things inside her body tore.

She wondered again about the mother of monsters and her gifts, because Audrey knew this birth should have been killing her, and somehow she kept going.

Baba Yaga remained between her legs, coaxing and mumbling, unconcerned. Jonathan muttered encouragement against her temple. May paced, chewing at her nails. Everything sounded like senseless noise. She smelled her own blood, so much blood, the birth fluids, Jonathan and both their sweat, his tinged with fear and frustration and adoration. Hers tanged with pain, worry, and anticipation.

Hours ago, she panicked, convinced the baby was stuck and they were both going to die and there was nothing anyone could do.

The witch chided her, asking her what good would her mythos be about eating babies if she couldn't deliver them properly in the first place?

For some reason, it helped her feel better.

She drifted in and out of consciousness a few times, Jonathan's voice an anchor that pulled her back each time.

Now, she just wanted it to be over.

She panted, fresh tears falling.

"You're good, sweetheart, so good," Jonathan murmured, and she let out a sob.

She wanted to hold their child, because they would, together. They would, and . . .

Audrey let out a growl to rival Jonathan, Baba Yaga barking orders about pushing again, and harder, and now, and Audrey listened even though she felt like she was ripping in two, and *she couldn't*, but then the pressure gave with a rush.

"Again, girl, almost done."

The next push was easier, like her body knew what to do, and with a slick slide, the baby left her body. She turned her head into Jonathan's neck, sobbing, and he soothed her, shushing, and a second later, there came a sharp wail, once, twice, and then a steady cry.

"A boy, then," Baba Yaga said, bringing the squirming, tiny baby toward her. She clutched him to her chest, staring down, vaguely aware of Jonathan using the eversharp knife to cut the cord. The afterbirth came without trouble.

"She's still bleeding," Jonathan growled, a desperate lilt to his words, frantic need, the scent of him, his rising panic, nearly drowning.

"And were she still human, she wouldn't stop. Yet she heals. God and angel, remember?" Baba Yaga waved a bloody hand in his direction, clicking her tongue. "Vileblood in gifts, but not in curses."

Jonathan relaxed a fraction, but Baba Yaga was right. She felt her body righting itself, knitting back together, but she still felt woozy from the blood loss, her entire world hazy as she cradled the life they'd made in her arms.

"So small," Audrey whispered. Their baby stopped crying, going utterly still at her voice. He was damp, slick with birth and blood, with dark curls wetted to his scalp and angry tight fits. He barely overfilled her two hands, and he almost weighed nothing, his limbs long and skinny, but he was whole. A whole, tiny person that came from her body. "Look at you."

And he looked up at her face and blinked a few times, and Audrey's breath caught.

His eyes were a clear, beautiful hazel.

Jonathan's hand cupped the baby's head, so huge by caparison.

"Early, but healthy. He's small yet, and will catch a chill easy, so extra blankets. Let him suckle; both of your bodies know what to do." Baba Yaga took the bowl and rags, dropping them in the sink and pumping to wash her hands. She brought over a bundle, wrapped tight. "There are a few ways to deal with the afterbirth, but it has power. Kept it safe until you decide."

"Thank you," Audrey said. "I don't know how—"

"You do," Baba Yaga said, firmly. "I can give you three hours rest, then I'm dropping you at the Nizhny border. You already know how you pay this debt." The witch clapped her hands. "And this boy needs a name."

Audrey laughed, resting her forehead against Jonathan's cheek as he petted his son's head, looking absolutely lost. They'd never talked about names. He wailed then, snuffling at her breast, and after a few angry snorts, he latched.

Baba Yaga waved to May. "Come, dhampir, help me with my weeding, and give the new family a moment's privacy."

They left and Audrey sighed, nuzzling Jonathan's cheek, inhaling the wonder in his scent—that had to be what she smelled, because she'd never scented anything like it on his skin before. Profound and gentle and perfect.

Then she grinned and whispered, "We could call him Junior?"

Jonathan laughed, really laughed, a full blow guffaw that had her giggling, then wincing, her stomach aching and empty. He knocked his head against hers, rolling his eyes before he gave her a soft, sweet kiss, and whispered, "Told you already, anything you want."

Chapter 35

Three hours went quick. Audrey dozed as their son fed, then napped on her chest. When she woke, she couldn't believe how much her body had already recovered from the birth. The benefits of being vileblood . . . No, not vileblood, and no longer human? God and angel? A concept Audrey was having trouble wrapping her mind around, but being able to heal quickly? Gods, it was a boon after everything. It didn't shake the bone-deep exhaustion, but it was a good start.

The baby was furious when she handed him to Jonathan so she could dress, squalling and thrashing as soon as he was taken from her arms. A sharp scold from his father and he startled, then stared at Jonathan in fascination. Baba Yaga helped her make a wrap tight around her body and then tuck him away safe and warm and happy. A minute later, he slept again. Jonathan bundled her up the rest of the way, and May waited by the front door.

"I know I'm trying to help your daughter," Audrey said as Jonathan packed up the rest of their belongings. Baba Yaga had cleaned up all evidence of their presence, rocking in her chair again, same as when they'd first found her. "But thank you, for everything."

The witch nodded once. "What Rina considers family is mine in bond as well. This kind of magic is deep and dark and strong."

Those were . . . extremely powerful words from an Aperien like

Baba Yaga. Just speaking them dampened the air with her magic, the scent unmistakable. It wasn't a simple statement; it was a claim, and the world heard.

Audrey only nodded, remembering Baba Yaga's explanation of the risk she posed to Rina's dreams and to Nizhny itself. It seemed better not to draw any more attention to the matter.

"Be well, Audrey Gunnar of Nizhny," Baba Yaga said. "And Jonathan Gunnar of Nizhny." Her single, yellow eye drifted to May, who stilled. The witch hummed in pleasure, enjoying May's fear, then chuckled. "And Maythorne, soon to be of Nizhny."

Then she looked at her fire, rocking again, and Audrey knew in her bones their time here was done. Gods, she wished Rina could somehow see her mother. But she would, someday. She could give Rina that knowledge at least, that someday she would be reunited with her mother.

Jonathan took the lead, May at her back without prompting. Audrey was certain May wanted to run out the door as fast as possible. Audrey pulled her coat tight, both hands holding *their son*, she thought with an utterly ridiculous grin. Jonathan perked a brow at her as he turned the door handle, and she just grinned right back at him. He opened the door, and the undeniable scent of home came with the breeze.

They all stepped out and down from the porch, and Audrey didn't need to look back to know the hut was gone.

They stood at the very north end of Nizhny. She could make out the lights on the horizon from town, a soft, gentle glow. And she knew the scent of taiga, recognized Aspen's magic on the breeze. Not even twenty feet and they'd cross into his forest.

"Let's go," Jonathan grunted. It wasn't sunrise yet, giving them time to get to the station before May burned again. Audrey never thought she'd be happy to walk more, but she nearly floated as they crossed into Aspen's forest and couldn't help a laugh when the trail twisted through the trees and they passed a good five miles in less than a minute.

She knew Aspen didn't show himself because May was a stranger, but she pressed a palm to the last pine on his border, rested her forehead against the bark, and whispered thanks. She felt him in the air.

They made it about half a mile before Tomas came running over the hills between their homesteads and the border parcels. Audrey's heart skipped at the sight of him. He stumbled, then hooted, then ran at them, mud flying as he waved. She laughed, while Jonathan only shook his head, and then Tomas was on them, throwing his arms around her in a crushing hug.

The baby squealed, startled awake, and Tomas jumped back so fast he would have fallen over if Jonathan didn't catch his arm.

"Oh shit, I'm sorry!" He blinked, and blinked again, leaning forward to peek into Audrey's coat. Her son fussed a few more times, squirming, but a few pats and soothing noises and he settled down to nurse again. "Wait . . ." Tomas pointed. "But . . ." Then he pointed to Audrey. "You. Baby. And you? You're okay? You're okay?"

Audrey laughed, her eyes stinging as she reached out to touch Tomas's cheek, then pull him close into a half hug. He kept blinking; she smelled the tears he fought as he stared down in wonder at the new, tiny life in her arms. "We're okay. We're all okay."

"Thank gods," Tomas whispered, his head falling on her shoulder, and she kept him close for a minute. He was only a few years younger than her, but his life had been so limited and so dark until Nizhny. They'd become his family, and they'd had to leave him here, worrying, in the house next to their empty one.

"We're okay," she whispered again. Tomas nodded, sniffing, still peering down at the baby nestled against her, who now had a very furrowed, angry little brow while he nursed, so grumpy.

Tomas laughed then, wiping his nose as he pulled back. He slapped Jonathan hard on the shoulder, who growled at him. "Looks like his dad, all broody-face, huh?"

He barely had time for a yelp before Jonathan tackled him into the mud. Audrey laughed as they wrestled, Tomas begging for mercy before Jonathan hauled him back to his feet. Then Tomas frowned when he noticed May lingered a few paces back, his nostrils flaring.

"She's a friend," Audrey said. "We wouldn't have made it back without her. This is May. May, Tomas."

Tomas relaxed immediately. "Cool, thanks. For getting them home, you know?"

May shuffled her feet. "Sure, no problem."

Tomas leaned to the side, looking around May, before he asked, "Where's Aster?"

Audrey sobered as she took Tomas's hand, exchanging a glace with Jonathan. "It's a long story, but Nizhny is in trouble. We need to get to Rina now."

Tomas ran ahead, so by the time they reached the station proper, Rina was stomping her way up the rails to meet them, pulling on her coat, with Virtue jogging to keep up with her long stride. Tomas sat on the station steps catching his breath, Innocence hovering over him, focused on their approach.

Gods, seeing them all again, Audrey couldn't help it. She was crying before Rina reached her, scoffed, and embraceed her. She was more observant than Tomas and stalled, picking up on the way she held her arms, the bundle against her chest instead of a bulging stomach.

"A son?" Virtue asked from beside Rina, her smile radiant, the succubus always stunning even in her plain sleeping robe. She canted her head, curious as she said, "Healthy and whole, like his mother?"

"Yes," Audrey whispered, pulling back the coat so they could both peer in, the view mostly a head of dark curls, lulled back to sleep by the walk down the rails.

"Gods," Rina said, dragging a hand down her face. "I'd heard nothing for weeks. We didn't know what to think." Her gaze darted over Audrey's shoulder, taking in May, giving the dhampir a stiff nod in greeting before frowning at Audrey and Jonathan in turn. "Tomas said there's danger?"

Then Aster hadn't gotten word or it had somehow been intercepted.

What she wouldn't give for a happy, perfect reunion, but they didn't have time. "Dimitri has an army coming on the rails. Tomorrow."

Rina's expression went so utterly cold. The fury Audrey scented from her was more terrifying than Baba Yaga's hut. The Aperien, Nizhny's leader, gave a single, stiff nod.

"Let's get you warm, then you'll tell me everything."

Chapter 36

They sat huddled close around the tavern fireplace, speaking in whispers though no one was around to hear. Only E had joined them, already waiting when they came inside, with a stoic nod. Being inside Aster's tavern while she was likely in danger really drove home the desperate dread of their situation, despite finally being *home*.

Maybe it was better this way. With the news fresh, maybe the shock of it would make Rina more flexible. Audrey almost laughed at herself for such a wistful hope.

Audrey introduced May without giving her name before anything else, making it clear beyond any doubt they'd be dead or rotting in a Pen without the dhampir's help. May, for her part, kept quiet, still unsure about her place. Virtue made them all a light meal with warm drinks. Frode and Hertha arrived a few minutes later. Rina, Innocence, Tomas, and E all settled in while the baby slept in her arms and Jonathan sat beside her, his hand on her thigh the entire time.

There would be time for stories later, but for now, the most pressing matter was the army coming for their home. She considered telling Rina about meeting her mother as an opening, but the steel in Nizhny's leader was answer enough; the battle came first. Audrey explained Nikita's warning, gave her the numbers as she remembered them, the threat of which she didn't need to elaborate on. They'd be outnumbered thirty fighters to one, at least, and that didn't count the two dragons they'd brought in to "help move the lumber" during the recovery efforts. That also didn't account for any changes since they'd fled Moscow. There was a good chance once they were discovered missing, Dimitri might have upped his offensive.

Audrey was impressed by Russian cursing now that she understood it. Rina went on for a few minutes, a vent of frustration that ended in her throwing a chair against a wall before Virtue coaxed her down by reminding her Aster would not be happy about the chair.

"She's in Moscow still?" E asked then, turning the conversation while Rina paced and Virtue walked with her, the pair speaking in hushed tones. Audrey did her best not to eavesdrop. Jonathan wasn't trying at all.

"I don't know. She stayed to act as a distraction." Audrey sighed, her hand running back and forth over her son's tiny body through the blankets; she couldn't seem to stop, needing the reassurance that he was still there as he slept quietly against her, a comforting, warm weight over her heart. "She said they wouldn't be able to keep her, and she'd head home as soon as she could."

E didn't seem overly concerned about Aster. No one did, really, which eased Audrey's mind a bit. Aster might be an Aperien, but she was her friend, and she hated the fact they'd left her behind. She hated the entire situation.

No matter how hard Rina worked, how hard they all did for the family they'd created here, at any time it could be threatened by a greater power. Even Rina's own mother was a threat simply by having stronger magic by nature.

She smelled Rina's pain, her fear, the frustration over a failure she had no control over. With the weight of an Accorded power behind Dimitri, what was to stop him?

Her heart lurched.

Audrey let out a sharp breath; gods, it was so obvious, wasn't it?

The answer was right there, and it always had been.

What had May said? If you can't beat them, join them, and fight back inside?

Rina was going to hate this.

Well, if anyone could make a case for what needed to happen next, why not an esquire?

Audrey scoffed softly, realization settling over her in a warm, welcome blanket. Baba Yaga hadn't helped her with her son's birth to get them here fast enough to warn Rina of the threat to Nizhny.

Baba Yaga had saved her life so she could help Rina accept a way to save Nizhny from herself.

"Rina," Audrey said, her voice carrying across the tavern, speaking in Russian. An unspoken request: listen. *Please*, she implored with her tone, with her expression, while holding her child, Jonathan's son. A future that not even a day ago had seemed impossible. "There's an answer."

Rina looked to the ceiling with her hands on her hips for a moment before she turned. Her icy-blue gaze, the fierce leader and woman Audrey had come to respect, to call friend, to love as a sister.

Did she already know? Did she know the way to save her dream?

Could she accept it?

No, Audrey knew, not without help. "You have a favor from Theodore." Rina's brow furrowed. And then a sneer twisted her expression. "You haven't failed, Rina, not yourself, not Nizhny or any of us, or your parents." Audrey refused to flinch.

"No," Rina all but snarled. "The answer is no."

And then she left, the fury in her exit thickening the air, the station doors slamming heavily as she stormed out into the night.

No one spoke, not even Virtue, who watched the doorframe still rattling from Rina's departure. A heartbeat, then two, then five and ten, and Audrey stood with Jonathan's help, but he didn't stand.

It was the old smith who finally broke the laden silence. "You mean to have her join the Accords."

Audrey looked to him, nodding without hesitation. She tried to imagine a day where she couldn't bring this kind Aperien—he was, no matter how gruff he pretended to be—warm cookies so she could find his smile when he didn't think she watched him.

The nod E gave her in return was barely a ghost. "She'll fight you."

Audrey lifted her chin. "She'll try."

Virtue's laugh was humorless. Everyone else sat in varying states of disbelief, frustration, displeasure and, Audrey noted, uneven levels of acceptance colliding in their scents. They knew, all of them did, that they died on principle or ran and lost everything. There was no middle ground, but there was also no one besides Audrey who had a chance to convince Rina to take a third option.

She didn't know why she knew, but she did. Maybe it was Baba Yaga's words, maybe because she'd broken an impossible curse with nothing but love, and while she loved Jonathan and their child more than anything in any world, she also loved her home and everyone in it.

She wasn't Audrey Doe of the ESC slums, lost and forgotten.

She was Audrey Gunnar of Nizhny, a wife, a mother, and a friend. And a fighter, even if she never lifted a blade.

Audrey soothed their son when he wiggled and snuffed in his sleep, annoyed by all the chatter, at his mother moving again so soon after he'd fallen asleep.

Now was as good a time as any for him to learn how to fight for what he loved.

Rina stood at the rail station where passengers disembarked, not so far from the station, the heart of Nizhny, the first place she'd bled and lost to bring a new home to these wild dangerous lands. She was a sight for all she lacked in magic. She always had been. Audrey smiled as she watched her friend, the woman she'd stand with and fight for, even if it meant pushing when Rina wanted to pull.

Her hair was loose, a heavy tangle of blond against her dark leather armor. A thick boot propped up on the wooden rail, her eyes closed and her expression unreadable. She inhaled and exhaled with purpose. She held her father's blade, the great sword sheathed but leaning next to her, like he stood beside her to offer solace, perhaps advice, maybe even peace among memories of love. A reminder of what she fought for.

The Aperien carried herself with pride, with a stern hand, and with a beautiful heart. Her witch blood didn't give her magic, but Rina possessed her mother's fortitude. Now that Audrey had met Baba Yaga, she wished she'd had the chance to know her father as well. A hero, one who embraced his nature as such, and whose love turned a villain into an Aperien willing to kneel to save her own daughter in turn.

Audrey didn't mask her steps, her boots sounding against the platform as she scaled the few stairs. That's when she noticed for the first time the blade hilt, trapped in Rina's clenched, gloved fist, had an odd yellow stone set in the pommel. An unforgettable color. Beside it hung a silver bauble on a short chain: Theodore's favor.

"Your mother says hello, by the way, and wants you to know she's not a loony eating mushrooms out in the swamp."

"She . . ." Rina blinked her eyes open, surprised by where Audrey chose to start the conversation, then huffed a laugh. "Good to know."

"She wants to come to you, but she said she can't."

"That so."

"Her magic is too strong. She'd take Nizhny without meaning to and change what you've made. She doesn't want to do that to you."

Rina hummed, gaze flicking to the horizon. The direction of Moscow. "No mind what I might want, is it?"

Audrey considered Rina for a moment, catching the fierce scent of her fury, nothing short of a raw, open wound. She tasted the grief for what Rina'd already lost and what was at stake right now. Audrey had learned that scent from Jonathan in the moments where he'd truly believed she would die. Rina's hurt was a deep well, one she kept to herself. Audrey wondered if Rina knew she could sense it now.

Was it a matter of trust that she wore these emotions on her skin? Or had they finally become too much for any single person to shoulder alone?

It didn't matter, so Audrey waited until Rina was ready.

"You ask me to become what I hate to save what I love."

Audrey shook her head. "It's not so simple. When I got on that train? I thought I'd get to Moscow and hate it. In my mind, it was no better than the ESC. I made this contract with you, and I expected to see the same abuse I saw all over the slums when I was indentured. I kept waiting for all the ugly to come through, that humans were nothing more than slaves."

"Ah, the shine blinded you then?" Rina smirked sideways at her, then back out across the taiga. The argument lacked heat.

"At first," Audrey admitted. "It's very pretty. But no, the more people I met, the more I realized that as much as I hate how uneven power is spread in this world, Moscow is not a den of rotting evil."

Rina chuckled, and when she didn't argue, Audrey went on. "Your uncle changed his mythos and gave a huge portion of the world's population stability. He agreed to the Accords, put his anchors and his magic into keeping what he could safe. The power disparity is still disgusting, but the people there are happy and at peace."

"I know," Rina said with a shrug. "Koschei this Deathless is not the monster from his myth. My father was his counter in so many tales and wouldn't have called him brother if he hadn't truly changed for this world. But he's also no savior. None of the Accorded leaders are. They might think so, they might claim neutrality from their palace of ice, but you've seen how they wield that power when it suits.

"Your husband and his kind. Virtue and hers. My mother, forced away when she became a risk. This world still fails us when we need it most, over and over again." Rina rubbed her face, then turned toward Audrey fully, gesturing at her child, not even a day old yet, bundled over her heart. "That's the future you want for him, is it?"

"I want him to *have* a future. Here. With you to protect him."

Rina laughed, and the sound was ugly. "You see it right now; I can't protect shit. Not who I love, not what I've promised. I'll never be strong enough to stand, so instead we'll be unmade and the Accords win again. Look at Virtue. She served them, she believed in the Accords, and as soon as they could, they drove her out. Audrey, there is no freedom or safety for us under that yoke."

"And you can't change that from out here," Audrey countered. "Fight them on their ground, for all the reasons you founded Nizhny in the first place. For Virtue, for the Clan. For anyone else who'd be cast aside in the future. And if I could change an Accord law, just a human girl, imagine what Katerina Yaga could do?"

"Only a human girl, hm? You'd still breath out that nonsense?" Rina asked. "Just a human girl wouldn't be standing here, alive, after having a vileblood's child." She pointed a finger in her face, almost touching her nose. "I knew, in my bones, that day that fucking archivist came to me, damn near begging take you and Gunnar in. Hells if I'd walk from a favor like that, but I knew. Mother used to say I had a nose for fate when it came sniffing around, even if I didn't have any magic."

Then she snorted. "And gods, the pair of you. Ridiculous. If I'd had any doubts, they fled the second I saw him look at you. And now? You've broken the most powerful curse of our age, a new breed of duster in your arms, and you're not even human at all anymore, are you?"

"That's not important right now, Rina."

"Isn't it? Because you're telling me, a savage with a blade, I'm going to change the Accords? Me?" Another laugh, a bit more brittle this time. "You'd think I'd even be able to consider it if you were going to fuck off and die in another fifty years?"

Audrey shivered; that, she hadn't considered. Gods, the thought hadn't even crossed her mind. Vileblood didn't die from age. Aperiens didn't either, hybrids or otherwise. Not only had she been given a future, she'd been given an eternity to treasure it.

"I don't think you're supposed to be the one crying," Rina said. She rested her forehead on the pommel of her father's blade and sighed. Did she know, Audrey wondered as she wiped her cheeks, how close that brought her to both her parents?

"I want to spend forever here," Audrey whispered. "I want to help you with paperwork, because I know you hate it. I want to argue with you about treemen and take your wolves and make you mad, over and over again, as long as it means we can keep our home. The home you made, Rina.

"I want to help you fight them. We can start with Virtue and her kind. I know the laws, and what I don't know, I can learn. Whatever you need. I'm not going anywhere Rina. None of us are. You gave us Nizhny, and we will do whatever you need to keep it. You are the beating heart."

Audrey touched her shoulder. When Rina didn't shrug away, Audrey squeezed.

"I'm compromising everything if I do this," Rina whispered.

Audrey brushed the hair back from Rina's face and shook her head. "No, you're not compromising yourself. *You* are this dream on the taiga, Rina. The core, your values, your strengths, they aren't lessened because you bend instead of break. If you let Nizhny die because of pride, that would be the compromise, and I think the only way you'd be able to walk down that road is because you know you'd be gone at the end of it."

Rina arched a brow as she rose to her full height, slinging the sword over her back. "Bold words, just a 'human' girl." She closed her eyes, gathering herself, and when she glared down at Audrey this time, those icy-blue eyes gleamed. "Then I order you to stay. You and all your brats and your grumpy lover."

Audrey laughed, wiping her eyes. "Husband. I'm Audrey Gunnar of Nizhny."

She felt . . . something. Deep down in a place inside her that didn't have a name, or maybe it did? Saying it was her heart was too simple—her soul, not profound enough. It was *more*, heavy like tangled ropes made from truth and hope and dreams and probably some kind of magic only gods and angels touched.

Audrey exhaled, let herself sink into the that feeling, into this new part of her, because she wasn't just a girl anymore, and she hadn't been, not since one man loved her enough to teach her she mattered.

She repeated her name as she watched Rina's smirk spread into a nearly feral grin. "I am Audrey Gunnar of Nizhny, and I swear on everything I love, that this is my home and my family, and I will protect it with you. Always."

"Good. Now, Theodore better answer this favor and fast. And you can make me sound as noble as you like," Rina called over her shoulder as she stepped off the deck in a half-leap, grunting against the landing and cracking her neck. "But when Dimitri shits his pants tomorrow, I'm treasuring that fucking memory until the entire damn world comes crashing down around us all."

Audrey grinned, really grinned, and said, "So will I."

Chapter 37

Audrey hated leaving her tiny, helpless newborn son with anyone else besides herself or Jonathan, but she trusted Virtue with her life, his life, and Jonathan's life, and she really needed to take a deep breath. Maybe three or four, so she wasn't in the middle of panicking while they faced down Dimitri Syn Koschei and his army.

They'd been back in Nizhny less than twenty-four hours as the unscheduled Moscow train rolled into the station. Almost everyone had gathered except Virtue, Innocence, Tomas, and May, who were all tucked away in Audrey and Jonathan's cabin.

Audrey's fingers twitched, and she fumbled until she found Jonathan's hand and squeezed his fingers. He gave her a soft grunt. "Kid's fine, probably still asleep."

"I know. I'm fine."

Jonathan hummed; he didn't believe her, and she was lying, but whatever. To the gathered group, he asked, "This asshole is really going to come in on the train with a few friends, announce his plans, and he's that confident we won't stab his fucking ass?"

Rina snorted, the grin she shot Jonathan positively shit-eating.

E leaned on the nearby fence, picking at his dirty fingernails. "Arrogance is a weapon."

"Very true." Theodore stood with his hands folded behind his back, clad in his finest archivist attire. After all, he represented the Accorded

Territories for this exchange as proof of Nizhny's newfound status.

Theodore had more than come through on his favor. Within only a few hours, he and Rina left for a pocket plane summons, a neutral magically sealed area where the Accorded leaders and an Archival Tribunal gathered to hear Katerina Yaga's proposal for Nizhny to join the Accords.

Audrey was both relieved and disappointed she couldn't attend.

The vote had been unanimous, even the Deathless himself approving Rina's gambit and congratulating her before leaving the summons to return to Moscow. What a dinner that was going to make, Audrey mused, when Dimitri returned home with his tail tucked and his army unused. There might have been a time she sympathized with the heir of a man who could never die and had no use for the son who begged for his attentions. That was before she'd met Dimitri, and he'd proven time and time again to be nothing more than a raging asshole in a fancy, ugly suit. Jonathan's words, not hers, be she couldn't help but agree with him.

Audrey still held her breath. Uneasy. Worried. She felt empty without her son in her body, more so without him at her breast. She hated for one more day they treated their child like a dirty secret, but they didn't want to give Dimitri any possible advantage.

She wasn't pregnant; Dimitri couldn't prove any wrongdoing on Jonathan's part. While they'd pieced together a picture from May's research, nothing in her notes contained hard evidence. She wore E's necklace, reinforced to conceal the fact that she was no longer human at all.

She felt the rumbling through the soil before she heard the train and stacked her spine. Why was she still so worried?

Jonathan brought their joined hands to lips. "Steady there, sweetheart."

"I'm trying," she mumbled, but her heart raced anyway. So much was at stake, and had been for so long, it was hard to let go of the worry that had plagued her for months.

Rina moved forward from the group, and Audrey couldn't help a grin. Aside from Theodore, everyone dressed as they might for a normal day in Nizhny. Muddy boots all around. E's hands were filthy from his smithy. The Clan hung back from the rails a few paces, but they wore their working gear, gathering loosely as if they'd been interrupted from more important matters. Even Rina looked like she'd rolled out of bed a few minutes before; she'd dressed down from her minimal effort she'd put in for the Tribunal's sake. Audrey wore the doeskin pants Jonathan made for her, done with fancy dresses.

Levity vanished with the train's approach, and for all the confidence of the gathering, Audrey could still scent unease. The Accorded magic that bound the territories wasn't impermeable; it didn't prevent those under the bindings to break the rules, but rather ensured consequences for those who did.

If Dimitri was a true fool, he could attack anyway. By the time the Moscow Dominion paid the consequences—in case of an infraction so dire, exile from the Accords and a blood price drained from the Deathless himself—Nizhny would be long overrun and her friends and family dead. Audrey found it hard to imagine the man so desperate for his father's approval would make such a dire mistake, but fear of the possibility weighed heavy in her gut.

She'd convinced Rina this would work. She'd asked her friend to trust her judgement, to believe in her assertion this was the best way to save her dream. Gods, she'd sworn in trade with Baba Yaga for the birth of her son in exchange for seeing Rina and Nizhny preserved.

If she was wrong, everyone would pay the price for her mistake.

The train rolled into view, chugged black smoke from the coal engines as it ambled closer and closer. And two dragons, Arthurian in their flaming red scales, violent wingspan, and lashing, barbed tails. Firebreathers by the coloring, each at least a century old based on the size. A single fly by, and they could scorch her home to ashes. The beasts circled in the distance, remaining outside the south border of Nizhny proper, setting down in the clear-cut land from supplying the Dominion with lumber for restorations in the eastern province. The train kept on, and no one spoke as it crept up the line and eventually came to rest outside the station entrance instead of at the passenger disembark.

Rina kicked up her sword, resting it over a broad shoulder, and headed down the line to meet where Dimitri intended to exit. The front doors, as if a king returning to his castle. Everyone followed her without a word, Audrey slipping her hand from Jonathan's and wiping her sweaty palms on her pants before taking a deep breath in and out. A little longer, and they could go back to the cabin, she could hold her son, and this mess would finally be done.

The engine steamed in the cold air, hissing as it came to rest. Audrey was surprised when Dimitri himself stepped from the train first, dressed in the finery she'd expected but without the cane this time. His personal guards followed tight on his heels, all dusters of various bloodlines, all dressed to the teeth in Dominion colors, with the Deathless's emblem blazoned on their armor. Today they were dressed for war, not for the show she'd seen outside his home in Moscow. Golden chain mail, plate mail, and shields. Weapons of all kinds on the dozen men who flanked him now, helmets adorned with bright red plumes tucked under their arms. Even the train itself was adorned, Dominion crests painted up and down the cars.

Audrey exhaled; this was good. Dimitri was here on the Dominion's behalf. Considering the timing, he'd left the eastern border before Rina's meeting with the Tribunal concluded.

He had no idea what he was walking into.

And the Deathless either hadn't been able to contact him in time to divert Dimitri from his plans, or he hadn't bothered to try.

Or they'd decided Nizhny was worth the consequences.

Audrey found the last option hard to believe, not after meeting Koschei as a simple man who enjoyed art and keeping his Dominion stable.

"Cousin," Rina drawled, leaning against the handrail with her father's sword beside her hip. "I thought last time you were here, we talked about how much I dislike unregistered visitors." She canted her head at him, and Audrey swore she yawned before she added, "Nizhny isn't a place to entertain yourself when you're bored at home."

"Cousin," Dimitri returned, striding right up to Rina, his chin high, his smirk and arrogance confirming he didn't know about Nizhny's newfound status. "Self-important as always, I see."

Rina motioned between them. "Pot, kettle. Why are you here, Dimitri? Must be important for you to show up with an unscheduled train, a fancy retainer, and two dragons. Does daddy know?"

The flicker of irritation across Dimitri's careful mask was so quick, Audrey almost missed it. Then he smiled, bright and white, and might have been quite handsome if she didn't know the man underneath.

"The Deathless is well aware of my presence and purpose in Nizhny this morning."

"When's the last time you spoke with him, I wonder?" Rina asked.

For the first time, Dimitri hesitated, and his gaze snapped to her, then Jonathan, but then back to Audrey. She lifted her chin, meeting the cold, calculating stare. Then he took a longer moment to study the others gathered at the platform, which was most of the Nizhny population, and his eyes widened slightly when he saw Theodore in his archivist robes at the back of the group.

"Not in the last six hours or so, I imagine," Rina added. Dimitri's focus snapped back to Rina, and she shrugged. "Big news. He probably wanted to tell you in person." She waved a hand. "You go first, though. Since you came all this way."

Jonathan chuckled beside Audrey, and Dimitri stopped trying to contain his scowl. "That vileblood trash you keep on your payroll is in his violation of his parole. Not only did he attack a Warden in Moscow—who was merciful enough to let the transgression pass—he's broken the most basic tenet of the Accords by endangering your precious human pet." The disdain in his expression when he turned his attention back to Audrey made her clench her fists so hard they ached. "She's whored herself out to him. She carries his spawn."

Audrey stepped forward, ignoring the low growl from Jonathan, the frustration in his scent, no doubt because she was putting herself at risk even though it had always been expected.

"I'm not pregnant," Audrey said as she joined Rina. "You've been misinformed."

"Hells of a mistake," Rina added, "Being as you felt the need to drag fucking dragons all the way out here to stick your nose in another Accorded Territory's business."

"She's lying, and you just accept this?" Dimitri sneered the words, missing the bigger picture as he jabbed a finger in Audrey's direction. "I have documentation of her time in the capital, dealing with an apprentice at the Dominion Blood Clinic to try and find a cure for the vileblood curse and her condition."

"I'm not pregnant," Audrey repeated, gesturing at her body, which showed no outward signs of her recovery. In fact, even without the aid of E's necklace, her body was completely back to normal aside from swollen breasts from feeding her son. Her new blood, or rather the lack of human blood, had healed all signs of the pregnancy overnight. It still made her head spin, but now wasn't the time to think about it. "Did you bring your magic reader?"

"How utterly *tragic* you lost the abomination festering inside you. It changes nothing about his crimes." The callousness in his tone felt like a slap, but she somehow kept her expression detached.

Dimitri stepped back when Jonathan stepped forward, his fury burning her nose out, and Rina held out an arm to block his advance.

"Even if all this was true, a missive would have sufficed," Rina said. "Or do you truly believe I can't handle my own affairs? That I secretly yearn for your intervention after all these years, cousin?"

"Clearly, as you rely on a vileblood and his plaything to handle those affairs, even when summoned by the Deathless himself."

"Insult my wife one more time, you fuck, and I'll intervene right here, right now," Jonathan snarled.

Dimitri laughed. "Ah, yes, please add threatening an envoy of the Dominion to your list of offenses, with official ears within range, no less. Availian, I trust you'll be scribing all this for preservation, of course." To Rina, he said, "Come, cousin, you know why I'm truly here. And you know damn well I didn't bring dragons for a vileblood. My father offered you a peaceful transition to join the Dominion fold and retain some of your pride and dignity, and you spat in his face with this farce." He waved at hand at Audrey and Jonathan. "You denied the olive branch, so here's the boot, Rina. I have no problem rebuilding on the ashes of you and your misfits. Better the world without them all. Or maybe you care more about your people than your pride and are finally ready to put yourself where you and your mother belong: under your betters."

Rina snorted and craned her head back as Theodore moved beside, his hands folded behind his back. "Hey, Availian, you taking notes like he said?"

"Yes, I am. For preservation, of course." Theodore didn't posture, magically or otherwise. Even with her new senses, Audrey couldn't pick up more than his natural scent, which she now knew was his dragon and god blood, because there was only so much powerful Aperiens could do to suppress their natures without actively trying. Theodore simply didn't flex that power, and he didn't need to do so. His reputation and his crisp calm accomplished as much in spades.

Dimitri's confidence waned slightly, realizing that Theodore spoke to Rina and not him.

"My cousin has never been a great listener," Rina noted, grinning now like a cat with the cream. "Maybe he needs someone to say it again? Louder maybe?"

Theodore inclined his head to Rina, and Audrey knew him well enough to catch the twinkle of mirth in his gaze before it darted back to Dimitri. "Yes, I will record the threats made by Dimitri syn Koschei, on behalf of the Moscow Dominion, upon the newest member of the Accorded Territories, Nizhny, under Katerina Yaga."

Silence echoed, followed by shuffling through Dimitri's guards as they shifted in their armor. Dimitri stared, his face paling, the shock leaving him speechless for a good fifteen seconds before he shook his head.

"Impossible. A new territory cannot join the Accords without a vote."

"Happened last night, probably while you were on the train over," Rina answered, crossing her arms now, giving up on the impression of bored and morphing into threatening. "The vote was unanimous."

Dimitri glanced at Theodore, who nodded. "I arranged the tribunal myself and attended. Nizhny is part of the Accords. I trust you are aware of the consequences of violating the Peace Accord. No territory may act against another in matters of war, to secure the stability of our world. And this means any threats you make are in your father's name."

The moment stretched, Dimitri utterly off guard, his expression twisting and stuttering between a hundred different emotions at once. Audrey was close enough to scent him, but what she caught, at least what she guessed came off his skin the most intensely, was desperation.

Theodore remained unmoved and stoic, but Rina grinned like a hyena, enjoying every second of humiliation her cousin suffered, and she didn't need to look at Jonathan to know he openly gloated. E said nothing, but the smith always looked cold and condescending to strangers, worse to those who'd insult what he valued. Audrey kept her expression calm, contained, but he must hate her on principle at this point, given that she'd played a huge role in this outcome—even bigger than he might imagine in this moment.

But desperation and fear drove people to do horrible, foolish things.

And it wasn't a risk Audrey was willing to take for any level of petty satisfaction. Too much was at stake.

"Your father wouldn't have sent you here to make a fool out of you, Dimitri," she offered quietly. She didn't dare move closer—too risky, and Jonathan might lose his composure if she put herself in too much danger in this volatile moment, which would only increase Dimitri's aggravation. "The tribunal happened very quickly, and he likely wasn't able to get word to you in the short time before you arrived. I might not know your father well, but the Deathless I met takes great pride in the Dominion and your people. He may have condoned your wishes to claim Nizhny and bring it into the Dominion, but that was before. Everything he's done points to a man who uses power when he needs to, but not when it would strip protection away from everything he's built since the Aperien Event."

The hatred in Dimitri's expression might have chilled her when she'd walked through Moscow as a human, but she wasn't that girl anymore. She lifted her chin, held his fuming gaze, and wondered what she would say to her son, years from now, if she ever found herself standing right here while her child edged up to a choice she knew he would come to regret.

"Breaking what he's built is not the way to earn his favor," she added, whisper quiet. "You can be better than this." She didn't tell him he was better, because she didn't believe it, but she did believe that anyone could change if they wanted it badly enough. And that's what she believed when she said those words and didn't blink as she did.

Dimitri rolled his eyes. "How trite," he sneered at her, but the desperation waned from his scent, and the tension bled back from Audrey's shoulders as he turned to Rina. "You win this round, cousin, but I won't forget this."

"See that you don't," Rina answered. "Now get the fuck out of my territory."

Audrey shivered, but the words came from an Accorded leader now, and the magic already seeped into the air, the soil, the world. And now Audrey could sense these things, not simply the awareness that came from Jonathan's blood but her lack of humanity.

She was Aperien now, not even a simple duster. God and angel.

And the world around her knew.

The train left within five minutes, Dimitri offering nothing else as his guards followed him back into the car. The dragons took wing after the train headed down the line and out onto the taiga, the danger over, at least for now, retreating back to the Dominion, now their Accorded peer.

Rina turned to Nizhny, to the people she'd defend to her dying breath, cool and collected as she said, "Now that shit's done, I need a fucking drink.”

The Clan cheered to that, and Audrey couldn't help but laugh as Jonathan slung an arm around her shoulder and tugged her close. Rina jumped from the landing, and E followed with a nod to Audrey, leaving her and Jonathan with Theodore.

"Well done, esquire," Theodore said, his expression fond.

"Couldn't've done it with you, Maxy," Jonathan drawled as he gave him a rough pat on the shoulder.

Theodore narrowed his eyes in confusion, then sighed. "Serves me right, I suppose," he muttered.

Audrey covered her mouth, giggling. "He was very upset about your manners, Theodore Maximilian Avialian."

"Gods on high," he grumbled, stepping down with his perfect grace. "I'm not having this conversation." He headed toward the tavern, following the singing Clan members, his back stiff and steps hurried.

"As much as I'd like to harass him more, we should get to the kid before he gets grumpy."

Audrey hummed happily, leaning into him as they headed toward their cabin.

"And I still fucking hate train days."

Epilogue

"He takes after his mother," Theodore said, the baby little more than a squirming mess of blankets in the crook of his elbow. "Thankfully."

Jonathan grunted from the other side of the couch, sprawled out and at ease. Audrey sat between them, smiling as Theodore made a face and their son cooed.

"But you haven't decided on a name?"

Audrey sighed; feeling guilty as a mother, she was learning, never eased. "We never talked about it," she admitted. "There was just so much else. It feels unfair to decide in a rush." She reached out and brushed the dark curls from her son's forehead. "But this hair? All Jonathan."

Theodore lifted him up, swinging him until the baby gurgled. Audrey laughed as his voice pitched high when he said, "Let's just hope he isn't as grumpy, yes? Yes."

"Hilarious, Maxy," Jonathan drawled and rolled his eyes, all stoic on the outside despite his scent radiating with warmth as he watched Theodore play with their son.

Theodore didn't acknowledge the barb at his middle name. "Grumpy and unbearably rude," he cooed instead.

It had only been two days since Nizhny joined the Accords. Three since they'd finally made it home, and not even four since her son's birth. Since her uncertain life became a future that seemed almost limitless.

Almost.

A knock, and the door swung open, and Audrey was on her feet and crushing Aster in a hug before she crossed the threshold.

"Come now, it has barely been a month. Now, let me see this baby who breaks all the rules already?"

"Aster," Audrey babbled, but the cornflower wraith shook her head and patted her cheek.

"We have time for stories, Miss Audrey." Aster laughed when she groaned at her. "But I do have a surprise for you." She canted her head toward the open doorway.

The pegasi grazed outside.

Much later, night heavy on the taiga, Nizhny quiet and calm, her son nursed as Audrey rested on the couch. Jonathan and Theodore shared a fancy whiskey E had provided earlier in the afternoon. The smith was passed out cold in the armchair, snoring softly, an empty plate with only cookie crumbs in his lap. Rina sat at the table, leaning back in the chair with her arms crossed, eyes closed as Virtue braided her golden hair. Aster sat across from them, smiling as she ran her fingers over the cornflowers in the vase. Tomas, Innocence, and May had retired to Tomas's cabin a bit earlier; the pair agreed to host the dhampir in their spare room for the time being.

Audrey and Jonathan had finished the story of their time in Moscow only a few minutes earlier.

Theodore spun his glass, empty now, and yawned. "Warden Pyriel is in Moscow, then. He will come here, and soon, to try and uncover his predecessor's fate."

Rina grunted, and that was all they got from their fearless leader. Not that Audrey blamed her. She'd stood before an Archival Tribunal for Jonathan's hearing. Exhausting didn't begin to cover the experience, and she'd only argued for one duster's parole.

Rina had committed a portion of her power, the Aperien strength of her blood, to bind Nizhny to the Accords under her rule.

Audrey was surprised the woman was still awake.

"I left three days after Audrey, Jonathan, and Maythorne fled. He remained in the capital as an honored guest," Aster said, her gaze drifting to Audrey, thoughtful. "This Pyriel is not what I expected."

"Nah," Jonathan said. "Dimitri could have moved on me. Audrey passed out, and I think the angel wanted to help, saw her falling or whatever, but . . ." Audrey shared a look with him, knowing, and he shrugged. "I reacted."

"The way he watched afterwards was what drew my attention," Aster said. "Yes, he declined to see Gunnar punished, but it was more than ego and misunderstanding. He saw Audrey's fear, her response to an angel sending her into a panic so blind she collapsed." Aster tsked. "And he failed to take this on insult."

"No," Audrey said quietly. "He knew there was more to the story. And he knew who we were. Dimitri made sure of it. If he didn't suspect anything strange before regarding Kushiel, he does now. He's going to come here. I'm sure it will be obvious we won't be coming back to Moscow, well, ever."

Jonathan smirked. "Shithole, anyway. Much nicer here in the mud."

Audrey grinned at him. Gods, she loved him. And she got to keep him, provided another angel didn't come to try and take him away from her.

She put that worry under a tight leash. It would bother her until resolved, but she wouldn't let it drive her into a panic or let fear rule her. Her Nizhny family stood strong when Kushiel came to threaten her and Jonathan. They would face whatever this next angel brought to their borders, together, with Theodore's help and Accorded backing.

"What's next?" Audrey asked Theodore, running her hands through her son's hair, the most precious part of this new future. One she would never stop fighting for.

"I've been busy while you were in Moscow," Theodore said. "I've put in a specific acquisition with an old friend." He rubbed his chin. "And if everything has gone to plan, they should be on their way to Moscow with exactly the kind of help we need for dealing with Pyriel's inevitable arrival, and the truth of what happened with Kushiel."

<u>The Earthen Calamities Series:</u>

Dreams on the Taiga: A Novella

Dreams on the Taiga: Audiobook

Blood on the Taiga: Nizhny Book 1

Cursed on the Taiga: Nizhny Book 2

Legends from Ashes: A Novella – Free Newsletter Signup

Feathers of Trials and Truths: The Acquisitionist Book 1 – Coming June 2025

www.eandersauthor.com

Acknowledgements

Whew! This book was a doozy.

I remember complaining to my wonderful friend, book coach and fellow author Jocelyn Lindsay about how hard CURSED ON THE TAIGA was to write compared to the first book in the series. She smiled at me and said (in a much nicer way): "Duh, you're writing about your own trauma in this book." Huh, funny how she's right so often.

I had an early miscarriage before I got pregnant with my son. And my pregnancy was really, really tough. I had hyperemesis gravidarum and was in the hospital three days a week for IV treatments, which also meant months of bed rest, and hip issues afterwards. My eighteen-year-old cat, who had been with me for half my life, died when I was five months along. I dealt with prenatal depression and had a cesarean. After the birth, I split my stiches, and faced post-partum depression and serve anxiety disorder.

Needless to say, things didn't go how I'd hoped or expected. Writing Audrey's experience with a cursed pregnancy, with all her fears, sickness and frustrations, definitely reflected some of mine before, during and after my own pregnancy. And sometimes it's hard to talk about, because pregnancy and motherhood are supposed to be beautiful and amazing parts of our lives. I hope those of you out there who faced challenges during your own pregnancies, however small or large, feel seen after taking this journey with Audrey.

A big thanks to Jocelyn again, who has been with me every step of the way for THE EARTHEN CALAMITIES and continues to be awesome sauce.

To my beta readers for this round: Heather, Darci, Cameron, Jenn and Matt. Thank you, thank you, thank you!

To all my newsletter subscribers for reading all about my nonsense, my books and my frogs. To Lori Diederich, proofreading extraordinaire. To 100covers and my project manager Shanna for the continued awesome work on covers and graphics. To everyone who read BLOOD ON THE TAIGA, and extra thanks if you left a review!

To Emily McKay for being a sounding board about all things motherhood, ADHD, writing and questionable smut choices. To spicybookgirly for being my biggest cheerleader for Audrey and broody-brood Gunnar on Instagram.

To everyone who came to my first book signing and made it amazing: Heather, Dany, John, Whitney, Diane, Traci, Zerelina and her son, Kristen, Jocelyn and Joyce.

To the B&N Bellevue peeps: Dennis for FFXIV chats and helping me with consignments, and Jamie for writing me the most amazing recommendation for BLOOD ON THE TAIGA, and both for hand-selling my debut! To Alyssa, Anna and Natalie for taking care of my consignments at other B&N locations.

As always, to my family. My parents and my brothers for always being supportive and coming to buy out my debut novel at Barnes & Nobles the first week of release. A special thanks to my sister-in-law Darci, who is a nurse and a doula, and answered all my pregnancy questions as a beta. To my niece Isabell, because meeting her made me want to become a mom some day.

To my son, Ethan, because without him, this book never would have been possible, let alone the amazing gift of being his mom.

And always to Erik, my husband, who is my very tolerable and always supportive other half, be it for books, frogs or any other shenanigans I get myself into.

Love you all!

In memory of the late Toe, the angry tomato frog, who was my very first fantastic frog.

About the Author

E. Anders lives in the Pacific Northwest with her husband, son, two cats and sixty-three fantastic frogs.

Her newsletter, FANTASY AND FROGS, features: updates about her published and upcoming fantasy novels in THE EARTHEN CALAMITIES series; pictures and videos about her many pet frogs; links to free eBooks from other indie authors; and random things she loves that are not limited to but mostly - as you probably already guessed - about books and frogs.

9 798989 180752